Wild Sign

BY PATRICIA BRIGGS

The Mercy Thompson novels
Moon Called
Blood Bound
Iron Kissed
Bone Crossed
Silver Borne
River Marked
Frost Burned
Night Broken
Fire Touched
Silence Fallen
Storm Cursed
Smoke Bitten

The Alpha and Omega novels
Cry Wolf
Hunting Ground
Fair Game
Dead Heat
Burn Bright
Wild Sign

Aralorn: Masques and Wolfsbane

PATRICIA BRIGGS

Wild Sign

orbitbooks.net

ORBIT

First published in Great Britain in 2020 by Orbit

A CIP catalogue record for this book
is available from the British Library.

HB ISBN 978-0-356-51367-6
C format 978-0-356-51368-3

Printed and bound in Great Britain by Clays Ltd, Elcograf S.p.A.

Papers used by Orbit are from well-managed forests
and other responsible sources.

MIX
Paper from
responsible sources
FSC® C104740

Orbit
An imprint of
Little, Brown Book Group
Carmelite House
50 Victoria Embankment
London EC4Y 0DZ

An Hachette UK Company
www.hachette.co.uk

www.orbitbooks.net

For Collin, Amanda, and Jordan.
Here's to less interesting times.

PRELUDE

SUMMER: NORTHERN CALIFORNIA

Sissy Connors, PhD, checked her GPS, adjusted her backpack, and continued her trek into the mountains. Common sense told her there must have been an easier way, but none of the trails on the USGS map seemed to go exactly where she needed to travel.

She was an experienced hiker—her doctorate was in botany and her field study trips sent her to the edges of the world, looking for oddball plants that might contain the cure for Ebola or MRSA or some other disease. Elvis, her half German shepherd, half who-knows-what-except-it-was-big who trotted beside her, was experienced, too. Generally, he would trot back and forth, investigating anything he found interesting, then checking in with her before exploring again. But for the last five miles he'd stuck to her side like glue. He didn't look nervous, precisely, but the last time he'd done this it had been because a cougar had been stalking them.

This *was* cougar territory. Elvis's attitude had her paying attention to the branches of the trees she was walking under, but other than some porcupine sign, she hadn't found any indication she and Elvis weren't the only living things for miles.

She didn't think it was a cougar making her dog cling to her side, because she felt it, too. The air was . . . different. In her years of wanderings, she'd explored places that were sacred, where every step forward felt like a sacrilege. She'd discovered secret meadows or caves that welcomed her presence. She'd hiked through places that made her stomach turn—even though her normal senses found nothing wrong.

This had all the hallmarks of one of those hikes. She found some comfort in trailing her fingers in the big dog's ruff as they climbed.

It was hot and the last few miles had been uphill. She stopped in a shaded place, took out a canvas water bowl, and filled it from her canteen. She set it down for her dog and took a good swig herself. She was near her goal; she'd been circling it for a while, trying to find a negotiable path through the mountainside.

"Dad," she told the empty air. "I know you like to be an off-grid hermit, but this is ridiculous."

She found it an hour later—fifteen minutes after she swore she was going to turn around and start the two-day hike back to her car. She passed the rock face of yet another cliff—and stopped.

A petroglyph.

Tired, sweaty, and frustrated as she was, she couldn't help the smile of wonder. She reached out but did not touch it. The marks were perhaps two feet square, and they formed a symbol she hadn't seen before. Like the legs of an isosceles triangle, two lines rose from opposite edges of the petroglyph and met with their vertex angle at the top of the figure. Each of those legs was crossed by three upward slashes.

She took a step nearer—and realized there was a steep trail up the side of the cliff, tucked into a crack in the rock she hadn't been able to see from where she'd been standing. There was no sign it was a trail to her father's camp, but it headed in the right direction.

She crawled up the steep trail—helping Elvis up ahead of her with a hand on his rump when he couldn't find purchase on the sheer rock. It wasn't quite steep enough for her to use her climbing gear. She had to crawl out through a hole between a tree and a rock the size of a small house to get to the top. If the thought of getting Elvis back down in one piece hadn't been so harrowing, she might have given up. She hoped she could find another way back once they were at the top.

Finally, she surmounted a particularly difficult bit and found herself in a small meadow surrounded by dense forest.

They had tucked the buildings in under the forest canopy so well it took her a moment to see she had reached her goal. But once she noticed the first building, her eyes started to pick out the rest of them.

There were a few tents, but most of the living spaces were actual cabins or yurts. It was more than an encampment—a whole town, really, complete with one tidy cabin marked by a small hand-painted sign that read USPS—Wild Sign.

It was much more civilized than she had expected her dad to tolerate. It took her a minute to realize it was too quiet.

"Hey!" she called. "Dad?"

She waited. Then she tried, "Dr. Connors, it's your daughter, also Dr. Connors!"

But only the wind answered.

SUMMER: MISSOULA, MONTANA
PREVIOUS TO THE EVENTS IN *BURN BRIGHT*

"I am never going shopping again," Rachel said solemnly before tossing back the whiskey shot she'd requested from their server. She was a small woman with curly brown hair and a rounded build. She'd managed, somehow, to escape the hyperfit look most of the werewolves acquired. Anna had thought Rachel had ordered the whiskey because that was what Leah had ordered, but watching Rachel put the liquor away made Anna reconsider.

Anna sipped at her own drink without enthusiasm. She should have ordered whiskey, too. Specialty cocktail or not, her drink tasted like paint thinner. Doubtless the high alcohol content was supposed to make up for the taste, but as a werewolf, Anna didn't even get much of a buzz from it.

If she had been in this little intimate back room of the restaurant with her mate, she'd have laughed, put it aside, and ordered something else. But she was in if not precisely the company of enemies, then certainly *dangerous* company. It was important to maintain the appearance of competence. Competent people, she was sure, did not order drinks they did not like just to impress people with their nonexistent sophistication.

Rachel set her glass down and told it, "No more fitting rooms for me."

Anna grunted in sympathy.

"That," said Sage accusingly, tipping her glass toward Anna, "was a Charlie grunt. No men allowed on this expedition means no grunts."

Model-beautiful Sage was the only person allowed to call Anna's mate Charlie—not excepting Anna herself. Sage treated him like a big brother. And, Anna thought ruefully, Charles treated Sage as if she were any other member of his father's pack: to be protected but also to be held at a distance. Only with his brother and his father did the impassive shield he kept around himself loosen. With Anna he had no shield—Charles belonged to Anna with all his complicated soul and uncomplicated heart.

Anna would much rather be curled up with him in front of the fire or eating something one or the other of them had cooked. Instead, she sipped at her paint thinner at a restaurant in Missoula, the better part of two hundred miles away from home, at the tail end of one of Leah's females-only shopping expeditions. Anna was pretty sure there was no clothing store, shoe store, or makeup counter in Missoula they had not explored.

Anna's feet ached, and she saw Rachel slide out of her shoes and flex her toes when she thought no one was looking. Even Sage, the shopping queen, was rubbing her left calf. Only Leah, in four-inch heels, looked perfectly comfortable. Anna frowned at Leah's feet— maybe Leah wasn't crazy for spending ungodly amounts of money on her shoes.

Leah, the Marrok's mate, used the shopping trips to Missoula or Kalispell as bonding time for the women in the Marrok's pack. Usually they were something anyone without a Y chromosome could attend, but this time Leah had limited it further: Anna, Sage, Leah, and Rachel. Anna was pretty sure the trip had been designed to get Rachel, who had come into the pack only a month ago, comfortable enough to open up.

Rachel was not a permanent pack member; she would be with them only until the Marrok found a place for her that he liked. Somewhere safe. As Anna well knew, even werewolf strength didn't help

5

you when your abusers were werewolves, too. Rachel had come to them after her pack had undergone an extensive reorganization. No one had been killed, but her old pack was under new management, the former Alpha moved to a different pack where he was not in charge. Outside of the Alpha, Rachel had been the only wolf extracted from the situation.

Rachel hadn't said a word above a whisper since she'd arrived two weeks ago, and Leah or the Marrok (or both) had decided to do something about that.

Shopping.

Anna smiled into her house special cocktail as she pretended to sip. After two hours of trying on clothing, Rachel had forgotten to be intimidated and had joined the chorus of moans when Sage had found a dress that made her look fat.

Tall and slender, with gold-streaked brown hair and deep blue eyes, Sage looked more like a fashion model than most of the fashion models. Finding something that made her look bad had been quite an achievement. Distraction and bonding over bad fashion had broken through the shell Rachel had worn and revealed a quiet but naturally cheery soul.

Leah, for all of her faults, was good at her job. And the semi-good-natured ongoing rivalry between Leah and Sage (that Anna was convinced they both enjoyed) served as a reminder that no one in this pack needed to worry a more dominant wolf would overreact to a little snark. A reminder that the Marrok's pack was safe.

Anna had probably been included because she was an Omega wolf. Without trying, she pulled the tension in the air down to a manageable level and made people feel comfortable around her. This wouldn't be the first time she'd been recruited to help with a damaged werewolf. Now that Rachel was talking, Bran would be able to figure out where she would fit in best, whether that was in the Marrok's pack or somewhere with less potential for violence—most of Bran's pack were there because a lesser Alpha would not be able to control them.

Food came eventually, and in the middle of eating her steak, Rachel broke into the conversation with a total non sequitur. "I feel like a failure."

Sage reached out and covered her hand. "Why is that?"

"I'm a werewolf," she told Sage. "And I had to run away from my problems because I couldn't protect myself."

"Me, too," said Sage promptly.

Rachel's eyebrows shot up and her mouth opened in surprise. Anna had noticed throughout the day that Rachel was sporting a case of hero worship for Sage. Anna understood that. Sage had been the first to welcome Anna to the pack, too. Sage made it a point to protect newcomers until they could stand on their own two (or four) feet. She was an effective protector; her reputation as a fighter left most of the pack unwilling to push her too far.

Privately, Anna thought the way Sage called Charles "Charlie" also helped her in her efforts to cow bullies. Most of the wolves in the pack were a little afraid of Anna's mate. None of *them* would have dared to give Charles a nickname he disliked.

Sage nodded at Rachel. "One wolf cannot stand her ground against a whole pack." She cast a mischievous look at Anna. "Wolves whose last names are Cornick excepted." She returned her attention to Rachel. "Even Charlie had to bring Asil along to straighten out the mess your old Alpha made of his pack, Rachel."

That wasn't why Asil had gone. Asil had been sent so there would be no chance of any defiance that would force Charles to kill someone who might otherwise be saved. Charles alone was terrifying. Asil was a legend. No normal wolf would even imagine disobeying the pair of them.

Sage nudged Anna's leg underneath the table. At least she thought it was Sage. It might have been Leah. Anna was supposed to share her story to make Rachel feel less alone. Oh goody.

"Me, too," Anna muttered unenthusiastically. "I spent my time in purgatory."

"But you are an Omega," exclaimed Rachel. "No one would abuse an Omega wolf."

Anna would have let that stand, but Sage said, "They did. They forced the Change on her and followed up with several years of rape, pimping out, and beating."

Anna pushed her plate aside because she wasn't going to be able to eat after that. "Yes," she said. "And I needed rescuing, too, Rachel. But this isn't a 'my life was worse than your life' contest."

Trying to avoid seeing Rachel's expression, Anna met Sage's eyes accidentally. The other wolf immediately dropped Anna's gaze, and there was a faint flush on Sage's high cheekbones. Did Sage feel like it was a contest? Anna grimaced.

"Is that what life as a female werewolf is?" asked Rachel in a sub-dued voice. "Abuse? Looking for a protector? A rescue?" Rachel was tiny, maybe two inches shorter than Anna. Next to Sage and Leah, who were both very tall women, Rachel looked fragile and de-fenseless.

"Remember what pack you are in," Anna told her. "There are hun-dreds of female werewolves out there—and the Marrok only brings in one or two women a year who need assistance."

"Don't forget werewolves can live a long time," said Sage, pulling

Anna's uneaten dinner over and shoving her clean plate in front of Anna. "We all, male and female, are likely to run into a bad Alpha or some other kind of abusive situation at some point. The trick is to not join the other side of the equation and become abusers ourselves."

Leah pushed her own empty plate aside and downed her fourth shot of whiskey neat. "I think it's a matter of choosing your mate well."

Sometimes the older wolves showed the effects of being raised in an earlier era—like Leah's assumption a good mate was the cure for all problems. Anna was pretty sure no one else at the table believed the cold relationship Bran and Leah had was a good thing. It wasn't abusive—not quite. Not physically abusive, anyway. But Anna would have lasted a month, tops, in a relationship where her needs were met with attentive care—and not an ounce of affection.

But no one could say that, of course. Though there was something in Leah's face that made Anna wonder if Leah knew what they were all thinking.

"How did you choose Bran?" asked Sage.

Huh. Anna had presumed Sage, at least, would have known the story. There were a lot of things that everyone knew except Anna, and she'd assumed the details of Leah and Bran's courtship had been one of those. Anna knew better than to go around asking questions about the older wolves' pasts. If they wanted you to know, they would tell you. All Anna knew about how Leah and Bran met was that Bran had gone off to find a mate and had come back with Leah.

Leah played with her napkin, making her newly polished nails glitter in the deliberately dim lighting. She glanced around, as if looking for witnesses. But she had reserved a private room for them, and the other two tables in the room were empty, the door was shut, and there was no sign of waitstaff.

"I don't talk about it," she said shortly, in a tone of voice designed to put an end to the topic.

Sage was made of sterner stuff. She huffed a laugh. "I understand that, darlin'. Else I would know the story already. But now you've got to tell us—how did you get messed up with—" Leah raised an elegant eyebrow, and Sage grinned and altered her wording midsentence. "—ah, how did you meet our fearless leader?"

For a moment Anna thought Leah would balk, but finally she said, "My father and mother were missionaries called by God to educate the heathen savages." She took up her unused salad fork and peered at it, as if looking at her own reflection.

A lot of the old wolves still took for granted things Anna's generation tended to give more careful evaluation. Even so, Anna would never have thought the Leah she knew would have been able to utter such a sentiment seriously, but if there was sarcasm intended, Anna couldn't pick it up in Leah's voice.

"I was fifteen—the oldest of six children," Leah continued. What Leah said certainly had the ring of truth, but her casual tone hid more mass than the visible top of an iceberg did. "And Papa packed us all up in a wagon and headed west."

"This was when?" asked Anna. She might not know Leah's story, but she knew her husband's history. He'd been a child when Bran brought back Leah. "Late 1820s or early 1830s?"

History had not been her best subject, but living in a pack of wolves that encompassed individuals born before the *Mayflower* left port had upped her game. Leah's father's expedition west seemed pretty early. The Civil War and the California Gold Rush were both in the middle of the nineteenth century. The western expansion had mostly been driven by those two events.

Leah shrugged. "Maybe? I don't remember. Our church funded us to fuel the salvation of pagan souls." *There* was the thread of cynicism Anna had felt but not really heard. "Papa packed us all in a wagon—except for my littlest brother, who was only a few months old. He stayed with my aunt and her family. The idea was we would get settled and then my aunt and uncle would come join us."

She huffed an unamused laugh, and her foot began to tap a rhythm on the tile floor. "He had no idea what he was doing, my papa. Big dreams and no common sense. We ran out of food first. Then my little brother James broke his leg and died from the infection that set in."

She was speaking in a quick, light monotone—as if she couldn't bear to actually think about the words she was using.

"Two days later, one of our horses went dead lame and the other couldn't pull the wagon on his own over rough ground. For lack of any other plans, we camped next to a creek for a week or so waiting to see if the lamed horse would recover before we all died. The horses were pets, and Papa couldn't bear to shoot one of them just to feed us. He couldn't fish and Ma spent her time crying, but my oldest little brother, Tally, and I caught a few trout. Not enough, though. We were starving to death when *he* came."

The door behind them opened and a waiter came in to bus their plates. Leah pasted a polite smile on her face and ordered another whiskey in a voice slightly too loud.

Hesitantly, Rachel ordered red wine. As Sage requested water, Leah started humming under her breath.

Anna asked for water, too, but most of her attention was on Leah's music. Her humming was spot-on for pitch and rich enough to hint Leah might have a beautiful voice when she sang. Anna had never heard Leah sing. In the Marrok's pack, music was everywhere. Anna had assumed Leah just didn't have a good voice, that she *couldn't* sing, not that she *didn't* sing.

The door shut and they were alone again. No one said anything, unwilling for Leah to stop. The tune she hummed was compelling in the way "Bohemian Rhapsody," "Stairway to Heaven," or "In the Hall of the Mountain King" was compelling. Anna found that she leaned forward to hear more—and tapped her own foot in time with Leah's foot, which was giving a percussive beat that was counter to the rhythm of the song.

Sage's eyes were wide and she was staring at Leah. Sitting beside her, Anna could scent her unease. Fear, even.

It was Rachel, not Sage, who broke the odd spell, though. "What are you singing?" Rachel whispered. "I think I've heard it before—but I don't remember where."

Leah stopped, blinking rapidly as if she'd been caught up in the music, too.

"Where is that whiskey?" she muttered. Then she shook her head and lied, "Nothing, Rachel. It's just a song I heard once upon a time."

She seemed to hear the lie with a little surprise as it crossed her lips. But she didn't correct it, just shrugged and said briskly, "Anyway. Bran showed up. They saved me by Changing me into a werewolf."

That was weird. Changing someone was not a way to save someone who was starving. And who was "they"? Charles had told her Bran had gone off alone and brought Leah back.

Anna knew better than to ask about any of that, though. Leah hated Charles and that put a few odd kinks in her relations with Anna, Omega or not. If Anna questioned Leah about a situation she clearly did not want to speak about, Leah would clam up.

"You were fifteen?" asked Sage, an edge of outrage in her voice because, like Anna, she had been born in the last hundred years. "*Fifteen* when he took you for his mate?"

That was a good question. But it wasn't the first on Anna's list, her very long list. And she was pretty sure it was wrong, too. Someone—Charles, surely—would have told Anna if Leah had been only fifteen when Bran brought her back to his home in Montana.

Leah shook her head and said briskly, "Fifteen? Goodness, no. Twenty or more, I think. You know how time blurs after a while."

The "he" who had come upon Leah and her starving family had not been Bran, then. Five years or more between that day and when Bran had "rescued her" by transforming her into a werewolf. Leah had given them only the beginning and the end—leaving out all the interesting parts in between. Why had she started the story if she wasn't going to finish it?

Anna waited for Sage to address some of those questions, but evidently she'd decided to leave off questioning.

There was a long, quiet pause as Rachel finished her drink, Sage fixed her makeup, and Leah stared at her empty shot glass. Anna tried not to look like she was bursting with curiosity. Five years of something so important Leah wouldn't talk about it. Anna would bug Charles.

She took out her phone and texted him: Almost done. Do you know how and why Bran Changed Leah?

She'd been texting him on and off all day. She'd sent him a photo of Sage in the unflattering outfit—but not in the five hundred dresses/shirts/pants/skirts that made her look stunning. Anna wasn't an idiot. Charles hadn't replied to any of them. He must be out doing something. Bran liked to steal him to go hunting when Anna was gone.

She got a text back this time.

No idea. Da doesn't talk about it. But he doesn't talk about the past in general. Sorry for not responding earlier. Went for a run with Da.

Leah was humming again. Hearing it afresh . . . she could imagine it played by a full orchestra with timpani drums beating the same rhythm of Leah's toes, making Anna's chest buzz with the power of it.

Anna looked up from her phone and frowned at Leah. Understanding what a piece would sound like with different instrumentation was part of what had made Anna the kind of musician who got scholarships to Northwestern University. But this was more visceral than what she normally experienced.

She needed to interrupt it, so she said, "What *is* that song, Leah? Rachel's right. It's familiar but I can't place it." It made her want to go do . . . something.

Leah stopped humming but she looked lost in her own thoughts.

"Anna was a music major in college," Sage told Rachel. "Before the bad wolves got her."

Pulled away from the musical puzzle by Sage's words, Anna tried not to scowl. Anna hadn't wanted to go into graphic detail about her time in hell, for sure, so why did Sage reducing her abduction to the level of a Grimms' fairy tale make the hair on her neck stand up? Anna frowned at her mostly full cocktail, sure she was overreacting. Maybe she shouldn't drink things that tasted like paint thinner?

Leah touched Anna's hand and gave her a soft smile that made her look more beautiful than Sage for a moment. And no one was more beautiful than Sage. It wasn't a smile Anna had ever seen on Leah's face before—something, she thought, the music had brought out.

"I don't know the name of the song," Leah said, her voice a little rough, as if her throat were dry. She looked at the far wall, but Anna was pretty sure it wasn't what she was seeing. "I never did—or at least I don't think I did. It's been troubling me lately. I wonder what it means."

The waiter came back with their drinks then, and the topic of conversation moved on to something lighter. But the song Leah had hummed lingered in Anna's ears, along with a nagging sense of unease because of the unfinished story. It felt important. There had been five years between the day someone had happened upon Leah's starving family and when Bran and someone else had rescued her.

Rescued her from what?

CHAPTER

1

AUTUMN: ASPEN CREEK, MONTANA

Anna let her hands press the ivory keys of the old upright piano in a few preparatory chords, enjoying the rich sound. Music, for her, was not just an auditory experience—she loved the feel of the vibrations running through her fingers. The bass notes resonated in her core, leaving her energized and ready to play.

In all senses of the word.

She glanced over her shoulder and up at her husband's face. She wasn't sure anyone else had ever played with him. No one in their pack, for certain, including Bran. Oh, they played music with him, but they didn't play *games*.

The piano wasn't her instrument, but like most people who had ever attended college with the aim of majoring in music, she was reasonably competent. For this game, the piano was more flexible than her preferred cello, which was limited to two notes at a time, a few more with harmonics.

"Ready?" she asked him, then launched into the song without waiting for his response.

She hummed where the melody came in—it was his job to figure out the words. It didn't take him long this time. Charles, his warmth against her back, though he didn't touch her, began singing the lyrics to "Walk on the Ocean" with her two beats after she'd started humming.

The game had originated when Anna found out Charles hadn't heard of P. D. Q. Bach, who had been a favorite of one of her music teachers. A lack she had remedied with the help of the Internet. In return, Charles had shared a few singers he liked. Some of them left her cold. Some of them had been unexpectedly awesome. Of course, she had heard Johnny Cash before she'd met Charles. But Charles had turned her into an unabashed Johnny Cash fan—though she liked Cash's songs even better if Charles sang them. They suited his voice.

She would have loved Charles if he hadn't been able to carry a tune in a bucket, but Charles's facility for and love of music had been one of many unexpected gifts her mate had brought to their union. She had been so lucky to find him.

Gradually they had begun challenging each other, finding singers, groups, or songs that the other didn't know. It was the best kind of game: one with no losers. Either they figured out the song the other pulled out of their store of obscure or favorite songs (or obscure *and* favorite songs) or they didn't.

Sometimes they kept score—the loser to do dishes or cook or something more fun. But mostly they just enjoyed making music together—the game giving the activity more variety than it might otherwise have had.

Toad the Wet Sprocket, evidently, had not been a challenge at all.

Anna laughed in surrender, then sang the rest of "Walk on the Ocean" with Charles, letting him anchor the melody while she worked out a descant an octave above him—pushing her alto into a register mostly reserved for sopranos. Sometimes crafting harmonies on the fly could go terribly wrong, but this time it sounded good. Their voices complemented each other, which, even with good singers, wasn't always true.

"That's one of Samuel's favorites," Charles told her when they were finished.

Anna hadn't spent much time with Charles's brother; he'd left his father's pack by the time she'd joined, but she knew he was a musician, too. Listening to Charles, Samuel, and their father perform the old Shaker song "Simple Gifts" at a funeral had been the first indication Anna'd had that she'd married into a very musical family.

She'd thought her music lost the night she'd been attacked and turned into a werewolf. Charles had given it back. In return, she hoped, she had given him playfulness.

He bent down, put his mouth against her ear, and said, in a mock-villain growl, "You'll have to do better than that to defeat me."

The rumble of his voice sent chills up her spine. She loved it when he was happy. She was so easy—at least as far as Charles was concerned. She leaned back against him, then tilted her head up. He bent over and kissed her lips.

He started to pull away, hesitated, and came down for a second round. His lips were softer than they looked, sweeping from the corner of her mouth in a gentle caress before pressing her lips open.

His breath became ragged. His muscles, still warming her back, tightened until she might have been leaning against a wall instead of a living being. If there was anything sexier than being desired, she didn't know what it could be.

Her body became liquid as their lips lingered together, taking the gift of desire and returning it to him. His hand pressed briefly on her breastbone, just above her breast, his touch gentle. Then he slid his hand up until it covered the arch of her throat, fingertips spread to span her jawline, encouraging her to keep her head tilted for his kiss. As if she needed encouragement.

When he finished with her mouth for the moment, his lips brushed her cheekbone and over to her ear, which he nipped. The sharpness after the soft and light touch sent a shock reverberating up her spine.

"Mmm," she said.

He stepped away from her, breathing hard. His smile was sheepish. "That was a little more than I intended," he said.

She shrugged, knowing the dismissive gesture would be given the lie by her reddened lips and the arousal he probably would not have to be a werewolf to sense. "I am not taking any of the fault for that, sir."

He laughed, the sound low and soft. Hot. But he still took another step away—backward, as if he couldn't quite make himself turn his back on her.

"I have a song for you," he said. "I've been working on this for a while."

He grabbed one of the cases stacked along the wall of their music room and took out a flute. He gave Anna an assessing look and then pulled her guitar off the wall where it hung with several of his.

She had come to him with nothing, but she had the feeling, given the pleasure he took in giving her things, that her collection of instruments might outpace his in time. She took the guitar when he handed it to her.

"Just what am I supposed to do with this?" she asked archly, but she reversed her position on the piano bench so the piano was at her back and gave the guitar strings an experimental strum, adjusting the high E until the pitch was true. They were new strings, and the E liked to slip.

He didn't answer her, just pulled up a chair so he would face her when he sat in it. He dragged a low table over beside his chair and set the flute on it. Then he searched the cases and pulled out an instrument she hadn't seen him use—a viola.

"Oooo," she said. "Can I see?"

He raised an eyebrow but handed it over. "It's Da's," he told her.

She glanced in the f-hole and found a maker's ink signature and the date 1872. It didn't tell her much. She reached out blindly and he gave her the bow. She tested it, tightened a peg an eighth of a turn, and stroked the bow across the strings, smiling at the rich tone.

"Bran has good taste," she said, handing the viola and bow back to him.

He took more care in tuning it than she had with the guitar—as one does, she thought with amusement. Violas—like their little sister, the violin—were temperamental. When he was satisfied, he sat down, the viola held like a cello, instead of the more usual under-the-chin method.

"Ready?" he asked.

She rolled her eyes. "No? What are we playing? Or do I get to make something up? How about a key signature?"

He grinned. "I have faith. Join in when you are ready."

He picked up the flute and . . . he was right, she recognized the tune.

She'd been making an effort at reconnecting with a few of her friends from Northwestern. A few months ago one of them had shared a link to a self-proclaimed Mongolian folk metal band. They called themselves the Hu. They played modified traditional Mongolian instruments in addition to those more commonly found in rock bands. They also used a type of throat singing in which a single singer produced more than one note at the same time.

They sounded exactly like what she'd have expected musicians from Genghis Khan's troops to sound like if they'd been given the power of modern instruments. She loved it.

She'd shared their music with Charles, he'd listened to a couple of songs, nodded his head—and she'd thought that had been that. Apparently, she'd been wrong.

He began, as the original song did, with the flute, switching seamlessly to the viola, which he used to mimic the traditional horsehead fiddle. When he sang, he used the throat-singing technique—in, as far as she could tell, the original Mongolian.

It was a gift. He'd done a great deal of work—and he was a busy man—to prepare this song for her. For a quiet man, Charles was very good at saying "I love you."

When the song drew to an end, Anna, flushed with enjoyment and pleasure, applauded enthusiastically. "Holy cow. Just wow. I didn't know you speak Mongolian. You are full of surprises."

He put the viola away and gave her a lighthearted grin that lit up his face. "I just mimic. Doubtless my song would leave anyone who actually spoke Mongolian scratching their head. And I don't have the throat singing down right. There's a vibration technique I haven't figured out yet. I had to do that on the viola."

Anna hung her guitar up, shaking her head with mock reproof. "That's it. You might as well give up music altogether and go live on the top of a mountain, where you can wallow in your shame."

Big arms wrapped around her, pulling her back against him. She gave an exaggerated oof as if he'd squeezed out all of her air.

"Only if you come with me," he crooned. "Then I won't get bored as I wallow."

"What makes you think I could help you with boredom?" she asked in an innocent voice, pushing her hips back against him suggestively as one of his hands moved down, an iron bar across her belly, while the other moved up, pushing her hair aside to bare the side of her throat for him. "What is it you think we can do all alone—"

Upstairs, the doorbell rang.

They both froze. It was late for casual visitors.

"The door isn't locked," Charles growled.

"And anyone who is pack is likely to just walk in," she agreed reluctantly.

He didn't release her.

"Charles?" she asked.

He inhaled her scent. "I am second in the pack," he said with obvious reluctance. "If someone is ringing our doorbell, I have to answer."

She twisted in his arms and stood on tiptoe to kiss his chin, liking that she was going to smell like him for a while. Jeez, being a werewolf had changed her point of view on a lot of things, she mused, turning to climb up the stairs, Charles at her heels.

The phone rang—the landline that never rang but hung from the wall above the light switch like a tribute to the past. Charles stopped beside it.

"It's Da," he told her, then answered the phone.

Bran could make his voice heard in the minds of his wolves (and probably anyone else he cared to). He maintained that he could not hear responses—which was, Anna assumed, why he had decided to use the phone.

"Tell Anna to get the door," Bran said. "You need to let the wolf greet them." And then he left them with a dial tone.

Huh, she thought, meeting Charles's eyes.

He shrugged. He didn't know why Bran had bothered calling, either. Maybe just to make whoever was at the door wait a bit longer. Trying to work out the hows and whys of Bran's actions tended to leave Anna with a headache and no wiser for the struggle.

Anna obeyed her orders, walking the twelve feet or so to the door and opening it. She was still trying to work out what Bran's call had been about, so she blinked a little at the unexpected visitors.

The nearest, illuminated by the porch light, was a fortysomething black woman, looking athletic and smart in a white polo shirt with the FBI logo on one shoulder and dark blue trousers. Beside her was a short, fine-boned white man who could have been anywhere from his midfifties to midseventies. His hair, which had been dark, had been shaved completely off. His tan jacket and blue slacks fit him well and were free of wrinkles or creases. Still, he struck her as more fragile than he'd been the last time she'd seen him, and she wondered if he had been sick. He didn't smell sick.

For a moment she felt an automatic smile of welcome flow up toward her face, borne of a genuine liking for Special Agent Leslie Fisher and a generally favorable impression of Special Agent Craig Goldstein.

But they weren't supposed to know who she was *now* or where she and Charles lived. A wide streak of wariness shoved her smile aside as she contemplated the two FBI agents and wondered what this visit was about to change in their world.

"This is unexpected," she said.

As the daughter of a lawyer, Anna had a natural inclination to respect the law. But the FBI had no real jurisdiction over her. They would not be permitted to question her or arrest her or take her to trial without a great deal of trouble—maybe not even then. They were all on pack territory now.

She wondered if they understood just how dangerous that was for them. She certainly understood how dangerous their presence here was for the werewolves. This was above her pay grade, she thought. But it would not help matters to let Charles take over.

Leslie looked at Goldstein. Anna remembered that he'd been the senior of the two when she'd first met them. It seemed that still held true.

"We have some information for you, Ms. Smith," he said without apology. "We felt it was best delivered in person. We also felt that you were the best person to deliver it to."

Goldstein knew very well Smith wasn't her name—Anna didn't like him rubbing her nose in it. She and Charles had made it plain that Smith had been a *nom de nécessité*, and not their own—for heaven's sake, why else would they have used "Smith," notorious in fact and fiction as a false name?

Goldstein's words smacked of a power play—and Anna disliked politics intensely. Too bad her mate was only slightly more inclined to diplomacy than certain axe-wielding Vikings of her acquaintance. Which left the role of negotiator to her.

This, she thought ruefully, was bound to be a disaster.

Several years of being trapped in a pack where brutality was a fact of everyday life had given her some skills in negotiating with terrorists, however. She wasn't quite ready to put Leslie Fisher in that category, but it was probably best to assume the worst.

First, show no fear. This was much easier to manage with Charles waiting behind her than it had been when she'd been alone, especially since the FBI had sent people she knew and liked. This was probably not a hostile move on their part. Not yet, anyway.

"My name," Anna said, letting ice coat her voice, "is Anna Cornick." Since they were standing on her porch, they already knew her real name.

Second, give the appearance of cooperation—but don't give them anything you don't have to.

"He was trying to be tactful," Leslie said, though she didn't believe it.

Anna raised an eyebrow. "Werewolves can smell lies." This was something, like her name, that they also already knew.

Leslie flinched subtly and gave her cohort a grim look. The next sentence out of her mouth was the truth, and she sounded more like a professional agent than a friend. "I'm sorry for the surprise, but we do need to talk to you. Rather than advertising that the FBI came to call on you, can we come in?"

Anna crossed her arms over her chest and snorted. "This is a small town. Everyone already knows you're here. Sometime in the next ten minutes they'll look up your plates."

"It's a rental car."

Challenge accepted, Anna thought. "Helen Oxford has a sister who works in the airport in Missoula with the rental car agencies. She won't have any trouble finding out who rented the car."

"We drove in from Spokane, not Missoula," said Leslie.

"Rental car agencies are nationwide companies," Goldstein remarked to no one in particular. Then he said, "Point taken, Ms. Cornick. If you wish to discuss this on your doorstep . . ." He looked around.

They were surrounded by mountains and forest. There were no nearby houses. The closest neighbor was a half mile away.

". . . then I see no reason we cannot do that."

Invite them in, said Brother Wolf.

Anna glanced over her shoulder to see the red wolf standing in most of the available floor of their galley kitchen. She wondered, again, why Bran had decided to give the FBI a werewolf to look at.

It was not a bad idea to remind your enemy of who you are, she supposed. Though she hadn't thought the FBI were their enemies. She had considered Leslie a friend. But she couldn't afford them to be friends now.

"We have two items of business to bring before you today," Goldstein was saying. "We know some things we think you should know. And we'd like to start building toward a more formal relationship that could help us both."

Brother Wolf had said to let them in, but Anna wasn't sure it was a good idea. She was reasonably certain that Charles wouldn't tear into the FBI agents without violent provocation. And she was reasonably certain, having dealt with both agents in the past, that neither of them was likely to be violently provocative. But Brother Wolf was an entirely different kettle of fish.

We'll behave, Brother Wolf assured her. *You can let them in.*

"I see," said Anna. "Perhaps you should come in."

She stepped back, opening the door as an invitation. The open door also gave them a very good view of Brother Wolf. If the sight of the werewolf bothered them, neither of them let it show. They had met Charles's wolf before.

Anna waved a hand, directing the agents through the living room and into the dining area beyond. Leslie let Agent Goldstein take the lead, and Anna followed behind them.

Leslie paused, looking at the large painting hung over the fireplace. Other than the various instruments that were scattered about, it was the only piece of art in the room.

It was a new painting, still smelling of oils to Anna's sensitive nose. The smaller piece it replaced had been moved to their bedroom, both works by the same artist.

On one level, the painting was of a gray wolf—not a werewolf—standing in winter woods. But that wasn't the lingering impression it made. Whenever Anna looked at it, she could feel the tension drain away and optimism flood in to replace it. Anna had stared at the painting for hours, and she still didn't know how Wellesley had done it. Wellesley's work had always been spectacular—but this one, painted after his curse had been removed, was more . . . more something.

Asil had brought it over after Wellesley had left. It had come with a note that read: *For Anna.* He hadn't signed either the note or the painting.

"Beautiful piece," Leslie said, reaching out but not touching the canvas. "Who is the artist?"

"A friend," answered Anna. She had no idea if Wellesley would be interested in painting as a career again, or what name he would choose when and if he did. But she did think if he had wanted people to know who had painted it, he would have signed it. If she and Leslie were being friendly, she might have told her so. As it was, the words lingered in the air.

Leslie frowned at Anna but continued on to the dining room to sit beside Goldstein. Once she was seated, she glanced over her shoulder at the painting again.

Anna pulled up a seat opposite the two agents. Charles moved to her side and stared at them. Neither agent stared back at him, which was smart of them. Charles was not happy.

"We are," Anna began softly, "very interested in who told you where we live."

Goldstein nodded and put his briefcase—a battered leather case that had seen better days—on the table and opened it. He pulled out a thick file in a folder and held it out to Anna. Taped to the front of the folder was a thumb drive. When she didn't take it, he set in on the table between them.

"Most of what we know about werewolves has been gathered in bits and pieces for decades, if not longer." Goldstein's voice had a faint New York accent Anna hadn't caught before. "A slip here, a note there. A colleague of mine has been riding a hobbyhorse of werewolf lore for the entirety of his forty-year career at the bureau. You'll find most of the general information comes to us from the armed forces— apparently there have been a great many werewolves over the years who have served their country."

He pulled another file out with another thumb drive. "This is from the Cantrip archives." He didn't say how they had gotten it. "Cantrip has been fed information about you from various groups—some of them supernatural hate groups like Bright Future or the John Lauren Society. Some of them are other supernatural groups. One informant was a witch—and she provided them with the equivalent of a biology textbook. Her information was classified and only the very top echelon of Cantrip has access to it. There was a vampire, too, at some point. But he killed two of their agents and they killed him."

Leslie cleared her throat. "There is information in there you would not want to be public knowledge."

Anna didn't make any move to take the offerings on the table— that would be for someone else to go through. Goldstein did not say who had told them where Anna and Charles lived, which would have been more interesting information.

Charles had long ago hacked into the Cantrip database. He probably had hacked into the FBI files, too. The wolves knew there were people in the government who understood just what the wolves were and mostly who they were. It was not the government Bran was worried about—at least not yet. It was the public in general—and what the public would urge their government to do.

"You've obviously had this information for a while," she said. "So why the candor now? What do you mean to accomplish with this?" She waved her hand at the files on the table.

Goldstein smiled grimly. "Some of my superiors were quite stuck on Hauptman. It took some persuading to bring this here instead."

Anna didn't know what kind of reaction she was supposed to have, since the Columbia Basin Pack and Adam Hauptman, its prickly and extremely handsome Alpha, were the most famous werewolves on the planet—at least in the eyes of the purely human.

"Okay," she said. Leslie's face didn't change, but from Goldstein's expression, Anna knew her response hadn't been the one he was looking for.

"The FBI feels that the various supernatural groups pose a threat to the public. We are reasonably certain if all hell breaks loose, our superior numbers and weapons will leave us the last ones standing. But that only means we all lose."

"Yes," Anna agreed, having heard variants on this assessment—albeit from the werewolf side—for years.

"We feel with allies to lend us knowledge, finesse, and firepower, we could avoid the zero-sum ending. We need a large group, one we can trust—and who can trust us."

Anna must have made some sort of derisive sound, because Goldstein grinned appreciatively.

"For some levels of trust," he agreed. "The FBI is a large organization—and our upper management is politically appointed. We have . . . not involved the political appointees at this point. We do understand why you might be less than happy to ally yourselves with us. That's why I brought you our files, as a gesture of goodwill."

"Not much of a risk," Anna observed. "Since it's all information about werewolves—and we already know all about werewolves."

"Right," said Goldstein. "But you can find out how much we know about you."

Anna wasn't sure she believed that last part even if Goldstein did. But she didn't think that conversation would be useful.

She shrugged. "All right. So why bring it to us?"

Goldstein frowned at her a moment. He tapped a finger on the table and said, "I think our opportunity to ally with the fae died when that thrice-be-damned court let Heuter walk. Everyone in the courtroom, judge and jury, knew he'd raped and killed people who came from the supernatural groups. Everyone knew he'd raped the daughter of a Gray Lord and intended to kill her—and they still let him off because he was human and his victims were not. Do you remember the cheers from the courtroom?"

They had all been there.

His assessment of that situation was right on target, Anna thought. Gwyn ap Lugh, who went by the name of Beauclaire, was the most prominent member of the faction of Gray Lords who had been friendly toward humans. It had been his daughter who had been brutalized and scarred.

"Charles told me the world would have been better off if he'd just killed Heuter when he had a chance," Anna agreed. "It wouldn't have been just to kill a man who had surrendered—but what the courts delivered wasn't justice, either."

"I could have shot him, too," Leslie observed regretfully. "I thought about it pretty hard."

Goldstein grunted. "That ship has sailed. So, while we hope for a cease-fire with the fae, we are aware the fae will never trust us. My bones will be dust and Beauclaire will still remember a human court chose to protect their own monster rather than give a Gray Lord's daughter justice."

"That is a problem when dealing with immortal creatures," murmured Anna.

"The only other large and organized group we know about is the vampires. It is difficult for a chicken to make an alliance with a fox— you never know when you'll be eaten for breakfast," Goldstein said.

And the vampires were still allowing the world to pretend they didn't exist. It was easier for everyone concerned. An alliance would surely mean the vampires had to come out of the shadows.

"That left the werewolves," Leslie said. "But we didn't know how to approach it. We knew there were packs directed by Alphas. We even knew several of the Alphas *very* well—Hauptman, for instance. Then you and Charles came to Boston."

They hadn't mentioned the witches, Anna noted. Maybe they didn't consider them an organized group.

"Before that," said Goldstein, "we had always thought the wolves to be individual packs run by unaffiliated Alphas. As soon as we reconsidered, it wasn't hard to look at certain events and see the wolves are highly organized. That they are able to act as a single unit if necessary."

Anna controlled a snort. He made it sound like a business arrangement. Bran controlling the werewolves was more like shoving tigers around with cattle prods. Marginally effective, if potentially fatal to all involved.

"Is that person, the person in charge—is that you, Anna Cornick?" asked Goldstein.

She'd been stuck trying to make her tiger metaphor work. She had to blink at Goldstein for a minute to process what he'd said. She decided that was a good thing, because it wasn't hard to keep her face blank while she thought about what to do with his question.

"Why do you ask?" she said, without letting any expression enter her voice or face. Her years surviving in a brutal pack had given her that ability. "You know who I am. Anna Latham, age twenty-six, college dropout."

"Anna Latham, musical prodigy," said Goldstein somberly. "Who disappeared after work one night and was never seen again. Oh, her father and brother both say that she is alive. But no one else who knew her has heard from her. No concerts have been scheduled, though she used to do them as an invited guest."

She'd been working at reconnecting with her friends. Either the FBI had asked the wrong people or her friends thought she was in trouble and were trying to protect her. The concerts, though, were unlikely to happen. She missed performing to a big crowd.

"Werewolves are immortal," said Leslie very quietly. And Anna remembered how worried Leslie had been when she'd first met Anna that someone as young as Anna had been married to Charles—who did not look young, no matter the lack of wrinkles or gray hair. No one with eyes as old as his could look young.

"Isaac, the Alpha of the Boston pack—" began Goldstein.

"Olde Towne Pack," Anna corrected.

"Olde Towne Pack," Goldstein repeated, and she bet he wouldn't get it wrong again. "Isaac had no trouble following your orders."

That they had seen, anyway.

"I thought at first you were playing front man to Charles," Leslie said. "But he does your bidding, too."

And they had added two and two and come up with twenty-two.

Anna opened her mouth to tell them they were wrong.

Wait. See what they have to say. Do not lie to them, that could come back and bite us. But for now, let them believe you are leading the packs. It was Bran's voice in her head.

Aha. That was why Charles had had her invite the FBI in—so his da could listen from outside the house. It had taken her a long time to adjust to the difficulty of a private conversation with other werewolves around. The walls of her house were no match for wolf ears.

"I see," Anna said, because she had been ready to tell them they were wrong, and she couldn't think of anything else to say.

"*If* there is someone in charge, if that is you, we—that is to say, my . . ." Goldstein faltered.

"Superiors?" suggested Anna.

Owners, growled Brother Wolf, unhappy with Bran for asking his mate to put herself in harm's way like this.

"Colleagues," said Leslie, watching Goldstein. "Equals."

34

Goldstein had been with the bureau for more than twenty years, Anna recalled. He wasn't subject to political whim because he wasn't quite that far up in the bureaucracy, but Charles had told her Goldstein was right on the edge. He could have toppled into high office had he wished it. Leslie Fisher was on her way to doing exactly that.

"Our job," Leslie said intensely, "the job of the FBI, is to protect the citizens of the United States. We can do that better through an alliance with the werewolves."

"Who are citizens of the United States," said Anna.

"Yes," agreed Goldstein after a damning hesitation. "An alliance between the FBI and the werewolves will make everyone safer."

Anna wondered if that was true.

"We know an alliance will take time," Leslie said. "But today is a start."

Goldstein pulled out another folder and set it beside the other two. "To that end, as a demonstration that you might find us as useful to you as you are to us, we have a mystery for you."

"There's a town missing," said Leslie, pulling a folded-up USGS map out of the folder and laying it on the table. Someone had used a black marker to circle an area, then taped a slip of white paper next to the circle. Written in a neat hand in blue ink were the words *Wild Sign*.

Leslie tapped the marked space. "A group of people, as few as thirty or as many as forty as best we can tell, went up into the Marble Mountains in Northern California to live off-grid. The first of them set up about two or three years ago. Their settlement was illegal—the mountains are a mix of designated wilderness, federal lands, and tribal lands. Probably they thought they were on federal lands."

Lots of snow in the Marbles, Brother Wolf told her. And Anna got something that was very nearly a visual from him.

"We have confirmation it was an active site this spring, when one of the Forest Service rangers stopped in to check on them. One of the community wrote to his daughter and gave her this map. It was his habit to write to her regularly, but his last letter was this April—a few days after the ranger stopped by, in fact. When the daughter received no further correspondence, she hiked in and found it abandoned. They were just gone."

"Like Roanoke," said Goldstein, "they just all disappeared. Of the names we've found, none of them have relocated and none of their relatives know where they are."

"And this concerns us how?" Anna asked.

"Because it was finally determined that the settlement is not on either federal or tribal lands. It's on a private parcel owned by Aspen Creek, Inc.," said Goldstein. "Which is why no one tried to move them along."

He and Leslie were looking at Anna, and she had no trouble looking blank.

"Aspen Creek, Inc., was the owner of the condo you stayed in while you were in Boston," Leslie said. "And Aspen Creek is where you live. Where your pack lives." She hesitated. "Where the Marrok's pack lives."

The title "Marrok" was not a secret word, but it was one Anna had never heard from a government official before. Leslie's tone of voice and her pause meant she knew how important that term was. Anna didn't know what Bran wanted to do about his title being bandied about in the human halls of power, so she chose to do nothing.

After it became obvious Anna wasn't going to admit to anything, Goldstein's voice was dry when he continued, "And there is this: the original owner of the property was one Leah Fenwood *Cornick*."

A light knock sounded and the front door opened. Bran came in with a sheepish smile on his face. Anna had heard Charles's foster sister, Mercy, say Bran looked more like a pizza delivery boy than the Wolf Who Rules. She hadn't quite understood it until just that minute.

He wore a long-sleeved shirt that managed to conceal the hardness of his body, his shoulders hunched vaguely apologetically to match his smile. With a height that was just barely average and sandy blond hair worn a little untidily, Bran looked like a college student—or a pizza delivery boy.

"Hi," he said pleasantly to the FBI agents without quite meeting their eyes. He patted Charles on the head as he padded around to slip between his son and Anna.

"May I?" he inquired of Anna as he pulled the map over toward their side of the table.

"Be my guest," she said, unable to quite conceal her amusement.

He bent over the map. After a brief but thorough examination during which Anna returned Leslie's inquiring look with a shrug, Bran gave an abrupt nod of his head. He looked his son in the eye for a moment, tapped the table with one brisk finger, then exited the house with a wave over his shoulder that might have been directed at the FBI agents—or just the room in general.

They feel earnest, Bran told her after he'd shut the door behind him. *They at least believe everything they are saying. Tell them who I am. Tell them we will go looking. Tell them the rest of their visit might or might not be fruitful. The lessons Beauclaire learned are lessons we also take to heart. It might have been one of ours in the courtroom instead of Lizzie Beauclaire. I do not trust the humans.*

Anna drew in a deep breath. "Despite your flattering suspicions, I am not the Wolf Who Rules." She liked Mercy's phrase for Bran's title. "Marrok" didn't mean much to humans until she explained it. "Wolf

Who Rules" was self-explanatory. "The actual Wolf Who Rules just left through the front door. He believes you are sincere, but the lesson Beauclaire received—the lesson we all received—about how humans really think of us is concerning. *You* might not think we are monsters— or at least that we can be your monsters—but we don't believe the rest of the citizens of this country agree. That doesn't mean cooperation is out of the question, or that we won't be available to give a certain amount of aid—but don't consider us allies yet."

"You can't mean to tell us *he* is the wolf in charge." Goldstein's voice conveyed absolute disbelief. "I have met Hauptman. Hauptman would never take orders from someone like him."

"But they would take orders from someone like me?" asked Anna, amused.

"They do take orders from you. I've seen it," he said, as emotional as Anna had ever heard him.

Anna smiled. "I was Anna Latham the music student at Northwestern. I am twenty-six years old. I am married to the son of the Marrok—the Marrok who just left."

She let the smile fall from her face, because this was important. She liked both FBI agents and didn't want either of them to do something dangerously stupid—like underestimating Bran. "He is very good at blending in, my father-in-law. But don't mistake him for anything but a ruthless bastard."

Charles smiled, showing all of his teeth.

CHARLES SHOWERED FIRST, then dressed while Anna showered.

He wasn't sure he wanted to go running in the mountains of California on a wild-goose chase. Brother Wolf, however, was eager—it had been a long time since they had hunted in those mountains. Werewolves tended to be territorial, and Brother Wolf was no exception, but he loved to go exploring, too. And he wanted to share all of the extraordinary places they had been with Anna.

There was a cave, he told Charles. *Do you remember the cave?*

Charles did. "The Marbles encompass a lot of ground," he told Brother Wolf. He wasn't sure the wolf could read maps. "That cave is maybe twenty miles from where we're headed." He considered. "We might manage the lake with the big trout, though—if it's still there."

The Klamath River, like most big rivers, had been dammed and its path forever changed. New lakes formed and others gone forever.

Anna came into the bedroom with a big red towel wrapped around herself and nothing else. Her reddish-brown hair was tied up on top of her head, and there was a drop of water on his favorite freckle.

They were all his favorite freckles.

"Stop that, you," she said, but he could tell she didn't really mean it by the heat in her eyes. "We have bigger problems. What was your da thinking, strolling in there like some meek little lamb? I don't know if I managed to convince the FBI that he's the Marrok."

"That isn't urgent," Charles said. "He can convince them himself whenever he wants to. He came in to see the map—I think he knows something about what's happened. And he came in to see if he needed to kill someone. It is a good thing the FBI sent Fisher and Goldstein. If they had sent someone more twisty, Da might have decided to kill them to send a message to their owners." He used the term Brother Wolf had thrown out.

Anna grimaced. "I thought that might be it." She looked at Charles. "I would have defended them."

He knew that—and it would have been obvious to his da as

well. That knowledge might have been the thing keeping both agents alive. He didn't think it was because Bran was seriously considering an alliance.

"Unofficial offers from government officials are notoriously dangerous," he observed. "Secret alliances were the powder keg that blew up into World War I."

"That doesn't mean friendly relations wouldn't be useful," Anna countered.

He nodded agreement. "Friendly, yes. But wherever such a relationship ends up, it will be far short of an us-against-them alliance of humans and werewolves against all comers."

"Especially since Bran doesn't really like mundane humans," added Anna, wiping her cheek on the end of her towel.

Charles closed the distance between them. He put a finger over the towel where her breasts came together and formed a valley, but he left the towel where it was. He never touched her without her consent, and never would.

She smiled, and it was a wicked, hungry thing.

"Yes," she said.

CHAPTER

2

Charles spread the map that Goldstein had left with them on his da's desk. He had taken a silver Sharpie and inked in the boundaries of Leah's land before he'd left Anna sleeping in their bed and gone to find his da—as his da had requested before he'd left Anna and Charles to deal with the FBI.

Charles had known about the land, of course. He took care of all of the pack's properties, and the personal properties owned by his family. Taxes, upkeep, and, when appropriate, renters or rental agencies were all under his aegis. It wasn't the only section of land owned by the Cornick family, so he hadn't been too curious about it.

He'd thought his da had bought the property for Leah sometime in the nineteen forties—during World War II. But if her name had been on the original deed . . . He couldn't remember how that part of California had been settled. Had that been one of the areas settled by homesteading? That would mean Da had acquired that land a lot earlier than Charles had believed.

Bran studied the map for a minute and then shrugged. "I haven't been there in a long time. I doubt I could find my way there without a map and a guide. Too much has changed—the entire course of the river, logging, trails, and towns."

Charles nodded. He had the same problem. He'd traveled all over the west in the early nineteen hundreds. Some of that had been business for his da, and some of it had been to get away from his da. He'd been to most of the towns nearest to Leah's land at one time or another. He didn't remember much about many of them, and he doubted he'd recognize them.

"You are sending Anna and me to check out the missing people," Charles said. It wasn't a question.

"I don't like to send you there," his father replied, arms folded across his chest and an expression on his face so neutral that Charles knew Bran was very, very unhappy.

Since his da had sent him to some nasty situations over the years, Charles was intrigued.

"Do you know what could have happened to them?" he asked. "Is there something—*someone* dangerous?"

Bran frowned. "Yes. But I don't know much more than that. The only one who *might* be able to tell us something is Sherwood Post, and he's forgotten it all."

His da's voice held a growl that told Charles it was a good thing Sherwood was safely out of his da's long reach at the moment. Da had always blamed Sherwood for the memory loss, though from the outside it had seemed grossly unfair. Doubtless Da had reason for it—he usually did—but he hadn't shared it with Charles. At any rate, the old three-legged wolf was a member of Hauptman's pack now—and the Columbia Basin Pack was the only pack in North America that did not owe fealty to Bran Cornick.

Charles waited.

"Leah's been singing again," Bran said in an apparent non sequitur.

"What do you mean, singing?" Leah didn't sing. He hadn't thought about it much; some people sang, some people didn't.

Leah had used to sing, though, hadn't she? He remembered her singing when he was a boy. But there had been something unsettling about her when she had.

"Do you mean like she used to sing?" he asked. "When you first brought her home? Brother Wolf used to make us leave when she was singing. He didn't like it."

"Nor do I," admitted his da. The growl in his voice was almost subvocal, raising the hairs on the back of Charles's neck in response.

The obvious question was "Why not?" but Da's growl and the memory of Brother Wolf's unease kept him quiet. There had been something wrong about Leah's singing. Da would tell Charles about it when he was ready to do so.

Bran looked back at the map. "April was the last time anyone heard from the people living in this village?"

"That they know of," Charles said. He'd taken time to go through the file the FBI had given them before he'd left his house. "Dr. Connors's daughter is the only relative who has come out and identified her father as missing. The rest of the names they got from the post office box, but the relatives of those people have been singularly unhelpful. Apparently people who want to live off-grid are not big on communicating with the outside world. The last letter Dr. Connors's daughter received was dated early April. That seems to be the last communication from Wild Sign."

"Leah started singing last April," Bran told him.

"You believe there's a connection?" Charles asked.

"I don't like coincidences," Bran told him. "There is something magic in whatever she's singing. It feels like a summons of some sort. But I can't tell if Leah is trying to summon something to her, or if she's hearing a summons."

Charles looked up from the map. "Leah doesn't work magic." He was as sure of it as he was of his own name. "Not outside of pack magic. But you aren't talking about that kind of magic."

"No," Bran agreed. "It doesn't feel like her—she smells wrong for a while afterward."

Charles sat back. "Then why haven't you done something about it?" He didn't know what he'd do, but if Anna started smelling wrong, he wouldn't have sat on his thumbs for five months.

"At first she used to sing all the time," Bran said, and Charles wasn't sure he was talking to Charles until he looked directly at him. "Do you remember that?"

"I remember that she sang," Charles said. "And her song made Brother Wolf uneasy. But I don't remember her singing all the time."

Bran didn't seem surprised. "Mostly she'd stopped by the time we got back here, I think. You haven't heard her sing recently?"

Charles said, "No." It wasn't surprising. Neither Leah nor he sought out each other's company.

Bran nodded. "I was told, back at the beginning, to ignore it and hope it went away." He gave Charles a wry smile. "I wasn't told what to do about it if she didn't quit. I don't know what to do about it now—and the only person who might know—" He growled in frustration. "We didn't talk about it because we were worried that talking about it might give it power."

There were things that grew more powerful when spoken of—some of the fae, those who had died, demigods, and some of the spirits of place. Speaking something's name could draw its attention, and that held its own dangers. Charles could not immediately think of any kind of magic—not a magical being—made worse by speaking of it, but his da knew a lot more about magic than Charles did.

"You think there is something or someone yanking on Leah's chain," said Charles. "And that it is all connected to the plot of land where the off-grid squatters disappeared from?"

"I think so, yes."

"Tell me what you can," Charles said.

Da nodded. It took him a while to begin, but Charles was patient.

Finally, his da said, "I wasn't actually out looking for a mate when I left you with your grandfather. The wolf was restless and I couldn't stay where she . . ." He stopped speaking and his eyes flashed yellow with grief that belonged both to him and to his wolf.

Charles had heard stories of his mother from his grandfather and his uncles, not from his da. He knew the battles between his parents had lit the forest with their fury. He knew neither of them could speak more than a few words in each other's language. He knew their love had been a rare and amazing thing to watch. His grandfather liked to claim his only daughter had been soft and dutiful until she met Bran, and that made Charles's uncles laugh behind their hands. But Charles knew all of that secondhand.

When he had been a child, he'd pretended he would happen upon his mother someday. He dreamed of walking with her in the forest. He wanted to know the extraordinary Blue Jay Woman who had fought with Bran and won. Over his da's objections, she had carried Charles to term, fighting off the werewolf's need to change under the full moon. She had died in the process because the spirits exact a price from those who defy the natural order of things, and werewolf women were not meant to bear children.

Charles had known all of his life that his mother's death had been his fault.

So had his father.

Charles had understood from the beginning that his da left when he could no longer look upon the son that his mate had loved more than she loved life. Those around him had given him other reasons, but Brother Wolf had known, and anything Brother Wolf understood, so did Charles. There had been nothing special about the trip Da had begun that had ended with him bringing home his new mate, though later Bran had claimed he'd needed to find a mate to make his wolf stable after Blue Jay Woman's death.

Only in his own thoughts did Charles use his mother's name. He thought that was safe, that it wouldn't call her back from the land of the dead.

"You could not stay," Charles said softly. "I know."

Their eyes met—and it was Bran who looked away.

"I was running as wolf in the mountains, the wolf in charge, when I heard the call."

"A summons?" Charles asked.

Bran shook his head, thought about it a moment, then, unexpectedly, grinned as he nodded. "Yes. I suppose. I have no idea how he knew I was nearby. That was very early on—there were maybe ten werewolves west of the Mississippi. Possibly only two." He looked at the wall of books behind Charles. "All that territory and there we were with less than twenty miles between us. Sometimes I have to admit I believe in fate."

He looked at Charles again. "I had decided not to come back for fear of what I would do. Had that wolf not called me . . ."

The room hung in silence for a moment.

"I know," Charles said.

His da's wolf was not like Brother Wolf, who reasoned as well as Charles himself did, though sometimes with a wholly different perspective. His da's wolf would have destroyed the thing that took his mate from him, and his da had been running out of the willpower to stop him. The only option his da had was a final one. "I knew. Brother Wolf told me."

Bran nodded. "Of course."

Silence lingered between them. Charles had the feeling his da wanted to say something more but couldn't find the words. When Bran spoke again, it was to continue the story.

"My wolf spirit and I were battling, the wolf ascendant when I heard my . . . heard *him* call me." Bran pounded a closed fist on his chest.

"Heard whom?" Charles asked, though Da had dropped enough hints.

Bran smiled faintly. "Sherwood Post."

Charles nodded.

"He didn't call himself that then, of course," Bran said.

The smile, barely there in the first place, died away. "There wasn't much left of him when I found him—hide, bones, and determination. He had this girl . . . this woman with him, who was in worse shape. He was half-delirious and mostly incoherent, and it didn't help matters that I was still more wolf than man. Much of what he said made no sense to me, and so I did not make an effort to remember it.

"More than a hundred people dead, he said. Of those he'd escaped with, the majority were women and children." Bran shook his head. "He'd somehow managed to kill or subdue whatever was killing them or holding them—though he wasn't clear on either of those points. I understood it had something to do with music and wild magic. The woman who was dying was the last of the group of people he'd initially managed to save. I found the bodies of the rest later—children, mostly. A couple of babies looked to be very nearly newborn. After all the rest died, when Leah was the last survivor, Sherwood decided that she would live whether she wanted to or not. I think he was probably half-mad by then. He wasn't a healer like your brother, but he had power. I had the impression that he'd drained himself to the edge of death trying to save the others, and that affected his reason, too. Bereft of other, better choices, he Changed her—and then held her to life with his magic when the Change didn't seem like it had taken. It was killing him."

Charles sucked in a breath at the awful parallel. A stranger held to life by magic that was killing someone Bran loved. Just as Charles had killed Blue Jay Woman.

"I am not the mage he was," Bran said. "Even if the wolf had not been so near, I could not break into the spell he'd worked. I—the wolf I was—determined the only way to save Sherwood was to save the woman also. I needed to form a pack again, to pull one of them into my pack so I could feed them strength."

Bran had been running without a pack for a long time by that point, Charles knew, since long before he and Samuel had left Europe for the New World. Neither his da nor his brother had ever told him why, and Charles had never asked.

"Sherwood was too far gone, and too bound to the woman. If I tried to make him pack and he chose to fight, and I had reason to believe that he might, he would die." Bran almost smiled again. "So, for that matter, might I have done. Instead, I performed the blood and flesh exchange with her. With Leah."

He paused, his eyes on the map in front of him but his mind obviously on that long-ago day. His voice carried a note of wonder Charles was fairly certain his da didn't know was there.

His voice a bare whisper, Bran murmured, "Of all of those people, she was the last survivor, Charles. When I bound her to my pack, the first of all that pack, I understood why. Her spirit . . . so strong." He half closed his eyes and breathed in as if he were still in that desperate moment. Under the lowered eyelids, Charles could see the glimmer of gold. "Such determination, so much fight in her." He let out a breath and smoothed a fold in the map with a flattened palm. "But not, alas, enough strength to allow her to survive without help. And making her pack was not enough. She'd been ill for a long time, and fighting for her life through the Change for several days."

Surviving the Change was not something one usually did for days—or even hours. In Charles's experience, the Change from human to werewolf happened in under an hour or it didn't happen at all. He imagined the agony of it, to be hung suspended in the middle of a Change from human to wolf, neither one nor the other. The confusion would make the pain all that much worse.

"I think if I had been less broken," Bran said, "or less moonstruck, I would have made other choices, but I cannot know that. I could simply have let her die. I could have helped her along. Sherwood would have died, too—but that was a choice he had made."

His voice trailed off and his body went very still. "I have done a lot of things I am ashamed of," Bran said. "This was not the worst."

"You bound her as your mate," said Charles, who had seen where this was leading—had grown up with the result of that decision. "But you couldn't have done it without her consent."

He knew that, remembered the tension of waiting to see if Anna would accept him. A person could be forced into the Change. Could be forced into a pack. But the mating bond could not be forced—it required acceptance by both parties.

"Could I not?" asked Bran, his mouth twisting. "She had been forcibly Changed, left in agony, then forcibly bound to a pack. I don't think she was capable of giving consent."

Bran shrugged his shoulders as if he were trying to shed some burden. "I knew it then, and I know it now. I am not proud of what I did. I bound her wolf to mine by force. She was dying. She was dying and taking Sherwood with her." He met Charles's eyes. "I could not bear it, not after Blue Jay Woman. My wolf spirit was looking for surcease, and Leah's was trying to survive." He paused, then said, "I do not regret taking Leah as my mate, only that I did it without giving her an alternative."

Charles gave him a formal nod, though both of them could hear the lie in Bran's voice. Leah was not Blue Jay Woman, who had been fierce—but from all accounts also brilliant and charming. Leah was cold and methodical.

Charles remembered the cold-eyed, brittle woman his da had brought home and thought of her, for perhaps the first time, from his adult perspective instead of the perspective of the child he had been. He considered that woman now in the light of his da's revelations—a survivor. A victim. Not a jealous woman, perhaps, so much as a broken one. He could see it. No wonder his da had been so protective of her; guilt could drive a person harder than love.

"As soon as the mate bond fell into place . . ." Bran hesitated only a bare moment and continued, "Sherwood's magic fell away and I was able to pull her all the way into the Change. They both survived."

Bran took up a pencil and touched it to the map at the edge of the silver line marking Leah's lands. "I think they were somewhere in here when I came upon them. It was a clearing on the shoulder of a mountain. Sherwood didn't tell me much, but I got the impression he had dragged his little group of survivors as far as they could travel before stopping.

"We buried the dead while Leah recovered enough to travel." He hesitated. "She never said, but I am quite sure one of the children we buried was hers. After the first day, after Sherwood recovered his senses, he would not say a word about what he had fought, about why he worried when Leah sang. He told me only that it was dangerous to speak of. I believed him, believe him still. Leah told me once that she remembers that time in her life in snapshots of memories." He paused. "She remembers some faces, a few moments. But nothing concrete. She thinks Sherwood made her forget."

"And now something is happening and we can't ask Sherwood," said Charles. "Because Sherwood doesn't remember anything before the day the Emerald City Pack found him in the witch's cage, and Leah doesn't remember anything because of Sherwood."

"And I can't send him with you because he belongs to Hauptman now," agreed Bran. "Though I've got half a mind to make him go anyway. Maybe something about the trip would jog his memory loose."

His da, Charles believed, thought Sherwood's amnesia was something he could have overcome if Sherwood had been willing to try to remember who and what he had been. Charles wasn't so sure—he'd been there when they'd dragged him out of the silver cage, more skin and bones than flesh. Da had known the old wolf longer, but Charles thought that might be giving his da unrealistic expectations.

Bran had finally had it out with Sherwood one night behind the closed doors of his study. Charles didn't know what had happened there, but magic had leaked from the room and a dark voice that did not belong to his da spoke in tones that rattled the bones of the house, though no one who heard it could understand what it said.

The next day, Da had given the old wolf a new name: Sherwood Post, a name he'd claimed to have taken at random from a pair of books he'd had on his desk. Charles thought it was more calculated than that; he hadn't even known his da had a copy of Emily Post's book in his library. Bran had then forbidden any of his wolves who had known Sherwood before from speaking the wolf's old name. There hadn't been very many of them—the old Sherwood Post hadn't sought out werewolf company, and when he had, he'd often used names other than his own.

"I'm not sending you alone," Bran said. "I spoke to Tag, told him the pertinent parts of this story, and he has agreed to go."

"Tag," Charles said warily. Taking the berserker out in public was a risk.

Bran nodded. "Sherwood Post almost died. He thought he'd defeated it—I know this because he never went back, and he would have. But if he'd been sure, he wouldn't have worried about telling the story of what he'd faced. I need to send you with backup."

He clenched his hands and met his son's eyes. "I can't come. Risking both of us is unacceptable—and I need to stay here." He hesitated, then admitted, "With Leah. I don't like any of this. Tag isn't a mage—but magic slides off him in unusual ways, and he's traveled all over.

He's had encounters with more kinds of creatures than almost any-one I know."

Charles got up. "I'll tell Anna what we are doing." He paused. "I would rather leave her here. Tag and I both have some defenses against magic."

"But you can't," said his da.

Charles met his eyes. "No. If you are sending Tag, bringing Anna becomes imperative. If he goes berserker, she's the only one besides you who would have a chance of bringing him down."

"Yes," Bran said.

"You asked me to come here without Anna so you could tell me how Leah and this missing town might be part of the same story," Charles said. It was a guess, but he could tell from his da's face he hadn't gotten it wrong. "If Anna comes with me, I need to tell her everything."

Bran nodded. "I wouldn't ask you to keep this from your mate."

"So why did you make me leave her home?" Charles asked.

"Do you think," said his da, a hint of amusement in his voice if not his face, "that your mate would have let me get through the story without demanding more information?" He lifted an eyebrow, and his eyes, wolf eyes, laughed. "Or chew me out for how I treated both you and Leah?"

Charles thought about it.

Bran's face grew serious. "But these events have left my wolf a little unstable, and justified as Anna's rebuke would be, I am not will-ing to risk hurting her feelings—" He paused and said, "—or scar-ing her."

They were all—all of the pack—conscious of where Anna had been before Charles had found her. He was pretty sure she had no idea how hard they all worked to not be too scary. Some of that came from understanding what they owed her. Bran had not had to put down any of his pack for loss of control since Anna had become part of it. Charles wasn't sure he could remember a year without either him or Bran having to end one of their own.

No sane dominant wolf wanted to distress an Omega in any way. Stable wolves, mostly, didn't have to become one of Bran's wolves, but they had not had so much as a serious fight break out among their own since Anna had come. Even the most broken of the wolves did not want to scare Anna, because she was an Omega.

Charles nodded. "Are we coordinating with the FBI on this?"

Bran leaned back and sighed. "I appreciate them bringing this to us. But I judge that this is our problem. If the people disappeared from private property, it is not their jurisdiction."

"Are we interested in an alliance?" Charles said. "Not the one we were offered, with some secret-even-to-themselves collection of federal officials. But a real alliance with the mundane humans?" It seemed to him that a path could be cleared to doing so.

"What's in it for us?" Da said. "I don't mind this sort of . . . voluntary cooperation between us. But why should I enter into an agreement that would allow them to pull me into a conflict some idiot in Washington creates?"

Charles gave his da a shrewd look. He knew better than to tell his da that the strong should protect the weak. Da believed that all right; Charles had learned it from him. But even a torturer would not get the Marrok to admit he believed mundane humans should be protected.

So Charles said, "Because in the end, the human population holds all the cards. It would cost them, but they could kill us all."

"Point," Bran said. "But we are a long way out from having to make a decision on that."

"I have a few questions about Leah's story," Charles said, fairly sure their listener had left. His da might be more willing to open up now.

LEAH LEFT THE hallway outside Bran's study when the topic of conversation turned to theoretical politics. It wasn't her habit to eavesdrop, but she had heard her name and paused. When it became clear what they were talking about, she found herself glued to the floor.

She didn't know if Bran had known she was there. Or if he had intended to keep to himself the news that there was something going on in the mountains where she had been reborn, died, and been reborn again.

She'd never been back there, though she'd requested that Bran acquire the land after he had married her in the legal sense not long after he'd first brought her here. She couldn't even remember what her reason for that had been. A lot of her memories of those early days of their marriage were foggy.

She only knew some part of her still longed to return . . . home—which was an odd way to think of a place she didn't really remember and where she had lived so short a time. Another part felt it would be unwise to let that land fall to some innocent. It was sheer luck it had ended up in the middle of a wild area rather than on the edge of some settlement turned to town turned to city—luck and a rugged landscape that did not yield easily to the needs of mankind.

She wandered to her bedroom and over to the jewelry tower in the corner of the room. It was turned so she could observe herself in the full-length mirror, and she did so.

Straight dark blond hair, loose today, hung down to her shoulders in a shining wave. Large deep blue eyes surrounded by lashes she kept dyed, as she did her eyebrows, because they were several shades lighter than her hair.

She was tall and leanly muscled. She flexed her long-fingered, manicured hands. Her father had said she was built for work—it had not been a compliment. Bran said she looked like a Valkyrie. She wasn't sure if that was a compliment, either, though she didn't think it displeased him.

But no amount of grooming, of cleaning, of polishing, could erase the gaunt woman she had been, more animal than human, with dirty hair so tangled they'd had to cut most of it off. She looked at her muscled forearms and saw instead how they had appeared when she'd been so thin that both bones had shown through the skin. Sleek, smooth nails polished glossy red seemed more unreal than the filthy nails broken down to the quick.

And the stupid part of that? As clear and as visceral as the vision of that haggard creature was, she couldn't actually remember looking like that. By the time Bran had brought her here, she had been healthy in body and very nearly sane.

Very nearly.

She should go there instead of Charles, she thought. She had survived whatever it was once; she should be able to survive it again.

Her eyes turned to ice as her wolf nature rose.

"No," said Bran very quietly from the doorway. "You can't go."

He had known she was listening—there was that question answered. She turned to look at him.

"While it is possible that previous exposure to whatever it was Sherwood met up in those mountains might shield you," he said in a gentle voice she didn't believe for a moment, "it is my expectation that it would have the opposite effect. Magic isn't like a disease you can build up an immunity to. Mostly it works like a vampire bite. The first one usually has only a small effect, and that effect fades away over time. The second or third bite leaves their victims permanently trapped."

He crossed the room to her, dropped to one knee, caught her hand, and brought it to his mouth. Then, keeping her hand against his lips, he bowed his head and said simply, "I am not willing to lose you."

She raised her gaze from the top of his head and looked again in the mirror, where a rag-clothed, filthy, bony woman with empty eyes the color of a still lake stared back at her. That woman met Leah's eyes and began to sing.

"WHERE HAVE YOU been?" asked Anna sleepily.

She'd been vaguely conscious of Charles getting out of bed, but she'd drifted off before she could ask him where he was going. He usually did one last check on the horses before they went to bed for the night, but her internal clock told her he'd been gone for a couple of hours.

"Talking things over with Da," he told her.

She rolled over and watched him strip out of his clothes with lazy appreciation.

"Are we going to California?" she asked. "Do you want me to text Leslie?"

Charles climbed into bed beside her and pulled her into his arms. "No," he said, "don't contact the FBI. This is family business. Yes, we are going to California." And he told her how Leah came to be the Marrok's mate.

When he was finished, Anna said, "Your da should be shot. And I'm only withholding judgment on Sherwood because I don't know his side of the story."

"Yes," Charles agreed. "He thought you would see it that way." He paused and said, "I'm not sure I don't see it that way myself."

"I've only heard Leah discuss how she became a werewolf once," Anna told him, then recounted as closely as she could remember what Leah had said at the restaurant in Missoula.

"Huh," said Charles when she was done.

She gave him a mock punch in punishment, then flattened her hand on his bare chest. "So Sherwood Post is the only one who actually knows what happened? But your da never asked him what that was while Sherwood still remembered it?"

Charles grunted. "He told me he asked. But once Sherwood was cognizant again, he refused to talk about it. Da thinks Sherwood did not believe he had killed or destroyed whatever it was he fought. Sherwood believed merely talking about it was a problem." He paused. "And Da is pretty sure it was Sherwood who made certain Leah wouldn't remember it, either, that blocking her memory of it was part of how Sherwood was trying to free her from it."

"Wait a minute," Anna said. She'd known Sherwood for a while before he'd been shipped off to Adam Hauptman, but Charles's story had revised her understanding of the quiet and stoic wolf a great deal. "Mind magic . . . that's witchcraft, right? But Sherwood is a werewolf—and male witches are not usually powerful."

Charles drew in a breath. "Sherwood . . . the person Sherwood was, was a Power in the way my father or Bonarata is a Power. If one spoke of him, one would probably not call him a werewolf, even. That he was a werewolf did not define him in the way it defines me or you. I don't know what category he would fit into, but it would involve magic." He paused. "I don't know how he managed to get captured by the witches. My da is more than half convinced Sherwood let them take him in the arrogant belief they couldn't keep him—and found out he was wrong."

"So," Anna said, feeling apprehension she wouldn't have felt before hearing a bedtime story this serious, "are we going to California?"

"Yes," said Charles. "We are taking Tag with us."

"Because . . . ?"

"Because magic has trouble latching onto him for whatever reason."

"Like Mercy," Anna said in surprise.

Charles shook his head, but said, "Maybe. I don't understand the mechanisms of Tag's resistance. Mercy's immunity seems to be from the same heritage that allows her to change into a coyote and is far less reliable—and more effective when it does work—than Tag's."

"So we three are going to venture into a situation that disappeared a village and brought a legendary werewolf—no," she corrected herself, "a legendary *legend* to his knees and killed who knows how many people. You and I and Tag."

"Information gathering," Charles told her. "The idea is we go see what's going on, and return to discuss what to do about it with Da. We are not to engage the enemy unless we cannot help doing so."

Anna considered that. "Your father's orders?"

"Yes," confirmed Charles.

"Has he *met* Tag?" Anna queried.

Charles tightened his hold on her as he gave a huff of laughter.

More seriously she asked, "How many monsters can control people's minds?"

Charles sighed. "Witches—but not all of them. There used to be a couple of families who specialized in that kind of magic, but they disappeared after the Inquisition. That doesn't mean the rest of them can't do it."

"Sage was in the restaurant when Leah told her side of the story," Anna said somberly. "She was very interested."

They both contemplated that.

"Vampires can control minds, too," Anna said, breaking the silence.

"All of the fae can work illusionary magic," Charles said.

"And the music thing ties in pretty well with the fae, doesn't it?" Anna said. "The Pied Piper of Hamelin."

"That one just springs to mind, doesn't it?" Charles said. "I can think of a few of my uncle's stories, too—and creatures native to this land were far more plentiful than fae, witches, or vampires back in the day."

"So we are clueless," she said.

"Absolutely," he answered.

"Just making sure."

He laughed again. "Good night, Anna."

A few minutes later Charles said, "Asian magic works differently— their mages are not divided up into witches and wizards and sorcerers. I haven't had a lot of experience with it. But I do know they have creatures that could create this kind of trap."

"The Chinese came out to California with the railroad," Anna said. "And for mining, right? It's been a while since my American history class, but I associate all that with the Civil War. Were they here early enough to be Leah's monster?"

"All it would take would be one," Charles said. "The monsters of the Old World came over with the first of the explorers."

"Now that we have established it could be anything," Anna said, smiling into his shoulder, "can we go to sleep?"

"I called Samuel this morning," Charles said, his voice solemn. "I told him that I needed him to help us find a way to have a child."

Anna couldn't breathe, her heart pounded, and her mouth was dry. They had applied for adoption with a few agencies—but the waiting list was very long. She'd thought Charles was against other options.

She licked her lips and said, "What did he say?"

"Not to go out looking on our own. He is concerned that if the public—the human public—finds out what we are trying, there will be an outcry that will make everything more difficult."

"We talked about that," she said. It had been one of the reasons Charles had leaned toward adoption.

She felt Charles nod. "We did. He says to wait until he can make it back and he'll help. He has some ideas."

"Did he say when he would be back?" Anna asked. Charles's brother, Samuel, was traveling with his mate, a powerful fae named Ariana. The last Anna had heard, they were in Africa, and Samuel, who was a doctor, was working with Doctors Without Borders, though there had always been something vague about what, exactly, he was doing.

"No," Charles said. "He sounded . . . worried, I think. Unhappy. He wouldn't tell me why. Da says Samuel hasn't told him what's going on."

"Which doesn't mean Bran doesn't know," Anna said.

"Yes," agreed Charles. "And Da sounded worried, too."

"If there is anything we can do, either Samuel or Bran will let us know," Anna told him.

Her husband let out his breath in a huff of air. "This is true."

When the darkness pressed too deep as they both lay awake, Anna said, "Why is the music so important? Do you have any idea?"

He gave a deep sigh and she couldn't tell if he was relieved to change the subject or not. Children were something her husband had very complicated feelings about—and she wasn't sure he understood them himself.

As he spoke of parallels between magic and music and how they both could be used by various evil creatures, she felt his body relax. Monsters, she thought with drowsy humor, were apparently less frightening than children.

CHAPTER

3

Anna found herself, not unexpectedly, at the wheel for the California trip. Charles actively disliked driving, and Tag . . . Tag drove with a joyous abandon that probably had not been as hazardous when the most common mode of transportation had been horses. A horse could decide not to run off a cliff or into a tree no matter what Tag did or failed to do. Automobiles tended to rely on their drivers to avoid accidents, so it was best if Tag didn't drive.

They borrowed an SUV. Charles's single-bench-seat truck would have had a hard time containing the three of them. Charles was a big man and Tag was even larger, nearly seven feet tall and wide as an ox. Tag currently drove a Ford Expedition that would have held them all with room to spare if it weren't for the territoriality plaguing all dominant males. Tag could have ridden in Charles's truck, had they all fit, because Charles was easily more dominant than Tag. But Charles could not ride in Tag's vehicle—except, possibly, if he drove.

Anna had long since quit fretting about dominance issues except to be thankful she, as an Omega, was outside all of that. Bran had a small fleet of automobiles owned by the pack, and he made it available to them. The pack Suburban was neutral territory and plenty big enough for all of them. Charles rode shotgun and Tag stretched out in the backseat and went to sleep for most of the drive, for all the world as if he were a cat instead of a werewolf.

The first day had been mostly interstate, and they'd stopped shortly after crossing the California state line, staying in a hotel in Yreka. The second day, Anna found herself driving on a narrow highway barely two vehicles wide as it twisted through mountains only a little more civilized than those at home.

When she'd first moved to Montana, she'd driven these kinds of rural highways with a white-knuckled grip. Some of the roads around pack territory were little more than two ruts through the woods, so the narrow highway now only bothered her when they got stuck behind slow-moving RVs or semis.

They traveled along the edge of a mountain valley where the only sign of civilization was a few fence lines. She hadn't realized that California had places that were so isolated. The road followed the edge of a mountain, so she had no warning when they rounded a curve and found what looked to be a gas station, though it was hard to tell because it was all but buried in trees.

"Pull in at this stop," said Tag. His voice was high-pitched for a man as big as he was, and when he sang, he had a beautiful Irish tenor. Uncharacteristically he'd been upright and watching the scenery for the past half hour. The urgency in his voice made her wonder if he'd been keeping an eye out for a bathroom break.

Pulling into the gravel parking lot, Anna got her first clear view of the place. The battered, flat-roofed building sported a ruff of cedar shakes like a tonsured monk on top, and cheap paneling everywhere else. The siding was painted a blue that had once been dark but had faded to a blue gray.

There was a pair of old gas pumps out front wrapped in battered yellow caution tape, indicating that part of the business was no longer in service. The lighted beer signs in the small dirty windows obscured what lay beyond.

Despite the dilapidated appearance of the business, six cars filled the parking lot: four late-model SUVs, a pickup truck, and a dented, ancient Subaru. It might have been silver a few accidents ago but was now mostly primer gray. Anna pulled in on one end of the lot, her left wheels on grass instead of gravel.

"Is this a bar?" asked Anna.

"Sometimes," Tag admitted, pulling on his boots and beginning to lace them up without hurry. "Was a gas station when I was here last."

"You know this place?" asked Charles.

Tag grunted.

A Native American man opened the door of the business, whatever it was, and stepped out, staring at their SUV. He looked to be somewhere in his midfifties, though his short hair was still glossy and dark.

He was not overly tall, but when he stopped, folded his arms, and squared his stance, he looked pretty badass. Anna softly whistled the opening notes of the theme song of *The Good, the Bad and the Ugly*.

At the sound, Tag paused, looked up, and saw their observer. "Good. I was worried it might have passed to other hands."

Apparently they weren't here for a bathroom break.

Tag slanted a quick glance at Charles. "Do you mind if I go talk to him first? I think these folks might be useful, and they know me."

Charles, his gaze pinned on the waiting stranger, said, "These are friends of yours?"

His tone was odd, something Anna couldn't quite read. He'd seen something Anna had missed—or he knew something she didn't.

"'Friends' would be stretching it a bit," Tag said judiciously as he got out of the SUV, bringing a leather over-the-shoulder pack with him. "But we know each other."

He didn't bother to close his door as he strode over to the man who waited, so neither she nor Charles had to strain to hear, even with the sounds of the nearby river.

"Carrottop," said the stranger. "Long time since you came this way."

Tag said something in a liquid tongue Anna couldn't pinpoint, and the other man laughed.

"Call me Ford," he said, sounding a lot friendlier, as if Tag had spoken some sort of code when he'd switched languages. "And it is rude to talk in a language everyone doesn't speak. Your accent is atrocious anyway." He looked over at their SUV.

Charles opened his door, so Anna climbed out, too.

"Call me Ford," said the stranger again, this time to Charles. He wasn't looking at Anna, but she felt like he was very aware of her.

"Charles Cornick," Charles said after waiting long enough Anna could have spoken if she wished. "And my wife, Anna."

Ford rocked on his feet, looking at Charles a little differently than he had before, less welcome and more wary. He glanced at Tag. "You keep dangerous company, Carrottop."

Tag didn't lose the goofy smile designed to draw attention away from his cool gray eyes. "So do they."

Ford grinned appreciably, and the tension in the air dropped back to where it had been before Charles introduced himself.

"Welcome to the Trading Post," said Ford.

THE TRADING POST was a lot of things stuffed into one building. The room smelled of tobacco, coffee, and cinnamon, all overlain with a strong smoky scent, as if someone was smoking meat nearby. She'd smelled a little smoke outside—it was fire season—but this smelled less like burning trees and more like a cook fire.

The carpet was threadbare, with the floorboards peeking through here and there. Four card tables, of the folding sort, were squished together in one corner with chairs that looked like the same kind Anna's high school orchestra had used—cheap, easy to stack, easy to clean.

Roughly half of the space not dedicated to tables was stocked like a tiny grocery store, with refrigerated goods stored in a double-sided, glass-fronted fridge. One of the walls consisted of a big walk-in freezer. A hand-lettered sign on the freezer door advertised locker space available above a price list for beef, pork, and venison sold in quarters, halves, or whole.

The remaining space was a very basic clothing store carrying jeans, blue T-shirts, a variety of flannel shirts, and brown leather lace-up boots. A glance at Ford showed he had done his clothing shopping here, and his boots looked suspiciously like black versions of the ones the store had for sale.

Along the back wall, shelves offered enough ammunition to arm a good-sized militia. In the corner next to the shelves was a huge old metal safe that looked very much like it belonged in a Hollywood

Western-and-bank-robbery movie. Anna suspected it was more likely a gun safe than a bank safe, but there were no signs, so she couldn't be absolutely sure.

There were two other people in the store, neither of them Native American. One of them was a woman of about Anna's age with reddish-brown hair, and the other was a towheaded boy who looked about five. Both of them had also gotten their clothing from the store. Anna wondered where the drivers of the other cars were—and why people with cars didn't drive the hour or so to Yreka to get clothes.

Without a word to the others in the store, Ford escorted them to one of the tables. Charles pulled out a chair for Anna. Tag pulled out another and looked at it doubtfully. Anna got it—he was a big man for such an insubstantial chair.

"Sit," advised Ford. He glanced at the woman—but she was already bringing a glass water pitcher foggy with cold in one hand and four glasses in the other.

As Tag sat gingerly on the edge of the chair, the boy opened a door in the back and left the building. Anna caught a glimpse of him running as the door swung shut behind him. No one seemed worried about such a young child running out where there was nothing but forest, highway, and the river Anna had heard but not seen when she'd gotten out of the car.

"Here you are," the woman said, setting the glasses around before bustling back into an alcove Anna's first impression of the building had missed.

Tag opened his mouth, but Ford held up a hand. "Wait."

The woman brought out four plates, each holding a mammoth slice of berry pie. Beginning with Anna, she placed the plates around the table.

Anna, aware of undercurrents, waited for someone to do something. Charles glanced at Ford, but then looked at the woman directly as he cut into the pie and took a bite. His eyebrow rose and he made a soft sound.

"Huckleberry," he said in obvious approval. "I haven't had a huckleberry pie in a very long time. Thank you."

Which meant they weren't dealing with the fae. Charles wouldn't have said those words to someone who was fae. He would have praised the food, but he wouldn't have thanked anyone.

Anna was sure by now they were dealing with people who weren't quite human. The store smelled of smoke, of gun oil, of all the things lining the shelves and filling the fridge. But she couldn't smell the man who sat at the table with them, or the woman who'd served them—just as she hadn't picked up the scent of the boy.

The woman flashed Charles a big smile. "You're very welcome. If you folks need anything else, I'll be right outside," she said.

Then she left by the same back door the boy had used.

They ate their pie. Anna had become a fan of huckleberries since her move to Montana, but she wasn't fond of berry pie. Mostly they were—like this one—too sweet. The flavor was powerful—huckleberries were like that. She thought if they had used half the sugar, she might have enjoyed the pie. She didn't like it, but she couldn't stop eating it. She glanced surreptitiously at Charles, but he was eating the way he usually did—like a well-mannered starving person who wasn't sure where his next meal with coming from.

She was the last to finish, her stomach telling her it had been too close to the big breakfast she'd eaten. But she only felt overfull, not sick as she probably should have.

"Thank you," Charles said again, this time to Ford.

Tag opened up the shoulder bag he'd brought with him and pulled out an earthenware bowl. It was putty colored on the outside and reddish brown on the inside, the shape a little irregular. The bowl was shiny in some places and matte in others, as if the potter had made a mistake with the finish—or as if it were so old the finish had worn off in spots. Anna was pretty sure she had last seen that bowl on the bookshelves in Bran's office.

Tag set it on the table in front of Ford.

The man raised an eyebrow and Tag nodded. Ford took the bowl up in two cupped hands, turning it so it caught the light. He brought it to his nose and sniffed. He paused thoughtfully and set it, very carefully, back down on the table.

"We'd like information," said Tag.

Ford nodded at the bowl. "It must be some information if you brought this to pay for it."

"There was a group of people who had set up camp in the mountains," said Charles. "They called it Wild Sign. We think there were somewhere between thirty and forty of them. They went there to live away from civilization."

Ford snorted. Anna couldn't tell if it was a derisive snort or a snort of agreement.

"Wild Sign is on land owned by my father's mate," Charles said. "And two hundred years ago, give or take a decade, something lived in those mountains. We are given to understand the people who settled there disappeared sometime this spring. We would like to know where they went. My father is concerned that a danger in the mountains, one that killed a lot of people a couple of hundred years ago, is waking up again. He feels responsible." Charles hesitated, but then left that there. "We would appreciate any information you could give us."

Ford smiled sweetly. "'The mountains' is a lot of territory."

Tag reached into his bag again and pulled out a USGS map folded to display an area marked with a silver marker. Anna couldn't be sure it was the same map Leslie had brought them, but presumably it was marked to display where the encampment had been.

Ford did not look at the map but gave a sharp nod. "It was a town, not a camp, this Wild Sign you speak of, a town with buildings and a school. It started about two years ago, when four people built a permanent camp up there as soon as the snow was gone. By last winter there were forty-two of them. Or so I have heard—I have not been there."

"Who told you?" Tag asked.

"My nephew works for the Forest Service. He came upon them by accident—the young seldom have the wits to heed their elders' warnings. He told me they seemed to know what they were doing and required no help. He also said they were a cheerful and generous people, free with food and drink for wandering forest rangers. They were not on federal land or tribal land"—he gave a wry glance at Charles—"or their own land, but the owner did not come to object, and so they were left alone."

"Why didn't you visit them?" asked Anna. That "elders' warnings" was directed at something—and she wanted to know what it was.

"The mountains are vast, Ms. Cornick," Ford said. "Why should I have visited them?"

Anna waited.

"No," said Ford with a hint of a smile fading as he spoke. "We do not go there. None of my people." He shook his head ruefully. "Not unless we are young fools who work for the Forest Service, we don't.

And his mama has seen to it that he won't go again. We don't go to that place."

"Why not?" Anna asked, and found herself meeting eyes that were deeper than a moonlit night and of no color she could name, though a moment ago she'd have sworn they were the same shade as her husband's eyes. She felt as though Ford saw all the way through her, whereas she saw nothing she could comprehend.

He looked away from her, smiled at his hands. Then he reached out and pulled the bowl nearer to him, as if the answer to her question was worthy of that gift or payment. "Because there is something sleeping there we do not wish to awaken." He glanced at Charles and then away. "The creature your father is worried about, I'd reckon. There are not two such in our territory."

"What can you tell us about it?" she persisted.

He took his napkin and pulled a pen out of his pocket. He drew an upside-down V and three upward slashes on each side. "That's a wild sign for you," he said, handing her the napkin.

"Are you referring to the town?" Charles asked as Anna examined what Ford had drawn.

There was a primitive feel to the drawing, almost like a Viking rune, but it didn't look familiar. When she and her brother had been children, they'd learned a set of runes and written notes to each other. The runes had been real ones—at least the symbols they hadn't made up. But maybe this was from an older group of runes or from a different culture. Tag held out his hand, and Anna gave the napkin to him. He frowned at it.

Ford answered Charles's question while Tag scrutinized the napkin. "The town was named after the signs they found in the rocks and trees around there," Ford said. "They called them wild petroglyphs." He grimaced. "Even when they were carved into the trees."

"Who carved them into trees?" asked Charles intently.

Ford shrugged. "None of my people."

Charles frowned at him. "That was very near a lie."

Ford's eyebrows raised. "I am not fae, Marroksson. I am not bound by their rules."

"You know what that bowl is," murmured Charles.

Ford laughed. "Yes. And I know if I take it under false circumstances, I will not hold it long." He looked down and considered his words. "The petroglyphs, I do not know. They have been there for as long as my people have been telling stories. My mother would say they were made by the Before People, but I do not in truth know who they were. Nor does my mother."

"And the trees?" asked Charles.

"The trees, obviously, are much newer than the petroglyphs," agreed Ford. "Some of those were carved by the recent inhabitants of Wild Sign." He held up a hand to ask for patience. "But there are older signs, carved into the forest giants long ago, perhaps as much as two hundred years." He paused. "There was a village in that location for a brief time, though, again, my people have no other stories about them, as we do not go there."

Tag handed the napkin to Charles, who studied it.

"That is not the only sign you will find in the rocks up there," Ford said. "And the trees . . . I think people who want to escape civilization should know better than to carve all over the trees, don't you? But this sign is the one my mother taught me to watch for. And her mother before her."

"What is it that sleeps there?" Charles asked, though Anna had already asked that—and gotten the odd glyph for her trouble. Charles's question was more carefully worded.

Ford shook his head. "We may not speak of it." He smiled widely, and for a moment his face looked vaguely inhuman, though Anna could not point out what made her think so. "And since we have not spoken of it for generations, I do not, in truth"—he tapped a finger lightly on the rim of the bowl—"know what sleeps there."

"Do you know about the music?" asked Anna impulsively.

He looked at her for a moment, as if she'd said something very interesting. Then he raised his hands, held together so the thumbs touched, fingers curved as if he cupped something roundish. Then he brought them up to his mouth and blew lightly, as if he was pretending to hold some sort of wind instrument, an ocarina maybe, she thought. The oldest of them were shaped to be played the way Ford was using his hands. Or, she thought, given the rune that he was imitating, something like the ancient aulos, which was a pair of double-reeded pipes played together, one in the right hand and the other in the left. Versions of the aulos had been found all over the ancient world, though not, Anna thought, in the Americas.

Ford smiled at her intent look, then he indicated the napkin Charles still held. "It is the sign, is it not? An instrument being played?" He wiggled his fingers suggestively. "Or so I have always thought."

ANNA WAITED UNTIL they were out of sight of the old gas station before saying, "They didn't have a cash register."

"Probably because they mostly don't use cash," said Tag mildly.

Anna gave a snort of amusement. Served her right for beating around the bush. "Okay, so what was he? And were the woman and child the same? They weren't fae, right? I kept thinking they might be like Mercy—descendants of the old gods. But there is a . . ." Her voice trailed away as they passed a homemade sign that read *Bigfoot Country Souvenirs—10 miles* above the familiar hulking shape popularized by a film clip of a faked Sasquatch sighting.

"No," she said, glancing at Charles before she had to look at the road again. "No. You did not let me talk to Sasquatch without telling me what he was. I could have asked to see his real form." She paused. "I could have gotten a photo on my phone and sent it to my brother for bragging rights." Charles laughed, but Tag drew a quick, appalled breath.

"You don't want to get on his bad side," Tag told her. "Really."

"How would you know that?" Anna asked, because there was a hint of a story in his voice.

"I slept with Ford's sister once, a long time ago, and he would have ripped me to pieces except she threatened to kill him for hurting me. It was a glorious fight, though, before she intervened." He paused and smiled softly, distracted from his point.

"You slept with"—Anna changed the ending of her sentence midway through—"Ford's sister."

Tag's smile softened even further. "Breeze. She thought I was one of them, I thought she was who she said she was. We were both surprised." He sounded amused.

If Tag hunched a little, he would bear a certain resemblance to the hulking Sasquatch on the sign.

Tag laughed, and like his voice, it was unexpectedly high-pitched. It was the kind of laugh that invited listeners to laugh along, even though the joke was on him. He shook his head, and his eyes were a little soft as he continued, "But that's not why he helped us today. I think he was impressed that the Marrok's son came with me."

"And because of the bowl," Charles said. "How did you happen to bring that?"

"Your father, after informing me I was going to be your backup on a dangerous mission along the Klamath River, where he knew I'd had plenty of adventures—and he emphasized the 'plenty of adventures.'" Here Tag's voice grew indignant. "How did he know about that, I ask you? I never told . . ."

When his voice trailed to a halt, Anna glanced at Tag's face in the rearview mirror and saw him reconsidering.

"I guess I did tell Samuel about it once," he said sheepishly. "And Asil." He made a humming sound, and his voice was very cold when he finished, "And Sage."

Sage had betrayed them all in a thousand small ways before she died. It would be a while before they quit flinching at just how thorough that betrayal had been.

"What is the bowl?" Anna asked to change the subject—though she really did want to know.

Charles shook his head. "I don't know, and I'm not sure my da does, either. Something powerful that belongs here and not on my father's bookshelf. My uncle—my mother's brother—and Da had a rousing argument or six about the bowl. I think if he, my uncle, hadn't died so soon, he'd have talked my da into letting him bring it back. To them."

"So it sat on his bookcase," Anna said.

Charles nodded and gave her a smile. "*Da* couldn't bring it back. The Sasquatch avoid him. This was a good way for Da to honor my uncle and get something out of it in return."

"He might have been a little clearer in his instructions, then," grumbled Tag, stretching out on the backseat again. "What if I'd taken it to the Karuk tribal elders and given it to them instead? That was what I intended if I couldn't find Breeze's people."

"It would have worked out," said Charles comfortably.

"You know," said Tag conversationally, "if I had known how much Anna mellows you out, I would have gone on a road trip with the two of you a long time ago, Charles."

Charles growled—but they all knew he didn't mean it.

ANNA THREADED THE Forest Service road like a grandmother, wincing at every scrape on the car's paint. The road split, the right fork going to a campground with showers, lavatories, and other camping amenities. Next to that campground sign was a fire danger warning sign proclaiming extreme conditions.

In this area, at the tail end of a very hot and dry summer, the fire danger was real. There were active fires in Oregon, just over the border—which was why Charles had not considered hiking in from the Oregon side, though it might very well have been a shorter way.

They took the left fork, and seven miles of rough going later, the road ended at a second campground, this one much less friendly. They drove by several campsites to take an isolated one, far from the primitive toilets.

As soon as Charles got out of the SUV, he could tell the campground was completely empty of ecotourists. The first campground had been full of RVs and bright-colored tents, and it seemed odd this one was deserted. It was the middle of the week and the fires in Oregon might have given people some pause about camping so nearby—

he could smell the smoke on the air here even more strongly than he had at Tag's friends' business.

He took a deep breath and smelled nothing unusual.

Tag gave him a look as Anna buried herself in the back of the SUV. "Uneasy?" he asked.

"There's no one else here," Charles said.

Tag nodded. "It's isolated, and we're at the end of camping season. From here on out, campers chance snowstorms and rain. But I'd guess it's the warning sign we drove by on the way here."

Charles frowned at him.

"Bear," said Tag. "Yesterday a ranger found a bear nosing around this campground because someone tried to bury their garbage instead of hauling it out. They advise people not to camp here unless you have an RV."

Charles snorted. "You wouldn't get an RV in here."

"And if you did, you might not get it out," agreed Tag.

One mystery solved, Charles helped haul camping things out of the SUV.

"Do we need to set up the tents?" Anna asked when Tag started to pull his out. "There's a lot of daylight left. We might even be able to reach Wild Sign before dark."

By Charles's reckoning they were a little over forty miles away as the crow flies. If this area held true to other mountains he'd been over around here, their actual path might be sixty miles or more. If they had been hiking on foot, it would have taken them a couple of days, but on four feet—Anna had it about right.

"No," he said. "We'll make camp here today and leave it up while we head in." He looked into the woods and lowered his lids, letting his senses roam out around them. "I don't think arriving at Wild

Sign as night falls is our best plan. There is no urgency—whatever happened to those people happened months ago, and whatever we need to deal with up there is probably not the only thing roaming these woods."

"Like the bear," said Tag.

A grizzly could kill a werewolf or two, but generally left them alone. Charles wasn't worried about bears, and neither was Tag. These mountains had an uncanny feel—and however guardedly friendly Ford had been, Charles did not want to confront a Sasquatch out here unless he absolutely could not avoid it.

They ate sandwiches and made camp. Anna and Tag played double solitaire, which seemed to engender a lot of yelling, mock grumbling, and laughter. Charles read for a while, then put his book aside, stretched out a bit, and closed his eyes.

Waiting to head out until morning had been a practical decision. But sitting on a camp chair with his feet up on a stump, pretending to be asleep, Charles felt a contentment that had nothing to do with the possible dangers they were going to be facing tomorrow, though it was true Brother Wolf gloried in the adventure.

Cheerful voices echoed in the quiet woods as Anna and Tag bickered about how best to cook their dinner, whose ace got played first, and *whether* to cook their dinner (because werewolves weren't picky about raw meat, even if human teeth had trouble ripping through a steak). If anyone else had been arguing with Tag that way, they would end up thrown through a door or into a tree when he decided to take offense instead of laugh. Tag's temper was a quick switch.

But Anna was an Omega and Tag her devoted follower. She could even tell him the French lost at Waterloo without him going ballistic—

or at least, Tag's ballistic would be more measured. So they squabbled happily until Anna persuaded Tag into a duet.

Tag's voice was a soldier's voice, learned on long marches between battlefields, which made it very well suited to the outdoors. Anna's sweet alto was better trained and she knew how to make her singing partners sound good. Their singing would have benefited from the addition of a baritone or bass, but Charles was content to listen, Brother Wolf lulled into contentment as a prelude to battle by Anna's presence and the forest setting.

There was no campfire. The fire danger was too high—and he thought they were illegal in California even in the spring. They'd brought a propane stove for cooking.

He fell asleep surrounded by the sounds of the evening: the wind in the trees, his wife's sweet voice—and the crackle of a campfire that wasn't there. It did not surprise him to find himself engaged in a game of chess with his uncle, who had been dead for two centuries, more or less.

BUFFALO SINGER'S FOREFINGER, which he tapped lightly on the edge of the table, was twisted from a fall when he'd been a boy, and he had a faint scar on the corner of his mouth. Charles had remembered the finger, but he'd forgotten about the scar. His uncle, only fifteen years older than Charles, had not been an old man when he died.

Buffalo Singer had been the one who most often took the boys on teaching expeditions or trained them in fighting, endlessly patient with the youngsters. He was the youngest of Blue Jay Woman's brothers, and though he never played favorites, he had a softness for his dead sister's son.

Bran Cornick had taught Buffalo Singer chess and found in him a worthy opponent. Buffalo Singer had taught Charles. Bran had taught Charles what he needed to know about being a werewolf and a little about dealing with being witchborn; he did not play with his son.

The battered chessboard balanced on a folding table made of sticks and buckskin—a device his da had fashioned for the purpose. Charles and his uncle sat on either side of it, staring at the board and thinking about possible moves. Charles had always thought those long evenings of motionless attention were how he had learned patience.

A commotion behind them had Buffalo Singer rising to his feet, a welcoming smile on his face—and Charles realized what day in the past his dreaming had returned him to.

Da was home, riding into camp with a strange white woman riding beside him. Horses were rare still, and his father had left on foot. These two were both chestnuts, and one of them had a great splash of white on her face that came down over one eye—and that eye was blue.

Bran dismounted and handed the reins of his horse to Charles, which surprised him. After a long journey, his da usually avoided noticing his son for as long as possible. But today he gave Charles a nod of thanks and then took the reins of the blue-eyed horse and gave them to Charles as well.

The woman slid down, landing lightly on her feet. Charles had time to notice both of her eyes were as blue as the horse's eye—and Charles had never seen *anyone* with blue eyes—then his da spoke to him.

Charles knew it was to him because Bran used English. Charles was the only one besides his da who spoke English in the whole camp.

"This is Leah, my mate."

Then he turned to the rest of the camp and introduced her again. Charles looked up at the woman who would, the dreaming Charles knew, never be his mother and saw indifference. It didn't matter, that boy told himself. He had his uncles and aunts and his grandfather, who all loved him. He did not need this woman as his mother.

The dreaming Charles saw something else. He saw Leah's cheeks were gaunt and her hands shook when she wasn't paying attention. He saw the wildness of the wolf in her eyes—and a bottomless, aching, unassuageable grief too deep for tears.

He remembered his da had told him one of the children he and Sherwood had buried had been Leah's.

In the way of dreams, Charles found himself seated on the ground, once more facing his uncle. But there was no camp, no Bran or Leah, no other people at all. The forest closed around them, dark and endless—but not dead. He could hear the birds and squirrels chittering at each other, feel the insects going about their business. Far away an eagle cried out.

Buffalo Singer's clever, callused fingers slid a pawn over to capture Charles's queen. He tapped the fallen piece with a finger.

"You be careful of her," he told Charles. "If you lose her, you lose the whole game."

Charles took a careful look at the rough-carved queen who only vaguely resembled a woman. His da had many talents, but carving wasn't one of them.

He looked up at Buffalo Singer and asked, "Who is she?"

But his uncle merely shook his head.

Charles turned his attention to the chessboard and studied the game, trying to see where he'd made the mistake that had caused him to lose. It felt like it was important to see where he, where Charles, had gone wrong.

His uncle reached over with a bent finger and tapped Charles on the forehead. "Keep a sharp eye out. The story is about her."

"Dinner!" called Anna cheerfully from somewhere.

His uncle looked up, a quick grin crossing his face. "I like her," he said. "She's feisty."

Charles looked up into Anna's face. "I like you, too," he told her.

She laughed and kissed him. He liked that, too.

CHAPTER

4

They found a trail at midday. It looked just like several others they'd found. But this one, unlike the others, carried no recent human scent.

Tag discovered a candy wrapper, battered and faded to pale colors by the sun and weather. Charles nosed the wrapper, and after a moment's consideration, set off on the trail. There was something—maybe it just headed in the right direction—that distinguished it in Charles's mind from the others. Maybe the spirits who lived in the forest directed him. With Charles it was hard to tell. Tag waited for Anna to follow, and he took up the rear.

Save me from protective males, thought Anna with half-irritated amusement. She was a freaking werewolf, for heaven's sake; she could take care of herself.

We protect our most dangerous weapon, Brother Wolf assured her.

Anna chuffed a laugh. She knew that Brother Wolf was serious. He could joke sometimes, but he never mocked. She just had no idea what prompted him to consider her more dangerous than Charles . . . or Tag.

The woods around them were full of deer, and at one point she caught the distant scent of elk. Coyotes abounded; one trailed them for a few miles out of curiosity. Twice, early in the morning, they had come upon bear sign—probably the bear that had been seen at their camp.

The woods were subtly different from those at home. Anna wasn't a botanist, so she didn't have names, but the evergreens were more diverse and the undergrowth smelled strange. The atmosphere of the land around them was different from home, too.

Charles talked about manitou sometimes, the spirit of a place, sort of an upper-level naiad or dryad, she thought. She'd come to her marriage with a better education on Greek and Roman beliefs than on those of Native Americans, and she still tended to conflate the vocabulary where the cultures intersected.

She didn't have the senses, the ability, to see spirits the way Charles did, but there was a flavor to these woods that was different from the feel of the woods at home. Maybe something was sifting through her mate bond besides the general feel of caution overlying Brother Wolf's fierce joy in this hunt. Maybe she just had an overactive imagination.

Though a lifetime of summer hikes with her dad and his handy-dandy pedometer (his words) had given Anna a very good sense of how far she'd traveled when walking on two feet, she had less of a feel for distance traveled while on four. They had set out at first light at a steady, ground-covering trot they could, and did, keep up all day.

So she didn't know exactly how far they had traveled, maybe as much as fifty miles, when they started to find the sigils carved into the trees. Some of them were familiar, as if whoever had carved them had access to the same set of Nordic runes Anna and her brother had used.

The two of them had used it as a simple replace-the-letter code, but upon finding one of their notes, her father had pointed out that scholars were pretty sure the original users of the old runes had used them as symbolic of whole meanings rather than as parts of words, like letters were.

Probably, he'd told them, the runes had been used as magical symbols. Not that her father had believed much in magic back then—he was a believer in cold logic and science. He was a little more open-minded now that his daughter was a werewolf, but she knew he still thought there was some scientific reason for her ability to transform.

At any rate, admonished by their father, she and her brother had tried to find the linguist-assigned meanings for the runes and use those. But since they had had very little use for words like "horse" (they lived in town, where there were no horses) or various Nordic gods, they had given up and gone back to using it as a simple code with a few runic-looking letters they made up themselves to stand in for the extra letters. But she remembered some of the symbolic meanings.

A square sitting on one corner with two lines extending down at a right angle from each other was one that meant "property" or "belonging to" with a sense of rightful ownership, an inheritance. She remembered it because it looked to her like a goldfish nose pointing up and tail pointing down.

The goldfish rune was a few seasons old. The one just above it, so new that there was sap beading up in some spots and the wood revealed by the broken bark was raw, was the rune that Ford had given them. Ford had thought it had something to do with music. It certainly looked more like a musical instrument than the goldfish looked like "property."

Charles, realizing that Anna had stopped, came back to stand shoulder to shoulder with her.

A claiming, Brother Wolf said. And Anna knew that he knew something of runes, too. Or maybe, if there was magic in these runes, he read the intent.

Tag huffed, lifted a leg, and marked the tree in approved werewolf fashion. Then he raked the ground in front of the tree and gave Anna a laughing grin full of teeth. Anna could feel Brother Wolf's amusement—but she could also feel his rising excitement. They were closer to their prey.

Once she knew to look for them, the runes were all over—most of them not the one Ford had warned them about, the musician one. Some of the runes Anna was pretty sure were made-up. Most of them had probably been carved in the last couple of years judging by the way the sap dripped out of them. But there were older trees, forest giants, whose trunks held runes distorted by years of growth. All of that tallied with what Ford had said—which meant they were on the right path. Not that she had ever doubted Charles could find their way to Wild Sign.

With Ford's description of petroglyphs in mind, she kept an eye out for marks on the rocks or stone outcroppings, but didn't see anything. The sun was starting its trek downward when they topped a steep climb, the trail more like a suggestion up an almost-cliff, and found themselves in an open flat meadow surrounded by trees. Underneath the shelter of the forest canopy, fitted neatly into the shadows of trees and the swells of land, were the buildings of Wild Sign.

Charles changed. He wasn't the quickest shapeshifter she'd ever seen. Mercy, his foster sister, could grab her coyote form in a blink of an eye—but she bore a different power. Today, Charles only took two breaths to make the shift that took any other werewolf of her acquaintance at least ten minutes longer. He'd told her it was because he'd been born a werewolf.

But that he arrived in his human form fully clothed . . . that was a different magical gift. His clothing at the end of a change was usually jeans, boots, and a T-shirt. And most of the T-shirts were his favorite color: red. But his magic could be capricious; she'd seen him end up in buckskins a time or two. And once, very oddly, a tuxedo. He looked good in a tux, but she'd never talked him into wearing one again. That particular tux had ended up in pieces he'd thrown away— the damage, she thought with an inward smile, had been her fault.

This time, he wore jeans and boots, but his shirt was a flannel button-down in a gray-green that blended into the forest nearly as well as Wild Sign. She wondered what that said about his current state of mind.

Anna, feeling the need for fingers and speech while she explored, changed back to human, too. Her change took a good deal longer. When she lay, panting and sweating, on the ground, Charles crouched by her, offering her one of the canteens from the pack Tag carried strapped to his back.

She took three big gulps of water, waited a breath, and drank some more. When she handed the canteen back to him, her hands had quit shaking. He helped her to her feet and presented her with her clothes, retrieved, like the canteen, from Tag's pack. She dressed, did a few deep knee bends and toe touches to make sure all of her parts were working as they should be. And all the while she took in the camp—no, Ford had it right, took in the town.

"I picked up five scents," Anna said, slipping on a pair of tennis shoes. "And maybe one more, but it is older. I got hints of a lot of people but nothing strong enough for me to follow."

Charles nodded. "It last rained six weeks ago. The information I have is that, on the strength of Dr. Connors's report, they sent in a chopper to investigate—a county deputy; the local Forest Service law enforcement officer; two rangers, one of whom is also part-time law enforcement for the Karuk tribe. The fifth scent, which was laid at the same time, I presume to be the pilot."

That hadn't been in the information Leslie had left with them.

"Maybe the older scent is Dr. Connors, then. No one else has been here in a while," Anna said. "Shouldn't there have been people looking?"

"For what?" Charles asked. "They know there was a settlement here and Dr. Connors's father is missing. But no one else has been reported missing—they are only gone. Law enforcement investigated this site thoroughly and found no signs of violence. They are looking for Dr. Connors Senior as well as the people who had mail at the drop box in Happy Camp—which is the nearest established town—but that is best done electronically. They don't think there is anything else examining the site can teach them."

Anna nodded. The report had said they'd found no signs of violence. No signs of rapid departure, though some personal property had been left behind, along with fourteen permanent structures, three yurts, and evidence of tents.

"If this were on federal or tribal lands, they'd have come back and cleaned up," Charles added.

"But it belongs to Leah," Anna said. "So it is out of their jurisdiction."

Charles nodded.

"I do have a question, though," she said. "With all of the runes scrawled over the forest around here, why aren't there any legends of Viking settlements in Northern California? Like the ones in Newfoundland or Minnesota?"

"The one in Newfoundland is real," Charles observed seriously, though Anna had been joking. "And no one has seen the runes here."

She'd missed something. She frowned at him. "After the first one—the goldfish below Ford's musician—I saw several hundred runes. They aren't exactly unobtrusive."

He laughed—which was distracting, because he was beautiful when he laughed, especially with the edge of gold gleaming in his eyes.

"A goldfish?" Charles's amusement bled into his voice. "It's called Othala, though I see how you'd think it looks like a goldfish."

"The goldfish with the musician on top," agreed Anna smugly, because she enjoyed making Charles laugh. "But seriously, there were runes all over the place. How could anyone miss them?"

"Witchcraft," said Charles. "Someone warded the trail—that's what all those runes were. I doubt most people would even have noticed the first one before they found themselves wandering off somewhere else."

"That's why you picked the trail," Anna said. "Was there magic?"

He shook his head. "I don't know why I picked it. It just felt right. But it stood to reason there must be a trail of some sort. One of the things missing from the report Goldstein and Fisher left for us was a note of how the people who lived in Wild Sign traveled back to civilization, which they obviously did, because they had a post office box—a real post office box—in Happy Camp. Law enforcement used a helicopter to get here. Dr. Connors's daughter either has magic of some sort or she found a different way in. I . . ." He shrugged. "We are not what it was guarding against, so it let us in."

"What were they hiding from?" Anna asked. "The people at Wild Sign, I mean. Do you think it found them? And maybe that's what happened to them? Do you feel anything here?" She couldn't help a little shiver as she glanced around, looking for a nonexistent threat. She knew it wasn't there, because if there had been a threat, Charles would be more concerned.

Charles, ignoring her wariness, shrugged. "Other witches? The warding was all white magic—and laid by more than one person. And there is one thing white witches fear more than anything else."

"Black witches," said Anna. All witches started out as white. A white witch drew her power from within herself. A gray witch drew power from the suffering of others, from other people's pain—but not from unwilling victims. A black witch tortured and killed for power—and white witches were their favorite victims.

"Do you think Wild Sign was settled by witches in the first place?" Anna asked. "Like some sort of white witch sanctuary? Did a black witch—or black witches—come destroy them?"

Charles glanced around at the deserted town. "Hopefully we'll find some answers here. Keeping in mind there were several witches here, I think we should stay together."

Because Charles could tell if someone left a magical trap for the unwary.

"What about Tag?" she asked.

Tag hadn't bothered taking human shape before he set off exploring on his own. She couldn't see him, but she could feel him through their pack bonds.

"Tag should be all right," Charles said. "He knows his way around witchcraft. Where would you like to start?"

Anna brushed off the last of the tingles left over from her change. She was conscious of a deep and growing unease, as if something were watching—or waiting. It hadn't bothered her until she'd changed back to human, so it probably wasn't anything real. She had a lot less imagination when she ran on four feet. Still . . .

"Do you feel something wrong?" she asked.

"Nothing definite," he said, which wasn't a no. "The witchcraft doesn't bother the wildlife, but it's keeping the usual forest spirits at bay. That makes this place feel even more empty."

He took her hand.

Immediately the eerie effect of the empty town lessened and the knots in her stomach eased. She was a werewolf, she reminded herself. Whatever had happened to these people, it had happened months ago. But it was Charles's warm hand wrapped around hers that reassured her enough she regained a bit of the excitement she'd been feeling since she'd first heard of this place.

It wasn't quite a lost civilization, but sure as God made little green apples, it was a mystery. She felt a little ghoulish for the thrill—she was pretty sure the only way the people who had lived in Wild Sign could be silenced for months was if they had been killed. But it looked like no one else was pursuing this the way they—her pack—could.

"Let's go look at the post office," she said. "Maybe we'll find some clues about who lived here."

The post office was easy to pick out—it had its own sign. The door was ajar and the two windows were open to the air, the shutters designed to protect the interior from bad weather still hooked back.

There was a flutter of black wings and caws when Anna stepped inside. Even after the birds had escaped out the windows, the interior smelled of crow. It wasn't a large space, maybe ten feet by ten feet. Shelves lined the wall opposite the door, empty of everything except a couple of birds' nests. A newish, dust-covered camp chair emblazoned with the name of its manufacturer had been shoved against the shelving—Anna could see the drag marks in the dirt floor.

"They cut this lumber themselves," Charles said, a hand on one wall. "It was well done, but there's just a little more irregularity than you'd expect to find in commercially produced boards."

"I don't see any clues here," Anna said, glancing at Charles to see if he had noticed something, something more than the lumber origin. But he shook his head in agreement.

So she said, "Your turn to pick where we go next."

"Latrines." He backed out of the post office and brushed aside a spiderweb trying to attach itself to the back of his neck.

She found herself grinning—because the speed of his decision had indicated he'd been thinking about it, and it was a very good place to look . . . and because it was honestly the last place she'd have suggested.

She followed him toward another clearly marked building behind the post office and a dozen yards downhill. She hadn't noticed it before, but like the post office, there was a sign hung on the wall that read *The Lavatories*. There wouldn't have been a real need for signs in a town this small. Someone must have enjoyed making them. Maybe the same someone who cut the lumber they'd used for their buildings.

"The Lavatories" was twice the size of the post office. There was a ladies' entrance and a men's, and each of them had two curtained stalls with composting toilets inside. Anna's experience with composting toilets was nonexistent, but Charles didn't flinch at opening them up and examining the waste receptacles—which were empty. All of them.

"Either whatever happened occurred just after they emptied the compost," commented Charles, replacing the last one, "or they emptied them out themselves in preparation for dismantling the camp."

"You think they knew they were abandoning camp?" Anna asked.

He shrugged. "It's too early to tell. But I do think four composting toilets are not enough for forty people. They'd fill up with waste too soon. They require a little time to decompose."

"Maybe some of them had their own?" suggested Anna. "Or maybe there are other lavatories hidden in the trees somewhere?"

He nodded.

"Where next?" Anna asked. "Cabins, tent remains, or yurts?"

"Let's check out that big yurt," he said after a moment's thought, indicating the building he had in mind with his chin.

The yurt he'd pointed out was at the far end of the town. And as they walked, he said, "If someone were abandoning a town, what would they take with them?"

"Not wooden buildings," Anna answered promptly. "Or composting toilets. If you don't care about the environment or leaving the forest a better place for you camping in it—" Another of her father's adages. Come to think of it, he probably knew all about composting toilets, Anna decided. "Then the tents are pretty easily replaced. Though people using composting toilets are probably not the sort who leave their junk all over for someone else to clean up."

Charles nodded and stopped by the big yurt. The outer fabric was forest green, a little darker than his shirt. He touched it.

"Sturdy," he said.

They walked around the yurt until they reached the far side, where the door faced the forest rather than the town. It was real wood and hand carved, with the trunk of a tree running up the hinged side, a raccoon peering around the edge with comically wide eyes.

A post had been buried in the ground beside the front door with fingerpost direction signs on it. One sign pointed toward the rest of the town and read *Wild Sign 20 feet*. Another, just below it, read *Adventures ½ mile*. The one at the bottom of the post read *Tottleford Family Yurt*. There was a pair of eye hooks on the bottom of that sign holding another that read *Right where you're standing*.

It made her feel wretched. It wasn't looking too promising for the residents of Wild Sign—and she *liked* the Tottleford family, liked the mysterious sign maker, too.

Anna couldn't help herself—even knowing no one was here, she knocked at the door. No one answered.

The door had no doorknob and it didn't just push in. Charles examined it for a minute, then pulled on a leaf set among the other leaves carved into the left-hand side of the door about knee height for Charles. It came loose, attached to a piece of twine threaded through from the other side. She heard a board slide.

"Pioneer trick," Charles said. "Though usually it's just a string all by itself. If I let the string go with the door shut, the latch will fall back down. It's not a lock, just a way to keep the door closed."

He pushed the door open, but stopped suddenly and put out a hand to keep Anna back.

"Witch," he said in warning.

Anna could sometimes feel magic—though not like Charles. She was a lot more aware of magic in her wolf form; her wolf was better at accessing pack magic, too. She trusted her mate's judgment and waited while he did whatever he felt he had to do to fix matters. The air was musty, but she also caught the faint smell of herbs and the various scents of an active household.

"It's safe enough, I think," he said to Anna. To the room he said, "We come seeking answers, no harm to this home or the family it encompassed."

He tilted his head as if listening for something, then walked on in. Anna couldn't tell if he'd gotten an answer or not.

She'd been in a few yurts before but never one this large; the interior was at least as big as their living room, dining room, and kitchen at home.

The floor was made from closely fitted planks, and shoulder-high movable partitions constructed of wood and fabric separated off rooms. In the bedroom area, there were four hammock beds, one larger and three smaller, as if for children. In another space, a kitchen-type station was arranged on a section of wall. A large bucket stood by a canvas camp sink, with a dipper hooked over the rim of the bucket. The camp sink drain slid through the fabric side of the yurt to the outside. A half-size fridge proved to be clean and empty— but still cooling.

"There is a farm of solar panels somewhere near this yurt," Charles said, though she hadn't thought he was paying attention to what she was doing. He'd pulled back the curtain on a small private area, which turned out to be a bathroom with another composting toilet. "The report made note of them."

He opened the waste container. "Empty," he said.

"It looks like they cleaned up," Anna said, moving on to the bedroom area. "It looks ready for the next set of guests." She peered into one of the four hampers lined along the wall. "Except they left all of their clothing."

There was a small bookshelf stuffed with books. The bottom shelf was filled with children's books, the next two with well-loved paperbacks—but the top shelf held treasures. Anna pulled out a battered copy of Chambers's *The King in Yellow*, which proved to be an 1895 edition. She slid it back and pulled out *The Outsider and Others* by H. P. Lovecraft. She thought it was a first printing, but she didn't know enough to be sure. There were maybe a half dozen decrepit copies of the old pulp magazine *Weird Tales* from the nineteen thirties; each of them was dated in black marker scrawled on its clear plastic wrapping.

At Charles's quiet hum, Anna looked over to see him stopped by a small folding table, his face intent, nostrils flaring.

"She left her tarot deck," Charles said neutrally, and Anna noticed a thicker-than-normal deck of cards among the other objects on the table.

"The decks are usually highly personal, right?" Anna asked, joining Charles. Her human nose wasn't keen enough to smell anything more than that the items on the table did indeed belong to one of the people who had lived here. But if Charles said it was a woman's tarot deck, she trusted it was so. "Is it something she'd have left behind?"

"That depends upon the witch. This doesn't feel like a witch's personal deck—those sometimes are almost animate." He touched the deck and shook his head.

He surveyed the room with a frown, turning in a slow circle.

Anna, not knowing what he was looking for, stayed back. Then he glanced up.

She followed his gaze to the ceiling. The ceiling of a yurt consisted of wooden rafters fit into a central ring, which had the same sort of essential importance to a yurt a keystone had for a stone arch—it was the single item making the whole structure work. In the other yurts Anna had seen, the ring had been just that—a plain laminate wooden ring. This yurt's ring was a series of three rings, which looked more like a wheel.

"That," she said finally, "is really beautiful."

Like the door, the rings forming the wheel were carved. Leaves wound around and through the spokes of the wheel, and little carved animals peered out in a way that reminded Anna of the raccoon on the door. The smallest ring and the largest were inscribed with runic symbols.

"They would never have left this behind of their own free will," said Charles solemnly. He held up a hand toward the wheel and closed his eyes for a moment. When he opened his eyes, he said, "This wheel has been used by generations of white witches, each leaving a blessing for her descendants." He held up a hand, fingers splayed. "I didn't feel it when we first came in because it is sleeping."

"What does that mean?" Anna asked.

He shook his head. "I have no idea. She might have shielded it before she left—or it might be this way because she died. But she would not have left the wheel, even if she had to leave everything else. Not unless there was simply no time to take the yurt down. But they took time to clean the composting toilets."

"Well." Anna sighed and followed Charles out of the yurt. "We didn't really think that they left willingly, did we?"

Charles closed the door behind them, listening for the latch to drop back into its bracket. He put a hand on the door and whispered, "Peace to those who sleep."

"Found a few things," said Tag, striding toward them. At some point he'd changed back to human. He'd dressed but was barefoot, having declined to carry the weight of his boots for the trip. He ran around the forest at home without shoes a lot, too.

CHARLES FOLLOWED BEHIND Anna and Tag as they headed over to the post office. Tag walked with energy, bouncing around like a puppy as he questioned Anna and responding to her story of their explorations with exuberant gestures. A person, Charles reflected with amusement, might be fooled into thinking Tag was just a big, happy sap. Around Anna, Tag was either lazing around like an overly large cat or vibrating with enthusiasm. Around Anna, Tag kept the lethal berserker tidily out of sight—because around Anna, he could.

It made Charles happy to see Tag like this. They hadn't had to execute any of their old wolves since Anna had come—and some of those old wolves were almost stable again. Tag was only one example, and not the most striking. The pack was better with Anna in it, in ways far more subtle than he or his da had expected. They had hoped for calm—they had not expected happy.

There was a battered old blue canvas bag up against the wall of the post office. Tag surveyed it with an air of smug accomplishment.

"Mailbag," he told them, then gave them a sheepish look. "Or at least, there are letters in it. I don't think that it is an official US mailbag."

Charles gave him a look. Brother Wolf thought Tag had found

something else, too. Tag caught his eye and nodded. Yes. The bag was only the first of Tag's discoveries.

The mailbag had been out in the elements for months, and it carried only eight letters—all of them from the inhabitants of Wild Sign. Tag, without the pesky scruples normal people were burdened with, had opened all of them, looked through the lot, and stuffed them back inside so he could present them singly to Anna.

"From the dates, these folks weren't real keen on letter writing," Tag said dryly. "This looks to be the product of about ten days."

Anna sorted through the letters. "Eight letters, all from two people," she said, handing a pair of envelopes to Charles.

They were both from Carrie Green, Wild Sign, CA, no zip. They were both checks. Presumably they had each been wrapped in the plain white paper now tucked to the side of the checks in the envelopes. There was no bill or note with either.

One, addressed to Happy Camp Mini Storage, seemed self-explanatory. Usefully, the locker number it was paying for was written on the check. If the owner of the storage facility hadn't already cleaned out the locker for nonpayment, it might hold some clues—though Charles didn't think the odds of that were high.

The second was addressed to Angel Hills and was for a significant amount. On the note line of the check, Ms. Green had written simply *Daniel Green*.

"Sounds like a rest home," Anna said. "Or maybe an apartment, but for that amount, my money is on some kind of extended care facility."

Charles agreed.

The other six letters were from Dr. Connors to his daughter, Dr. Connors. They were written on sequential days—April 14, 15, 16, 17,

18, and 19. Other than the date and the "Dear Dr. Connors the Younger" salutation, they were all written in code.

Dr. Connors did not want anyone to read his letters except for his daughter. Charles thought about why someone living simply in the woods would not want his mail read.

The coded letters, like the warding signs carved into the trees, supported the hypothesis that the people of Wild Sign were hiding. The yurt he and Anna had explored had belonged to a white witch, and the whole area had a—well, not a real scent, but maybe a psychic scent he associated with white magic.

A group of white witches might very well have abandoned the town in a slow retreat that allowed them to tidy up after themselves— but not take much with them that might slow them down. He thought of the yurt ring—and he decided he was still of the opinion that any witch who owned such a potent protection would never willingly abandon it.

Possibly Wild Sign and what had happened did not have anything to do with Leah's troubles here two centuries ago. From the stories Charles had heard, Sherwood had been a thorough man. Da hadn't thought Sherwood would have left some monster for anyone else to handle. Possibly he'd rested, then gone back to clean up the mess he'd left. Bran wouldn't know—he hadn't communicated with Sherwood between that time and when the wolves had rescued him, three-legged and amnesiac, from the cellar of a black witch's home nearly two centuries later. Possibly whatever Leah had faced was gone, and something else, black witches maybe, had happened to Wild Sign. Maybe it was a coincidence that Wild Sign had faced troubles in the same place. But coincidences, in Charles's experience, were as rare as hen's teeth.

Charles had been shuffling through Dr. Connors's letters, Anna peering around him to watch, though she'd already been through them. She stiffened and closed her hand around his forearm.

"Are all of these the same letter?" she said slowly. "I didn't notice it looking at them one at a time. But don't they all look alike to you?"

She was right.

Anna took the letters from him, found a bare space on the ground, and set them out. She crouched, then sat down so she could see them all at once more easily. When the wind tried to play with them, she grabbed some rocks and weighed them down.

Tag knelt beside her wordlessly. After a minute he rearranged the letters in time order.

"Same letter," Tag said, and, reaching out, he tapped the newest letter. "And when he wrote this last one, he was a lot more upset than when he wrote the first."

Charles had never been much of a letter writer, but his father had. When email had replaced letters for communication, Bran had been unhappy. Because the letters were more personal, they carried scents—and handwriting, which, with certain well-schooled exceptions, were seldom just lines on a page. Here, as Tag pointed out, it was easy to see the hand holding the pen had gotten shakier and more emphatic as the days had moved by.

"We need to find Dr. Connors's daughter," said Anna. "Fortunately the FBI left us her number. If we had a cell phone, I'd do it right now."

They'd left their phones behind. Charles was too cautious to bring traceable technology anywhere he wasn't sure he wanted the government to know about. It did mean they couldn't call for help, either. But Charles figured that if they found something the three of them couldn't handle, all that calling for help would do was get their help killed, too.

"We will call her when we get back to camp," Charles said.

In the meantime, they stuffed all of the letters into one of the envelopes. Then Tag produced a piece of twine to tie them together and put the resultant bundle into his pack.

He lifted the moldering mailbag. "Do we need this?"

Charles shook his head and Tag let the old bag fall.

"Found it by the side of the creek over there," said Tag, pointing vaguely south and downhill. "Don't know what it was doing there. Maybe wild animals dragged it around. Maybe someone just dropped it where I found it. Makes as much sense as anything else I've seen here. I found a couple of other odd things by the creek, too."

"What did you find?" Anna asked as they started off with Tag in the lead.

He shook his head, and Anna gave him a gentle shove that had Brother Wolf sharpening his gaze on Tag and stepping to a better attack position. But Tag just laughed.

"It's better if you see 'em. Faster, too," he said. "I'd be all day describing, and Charles would take one look and tell me a dozen things I didn't notice."

Anna gave a huff of amused agreement and slanted a look at Charles. Brother Wolf wanted to preen at her recognition of their prowess. Charles just smiled at her.

Tag led them down the hill, toward a busy creek meandering around the side of the mountain. They encountered a path when they were about halfway there, and Charles looked back up the hill to see where it led to in Wild Sign.

"The smallest yurt," said Tag, answering Charles's unasked question. "Smelled like witches, too. White ones. I didn't go in, though, because I was still running as wolf. That yurt and the one you and Anna explored, several of the tents, and two cabins all smelled of them. Too many witches in this place to be coincidence."

Charles nodded agreement and Tag looked pleased.

Someone had cleared a stretch of bank of the stream and piled stones to keep back the grasses and bushes. They had dropped a tree across the creek, trimmed off the branches, and then used an adze to flatten the upper side of the trunk and make a passable bridge.

There were signs that the stream was a lot deeper in the spring, maybe tall enough to cover the top of the tree-cum-bridge, but it was still plenty deep. It was hard to be sure, because the water was very clear, but Charles judged it waist deep where it pooled next to the tree-bridge.

Tag took them across the bridge and then led them off the trail to where a thicket of willows, their leaves bright autumn yellow, grew in a section of spongy ground. Someone with big claws had, very recently, ripped up a swath of waist-high grasses and young bushes to reveal the dead.

"They killed them before they left," Anna said, sounding faintly sickened. "These were witches. Did they sacrifice them for power?"

Charles knelt beside one of the skeletons. It wore a collar with a two-year-old expired rabies tag and an ID tag. The ID tag read *Bear*. Below the name was a phone number. On the other side the tag had been engraved with a heart. Charles rested a hand on the skull and waited to see what it could tell him.

He shook his head and met his mate's anxious gaze. "No. Killed cleanly without harvesting anything." There was a hollowness to the feel of creatures killed by witches in order to gain power. This dog had not been fed upon by black magic.

They found seventeen skeletons without much effort. Fourteen dogs and three cats. Charles thought that there might be more hidden under the bushes, but there was no need to disturb them further.

"I only discovered them because someone had spelled their grave to keep predators away," Tag said. "Predators other than werewolves, anyway. Spell wasn't strong, and it gave up as soon as I started digging."

Charles had wondered. Mostly skeletons left on the surface were scattered by scavengers. Anna was reading the collars. He stifled the impulse to stop her. He would have saved her the pain—but she was an adult. She knew what she was doing; it wasn't his job to protect her from her own decisions.

"Kriemhild," she said. "One of the names given to Siegfried's wife in the Norse sagas. I always liked it better than Gutrune, which was the one Wagner used."

Anna sounded like her normal self, and she was holding it together. But he could tell the dead pets had brought home the knowledge that all of the people who had lived here were probably dead. He thought so, too.

This killing field, like the carefully cleaned composting toilets, had the feel of duty. The kind of thing a dying person might do— clean up his mess so no one else had to. Killing their pets because there would be no one to take care of their dependents—and a good person would not allow these animals to slowly starve to death in the wilderness. Or possibly they had been protecting the animals from whatever had happened to the citizens of Wild Sign.

Charles wasn't sure yet exactly what it said about what had happened to the people in Wild Sign. Their story was just starting to take shape for him.

"Siegfried's wife," Tag was saying. "Someone liked opera?"

"Someone liked old Norse sagas," Anna said. "Gutrune was Wagner's choice for the *Ring* cycle, and this dog was named Kriemhild."

"Old Norse sagas aren't outside of the ordinary among the witchborn," Charles observed. "Or it could be there is an anime series or heroine of a computer game with that name."

Anna smiled at him, a genuine smile despite the edge of sadness remaining on her face. That had been a reference to an in-joke between them. He missed a lot of pop culture references, and she liked to tease him about it.

"If they didn't use their deaths for power, why did they kill their pets?" Anna asked.

"If they had to leave them behind," said Tag, "it would be a kindness to put them down rather than let domestic animals loose to fend for themselves out here."

"Sounds right to me," said Charles. That Tag had come to the same conclusion Charles had made it more convincing.

Charles couldn't think offhand of the exact circumstances that would allow a group of people time to clean up their camp and kill their pets before disaster overtook them—it spoke of a resignation that seemed oddly wrong. The people who had come to this mountainside and created a place where they could be safe did not strike him as the kind of people who would be resigned to their deaths. Wild Sign was an optimistic place, built with ingenuity by people fighting for a good life. The kind of people who had lived here should have fought—and there was no sign of any kind of battle.

"Charles?" Anna said, her voice thin.

He knelt beside her to see what she'd found: the top of a small skull, suspiciously round. A shape more common among humans than dogs.

Gently, he unearthed the rounded skull, Anna tense beside him. He couldn't help the sigh of relief he let out when he turned it over to see the skull supported sharp canine teeth. He kissed the top of her head.

"Chihuahua," he said. "And that makes eighteen."

She took a deep breath. "Someone needs to dig through these," she said. "If they killed their pets . . ."

"I'll do it," Tag said. "While you and Charles go through the rest of the camp." He reached down and held out his hand; Anna took it and let him pull her to her feet. "Come on. I have something else to show you."

He tugged her after him without releasing her hand. Charles couldn't tell if Tag was trying to comfort her—or himself.

Charles rose, but instead of following them, he raised his head and drew in a deep breath, letting Brother Wolf sort through the information the air held. Outside of the normal scents of a forest, he detected the faint trace of witchcraft lingering all around Wild Sign, though that was more intuition than scent. There was acrid smoke from distant fires.

Finally, he attended to the subtle scent he'd been catching the whole time they'd been there. He thought it had been strengthening every hour they stayed, but it was difficult to be certain. Like the feel of witchcraft, it was not quite something he could smell.

He waited until Tag and Anna were farther away and tried again. This time he was sure it was stronger than before—and not as unfamiliar as he had thought.

Unbidden, he saw Leah as she dismounted from her blue-eyed horse once more. He'd been close enough, holding his da's horse next to Leah's, that he'd caught an unfamiliar and unpleasant scent—an odor he had not perceived with his nose.

Had it really been the same? Or was he trying to find threads between what had happened to Leah and what had happened here at Wild Sign? He wasn't sure he could trust his memory of a trace so old. But Brother Wolf was sure it was the same . . . and Brother Wolf also thought they had let their charges get too far away if there was a possibility of danger.

He hurried after Anna and Tag, who had started back down the trail. He slanted a glance at the sky. They would stay another hour, he decided. He wanted to get them away from this place before the scent grew much stronger.

5

A quarter mile along the trail they came upon a sign that read *Here there be Music*. Charles was becoming quite fond of the signs scattered around the settlement with abandon. He wondered if the sign maker had intended a large-scale pun on the name of the town.

Here there be signs, thought Brother Wolf with amused agreement. *Signs in the Wild.*

Brother Wolf had not spoken to him in words before they had found Anna. He was pretty sure it was because Brother Wolf didn't trust Anna to read the images he'd used to communicate with Charles.

Our da always regretted he didn't take the time to learn our mother's tongue, Brother Wolf told him unexpectedly. *He always wondered what stories she would have told him, what thoughts of hers he will never know. If he could have talked her out of dying had he been able to argue with her more effectively. I chose not to make the same mistake.*

Charles wondered how Brother Wolf knew that, because he was sure his da had never said so much in his hearing. Not that he remembered, anyway.

Given the sign, Charles wasn't entirely surprised when the trail dropped through a copse of trees and ended in an amphitheater. Most of the basin was natural, a trick of the regional geology that backed the flat clearing with stone cliff faces to reflect sound on three sides.

But it wasn't untouched by human hands. Nature had never gathered all of the seat-sized boulders into a circle. They weren't large boulders; a strong human could have rolled them, or they could have used the four-wheeler he'd seen signs of. He wondered absently if they'd taken the machine with them or if it was somewhere around here, hidden in the forest, even as he registered that some of those stones had been there much longer than three years. Had Leah's people moved them? Had there been a Native tribe here at one time?

The tree stumps had been moved here during the time of Wild Sign, though; he could tell by the chain saw marks. The stumps had been used to fill in the gaps between rocks, as well as to form the bottom half of the arrangement, so there was a full circle of crude seating. Wild Sign folk, at least, had not used the area to perform before an audience; they'd used it to perform for themselves.

The amphitheater alone would have been interesting enough for Tag to bring them here. But he'd had a better reason—Charles understood why he'd wanted them to see it rather than explaining. The impact was startling.

Tag had stopped beside Charles, waiting until Charles looked at him with a raised eyebrow before speaking.

"I said it was weird," Tag said, and Charles reflected that Tag was a musician, too. He'd understood the meaning of what he'd found here.

Instruments, battered by months of wind and weather, lay where their owners had left them. Guitars, a couple of violins, at least one bodhran, and a tarnished flute were balanced on the sitting stones. What looked like the remains of a bagpipe were strewn across the ground, with grass growing thick around them.

Anna, who had gone ahead, picked up one of the guitars. The gentle motion caused the neck to separate from the body. Rain could have done that, Charles thought, swelling the wood until the glue gave.

"It's a Martin," Anna told them. "Custom. Hand inlay work." She turned it toward him so he could see the mother-of-pearl designs on the fretboard and body.

A custom Martin was expensive to be leaving out in the weather. Without being able to play it, it was impossible to accurately assess the price, but a guitar like that started around ten thousand and could go as high as someone was willing to pay. She set it down gently, as if she was worried she might hurt it further.

No, thought Charles grimly, this had not been some orderly exodus where people had fled the threat of predators. He didn't know a serious musician who would have just left their instruments to rot—and not because the Martin was worth money. Unlike the careful laying out of their pets, this was disrespectful. He didn't know what had gone on at Wild Sign, but he would find out.

He strode forward with the intent of joining his mate, took five strides, and stopped dead as darkness sent the hair on the back of his neck crawling. It wasn't magic, this feeling. On old battlefields, pain and blood sometimes twisted the spirit of a place until merely standing on such ground made a man's heart ache—or caused fear to rise through his bones. In old jails and psych hospitals, the spirit was so damaged it could make it hard to breathe.

A stride behind him, Tag swore, feeling it, too.

Something very bad had happened here. Not, he was pretty sure, whatever had made the people of Wild Sign leave their musical instruments behind. Something like this did not happen in a season. Two years after the Battle of Little Bighorn, Charles had felt nothing while he'd traveled over that ground. Ten years later, the spirit had been so heavy with sorrow, he had stood alone in the darkness and cried for those who had been lost.

This darkness of spirit had been here before the people of Wild Sign had decided to make this ground into a gathering place. It would have taken more than half a year to grow darkness this deep. He wondered why a group of witches would have thought it a good idea to come here. Did they have no common sense at all? How could they not have felt this?

"There's something bad about this place, isn't there?" Anna asked, watching them. "I thought maybe I was just spooked because of the dead animals and the abandoned instruments." She looked around. "I don't like it here. What happened to these people to make this place feel so awful?"

"It's not the Wild Sign people," Tag said, his voice certain. "This"—he swept a hand wide—"feels like Culloden." Interesting, Charles thought, that Tag's mind, like Charles's, had gone to another battlefield for comparison. "It would take a great deal of horrible to make the deaths of forty people resonate in the land."

While Tag had been talking, Anna's toe had sent something rolling on the ground. She'd bent down and picked it up—a recorder.

Doubtless there were other instruments scattered about and hidden by a season's growth of grasses. Absently she knocked it against her leg to dislodge the dirt.

"My da said Sherwood told him there were over a hundred people here, and everyone but Leah died," Charles said. He wasn't sure a hundred deaths would be enough to make the land feel as it did.

He closed his eyes, trying to get a better feel. He missed the little spirits of the woods who sometime gave him clues.

Brother Wolf said, out loud so everyone could hear it, "This feels like a place where sacrifices were made."

Anna nodded her head. "It feels tragic."

She lifted the recorder to her lips, almost absently. The note rose in the air, pure and clear, the stone walls behind them pushing the sound out. Like the guitar, it was a fine instrument. Unlike the guitar, it had survived somehow undamaged from its exposure.

Anna played a quick scale first, to check it for tune and playability—and to let her fingers get used to the hole placements. It was what Charles would have done with a strange instrument, too. You had to know your partner before you could make proper music.

Typically, his Anna's first instinct was to make things better, and music was always her willing tool. She started out in a minor key, trying several songs before settling on an old Irish tune. He and Tag waited where they stood, caught by the music.

The old words sang through his head in time with her playing:

> *The Minstrel-Boy to the war is gone,*
> *In the ranks of death you'll find him;*
> *His father's sword he has girded on,*
> *And his wild harp slung behind him.*

It was a song suited to this time and place, with its melancholy themes of death and beauty, war and music. Charles became aware something was stirring in response to the music—something, here and now. It made Charles uneasy. He could not tell if it was something physical or spiritual. He couldn't tell if it was for good or ill.

He wasn't the only one who felt it. Tag had started to sing along—had gotten as far as "in the ranks of death" before he quit singing in favor of watching the land around them with battle-honed alertness.

> *"Land of Song!" said the warrior-bard,*
> *"Tho' all the world betrays thee,*
> *One sword, at least, thy rights shall guard,*
> *One faithful harp shall praise thee."*

"Do you feel that?" Tag asked Charles in a soft voice that didn't interfere with Anna's song. "Something . . ."

Charles nodded, trying to isolate what was happening, but the twisted feel of the land kept getting in the way, tangling his senses— he could *hear* her sing the words. And he knew she could not possibly be doing that. She was playing the recorder; he could see her with her lips clearly closed around the mouthpiece. But even so, he could have sworn he heard her voice.

> *The Minstrel fell!—but the foeman's chain*
> *Could not bring that proud soul under;*
> *The harp he lov'd ne'er spoke again,*
> *For he tore its chords asunder;*

Anna turned away from him, playing to another audience, someone . . . something other than them.

"She's singing," Tag said, sounding worried. "Can you hear it? How is she doing that? Should we stop her?"

"Yes," said Charles, but he made no move to do so.

> And said, "No chains shall sully thee,
> Thou soul of love and bravery!
> Thy songs were made for the pure and free,
> They shall never sound in slavery."

The words echoed, and the music was amplified by the natural acoustics of the amphitheater into something much more powerful than a musician should have been able to get out of a little recorder. Even a musician as good as his Anna.

Driven by the urgent feeling that something was wrong, Charles started to move toward her. It felt like slogging through mud. Only then did he realize he'd been caught in the music, too. There had been magic at work—though, he thought with grim self-directed anger, that revelation should have hit him when he'd heard, impossibly, the words of her song.

The magic had lessened when she'd quit singing, having finished all the lyrics. The sweet voice of the recorder continued as Anna played variations on "The Minstrel Boy." He needed to get to her before she found another song; he was fairly sure when she found one, they would be caught in its spell again.

He had to free her.

"I can't move," said Tag tightly, berserker rage shadowing his voice, making it rasp.

"Wait there," Charles told him with authority he hoped Tag could hold on to. In a gentler voice he said, "Anna, love, put the recorder down. The song is over, the last verse sung."

She ignored him.

She can't hear us, Brother Wolf told him.

He wanted to see her face. He had to wade through the sticky magic to get to her—it wasn't only Tag who was riding an edge. Since she hadn't responded to his voice at all, he changed tactics.

"Anna," he barked. He tried reaching through their mating bond again; he'd been trying to touch her through it since she'd started playing. If she felt him, he could not tell.

Fight fire with fire, suggested Brother Wolf, though not in words. Instead, Charles got a vision of a backfire lit in the path of a blazing forest. *Sing.*

It was as good an idea as any. He chose a courting song Buffalo Singer had taught him, a song his uncle had learned from his father, who had learned it from his father before him. Like most of the songs his uncle had taught him, it had no words but plenty of meaning. It had been composed by Charles's great-grandfather as he sought to win the hand of the shy woman who became the mother of his children. It was a song rooted in love, carrying the weight of the generations of people who had sung it.

Charles had not sung this song since his uncle had died in his arms, raving with fever.

The rich notes filled him from his chest and up through his sinuses in a way most music did not, bringing with it the memory of men singing in the dark in the world of his childhood. As with Anna's music, the amphitheater gave depth and power to his voice—and so, in a way he did not pause to examine, did his memories.

Charles was forced to stop walking because he couldn't keep moving and allow Brother Wolf to sing at the same time—and the song was doing something.

He closed his eyes to better sense the flows and currents of magic that were mixing, driven by his music and Anna's trapped song. But he kept getting caught up in the voice of the tragic and broken land—he knew now why Brother Wolf thought this place had been used as a blood altar. It had that feel, layers upon layers of death.

He wasn't sure whether the land's twisted spirit was caught up in this or if it was something else. The not-scent he'd noticed earlier, the one that reminded him of how Leah had smelled when he'd first met her, was noticeably stronger than it had been before Anna had started singing. But he knew unraveling the magic in play was beyond his abilities right now. He'd have to go about it another way.

Brother Wolf joined in. As he did so, Charles was certain the tide of magic was about to change.

But when it stopped, it all stopped. There was no gradual defeat, no unraveling, no sense of victory. Just a sudden withdrawal of everything opposing Charles's attempt to defeat it. The air became clear and easy to breathe, the strange scent entirely gone.

Even the darkness that emanated from the land died away until he was tempted to believe he'd imagined it. Shadow-ladened land could be healed, but only by a great shaman over a period of months or years. It didn't just disappear.

Tag swore with feeling, for which Charles couldn't blame him. The abrupt cessation of whatever they had been struggling against made him feel like he'd been engaged in a game of tug-of-war and the rope had broken, leaving him sprawling (if only metaphorically) in the mud. It was disorienting on the verge of being painful.

Even so, Charles kept singing until he reached a place where his song had a natural stopping place. Breaking off untidily felt both ungrateful and unwise.

As Charles fell silent, Tag started toward Anna at a run, but stopped when Charles held up a hand. Charles was watching Anna's tensing back, felt the bond between them still shut painfully tight—but now it no longer seemed like outside interference. It felt as if she had rejected him utterly—which was not like his Anna. The scent of her fear threatened to send Brother Wolf into a frenzy.

"Anna, my love?" Charles said softly, knowing his struggle with Brother Wolf did not show on the outside.

She turned then, staggering a little—for which he could not blame her. Her face was composed, her body controlled, but all the same she reminded him of a deer, ready to flee at the slightest movement. Her eyes were terrified. He hadn't seen that look on her face in a long time.

What had the music done to her, to leave her panic-stricken and afraid?

She tried to speak, but had to lick her lips. "Who are you?" she asked.

PACK MEETINGS ARE the worst, Anna told herself stoutly, trying, by the understatement, to buck up her spirits as she cowered in the back corner of the room, attempting to be invisible. She wished she were safe in her Oak Park apartment and not in the Western Suburb Chicago Pack's stronghold in Naperville.

She knew she couldn't really hide, not in a room filled with werewolves. She hated knowing it was going to be rough tonight—after this long in the pack, she'd gotten a feel for when trouble was brewing. She could feel the anticipation in the air. She hated that she cowered, head down, trying not to be noticed.

Her father once said she argued so much that when she died, she'd argue with St. Peter at the pearly gates. He'd been proud of her obstinance—he was a lawyer by profession and by calling. He would not recognize her now.

It was a good thing, she told herself, that she was not allowed to contact him anymore.

At first she'd tried to pay attention to what her Alpha said in these meetings, but she'd learned he could read her feelings through the pack bond. It was better not to listen than for Leo to know how much she despised him. He didn't like being disrespected.

She could tell by the tone of Leo's voice that he was ready to wrap things up, and her senses prickled at the heightened danger as the crowd of werewolves, who also picked up on Leo's cues, started to fidget.

He was looking at her. Justin. She forced herself to keep her eyes down as her breath stuttered and her heart raced painfully in her chest.

Calm down, she told herself. *Calm down. Panic makes him worse. Makes them all worse.*

Leo quit talking and people began to move around. Anna had found one gambit that sometimes worked to keep her safe. She'd taken note of where Isabelle was and charted a path toward the Alpha's mate's side. Sometimes Isabelle would take her part—and usually even *he* moderated his behavior in front of Isabelle, who liked to pretend she was a good guardian of her pack.

Halfway to her goal, Anna glanced up from the floor to make sure Isabelle hadn't moved—and met *his* eyes. He was pacing her through the crowd.

Cold terror numbed her fingers, because she knew that look, knew he'd decided she was his prey tonight. Again. It had been two weeks; she had hoped for three but had known it was unlikely. He liked her fear. Her pain.

Chest tight, she . . .

A deep voice wound around her, calling her, lulling her with gentleness. She didn't understand the words, but for a moment she felt safe. She . . .

. . . looked for Isabelle. But the Alpha's mate was no longer standing where she had been, and Anna couldn't locate her. A rough hand grabbed her hair and jerked her head back harshly.

We have you safe. You are ours. No hand will touch you if you do not wish it.

A deep throbbing music tried to surround her with safety, but it dissipated in the pain of Justin's human-blunt teeth digging into her neck, drawing blood. The scent attracted attention. Someone let out a low whoop that seemed to stir the whole room. The pack would join Justin's hunt tonight. She knew she was lost.

Safe, insisted the music.

"Anna, my love," said a deep voice.

And, abruptly, as if by magic, *everything* changed.

Instead of a dark room, too full of werewolves, too full of men, she stood in brilliant sunlight, wearing unfamiliar clothing, on the side of a mountain. Before her there was nothing but evergreen forest as far as she could see. It was autumn, she thought a little numbly, taking in the colored leaves of the undergrowth. But she knew it was summer.

Her neck hurt where Justin had bitten her. She turned around, half expecting Justin's hold on her hair to stop her. Expecting that he would be there—that this was some game he was playing.

Justin wasn't there. But she saw then that she wasn't in untouched wilderness. She was standing in an amphitheater of sorts, surrounded by a circle of rocks spread around the space as though they were intended to be seating. Scattered about the rocks were broken instruments. Maybe Justin had knocked her out and she was dreaming. It was the sort of scene her subconscious might come up with: the death of her music. But it didn't feel like a dream. It felt real.

Two men stood on the opposite side of the clearing from her. The larger of the two stood farther away, poised on the balls of his feet as if he were ready to move at any moment, held back by something just barely adequate to keep him where he was. His orange hair hung down in tangled waves over his shoulders. But it wasn't that one, huge and menacing as he looked, who drew her attention.

About halfway between her and the redheaded man was a Native American man with wolf-gold eyes. She could not look away from him, although she knew quite well what happened when she met the eyes of dominant males, even by accident.

He was big, too, with wide shoulders and graceful hands. He wore his hair in a long braid and, incongruously in a man with such masculine features, gold studs in his ears. In contrast to his rather extraordinary looks, his clothing was mundane: a green flannel shirt, jeans, and worn leather lace-up boots.

Dangerous. She knew that with absolute certainty. This man was dangerous.

"Who are you?" she asked.

Her breath was harsh, her throat sour with bile, as she struggled to accept her current situation and evaluate it while she was still trying to deal with the sudden change of place. She was in danger and she had no idea what to do about it. The urge to run was almost overwhelming, but she fought it back because fleeing would be a terrible mistake.

And some part of her remembered the moment after Justin bit her neck, remembered the harsh hands and the . . . and the . . . She had run then, she knew it. Knew it had done no good. They had outnumbered her.

She fought not to remember it. Not to remember the hands, the greedy mouths—to jump in time to afterward.

Afterward.

Afterward, when she was alone in her apartment, she'd sat fully clothed in her bathtub and pulled up her shirtsleeve. This time, she thought, dragging the silver knife down the inside of her wrist and watching the blood well. This time it would work.

And somehow, Anna knew that memory, of sitting in the bathtub so she wouldn't cause a big mess for someone else to clean up. That part was true, too. She looked down at her arms and saw long silvery scars. How could there be scars and Justin's bite still be bleeding?

"Hey," said the Native American man. He had a deep voice, the one she remembered calling to her in the darkness of her terror. Surely he hadn't been in the pack meeting room, though that had been where she'd heard him.

"Stay here, sweetheart," he said. "Stay with me."

She put her hand to the side of her neck, felt the sting of the open wound and the stickiness of blood. But she didn't look at her hand. She couldn't take her eyes away from the man who had spoken to her.

He was scary—she knew people were scared of him. How did she know that? And why did it make her sad? Jeepers, her mind was in a muddle. She had to cling to the present moment because she was in danger—later, when she was safe, she could figure it all out.

Why did she want to go to him?

Someone growled and she jerked her eyes to the second man. Second werewolf, she understood. They were both werewolves. His face was twisted in rage and her breath caught.

"Tag," said the first man without looking away from Anna. "Go back up to the sign. You are scaring her."

Tag. She should know that name. She *knew* that name.

She put her hands up to her face, covering her eyes. Stupid thing to do, the scared woman inside of her said. But there was something wrong with her vision; she was seeing two different things and she didn't know what was real. "Seeing" was the wrong verb, but she couldn't find a better one. "Remembering" wasn't the right word, surely.

"Anna." His voice was very soft.

She jerked her hands away from her face and saw that the other stranger, the one with red hair, had gone away. Her werewolf had taken a seat on the ground.

Hers.

"What is scaring you?" he asked. Then even more softly, "Why are you afraid of me?"

She knew not to talk to them, to the dominant wolves. That never went well. She'd been taught better. She raised her hand to her jaw, but that had healed a long time ago.

"Anna? Will you tell me? I would like to know what's going on."

She made a sound that was half laugh, half sob. She would like to know that, too. She opened her mouth to tell him about where she had been before she'd suddenly found herself here on the side of a mountain. Maybe he knew how she'd gotten here.

But what came out of her mouth was "Justin."

He half closed his eyes as they flared to an even brighter gold and his whole body twitched, causing her to flinch back. There was a long moment of silence.

"Justin," he said with deliberate calm she didn't believe. She knew what rage looked like—and knew that it was more dangerous when it wore a mask of composure. "Justin cannot hurt you ever again. Justin is dead."

Oh, how she wished that were true.

"No," she said. "I just . . . He was . . . He was . . ." She reached up to touch the wound on her neck, this time for reassurance. It hurt—he had just bitten her. She wasn't wrong. She had proof.

"I just saw him," she told the seated man. "He was just here—I mean, I was just there. With him." She remembered the smell of him, could *still* smell him on her skin, and it made her sick.

"Anna," the man said, "Justin is dead." There was finality in his tone. "Can you hear the truth when I speak it?"

She started to shake her head, then realized that she could. That he was not lying, or at least he believed what he said.

"Yes," she said. But how could Justin be dead? Had whatever magic that transported her to wherever she was now, had that killed him? And how would this man know? Had this stranger teleported her here somehow?

Deep in her gut, something was trying to tell her she had this situation wrong. But she didn't know how or in what way—and she had to deal with the present danger first. The present danger who was sitting twenty feet away from her, doing the best that he could to look nonthreatening. It wasn't a good act, but it mattered that he was trying.

The seated man caught and held her gaze again. Instead of scaring her, as all of her previous experience told her it should, for some reason his regard made her feel better, more centered.

"Justin is dead," he said again. "Leo is dead. They cannot hurt you anymore."

And from the certainty in his voice, she knew that to be true. Even if she'd just seen Justin, just seen Leo. She knew they were dead because this man told her it was so. *How did this stranger know about Justin and Leo?*

"I killed Isabelle," Anna said, her mouth so dry she could barely force the words out. Her head hurt with a sudden, eye-watering pain. She didn't know where the words had come from.

"Anna?" he said, and she focused on his voice. One true thing in a sea of jumbled events.

"You sang for me," she whispered, knowing it was true, though not what it meant.

"Yes," he agreed.

She opened her mouth to say something else, and that flash of pain struck her again.

CHARLES CAUGHT HER before she hit the ground. Doing it when he'd had to start from a sitting position meant he mostly just managed to put himself under her rather than keeping her from falling.

Though he could hear her heartbeat, feel the life in her body, he still put his hand on her pulse for reassurance. He avoided touching the bite marks.

She'd had them when she turned around after the music had died. She hadn't had them when she put the recorder to her lips, and he didn't know where she'd gotten them from. He hadn't smelled the blood until she'd turned around. They were human teeth marks, healing now, but they had been deep. The blood was smeared all over her neck and shirt.

He didn't understand what was happening. Justin had been dead for years, and if he had to pick out regrets from his long life, the fact that someone else had killed Justin before Charles had had the chance to do it was first on the list.

He pulled her limp body into his lap, curling around her protectively. Shuddering with the effort not to go kill something, someone, anyone. If there had been a physical enemy present, he would not have been able to hold Brother Wolf back.

Because Charles wanted to kill someone, too. He just didn't know who or what his enemy was. Was the recorder some sort of artifact? Whatever had happened to Anna had had something to do with the music, that much was obvious. He was very aware Ford had told them that the symbol on the stones and trees around this place, the one that kept the very guardians of the forest away, represented a musical instrument being played. It didn't take a genius to make a connection.

Brother Wolf warned him that Anna was recovering consciousness. He knew that he should set her down and give her space. She'd been afraid of him.

Of him.

He could not make himself let her go. She would have to push him away herself. If she pushed him away, if she was frightened, even Brother Wolf would release her. Charles only hoped that he could force himself to do the same.

She stirred. He made himself look away from her, giving her as much space as he could, knowing that it was not enough. He was going to scare her again.

He felt the sudden tension of her muscles as she woke. Felt a tremendous shiver travel through her body and the instinctive way she drew into the fetal position.

Brother Wolf howled inside him. They would find this thing that had hurt their mate and make it very, very sorry. He waited for her to struggle.

Instead, she burrowed against him with a wild sob, wiggling to get closer to him with frantic need. She made a noise, a guttural heart-wrenching sound that he couldn't understand. He wasn't sure that she was using words.

He held her while she buried her face against him and shook, grabbing his shirt so hard that she ripped the shoulder. He rocked her gently. Had they not been in the middle of this place that he distrusted, he would have sung to her.

Gradually she relaxed against him, her body shuddering now and then, like a child who had cried too hard to stop all at once.

"Anna?"

She pressed her head more tightly against him, but she didn't say anything.

He jerked his head up as a scent came to his attention, this one more real than the one he'd started to identify with their unknown enemy. This one he smelled, but it was the same scent. When he took in a deep breath, he could not smell it again. But he knew he hadn't imagined it.

Deciding that he wanted to get Anna out of Wild Sign, he stood up, holding her tightly to him, and headed back up the trail.

Tag was waiting for them at the sign at the top of the trail. He had shifted to wolf, which Charles appreciated. Tag's wolf could be counted on—not to be less ferocious or less crazy, but the wolf obeyed orders. Sometimes Tag had trouble with that when he walked on two feet. Charles could deal with Tag, but he'd rather not have to while he was trying to protect Anna. He didn't want to kill Tag by accident.

"I don't know," he told Tag, who was staring at Anna. "I think she's okay now. She'll tell us what happened when she's ready."

He hoped he was right.

He set her down briefly to secure the pack on Tag's back. As soon as his hands were off her, she began the change to wolf.

Charles waited. When he sensed that she was absorbed in her transformation, he gestured for Tag to watch Anna. While she completed the change, Charles ran back to the amphitheater and found the recorder. It looked ordinary enough and it felt inert in his hands. He took it anyway. He was back before Anna was aware he'd been gone.

It was a good sign that Anna had decided to change to her wolf, he told himself as she rose, somewhat unsteadily, to her feet. Anna's wolf was how Anna had survived the hell of the Chicago pack in the first place.

But he didn't like the way her ears were lowered submissively—*his* Anna didn't have a submissive bone in her whole body. The defensive hunch of her body threatened his control of Brother Wolf. Tag wasn't in a much better state. Anna wasn't his mate—but Omega wolves were to be cherished.

He put the recorder in Tag's pack. Then Charles went down on one knee beside Anna.

"Are you okay to travel?" he asked.

She met his eyes, gave an affirmative yip. He could feel her through their bond, a roiling incoherent mess of emotions and adrenaline. Movement, he judged, would help her work through everything.

He changed and headed toward camp.

On the trip back, Tag led and Charles fell behind. Anna didn't let either of them get too close—but she didn't range away from them, either. It was probably a very good thing that they didn't run into any hikers along the way. Charles wasn't sure that either he or Tag would have been capable of civilized behavior.

They arrived at their camp a little after two in the morning. No one had been near it since they'd left. Charles shifted to human to open the bigger tent—which he and Anna would normally have shared alone—and invited Tag in.

Anna seemed a little lost crouched beside the SUV, well back from either Charles or Tag. Charles knelt down and gestured to her.

She padded toward him, not unwilling, just wary in a way that hurt his heart. It had been a long time since she'd looked at him that way. He put his hands on her gently, but worked them into the fur on her shoulders until he had his skin on hers.

As when she had sat on his lap in the amphitheater, he felt nothing. No magic. She didn't smell of that strange something from Leah's past. There was no stain on her spirit that he could see.

He would have been happier about it if he had understood why everything had stopped so suddenly in the amphitheater. Magic didn't just stop, it dissipated—and that battlefield pall should not have disappeared at all.

He kissed her forehead and released her.

"I'm going to be wolf tonight," he told her. "I can sleep with Tag and you can go sleep in the other tent. Or you can stay with us."

She scooted past him, into the bigger tent. He would have felt better if she hadn't so obviously avoided touching him. He shifted to wolf and stretched across the entrance—which was a foolish thing. It would be as easy for an enemy to cut through the tent side as it would be for them to unzip the opening—easier, probably. If he'd really been worried about an attack in the night, he wouldn't have slept in the tent at all.

He'd resigned himself to a restless night—and then Anna curled up against his back. When Tag lay down beside her, she gave a little sigh and relaxed for the first time since she'd started playing that recorder.

Charles put his head down and slept.

CHAPTER

6

Anna woke with a splitting headache and a body that felt like it had been run over by a truck.

The last time she'd felt like that had been when she had gone to a party hosted by the first violin at the end of her freshman year at college—hosting that annual party was an unofficial requirement of the position of first chair.

They'd played the "Hi, Bob" game—another time-honored tradition. It consisted of watching *The Bob Newhart Show* and downing tequila shots every time a character from the show said, "Hi, Bob." She hadn't even known what *The Bob Newhart Show* was before that night. The next year she'd done it with orange juice instead of tequila—and she'd never again been able to look at Bob Newhart without feeling vaguely ill.

But she was a werewolf; she wasn't supposed to get hangovers. She tried to remember what she'd been doing. They'd gone to Wild Sign . . .

She rubbed her head when the memory wouldn't come.

Charles would have answers for her. She got up, found clothes to wear, and put them on. She wiped the back of her wrist against her nose and grimaced at the smear of blood. That was pretty weird. Had she been hurt? She felt a little dizzy, and her knees, which had been fine a moment ago, tried to buckle. A sense of urgency started to press down on her. Something was wrong. Or had been wrong. Or possibly would be wrong.

Charles, she reminded herself, her head pounding in time with the beat of her heart. Find Charles. She needed to get out of the stuffy tent so she could breathe. So she could push the panic away.

Anna unzipped the tent and stuck her feet into her shoes, which someone had set next to the tent door. It hadn't been her, because she'd come into camp as a wolf. She remembered that now. She'd gone to sleep, but she didn't remember shifting back to human. Given the discomfort of the shift, she found that a little disconcerting—but not as much as losing most of a day.

Charles and Tag were sitting in the camp chairs on opposite sides of the folding table that held the propane stove. Tag had a beat-up copy of Yeats's *The Celtic Twilight* in his lap and Charles had his laptop out—but both of them were looking at her with alert wariness. There was quite a bit of tension in the air, and she wondered what she'd done to put that look on their faces. Or maybe there was something else going on.

Her own growing tension had eased at the sight of her mate. Charles was good at making her feel safe.

"Um," she said. "Good morning?"

"Afternoon," said Tag politely. As if they'd encountered each other walking opposite directions on a sidewalk—and only knew each other by face.

"That bad?" she asked.

Charles still hadn't spoken. He watched her, she realized, with wolf eyes.

"Let's put it this way," said Tag. "What's my name?"

"Colin Taggart," she said.

"Have I ever hurt you?"

Was this a trick question? "No?"

The query in her voice was directed at his question rather than an indication of any doubt about what the answer was. He flinched, and she rolled her eyes.

"Of course not," she said impatiently. "What's wrong?"

As soon as she spoke, she realized that she probably could answer part of that question herself. She felt sick, and all she remembered about yesterday was heading out toward Wild Sign. She had a few vague memories that came and went. Mostly they didn't make sense—a canvas sink, a baby's skull that somehow wasn't a baby's skull, and the inlaid fretboard of a guitar. The fretboard made her sad, though she didn't know why. Something was definitely wrong with her.

"You sounded all right this morning, too," Tag told her, sounding ill-used and a bit whiny. His eyes didn't fit his voice. His eyes were watchful. "And then you ran, making a noise I don't ever want to hear coming out of your mouth again." Tag scowled at her. "I don't like to scare women. I especially don't like to scare Omegas. I really, really don't like it when it's *you* I'm scaring."

Well, hell, thought Anna, feeling guilty. All of the wolves were affected by her being Omega. When she was distressed, they reacted badly.

"I'm sorry," she said. "I don't remember it. I don't remember quite a lot." Tag, she thought, wasn't the only one who sounded whiny.

The headache felt like someone had grabbed her brain just behind her eyes and was digging in with claws. And wiggling the claws.

"Got that," said Tag. "What do you remember?"

But Anna was watching Charles, who hadn't said a word since she'd come out of the tent. He folded the computer in his lap with exaggerated care before setting it on the ground. He got to his feet slowly.

She couldn't tell what he was thinking with his quiet face and gold eyes. There was intent in his motion. She found herself taking a slow step backward, and her heartbeat picked up speed—

—*as it had that night she'd run in the pack's home grounds when Justin led the hunt against her. The guttural sounds of their cries, inhuman sounds coming from human-shaped throats,* rang in her ears. Though she knew that was impossible.

Charles stopped moving.

She aborted her instinctive movement to cover her ears—the sound wasn't real. That was over and done. Why in the world was she dwelling on that particular event now?

She reached for Charles through their bond—and only then realized that it was closed up tight. Maybe that was the reason her thoughts were so muddled. She would feel better if she could feel him; he might drown out the pain that was making it hard to think. She wasn't good at manipulating their bond, though she'd gotten better.

Visualizations were sometimes useful, so she tried to imagine herself reaching out and unlocking the door that stood between them. She pulled on it and the bond blazed open with a suddenness that she hadn't expected. As if she'd pulled hard on a swinging door at the same time that Charles was pushing it.

For a disorienting moment, she was seeing herself from his point of view. Her hair was tangled and there were traces of tears down her cheeks. She had a bloody nose again. Her shoulders were hunched in pain. (Well, she wasn't used to having a hangover any longer. It had been years.) Her pupils were dilated like a drug addict's, making her brown eyes look black. She looked small and fragile—something she'd never seen when she looked into a mirror.

Charles did something—it certainly hadn't been her—and their bond settled down to its usual gentle awareness. The weird feeling of perceiving herself from his viewpoint receded. Charles took a deep breath. She realized that he'd even been careful of his breathing, so he didn't startle her into running.

Which, she noticed, a part of her was still ready to do.

She had a sickening half memory of running through the woods in the dawn light—the path she had taken lay right over Charles's shoulder. Her awareness, as she had sprinted through the unfamiliar territory, had bounced back and forth between the present moment and that horrible night when she'd become the prey of the pack. That explained why it had come so easily to mind just now—though not why it had done so this morning.

She reached out her hand. Charles stepped forward and took it at once, his warm hand closing around her cold one. The physical touch helped hold off her imminent panic, though she didn't quite know why she was panicking. When his arms closed around her, her headache faded as well.

"It had to shut you out to get its fingers into me," she told him. And then wondered how she'd known that—or if it was true.

"What is it?" he asked, only it was Brother Wolf who asked, not Charles, his voice smooth and dark.

"The Singer in the Woods." She still wasn't thinking right—and there was something wrong with Charles. Why was it Brother Wolf who was talking to her?

She shivered and pressed closer to him, feeling as if she would never get warm again. "It's damaged. Hungry. Lonesome. It needs."

Something sharp dug into her mind, trying to lock the connection between her and Charles closed again. Anna screamed—she could hear the duet roar of angry wolves, her own and Brother Wolf—and the claws retreated, driven back by the sound.

She didn't lose consciousness, but it was a close thing. By the time her world righted again, Charles had dragged her into his lap, sheltering her with his body.

"Music," she said through the fog that was trying to feed on her. That mind-dulling miasma in her head was another kind of attack, she thought.

"What?" asked Tag, his voice very quiet. She looked for him and found him by the SUV nearly twenty feet away. He was crouched down, balanced on the balls of his feet and the fingers of his hands. His eyes were wolf-bright. There wasn't a lot of human left in him. And she remembered that she was an Omega and he was a dominant wolf—and there was nothing physical he could protect her from to relieve his fury.

She would have apologized, but talking was too much effort—and she had to get through to Charles.

"Sing." She fought to get the word out. When he didn't immediately respond, she worried she hadn't gotten it out in an understandable form. She tried giving him explicit directions. "Sing for me, Charles."

"Charles isn't with us," said Tag in a rough voice as unlike his usual melodious tenor as she'd ever heard him speak. "He hasn't been here all day."

For a moment she didn't understand what he was saying. Charles was wrapped around her—they appeared to be sitting on the ground, though she didn't remember how they'd ended up there. Her cheek vibrated with his near-silent growls.

Oh. She was usually better at telling which one she was dealing with, but she wasn't exactly at the top of her game.

"Brother Wolf," she said. "I need you to sing."

That had driven it off before, the Singer in the Woods. She remembered that, hearing Charles's voice, feeling it charge the atmosphere with his love, his power. But Brother Wolf did not respond.

Think, she told herself sternly, but it was getting harder to keep track of what she needed to do. She had not broken under the weight of what had happened to her in the Chicago pack. She was stronger than this. What weapons did she have?

Oh. Of course.

I am a werewolf, damn it, she told herself, and called on the change to take her.

For the first time, the transformation didn't hurt. Or more precisely, her head hurt so much that the familiar agony of her body reshaping itself barely registered. As the shape of the wolf took over her body, its spirit clothed hers. The wolf flowed over and through her, sliding through her mind and healing the damage done. Midway through the change, her mate's music, Charles's music, became part of her magic, lending her energy and purpose.

His voice melted into her bones, a staccato warrior's song that thrummed in her chest with its battle cry. There were words, powerful words that lent themselves to combat. She didn't understand them but understood their import all the same. Those words formed both shield and sword for her battle. Which did not come.

The thing that had its fingers sifting through her memories fled in the wolf's wake, in the face of her mate's song. She was left panting, sane, and, as far as she could tell, free of the Singer, whatever the hell the Singer was.

The raspy martial lyrics of a folk metal band in her ears, she closed her eyes and rested her still-aching head against her mate's shoulder as he sang the Hu's "Wolf Totem" in a land thousands of miles and eight centuries from the steppes of Genghis Khan.

As with the last Hu song he'd performed for her, Anna was pretty sure he would tell her he wasn't getting the pronunciation right with this one, either—but if he'd been at the head of a Mongol horde, they would have known exactly what he meant when he sang.

WHAT WITH ONE thing and another it was late afternoon before everyone was back to their human selves. Boneless in her chair, Anna licked her fingers clean of the last of Tag's spicy barbecue sauce. It wasn't sanitary, probably, but she wasn't letting any of it go to waste.

Besides, it made Charles's eyes heat up as he went over the last day with his da on the phone. And Anna would do almost anything to wipe the ragged expression off her mate's face. Her success at that lasted until her hand went to her neck to make sure Justin's bite mark was really gone.

One of the things that being plunged into the single worst memory of her life had done was to make very clear how hard Charles worked to empower her. Not only because Charles would always back her, but because he had taught her how to defend herself.

She could fight now, in whatever shape she wore. And she knew how to weaponize the natural abilities being an Omega gave her. If she ever found herself the prey of a crazed band of damaged were-wolves again, they could not hurt her. She was almost sure she knew how to quiet their beasts. How to make them hers.

The woman I am now would never have had to suffer at the hands of Justin. She told herself that, but she couldn't believe it. The memory of his teeth in her neck, his smell, his hands on her skin, was too near. Maybe tomorrow she would believe in her ability to fend off Justin.

Charles was watching her, his jaw tense and his eyes yellow.

Today, she decided, she wasn't going to be afraid of a dead man. She was going to flirt with Charles instead.

She put her index finger in her mouth and met her mate's eyes as the spicy brilliance of Tag's sauce filled her mouth. Charles flashed her a sudden grin and turned his back so she couldn't distract him anymore.

She got up and threw away her paper plate. Tag had done both the cooking and the cleaning for the meal and had returned to his Yeats. He was wearing earbuds with the volume low enough she couldn't hear it. His head was nodding as he read.

"Anna?" Charles said, turning back to her. "Da wants to hear your side of this."

"Do you have all your memories back, Anna?" Bran asked. She'd been politely ignoring their conversation until then. She couldn't help overhearing everything, a condition of being a werewolf, but she felt it was polite to pretend she wasn't.

"No," she said. Then paused. "I don't know, really. I remember most of what happened at Wild Sign, I think. I'm a little foggy from the moment I picked up the recorder until I woke up this afternoon. But the only part I don't remember at all is this morning. After we got back from Wild Sign, I went to sleep as a wolf. Around six in the morning I apparently shifted from wolf to human, panicked when Charles touched me, and made like a track star through the forest. They caught me, kicking and screaming—we are the only people at this campground, which is probably a good thing."

She'd been thinking about the noise. But she supposed it might also be good in another way. If there had been another group camping here, they could have been fresh victims for the Singer in the Woods. They had, she'd noticed, all adopted the name that she'd produced in the middle of its attack. She didn't know how she'd gotten it—one of the things she couldn't quite remember.

"Do you think the Singer poses a danger for others?" Bran asked. "People near you? Or people near Wild Sign?"

She held off her immediate "How should I know?"

"It hasn't tried for Charles or Tag," she said. "So maybe not people near me." She paused and said slowly, "Or not unless it succeeds in taking me over and can reach out to people through me."

That felt right. And it led her to another thought. Since she'd been wanting to smack Bran for how he'd forced Leah through her first Change, bonding, and then mating ever since she'd heard the full story, there was a bite in her voice when she said, "I think that you were really lucky Leah is mule-stubborn, Bran Cornick, or your mating could have gone quite differently."

She didn't give him time to respond—she wasn't stupid. Her voice was overly chipper as she continued, "Anyway, at the end of this morning's chase, Charles says he sent me to sleep with some sneaky magic trick. But I don't remember that, either."

"I see," said Bran. After a brief pause, he said softly, "And I have always known I was lucky in my choice of mate."

Charles's eyebrows raised.

"Doesn't mean that you weren't a bastard," Anna said. She probably wouldn't have said that if they hadn't been communicating by phone.

"Charles says that after you finished playing the recorder, you didn't know who he or Tag were."

Clearly he was done with the topic of the events surrounding his mating. Trust Bran to ignore her rundown on what she didn't remember and hit exactly where she *wished* she didn't remember.

"That's right," she said. "Whatever it was, while I was playing, it stuck me right in the middle of the worst moment in my life. In Chicago." Bran would understand. He knew about Chicago. "It did not feel like a memory and I had the bite marks to prove it."

"Bite marks?" Bran's voice stayed calm.

"Justin," Anna said flatly. "While he was still in human form, he bit my neck, blooding me to excite the pack. That was real. When I found myself standing in that gods-be-damned amphitheater facing Charles and Tag, I thought I'd been teleported from Chicago somehow. I didn't have a clue who either of them were, where I was, or how I got there. The last thing I remembered was the pack house in Chicago. As if all of my memories between that day in Chicago and the moment in Wild Sign had disappeared." Her voice was tight.

Charles held out his hand and she grabbed it as if it were a lifeline. It was solid, warm, and strong, and it made her feel as if she could breathe.

"The bite wound on her neck was still bleeding," Charles growled.

"I see," Bran said. "I've heard of magic that could make your body remember wounds it had suffered, calling that damage from memory into flesh. I don't remember where, or from whom, and I've never seen it myself." He hesitated. "Not that I remember." The very old wolves had lots of memories they couldn't instantly recall. "I'll make inquiries."

There was the sound of drumming fingers; Anna presumed they belonged to Bran.

"Sherwood Post doesn't remember his past," Bran said. "I thought—we all thought—it was because he couldn't bear to remember the way in which the witches removed his leg so it could not be regrown."

"You did not speak to Sherwood after he sent you back to Montana with Leah beside you," said Charles. "What if he came back here? To make sure the Singer was dead?"

"It does raise some questions," agreed Bran. "He was, in his own way, one of the most powerful magic users I've ever known."

That hung in the air.

"I always wondered how the witches got him," Charles said neutrally.

"Exactly," said Bran. After a moment he said, "Well—"

"You called it the Singer in the Woods." Leah's voice cut through Bran's. "The one who attacked you."

Anna hadn't known she was listening. From Charles's face, he hadn't known, either. Anna wondered if her dig at Bran would have gone differently if he'd been alone.

"Yes," Anna agreed. "I don't know where I got that—it doesn't feel like something I made up, though."

"No," agreed Leah. "I don't think you did." Her voice was tight. "I wish I could help. I don't remember a lot about that time, and most of it would not be useful to you." She made a soft sound and then said, "There is something about memories. We fed it with music, I think." Her voice grew hesitant, soft. "Not just with music. That was part of it. It did something with memories, too. But"—her tone turned ironic—"I don't remember exactly what that was."

"Were there witches?" asked Charles.

"Like you think there were in Wild Sign? I don't know," Leah said. "I'm not witchborn." She sighed. "It doesn't feel like being witchborn mattered very much to the Singer, but I can't be sure."

Silence fell and lingered.

"If I remember more, I'll let you know," Leah said finally, sounding . . . Anna wished she could see Leah's face so she could read it. She sounded odd. "I'll call Anna."

"All right," said Charles. "Thank you, Leah. Da. We'll keep you apprised."

"Be careful," Bran said. "Remember Sherwood."

"Yes," Charles said, and ended the call.

He looked at Anna. "I think we should have you contact Dr. Connors."

Tag looked up from his book and grinned wolfishly at Anna. "Charles and I are the muscle. You are our communications expert. By that we mean that you get to do all of the investigative work. We just get to kill things or, less interestingly, intimidate people."

Anna stuck her tongue out at him.

"He's not wrong," said Charles, deadpan. "Annoying, but not wrong." He still carried a bit of Brother Wolf in his eyes and the set of his shoulders, but if he was teasing, he would be okay.

Anna rolled her eyes. "Okay, Brute Squad, give me the phone number. Getting information means giving some back. What do we want Dr. Connors to know? And what do we absolutely not want her to know?"

"Why don't you play it by ear," Charles suggested. "Tell her we have some letters addressed to her and see where it goes from there."

"It occurs to me that I'd feel better about this if we hadn't opened those letters," Anna said. "In the household I grew up in, opening someone else's mail just wasn't done. I think my father would have forgiven murder before he'd have forgiven us interfering in the US mail."

"That's why we're making you call her," said Tag. "You can blame us if you'd like. In the household I grew up in, opening letters without ruining the seal was an art form. It's harder to make a modern letter look as though you haven't opened it. Not impossible—but I generally don't bother."

Charles consulted his laptop and gave Anna the number.

The phone went to voice mail, which was a bit anticlimactic.

"This is Anna Cornick," Anna said. "I have your number from Special Agents Fisher and Goldstein of the FBI. My husband and I have been up to Wild Sign and we found some letters addressed to you that we'd like to talk about." She left her number, repeated it, and disconnected.

"What was the name of the place that check for Daniel Green was written to?" asked Anna. "If I'm making calls, I might as well try them, too."

"Angel Hills," said Charles.

"There's an Angel Hills Assisted Living in Yreka," said Tag. He had evidently started looking it up while Anna had been leaving a message for Dr. Connors. "You have about ten minutes before their regular hours are over. There's an after-hours number."

Anna called and asked after Daniel Green.

"Are you a member of his family?" asked the receptionist.

Anna looked at Charles, who shrugged. Tag nodded vigorously.

"Yes," she lied. "This is Anna Cornick. I'm Carrie Green's . . . sister-in-law."

"Ms. Cornick, if you will stay on the line? I will get someone who is authorized to speak with you."

Elevator music played with static-aided awfulness. The person who'd turned Leonard Cohen's "Hallelujah" into elevator music should have been shot.

Eventually a deliberately mellow voice came on the line. "Ms. Cornick, this is Dr. Sheldon Underwood. Letty tells me that you are calling about Daniel Green?"

"That's right," Anna said. "Look, we were going through Carrie's papers and found a check—" It had been enough to buy a new car.

"Has something happened to Carrie?" he interrupted, losing the mellow tones.

"We don't know." Anna managed to make her voice sound weary. "That's what we are trying to find out. But no one has heard from her since this spring, and you know she lived out in the middle of nowhere. We can't find her."

There was a long pause. "Daniel is—well, if you are a member of the family, Daniel has good days and bad. But they were very close; she came here every month to spend time with him. We were concerned when she stopped. It is possible that she told him something. He told us, you see, that Carrie wasn't going to be coming around anymore. He might tell you more."

She opened her mouth to refuse—Daniel Green would know that she wasn't related to him. But Dr. Underwood had continued speaking.

"Daniel's memory isn't good, and some days he doesn't know anyone. But if you come in the morning on a good day, he's very nearly himself."

"I can come tomorrow," Anna said. "I'll bring the check. What time in the morning, do you think?"

"Tomorrow won't work," the doctor said firmly. "He's having a procedure in the morning. Perhaps the day after?"

She hung up the phone having confirmed a time.

Tag said, "So why are we visiting an old man with a faulty memory?"

Charles replied before Anna could. "Because witchborn is a genetic condition. If, as we suppose, Wild Sign was a witch colony, then there is a chance that Daniel Green is also a witch. He might be able to tell us more about Wild Sign—and possibly what happened there."

"He knew that Carrie— Do you suppose she was his daughter? Anyway, he knew that Carrie would not be visiting him anymore," Anna said. "Maybe he knows why not."

They were packing up the camp for a quick departure in the morning when Anna's phone rang.

"This is Dr. Connors," said a woman's voice.

"Anna Cornick," Anna returned. "We have some letters—"

"So you said," interrupted Dr. Connors. "Who are you and what were you doing at Wild Sign?"

"Wild Sign was located on property owned by my family, Dr. Connors," Anna said.

There was a little pause.

"Fair enough," she said. "What was in the letters?"

"We have no idea," Anna told her. "They were in code."

"You did open them," Dr. Connors said coolly.

"Your father and his friends built a town on my family's land," Anna said, her voice neutral. "Then they all disappeared—without reappearing anywhere else that the FBI can find them. Yes, we opened letters we found in a bag that had been discarded by the side of the trail."

"Letters," said Dr. Connors, and for the first time Anna heard something other than rigid self-control.

"Two from a woman named Carrie Green, both of them payments. Six from your father to you, dated sequentially from April fourteenth through the nineteenth. We didn't try to break the code, but they seem to be identical letters."

"I see."

Anna said, "Look, we are going to be down here for a couple more days. When I get home, I can scan the letters and email them to you. Or you can give me an address and I'll send them to you."

"You are looking for them, too, aren't you?" Her tone made it not a question. Dr. Connors gave a sigh. "I am staying in Happy Camp for the time being. Assuming you are still nearby, I can drive to wherever you are—or you can come here."

Happy Camp, Anna remembered, was the town nearest to Wild Sign. They hadn't driven through it on the way from Yreka, so it was presumably located farther down the highway.

"We're camping tonight," Anna said. "We can drive to Happy Camp tomorrow if that's convenient?" She glanced at Charles to double-check and he nodded.

"Is there something other than my father's letters you wish to talk about?" Dr. Connors asked.

What Anna could tell Dr. Connors really depended upon a lot of things that she wouldn't know until they met face-to-face.

"Maybe," Anna said. "Let's meet and"—she chose Charles's phrase—"we can play it by ear."

"Fine," Dr. Connors said. "Call me when you get to town." And she disconnected without further ado.

"Hardball player, that one," murmured Tag approvingly.

CHARLES FELT EDGY, uncomfortable in his skin. He had to work not to pace. Anna had tightened their mate bond back down when she realized that her inner turmoil was affecting Charles. He'd allowed it because she had enough to deal with without also brushing up against his agitation. She didn't need to know that blocking the easy flow of emotional communication only allowed him to hide his own struggles more effectively. Let her believe she was helping him.

Brother Wolf had been enraged that they had not perceived that Anna was still caught in that thing—whatever it was Anna had called it—in the Singer in the Woods' net. As a consequence, Brother Wolf had refused to let Charles direct their actions after Anna had run from them this morning. He hadn't trusted Charles to be able to keep her safe.

Because of that, they had almost lost her again, this afternoon. If she had not played it smart, if she had not been able to fight—she would . . . he didn't know what their enemy would have been able to do to his Anna. He was supremely grateful he hadn't had to find out. Brother Wolf, though, was ashamed.

He, Brother Wolf, had been ineffectual against it. He was not used to being helpless, but that had not been the kind of battle won with tooth and claw. If he had given way to Charles sooner, they would have been able to give Anna the help she had asked for when she'd asked them. By the time Charles wrested control from Brother Wolf, Anna had already saved herself.

Charles could feel Brother Wolf's guilt. But he couldn't do anything to help until his own anger at the wolf settled a bit. So it was good that Brother Wolf chose to be quiet.

He hated to see the bruised expression in Anna's eyes now, when she didn't think anyone was watching. He'd hated seeing it the first time he'd met her, in the busy Chicago airport. He'd wanted to kill whoever had put that look there then—and that had been before she was his. Before he knew her—his indomitable, intrepid Anna.

To keep from hovering over her, he buried himself in work. The Suburban had an Internet uplink and a place to plug in his laptop. So he'd started the SUV and sat in the passenger seat, where he wouldn't have to contend with the steering wheel.

He couldn't manipulate their accounts on an insecure system—insecure by his standards, anyway. But he could research and watch the world markets to make sure that he did his part to keep the pack safe. Fangs and sinew were all well and good—but money was a better weapon. He lifted his head to look out to the campground where Anna and Tag were playing blackjack with pine needles.

Money was a better weapon against *most* things, but not all.

It grew dark and they wrapped up their card game. Anna took a flashlight into the bigger tent. Tag busied himself with putting away the folding table and camp chairs. Charles turned off the SUV.

Tag came up to Charles as he finished closing his laptop case. Charles could feel the other wolf's trepidation. Tag was an old wolf.

He knew that Brother Wolf was unhappy, and Tag was smart enough to be worried about that.

"I'm going wolf tonight," Tag told Charles. "There's a nice patch of grass up there on that knoll—I found it while we were chasing Anna this morning. That will leave me close enough to come if something happens. But it should give you some privacy, too."

Charles caught his arm as Tag started to turn away. He pulled him into an embrace, kissing his cheek before letting him go. Letting Tag know that Brother Wolf was not unhappy with *him*. And that Charles appreciated his generosity and perceptiveness.

"Da chose well when he sent you with us," Charles told him. "Thank you for coming."

Tag huffed, but he looked pleased. "Well enough," he said. "But I'm expecting a fight where I can dig my fangs into someone and taste some blood. Otherwise, I'll count this as a wasted trip."

"I expect that we aren't going to get out of this without bloodshed," said Charles.

"Hopefully no more of Anna's blood," said Tag as he began to strip off his clothing. "I don't want to ever see that again."

Charles was in total agreement.

Anna looked around when he joined her in the tent. She was moving stiffly and held her head in a way that told him she still had a headache. But she welcomed him with a happy smile.

He thought she might be the only person in the world who was always happy to see him. Some of the tension between him and Brother Wolf faded away—and only a very little of that was the natural effect that an Omega's presence always brought.

She had their sleeping bags zipped up together and had stripped out of her daytime clothing. She wore an oversized T-shirt that hung halfway to her knees. It was emerald green, a color that made her hair look more red than usual. Giant white letters across her chest read *Werewolf?*

"New shirt?" he asked.

"Not that new," she said. "Mercy sent it to me a while back because she thought it was funny. I just haven't worn it yet." She turned around so he could see the back, where a ferocious Hollywoodized werewolf bared its fangs. Below the werewolf, across her lower back and butt, it read *Ware Wolf! Where Wolf? There W—agh!!!!*

He laughed. He hadn't expected to, not after the day they'd had. He closed the space between them and pulled her against him, her back to his front. He buried his face in her hair and just breathed in. They felt like the first easy breaths he'd taken since they'd walked into Wild Sign yesterday.

"Why don't you lie down on top of the sleeping bag and I'll see what I can do about your headache," he murmured, stepping back so she could do just that.

He'd taken off his boots at the door of the tent, but he stripped off his jeans and shirt so he could move better.

His brother, Samuel, was the healer—their da's mother's magic taking that path in him. Samuel wasn't a miracle worker; he couldn't raise the dead or cure old age or heart disease. But he used his magic to help people. Their da said it was the reason that Samuel spent so much time on his own out in the world with the humans—because it was the humans who needed his touch. Their da wasn't happy about it.

Charles couldn't do what Samuel could do. But if his contrary powers were willing, he could ease his mate's pain. He knelt beside her and put his hands flat on her shoulders.

"Do you need me to take off the T-shirt?" she asked, taking in his lack of dress.

"No," he said. He didn't need the distraction. "Just relax if you can."

He closed his eyes, breathing deeply, reaching for the well of dormant power that he seldom touched. This wasn't his mother's wild magic. This magic was hungry, violent, and raw; it came from the other side of his family line. Witchborn. But it wasn't the pristine magic of white witches, though he'd never fed it with anyone else's trauma. It had always felt like this. Not tainted, but not good, either, as if this magic was forever damaged by the blackness of his paternal grandmother's heart. It had taken Brother Wolf to show Charles that it was not evil.

He knew his da would have been repulsed by it, and so he had always been careful to hide this magic from Da. Charles was very, very careful about the kinds of things that he used it for. Like Brother Wolf, it could be difficult to control, and out of control it was dangerous to others. Mostly he tried to forget about it.

But it was good for this.

Under his hands, Anna's tight muscles began to soften. Charles wasn't really healing her, but Anna's sore muscles hadn't come from overuse. They had come from Anna's struggle to drive the Singer—to steal Anna's name for it—away. Her wolf had borrowed energy from her body to shield her mind. It was the way wolf magic worked.

Generally the pack never noticed the drain—most of their kind of magic was something they used for a few minutes or less. The kinds of things that took longer than that, like the constant magic used to make humans see dogs where there were werewolves, tended to be shared among the pack as a whole.

But Anna's wolf had battled for the better part of a day. And it had not been an easy battle. Efficiency only came when you understood what you fought. She had used a huge amount of energy, and it had damaged her body.

She would have healed with some rest combined with eating well—both he and Tag had been putting food in front of Anna. But he saw no reason that she should wait when he could do something about it.

If Brother Wolf had settled down sooner, he could have done this earlier in the day.

"Mmmpf," Anna said, her voice drowsy. "I don't know what you're doing, but it feels good."

He fed energy into his mate's body until it began washing back at him. He stopped—and was very, very careful not to take any of that energy back into himself, in case some of it was not his. He'd done that once when he had been very young, and he'd felt as though he was going to turn into the Hunger that Devours. Except that he wasn't hungry for flesh, not even human flesh.

He'd gone to his grandfather because going to his da would have been disastrous. It had taken days of the old man's prescription of fasting and sweats to make Charles feel normal again.

"Gray witchcraft," his da would have called it. "Poison" was what his grandfather had said. Charles just knew he never wanted to feel like that again.

Anna fell asleep with a happy sigh. Likely she'd have been asleep earlier if she hadn't been hurting. Charles moved away from her, found a comfortable position, and sat cross-legged, hands loose, eyes closed, and sought balance as a precursor to binding the witchcraft away again. If Anna hadn't been there, he'd have sung one of his grandfather's songs. He used those songs to heal his spirit and cleanse his mind the way a shower cleansed his body.

He paused. Had that been what Anna had done when the Singer caught her? She had played a lament to the broken land—which is exactly how his grandfather would have begun to heal it. It was a way of connection, of opening up to the damaged spirit.

He examined his memories of the events in the amphitheater and decided that was probably what had happened. Anna, like most people, was mostly blind to the spirits in the world around her, which didn't mean the reverse was true. A lesser musician might have simply been playing a folk song. But Anna didn't play music that way. She had opened herself to her audience—and *something* had taken her up on her invitation.

He considered the amphitheater with its haunted atmosphere, and wondered if Anna's actions had only been an accident. Brother Wolf had examined that recorder with all of their collective senses. He had discovered nothing that suggested it was anything other than a rather well-made instrument. But it had survived in the open air for months, even if it hadn't survived Brother Wolf.

Music, he considered, *as a trap*. Had Anna picked up that recorder from her own impulse? Or had there been something more sinister at work?

His patrilineal witchborn magic had taken advantage of his distraction and was leaking out into the tent, seeping into the ground. Likely a real witch would have considered this a result of failing to contain their abilities. *He* understood the magic was curious and bent on exploration. He centered himself and began the process of coaxing it back.

Charles was sweating and tired when he had his grandmother's legacy wrapped safely away again, the ground and the air in the tent free of inquisitive magic. He glanced at Anna, who had rolled over and was limp with the sleep of the exhausted.

He shifted to wolf and back to human, grimacing with the exquisite pain of the change. Had Tag not been on guard, he wouldn't have risked tiring himself out. But he didn't want to sleep beside Anna still covered with the sour sweat that he'd accumulated with one thing and another today.

He glanced again at Anna—but this time she was awake. She sat up and pulled off her shirt.

"No," he said. "You need to rest."

She gave him an imperious look that made Brother Wolf want to roll with joy. She wasn't afraid of him. The terror on her face before she'd run this morning . . . he would happily go to his grave if he never saw her look at him with that expression again.

"I need you," she said. "This is the first time I've felt good all day. All that I need now, to feel like myself, is for you to wipe away the feel of Justin's hands." She covered herself and shivered, looking away, whispering, "I have been smelling him on my skin all day."

He gathered her up and rearranged the sleeping bag so that they were both on the soft inner surface. Then he laid her back down with care.

"Where do you smell him?" he asked, instead of telling her that she only smelled of herself. He'd smelled Justin last night, too. If she could still scent that old hurt, he would not argue with her.

She raised her right hand and showed him her wrist.

He brought it to him and brushed his cheek against it before kissing it gently. He touched her wrist with his nose, watching her as he took in the scent of her skin. Just them. He brought it to her nose for inspection.

"Better?" he asked.

She closed her eyes, concentrating. Then she looked at him and nodded.

It took time. He would have thought it to be a seduction game had it not been for their mating bond, because by the time she acknowledged that she could neither smell nor feel Justin on her skin, they both were flushed and taut with desire. But they were mated, and he could feel her distress, feel it lessen gradually as he touched, kissed, and licked his way over her body.

He did not enter her until their bond was free of the shadow of spirit, and that tested his patience to the breaking point. Hers, too. As he slid into her, wet and swollen for him, he felt her delight break free and was forced to bite his cheek hard not to follow her immediately.

He was not some pup who thought only of his own pleasure. He was an old wolf. Controlled. But it was a near thing.

When they were finished, she lay on top of him, as limp and wrung out as he himself felt. Brother Wolf, satisfied at last, slept deep so that it was only Charles who held their mate.

Only Charles who growled low in his throat at the memory of the thing that had tried to take his Anna away. It would not hurt her ever again.

He would make sure of it.

Anna stopped at the other campground, the one with the showers. She was not going to face Dr. Connors while smelling of fear, exertion, and sweat.

Charles might be able to take care of that for himself by shifting back and forth, and Tag smelled of nothing more noxious than the evergreen he'd apparently spent the night under. But Anna felt the need for hot water to clean herself physically and metaphysically. Showers, she informed Charles, despite the fact that he wasn't arguing with her, were not a luxury but a necessity.

The shower building at the lower campground bore a large sign that read *Bathrooms are for registered campers only*. Anna, pulling towels out of one of the general supply bags in the back of the SUV and handing them out, reflected that she used to be a rule follower. She would once have gone dirty rather than ignore that sign. Being a werewolf had been good for her in many ways—from a certain perspective, anyway.

No one gave them a second look. By chance, Anna had the women's side of the showers all to herself. She could have stayed under the hot water for a week, feeling clean inside and out as the water drained away by her feet. She contented herself with briskly scrubbing her hair and feet and everything in between.

The men's side of the showers was silent by the time she turned off the water. But she didn't hurry just because Tag and Charles were doubtless both done and waiting for her. Dr. Connors had sounded formidable, and, in Anna's experience, women judged others by their appearance.

Anna briefly considered going for very casual, sending a message of "I'm so sure of myself I don't care what I look like." But the events of the past two days had left her unsettled. She felt like she needed all the armament at her disposal—that meant foundation and lipstick, as well as the carry gun tucked in the small of her back.

She was pretty sure that she was breaking California law with her gun. But Wild Sign looked as though it had been a colony of white witches. Dr. Connors's father had been one of the people living there. It did not mean that he himself was a witch, but it did mean that he consorted with them. If his daughter did the same, if she was a witch, there was no guarantee that she was a white witch.

Anna had had enough dealings with witches not to go in unarmed if she could help it—breaking the law or not. Especially since it would take a foolhardy officer of the law to try to arrest Charles Cornick's mate. She tried to feel guilty about the knowledge that there was no chance Charles would let her suffer for breaking the law.

Or, if not guilty, at least not quite so smug about it. But she didn't quite succeed.

She tucked her deep green silk shirt into black slacks, and then donned the holster and gun. To cover the P365, she slipped on a sandy linen jacket she'd brought along for that purpose. The jacket didn't look entirely out of place, though it would have been better if she'd brought brown slacks instead of the black. She was just glad that she'd gotten into the habit of packing nice clothes wherever they went. Charles's being the son of the Marrok meant that they often found themselves in unexpected formal situations.

Metaphorical armor and literal weaponry in place, she looked at herself in the mirror. Her hair was still wet and fell in loose curls. She considered putting her hair up to complete the look. But she wasn't going on a job interview, so she left it down. It would dry better that way.

Charles was wearing a long-sleeved ivory shirt she'd bought for him, the stretchy fabric clinging lightly to bone and sinew. He'd re-braided his hair and tied it off with a piece of leather the same color as the shirt. The jeans and worn black boots shouldn't have looked right, but they did.

He frowned at her.

"What's wrong?" she asked him, trying to get another look at herself. She hadn't seen anything out of place in the mirror, but maybe she had a pant leg tucked into a sock or something.

"You covered up the freckles," he said, folding his arms across his chest.

She felt her face light up. If she ever got a chance to really time travel, she'd go back and tell her thirteen-year-old self to quit worrying that her freckles would drive away any chance she had to date.

The scariest and sexiest man in the universe was going to pout when she concealed them with foundation.

She put her hands on his forearms and used that to lever herself up and him down so she could kiss him.

"Sorry," she told Charles. "But I'm trying for a professional look today."

She rubbed her lipstick off his mouth with her thumb.

"Even without freckles, she still outclasses us," Tag said.

Anna had to laugh. She was . . . ordinary. Something that neither of the men she was with would ever be. She turned to say something smart-assed back but shut her mouth when she got a good look at Tag.

His bright hair was pulled back in a tight ponytail. He'd lost the stubble on his face, which had a tendency to lengthen into a bedraggled beard before he did anything about it. He wore slacks and a casual jacket over a button-up shirt.

Other than the long hair—and the outrageous color—he would not have looked out of place working at a bank. Or at least he didn't look as though he intended to rob one at gunpoint—which was an improvement. And then he produced a pair of mirrored sunglasses straight out of the costume design for a 1970s antiestablishment movie sheriff and put them on.

Anna got into the SUV and started it, thinking about those sunglasses. She looked over her shoulder at Tag and cleared her throat.

"Um, why the cool shades?" she asked.

Charles belted himself in and snorted. "Vanity," he said.

"Hey," complained Tag, shutting his door. "I resemble that remark."

"Don't you mean resent?" Anna asked, pulling out of the campground.

Tag smiled and she got the full effect of all his white teeth—almost the only thing she could see of his features between the facial hair and the sunglasses. "Not at all," he told her.

"The shades come off before you leave this car," she warned.

Tag's smile got sharper. "Of course."

"If you laugh," said Charles, "you only encourage him."

And that made her laugh.

She found it interesting that she wasn't the only one who had dressed up to face Dr. Connors—outside of Tag's sunglasses. She knew why she had. She suspected that the men had done the exact same thing—for exactly the opposite reason: to look less dangerous. Or at least more civilized.

Happy Camp, California, was a very small town—about the size of Aspen Creek, though Anna was pretty sure that it had been bigger at one time.

Tag frowned, looking at a cleared area beside the highway. "Used to be a damn big lumber mill over there," he said, sounding a little disconcerted.

"Things change," said Charles. "When I was last here, there wasn't a real town at all. More a series of small encampments while people sluiced and dug and mined for gold." He turned his head to Tag. "Towns have life cycles, just like people do. They just take longer. It's not any easier when they grow than when they shrink. Just talk to Asil about why he left Spain."

Tag seemed to shrug off the odd mood. "Not on your life," he said. "He and I deal better when we stick to events of the present time. We were on opposite sides of too many wars to discuss the past. Here's a gas station, Anna. Might as well fuel the pig up."

He was right; the SUV got better mileage than she'd expected, but it wasn't a hybrid. The man working the gas station was a Native American somewhere in his fifties. He gave Charles a narrow-eyed look.

"Salish," said Charles.

The clerk smiled. "Fishermen," he said in satisfaction. "Karuk."

"Fishermen," agreed Charles gravely. "We drove down from Montana to do a little hiking. I'm Charles."

"Rob," offered the clerk.

They shook hands. Rob rang up their purchases—mostly water and Tag's junk food.

"Lots of hiking around here," he said. "Careful of fires. We've got one going about twenty miles away—started this morning. If you stay south or east of town, you should be okay."

"Appreciate it," Charles said gravely.

"Watch out for Sasquatch," said Rob, tapping the side of his nose.

"I always do," Charles agreed. "But I'm more concerned with the Singer in the Woods."

Rob's eyebrows went up. "That old story? Stay on the trails and you should be all right."

"I've heard that some people built a town up thataway," Anna said, unfurling her power a bit. Being Omega didn't have as much of an effect on normal people as it did on the werewolves. But it did seem to lower hostility. She didn't clarify where "thataway" was.

She hadn't needed to. Rob gave her a warm smile and shook his head.

"I heard that, too," he said confidentially. "One born every minute, isn't there? I heard that something happened to them, they disappeared like that Virginia colony of Roanoke. Smart people don't travel that way. My grandfather, he took me up near that place one time. Showed me a drawing someone had made on a rock—told me that if I saw that symbol, I should take it as a warning, like when you come upon a tree that a grizzly has marked. Something we didn't want to meet has that territory claimed."

"What did it look like?" Charles asked.

"Like an upside-down capital V with lines hashed over both sides. I heard that the place where those people put their camp had those marks all over it. Lots of beautiful country around here, beautiful river, good places. Don't know why people have to go poking hornet's nests."

He paused a second, then frowned at Charles with sudden suspicion. "If you folks intend to go hunting for Wild Sign, you'd better have good weapons."

Charles smiled. "Thank you for the warning."

Rob shook his head, but he had a smile on his face. "Young people always think they know best."

"It's a hazard," agreed Charles.

THEY CALLED DR. Connors from the gas station. She gave them directions to the cabin where she was staying at an RV park in town.

"The RV park has a cabin," said Anna cautiously.

"Don't they all," agreed Tag with a grin.

"Place like this," said Charles, "you get creative about making a living—or you move on."

The town showed signs of struggling, for sure, Anna thought. But it was set down in the heart of the mountains—she could see why people would fight to stay in a place like this.

Tag said solemnly, "You can feed your wallet, or you can feed your soul, but you seldom can do both at the same time." He took in a deep breath out his open window.

They turned, as Dr. Connors had directed, in front of the Bigfoot statue.

"Do you reckon they got the size just right?" asked Tag, looking up at the scrap-metal giant. "I admit the only time I saw them in their real shape, they looked at least that big to me. But I expect that was more terror than reality."

"Most men overestimate size," said Anna, deadpan.

Tag sighed dramatically. "I disappointed her in that department, that's for sure. She expected someone taller." He gave Anna a wicked grin from the backseat.

They pulled into the RV campground and drove around until they found the cabin Dr. Connors had described to them, parking next to an aging but immaculate Volvo station wagon.

As they got out of the car, a woman opened the door of the small cabin and stood on the porch, watching them. She was a little taller than average. Her skin was tanned dark and her shoulder-length brown hair was sun-faded and caught back in an indifferent ponytail. She wore cutoffs that actually looked like they had begun life as jeans, rather than having been bought that way, and a gray tank top that showed just how lean and muscled she was. Her bare arms sported a few scars, mostly thin stripes.

If Anna had to pick out a word for her, it would have been "tough." She remembered ruefully that she'd thought about going in jeans and a T-shirt instead of dressing for a boardroom. This woman evidently had had the same thought and made the other choice—or possibly not worried about it at all.

"Hello," she said as they approached. "I'm Dr. Connors. You must be Anna Cornick."

Anna nodded. "This is my husband, Charles. And our—" She hesitated too long and gave Tag time to chime in.

"Henchman," he said with a grin that widened as Anna frowned at him. At least the sunglasses were nowhere in sight.

She shrugged. "Henchman, Colin Taggart."

"Call me Tag," he told Dr. Connors, who did not appear to be charmed.

Well, thought Anna, at least she didn't run screaming. People who met Tag tended to one reaction or the other.

"We would like to talk to you about Wild Sign," Anna said.

"There's a picnic table around the back." Dr. Connors didn't give much away with her body posture. Nothing other than hostility. Anna couldn't decide if the hostility was a normal thing for Dr. Connors or if she was still mad about their opening her father's letters.

They followed her around the little cabin. Anna took the opportunity of pointing a finger at Tag and shaking her head. His grin didn't make her optimistic that he'd behave anytime soon.

The picnic table was right next to the back of the cabin, on the edge of a grassy expanse that stretched down between the various RV sites to create a park where guests could cook, sunbathe, walk their dogs, or anything else they'd like to do. Currently, they were the only occupants who weren't squirrels or birds.

Dr. Connors was staring at the picnic table she'd promised with an unhappy frown. Anna got it. Picnic tables were fine for eating with friends—but they were a little close quarters for strangers. Anna didn't think Charles or Tag would willingly sit at them the way they were intended anyway, because the table would get in the way of their rising to their feet in case of an attack.

Charles walked to the far side of the table and picked up the bench, carrying it around and placing it opposite the other bench with considerably more distance between them than the mere table had offered. He then made a soundless gesture that invited Dr. Connors to pick her bench.

She took the one nearest the table, Anna and Charles sat on the other—and Tag sprawled out on the grass, as a henchman, presumably, would.

Anna dug into her purse and brought out the letters. Charles had taken photos of them, so they had electronic copies. She handed all of the originals and their envelopes to Dr. Connors. Anna had to half stand to stretch across the distance. Dr. Connors took the letters carefully and set them beside her on the bench, tucking them under one leg to hold them against any chance wind. She made no move to look at them.

If Anna had been easily intimidated by awkward atmospheres, she would have been totally tongue-tied by now. But she'd been playing her cello solo since elementary school, and she'd performed before tougher audiences than a grumpy, antisocial white witch who, according to the FBI report on her, spent most of her time in the jungles of South America. The FBI hadn't known about the white witch part, of course.

Anna hadn't caught the scent herself, but Brother Wolf had whispered *White witch* as soon as the wind blew past them as they had been walking around the cabin.

"We"—Anna gestured at herself, her husband, and Tag, who was playing with a strand of grass—"are werewolves." Which was something she wouldn't have told Dr. Connors without Brother Wolf's information.

The only reason Anna knew she'd scared Dr. Connors was the change in her scent. Anna decided to let Dr. Connors believe she'd kept her reaction to herself. So Anna didn't offer reassurances.

"Around two hundred years ago," she said, "one of our kind encountered a being in the mountains northeast of here. He thought it had been killed, but he acquired the land, just in case. Ownership has remained with our pack. And the thing—we have heard it referred to as the Singer in the Woods—was inactive so far as we knew from that time until this. A few days ago, the FBI landed on our doorstep to tell us that there had been an entire town built on our land. Some *damn* fools apparently decided that a parcel of land in the mountains that was neither federal land nor tribal was a wonderful place to build an off-grid town. They were, as far as we could tell, mostly white witches like you."

She let the words hit Dr. Connors and then said gently, "And those foolish witches woke it up."

"I don't know about all of that," said Dr. Connors, sounding suddenly weary. "I am out of the country for months at a time, Ms. Cornick. The last trip should have been two months and turned into ten for—" She shook her head. "For reasons that have no bearing on today. By the time I got back, my father had been out of contact for months. That's not like him. Nor is writing to me every day for the better part of a week. He writes a letter to me every week on Wednesday. My mother, his ex-wife, gets a letter once a month. My little brother gets a letter written on each Thursday."

She raised her chin and stared straight ahead, swallowed visibly, and said, "Got. We all got letters."

"In code," said Anna neutrally.

"In code," Dr. Connors agreed.

"We are here to take care of whatever is up in those mountains," Anna told her. "But it would really help if we knew what happened in Wild Sign. We don't know what we are dealing with. My mother-in-law—who was here two centuries ago—only remembers bits and pieces. Those letters are possibly our only eyewitness accounts to a threat we need to neutralize."

"I don't know anything about a Singer," Dr. Connors said. "I sometimes stayed with my dad for a few weeks, but I had never been to Wild Sign until I hiked in looking for him and found the place deserted."

"At this point," said Charles, "we don't know that all of those people are dead or if they are just missing."

It was apparent in his voice that he didn't think they were missing. Anna caught Dr. Connors's flinch.

Charles caught it, too, and his tone was gentler as he said, "We need to find out what happened to them. So far, your father's letters look like they might be the best clue we have, but anything you know about Wild Sign could be useful."

Dr. Connors's jaw firmed.

Anna said, "We can do things that the sheriff's department cannot. We have the money and the personnel to throw at this investigation. Your best chance to find out what happened to your father is to help us."

Dr. Connors looked down at the letters, as if reorienting herself. "They are in code because his family has been hunting him since he ran away at sixteen. Off and on." She looked at Charles. "Connors is not the name he was born with. His family is one of *the* families. I won't tell you which one. If it was black witches who found them up there, I imagine you'll figure it out. If it wasn't, I won't speak their name where anything might hear me."

Her voice shook a little. Charles nodded, eyes a little narrow. Anna wondered if he could make a guess.

"It doesn't matter which one it was," he said.

Dr. Connors cleared her throat and continued her story. "From the time he was eighteen until he was thirty-two, they seemed to forget about him. He got his PhD in applied mathematics and went to work in the aerospace industry. Got married. Had me and my brother. Enjoyed a normal life until my aunt Diana, his sister, showed up in the middle of a lunch. I was five and my brother was two. We were having a picnic in the backyard. My mom ran and my dad tried to keep us safe from his sister. She did something that had him on the ground, and then she pulled a knife and started cutting him—as if we weren't there."

Her mouth was tight and the edges of her lips were white. "My mother was a police officer. She came back with her service weapon and shot Diana in the head. She kept my dad alive until the EMTs got there. He still has the scars." She stopped and swallowed. "Had the scars the last time I saw him. The shooting was ruled self-defense. But my dad left us that afternoon—left the hospital, left his job, left his life. And he *never* got it back."

She looked at Anna. "You know about witches. I found out later that he could have gone gray and stayed with us. But my dad . . . he was a gentle soul. He made my mom divorce him. Came to visit sometimes for a day or two when he felt it was safe. When we all figured out I was witchborn, too, he collected me for a whole year when I was about twelve or so. I don't have a lot of power. He taught me to hide it." She gave the three of them a sour look that didn't quite mask the fear in her eyes. "Apparently it doesn't work."

She'd be safe from witches, said Brother Wolf. *Witches can't smell a rabbit at five inches. She doesn't feel like a witch, she just smells like one.*

Anna was happy to repeat Brother Wolf's assessment. "As long as they don't have a pet werewolf, you're still safe from witches. Witches don't identify each other by scent."

There was a woman walking a big dog on the far side of the park-like area they sat in. The first person they'd seen up and moving anywhere near them.

"He'd found a group of white witches to travel with by then," continued Dr. Connors. Anna couldn't tell if Brother Wolf's reassurance had helped or not. "They were safer together—up to a point. If there were too many of them, their combined power could attract attention. So in small groups they would hike into remote places and set up camp, moving around a few miles here or there to avoid getting pushed out. Winters were rough up north or high in the mountains, but they learned how to manage because those places were safer."

The woman with the dog was closer. She was African American. Her dark hair hung past her shoulders, cornrowed and beaded with lapis lazuli–colored beads that matched the blue in the blue-and-gold shirt she wore. Raw linen pants stopped midcalf to reveal muscled legs and bright blue flip-flops. She had lots of curves, but the end effect was of general fitness.

The dog, who looked like he had a German shepherd somewhere not too far up his family tree, had been roving around her on a loose leash. As they neared, he walked alertly at her side, his intent gaze upon the werewolves.

"Audience approaching," murmured Tag.

Dr. Connors looked over her shoulder and her whole demeanor changed. Her face relaxed and the lines around her eyes softened. The other woman smiled at her, a joyous, bigger-than-life smile.

"Tanya, this is Anna Cornick; her husband, Charles; and their henchman, Colin Taggart." Dr. Connors didn't slow down or hesitate on the word "henchman," though it made both Tanya and Tag, who had come to his feet, grin.

"This is my wife, Tanya, Dr. Bonsu to her students, who fear her."

"As you are not my students, please call me Tanya," she said, taking a seat next to her wife. The dog sat alertly next to her, his eyes on Tag, his ruff slightly raised.

"We are werewolves," Anna told her, ignoring the way Dr. Bonsu's—Tanya's—eyes widened and she suddenly smelled of fear. Smart people worry when they are confronted with werewolves. Time would take care of that—but there were easier methods for dogs. "We should put your dog at ease with us before we go on."

Charles got up and the dog started to snarl at him—and then Charles met his eyes. The dog licked his lips and dropped all the way to the ground. Charles put his hand on the dog's forehead and waited. First the dog's tail started to wag and then he wiggled happily, licking at Charles's hand.

"Good dog," crooned Charles, giving the dog a pat before returning to his seat.

"That didn't take very long," Dr. Connors said thoughtfully, and a little unhappily. "I would have thought he would be more wary."

"No reason," Anna said. "We aren't going to hurt him—and my husband just told him that."

"As simple as that?" Dr. Connors sounded a little spooked.

Was she worrying about how easily a witch could subdue this means of defense? She should be. But that couldn't be Anna's problem.

"Dogs don't lie," Anna said. "Dr. Connors—"

"Oh, call me Sissy, please," said Dr. Connors, who was the least Sissy-like person Anna had ever met.

She smiled suddenly at Anna's expression and it took years off her face. "I know, I know. But I was cute when I was a baby."

She glanced at her wife, her dog, the letters on the bench beside her. Then she sighed.

"You want to know about Wild Sign. Okay. About a year and a half ago, one of my dad's people contacted him about this place in the Marble Mountains of Northern California where they'd put together a colony where they were safe from the black witches hunting them. He never told me why it was safer. I don't think he knew when he headed out. And he never told me in any of his letters—though I could tell that he *felt* safe there. That's the first time he'd felt safe since my mother killed his sister in our backyard."

She looked at Charles, having clued in, Anna thought, to the person who was really in charge. "Do you think that there is any way he could be alive?"

"We have not found human bodies," he told her. "Until we do, it is premature to write them off. But nearly six months is a long time to be missing."

Anna thought about what the Angel Hills doctor had said about Daniel Green knowing that Carrie wasn't going to be visiting anymore.

"What do you mean, human bodies?" asked Tanya. "Did you find other bodies?"

"Pets," Anna said. "All laid out in a row. Not sacrificed—we don't think. It didn't have that feel. But all of them dead—cats and dogs. Eighteen that we counted. We didn't excavate, so it is possible that we missed some." She paused. "Did your father like old Germanic tales?"

"Kriemhild?" said Sissy. "Kriemhild is dead?" She swore. "Dad wouldn't get a pet. He said he couldn't keep himself safe, so he had no business taking responsibility for another being. Except for the pets, Dad never referred to anyone by name in his letters. He didn't want to be inadvertently responsible for someone being hunted down. So Kriemhild belonged to the person he called the Opera Singer. I don't know if she actually sang opera or just liked it." She smiled wistfully. "My dad loved that dog."

She wiped her eyes furtively, then continued in a brusque voice, "There was also the Family of Hellions, who were Mommy Hellion, Daddy Hellion, Hell Bringer, Doom Slayer, and Baby Demon. Baby Demon turned six in December. There was the Sign Maker. He's deaf, I think, and was dad's lover for a while." She frowned defensively at the three werewolves, waiting for a reaction that didn't come.

"I'm pretty sure that the Hellion family are—*were*—the Tottle-fords," she continued. "I met Malachi Tottleford the year I spent with Dad. And I met his wife and two of their children later on." She gave a small shrug. "I would have called the bunch of them hellions, too.

"Anyway," she continued, "the Hellion family found the place first, so Mommy and Daddy Hellion were treated as de facto leaders." She hesitated. "I have all of the letters Dad ever sent me, but they are in storage. I won't be able to access them until we head back home next week—we need to get back because Tanya's teaching job resumes the following Monday. Anyway, I'll print them off and give you copies. I don't know that you'll find anything in them that will help."

"We were hopeful about the ones we brought you," Anna said. "They seem to be mostly the same—copies of each other. Only the handwriting changes between them. If you look at them in time order, you can see it."

Sissy pulled the letters out and looked at them. Her hands shook as she saw for herself what Anna had pointed out. After a minute, her wife put a hand on her shoulder.

"I see what you mean," Sissy said, sliding them back into their envelopes with hands that were still unsteady. "I can't translate them here. This is an older code we haven't used in years—I don't know why he switched back. If my brother still has his code key, I can get you a translation tomorrow. If not, I'll have to go to my storage locker in Colorado and sort through boxes of stuff to find it."

She frowned. "If you are looking for general information about the community, Tanya's boy crush spent some time up there last fall. Dad called him Snow Cone."

"That's right," Tanya said with a quick grin—though her eyes were worried. "Over on the far side of town there's a coffee shop in a little hut. And more days than not there's a snow cone stand. The kid—okay, I'm showing my age. He's in his early twenties and a little different. He's another traveler"—she gave her wife a warm smile—"like Sissy. He's a photographer." She held up a hand. "Wait a minute."

She handed the dog's leash to Sissy and trotted off to their cabin.

"He's been traveling for years," Sissy said. "He makes a little bit of money working as a ski instructor, fisherman, or guide. Things like that. But what he really does is take photos. He has three or four books out. I mentioned his name to an artist friend of mine, and he says he's the real thing—and of course Tanya is a huge fan. He is apparently a well-known photographer of remote places—and a mystery himself. There are no photos of him, no biographical information."

Anna knew of a photographer who did that. She straightened involuntarily and Charles slanted a glance at her.

"All that is calculated," said Tanya, bearing a large coffee-table-type book under her arm. "Mysterious photographers sell better than wet-behind-the-ears kids. Like that artist—the one who sold a piece of art for over a million dollars and then it self-destructed."

Anna recognized that book. She couldn't stop the anticipatory smile.

"Banksy," Sissy was saying. "One point four million dollars. *Girl with Balloon.*"

"Right," agreed Tanya. "The oldest of this kid's books was copyrighted six years ago. He must have been sixteen—you'll see what I mean when you meet him."

She handed Tag the book because he was the one who held a hand out for it. On the cover was an albino stag standing in a dark forest with fog rising from the ground around him, like a scene out of a fairy tale. The title of the book was *Bright Things*, the photographer listed only as Zander.

Anna had a copy of that book—and the other five, too.

"Zander is here?" Anna asked, feeling breathless.

Tanya grinned and nodded. "I know, right? Sissy had no idea, either." She patted her wife's leg. "Yes, he is here—selling snow cones." She rolled her eyes.

"My dad mentioned Snow Cone, that he came up to visit them last fall, though he didn't say much about him. But Tanya is the one who thought to stop and talk to the young man selling snow cones." Sissy shook her head. "If he had been Lady Gaga, it would have been Tanya scratching her head and wondering what the fuss was about."

"I know who Lady Gaga is," Tanya said indignantly. "I do live in the real world. Anyway, if you're looking for an eyewitness who lived up there for a while, Zander might be useful. But he's shy. If you take my advice, one of you should go talk to him." She looked at the two men and shook her head. "*Anna* should go talk to him. It took me five snow cones before he said more than ten words to me. If Sissy comes, too, he still won't talk to me."

IN THE END, Anna dropped Charles and Tag off at Happy Camp Mini Storage armed with the number of Carrie Green's storage unit. Meanwhile, she went to buy a snow cone from the stand, which was within sight of the storage facility.

The coffee shop was one of those miniature house–looking places. It was covered with cedar shake shingles that made it look vaguely hairy, appropriate for a shop called Sasquatch Express-O. It was set up as a drive-through, but the car lane had an A-frame signboard blocking it that read *Sasquatch hunting. Back at 4 p.m. so you can be up all night.*

There were two metal picnic tables between the coffee shop and the snow cone stand. The stand itself was a ridiculous thing. The functional part, a circular workstation about six feet in diameter, was covered with a cone-shaped plastic top painted a bright rainbow of color.

Anna thought the stand was supposed to look like a snow cone.

Or maybe an ice cream cone. Hard to say. A cardboard sign duct-taped to the side listed the prices for small and large cones in wide black Sharpie written in an even and readable hand.

On the top of the picnic table nearest the snow cone stand, a young man sat cross-legged with a guitar in his lap, the case open behind him. He looked like he was about Anna's age, maybe a year or two younger, but not much. He hadn't looked up when she parked next to the coffee shop. He didn't look up while she walked over.

Like his photographs, Zander—assuming this was Zander—was fascinating. Beautiful, too. But more than that. His hair was an odd shade between white and wheat, almost silvery. His eyes were deep blue. For some reason, after Tanya's description, Anna had expected someone small and slender—but he was the size of a proverbial lumberjack, a lean lumberjack without a beard.

He was singing the Cranberries' "Zombie."

He had a very good voice—not as good as Charles's; he lacked the timbre of her husband's voice, but he had range. And someone somewhere had taught him how to sing.

The guitar he played was a Gibson that was probably older than either of them. It looked a little battered, and someone who didn't know as much about music as Anna did might think it was a cheap guitar. But his old Gibson cost at least as much as the Martin rotting in the amphitheater, possibly more, though Anna's understanding of collectible guitar prices and models was hazy, beginning and ending with "old Gibsons are valuable."

He didn't stop singing when she walked up, so she belted out the song with him. He looked up at that and smiled widely. He sang better than he played, but he didn't play badly. When he was through with "Zombie," he transitioned into the old folk song "Molly Bawn" without a pause. Though he called it "Polly Vaughn" and had a few other variants to the lyrics she knew. Folk music was like that.

He grinned when she started the first verse with him, as if she'd passed a test of some sort. She followed his version of the old song with little trouble.

When they finished, Anna said, "I've always found that song to be pretty unsatisfactory. Man shoots wife. Claims he thought she was a swan. Oops." She blinked at him, then continued in sickly sweet sympathy, "That poor man, poor, poor man. Everyone feels sorry for him. How could he know it wasn't a swan he shot? The end."

"It should end with a hanging, do you think?" he asked, almost seriously. "But what if he really just shot her by mistake? The guilt he must feel."

"If he can't tell the difference between his wife and a bird, he needs to be hanged before he shoots someone else," she said dryly. "And that would put paid to his guilt, too."

"But it's a pretty song," he coaxed, his fingers dancing lightly over the strings as he played a few random chords. He glanced up at her through his lashes in a look she didn't think was supposed to be flirtatious. "A fun song."

"Yes," she said, though she didn't really agree.

"The Ash Grove" was a pretty song. "Mary Mack" was a fun song. "Molly Bawn" was a song about a bastard who murdered his wife and got away with it. But arguing with someone she wanted to extract information from didn't seem useful, so she moved the conversation along.

"Cool guitar."

He lit up with enthusiasm. "She's pretty awesome. I paid too much for her, but it's not like these ladies grow on trees." He nodded his head to the coffee shop. "If you came for coffee, I'm sorry. Dana closes up from two to four."

"I don't look like the snow cone type?" she asked.

He glanced at her silk shirt and jacket, shook his head, and laughed, an appreciative male sound. "No."

So her protective camouflage had worked on him, at least. But honestly, she didn't want a snow cone, so there was that.

"No," she told him. "You are right. Excellent snow cone customer sensing. I am not here for coffee, either. I'm here to talk to you. A friend told me that you'd spent some time up at Wild Sign last fall."

His face closed down, all the warmth gone.

"There's no one there now," he said.

"I know that," she told him. "I was just up there. The land they were on is owned by my family. We're trying to figure out what happened. Why the people abandoned Wild Sign and where they went."

"You hiked all the way in?" he asked.

"The day before yesterday," she confirmed.

"The day before yesterday," he said, then gave her a sweet smile, as friendly as if he'd never shut down.

She didn't know what about that made him change his mind about talking to her, but she was willing to run with it.

"Yes. And found a place that people put a lot of work into—and then abandoned. We—I feel responsible. It is our land. I need to find out what happened to them."

"I can't tell you that," he warned her.

"I didn't expect that you could solve the mystery for us. For me," she told him. "But the more information we can get, the more likely we are to discover what happened, how a whole town of people just disappeared. To that end, I'd like to know a little about what folks up there were like."

"People," he said after strumming a few bars of "Stairway to Heaven." Anna knew guitarists (especially guitarists who had worked in music stores) who would run screaming at the sound of the opening bars to that song.

"They were just people," he told his guitar strings.

Anna, who had learned to listen from her mate, waited.

"There was an air of euphoria, of joy, about Wild Sign," he said. "It felt like a little bit of paradise." He played a few measures that sounded half-familiar, but Anna couldn't place the song. "They didn't have a lot—not money or things. But it didn't matter. They had what they needed. A safe place to raise their children." He smiled gently, his eyes distant, and spun out a few more bars.

In the manner of guitarists the world over, he talked a little bit as he played, drawing a picture of Wild Sign for her using words rather than his camera. At first the images came slowly, but as he talked, the picture became richer, nuanced and clear.

She would have been happier to just listen, but she dutifully noted down names. Like Dr. Connors, Zander didn't know last names. But he did use actual first names—mostly. Dr. Connors Senior was Doc.

While he talked, his eyes on his fretboard, Anna brought forward her wolf self to check him out. He smelled of days camping in the sun and a little like cotton candy. He did not smell like witchcraft.

She thought, though, that there might be a little of that old earth magic—the kind that Wellesley, their painter, had. But to check that out, she'd have had to be on four feet, which would defeat the purpose of her visit—to get Zander to talk. It wasn't worth it for something so faint, maybe some sort of good luck piece that carried a bit of magic. The important thing was that, not being a witch, he could not tell her about any magic that happened in Wild Sign. She was probably not going to learn anything important from him.

Listening to his soft-voiced storytelling, she had the sudden thought that, other than his talent for music, he could not have been more different from her intense mate if he had deliberately tried. There was a sweet, almost innocent air about him. Sensual, but in the way of the birds in the air and the beasts of the field. Earthy.

Zander liked to talk—once he got started. Even with her, most of the time Charles preferred to be quiet. She thought that was one reason her mate liked horses so much. They didn't require words to communicate—they listened to his hands and body, and he heard them with more than his ears.

Zander might be shy, but he liked people. Though most of his photography was nature themed, he'd done one chapter in his Alaskan book on the people he'd worked with at the fisheries in Ketchikan. She could see it in the verbal sketches he drew of the people who lived in Wild Sign. She found out that Emily—who must have been Mommy Hellion—loved to cook and never went out without something purple on. Deaf from birth, Jack made signs to spread joy.

Charles liked very few people.

If she had met Zander before she'd been Changed, she might have fallen for him. Not just because she loved his art but because he was sexy and sweet. He reminded her of one of Wellesley's paintings—deep and rich with meaning. Every time she looked, she saw something new. Something that made her think.

But she wasn't that woman anymore. It was Charles, with his darkness, his violence and contrasting gentleness, whom she wanted to take to her bed, to share her life with.

She had gone through some truly awful times, but without them, she would not have had the courage to love someone like Charles. Charles, who had reached out of his own darkness to catch her. She had the strong feeling that Charles's act had taken even greater courage on his part, though he had never told her so.

"Sounds like you knew some of the people in Wild Sign before you went up?" Anna asked, focusing once more on Zander's words instead of his person.

"Sure," he said easily. "The world's wildernesses are finite, you know? There aren't many of us who are driven to explore them. After a while, some faces are familiar. Emily and her family—the Tottlefords—I met a few years ago in Alaska. But they're not the only ones I knew. I stayed a couple of weeks with Jenny and her husband at the time in the Andes."

Anna was pretty sure that Jenny had been Dr. Connors Senior's "Opera Singer" from the stories that Zander had shared. But she didn't want Zander to know that they had another source for information about Wild Sign, so she didn't try to confirm that.

"The Andes?" Anna asked. "In South America?"

He nodded. "Peru." But something about the music he was playing had caught her ear.

"What is that song?" she asked.

He smiled. "Do you like it?" He played a few more measures before he spoke. "It's something I've been working on. My only problem is that it sounds familiar to me. I don't want to take credit for someone else's work."

"I hear you," Anna said. "It sounds familiar to me, too." She sighed. "Doubtless I'll wake up in the middle of the night with the title, singer, and where I heard it last in my head. But it's not coming to me now."

There was a wordless call behind her. She turned to see Tag and Charles jogging across the street. Charles was carrying two fair-sized boxes, and Tag had a box and a bright-colored fabric bag.

She turned back to Zander. He'd closed up again, like a flower when the sun goes down. He did not look like someone who could be observant and funny or take world-class photographs. He wasn't playing that odd song anymore—he'd switched to "The Ash Grove."

She'd been thinking about "The Ash Grove" a little earlier. Music was like that, though; a chord progression could call up a dozen songs to any experienced musician. They'd probably both picked up on a chord progression in something he'd played earlier that was also in "The Ash Grove."

"Thank you," she told him sincerely. "I appreciate your help."

He nodded without looking up. "Let me know if you find any of them? I'll be here until the snow flies—October or thereabouts. Then I'll follow the wind." He looked thoughtful. "Colorado, maybe."

"I'll let you know," she promised. "Safe travels."

She met Charles and Tag at the SUV, where they were off-loading their burdens.

"Found some things?" she asked.

Charles nodded.

Tag said, "Good thing we went there. Or else when the owner of the storage facility had his next sale, someone would be the proud owner of the Green family grimoires."

Wide-eyed, Anna looked at the boxes and bag. "That's a lot of grimoires, right? They have to be handwritten?"

Charles shut the back of the Suburban. "It's the largest collection I've run across in one place." He glanced over at the storage facility. "They have a presence all by themselves." And that would explain the heavy feeling in Anna's chest as soon as she had approached. "Carrie had spelled the locker, or someone—or something—would have come looking for them."

Anna got into the SUV. "What are we going to do with them?"

"Make my da happy, I'd guess," said Charles. "Though between this and the fae artifacts we've been acquiring, Da is going to have to come up with an alternative storage plan. Eventually we're going to run into some things that shouldn't be stored together."

In her rearview mirror, Tag soundlessly mouthed *Boom* and made exploding signs with his hands.

Out loud he suggested, "Maybe we should turn the fae artifacts over to the fae."

Charles looked at him.

Tag raised both hands and said, "It was just a suggestion."

"What did you learn?" Charles asked Anna.

She shook her head. "Nothing useful, except that I won't ever be able to think about the people of Wild Sign as anonymous dead people anymore. Zander is observant and a good storyteller, but he's not a witch. He didn't notice anything odd."

"We should find a place to spend the night," Charles said. "We could stop here and get going early tomorrow. Or we can drive back to Yreka and stay there."

"I saw a place as we were coming into town. On the river," Anna said, suddenly exhausted and ready to be done for the day, even though it was only midafternoon.

"I saw it," said Charles. "That sounds good. Tag?"

"Don't care," he said. "Find me a bed and I'll sleep in it. Otherwise, I'll sleep on the floor. As long as you ward those books. If you don't, I'm through sleeping until this trip is over. My hands are still tingling and I don't think a shower is going to clean me up." He looked at Anna, meeting her eyes briefly in the rearview mirror. "The Klamath might just do it, though. Let's stay on the river."

Anna was suddenly parked in front of a building bearing a sign that read *Resort*. The engine was running and both of her hands were on the wheel, but she didn't remember getting here. It was just like the sudden dislocation from Chicago to the Wild Sign amphitheater, but instead of losing years, she'd just lost a few minutes. She hoped.

"Anna?" Charles asked, but not like he was worried.

She shook her head. "Just thinking."

"Tag," Charles said, opening his door, "why don't you stay here and keep an eye on those grimoires. Anna and I will book the rooms."

Yes, she thought with relief, *only a few minutes—ten or fifteen at the most*. Not enough to worry Charles with.

They took three rooms. One for Charles and Anna, one for Tag, and a third for the grimoires, which Charles deemed too dangerous to leave in the car.

"What ought to happen with them is burning," Charles said as they carried them in. "But that brings its own set of dangers."

Even Anna—who, like Zander, had not been witchborn—felt as if there was something crawling up her arms as she took the bag in. It was uncomfortable enough to distract her from what had happened driving here. What she carried was a lot scarier than her little memory lapse. She was careful to keep the bag from brushing against her leg.

"Is keeping them here going to cause problems for people trying to sleep here after we're gone?" she asked, putting the bag in the middle of the floor, where Charles directed.

"Not if I do my job," he said absently, seeing something that she could not.

"Do we make your job easier or harder?" she asked.

"Harder," he said.

She brushed a kiss on his shoulder—but didn't touch him with the hand that had held the bag. "I'll go take a shower, then."

RENDERING THE BOOKS harmless took longer than he'd expected. They had been ignored for a long time, and they did not want to be hidden again. He would suggest burning to his da. Strongly.

Anna had not been wrong. Someone sensitive might have trouble sleeping in this room if they left the books here very long. But a few days should be fine. He'd smudge the room afterward and that should take care of any permanent trouble the grimoires might try to cause.

Anna wasn't in their room, though she'd obviously showered. He wondered what she felt she had to clean off. She didn't usually shower twice a day. The room was steamy and smelled like the things she used in the shower: body wash, shampoo, and conditioner. He took in the scent and . . . Brother Wolf stirred uneasily.

Charles wasn't going to give in to that. He pulled off the shirt Anna had gotten for him and exchanged it for a red T-shirt. If Tag threw him in the river, he didn't want to tear up his good shirt.

But when he took the path to the river, he found Anna alone. She was sitting on a big rock, facing the river, her arms slung around one of her legs that she'd pulled up to her chest. Like Charles, she had discarded her good clothes and now wore jeans and a black tank top.

"Hey," he said to her, because she hadn't turned around when he'd come up to her. The river was loud and the wind blew in his face, but she still should have heard him.

She turned to look at him—and for a moment he would have sworn she didn't know him. Then her smile filled her face and her eyes came alive. "Sorry," she said. "I was just trying to remember a song."

8

Anna still hadn't talked to Charles about the weird glitch in her memory by the time they were getting ready to head out for Angel Hills Assisted Living.

After a good night's sleep, she'd begun to think that she'd made a mountain out of a molehill. Nothing bad had happened. It hadn't felt like an attack—not like when something had been looking for a way into her head after they'd gotten back from Wild Sign. Maybe it had just been a leftover from her experiences with the Singer in the Woods, a hiccup.

As she got dressed for the day, she decided she'd talk to Charles if she experienced something like that again.

Charles came back into the room after his shower and said, "I think we should keep the rooms here at the hotel until we set out for home so we can leave the grimoires in their room."

Anna had noticed that he tended to speak about the books as if they were alive, which she found disturbing. She couldn't see Charles doing that by accident. She wasn't excited about driving all over Northern California dragging the books around with them like bait for any magically inclined whatsit who happened by.

Still, there were problems with leaving them in the room while they ran around looking for clues. Doubtless Charles knew all of the pros and cons, but she couldn't help worrying.

"You want to leave them locked in a room that every maid and manager can just waltz into while we're gone?"

Charles nodded. "That's a consideration, but they seem a little understaffed here."

Anna had gone back to the front desk for more towels the night before, because the only person on duty was the teenager at the front desk.

"A 'Do Not Disturb' sign should keep their overworked staff out while we're gone. And if they go in, all they will see is a box and a bag of old books. The warding should be enough to keep anyone from accidentally getting into trouble—and if someone tries to get to them through my wards on purpose . . ." Brother Wolf grinned eagerly. "We'll have a nice hunt." Charles dimmed the grin down a bit. "I think it's unlikely—given that they sat undisturbed in a storage locker for half a year." He frowned at the wall between their room and the grimoires'. "It's not ideal, but it's the best of bad options."

They left the books behind a door protected by the *Do Not Disturb* sign and a hotel lock anyone who worked at the hotel could open. None of them were happy about that except for Tag, who was visibly more cheerful the more distance they put between them and the books.

Anna, who had been watching for it, noticed that the old gas station was deserted except for the decrepit Subaru.

Charles must have seen her look, because he said, "It's early for businesses to be open."

"I was just surprised it didn't disappear after we left it," she informed him. "Like any self-respecting Sasquatch dwelling would."

"They aren't the fae," Tag observed from his sprawled position in the backseat. "It's too much work. They have to be really trying to impress you to do something like that."

Something in his voice made Anna suspect that he had been wondering if it would be gone, too.

THEY ATE BREAKFAST in Yreka, then set out for Angel Hills Assisted Living, following the SUV's GPS.

"Are you sure we are heading to the right place?" Anna asked as they bumped over the rutted dirt road. "Most assisted living facilities are somewhere an ambulance can actually reach."

Yreka was edged with hill country, and they were nine miles up a road that ran around those hills. It had been four miles since they had seen the last house.

"If we reach the GPS's target and it's not right, we can go back to Yreka and ask around," Tag said.

"Angel Hills doesn't have a website," said Charles. "Or much other information on the Internet." He gave a thoughtful grunt.

"That's odd," agreed Anna. She held the steering wheel steady as a rut tried to force the SUV to the side. "Most assisted living places have to advertise for clients. Maybe Yreka is small enough that word of—"

They topped a rise and found themselves abruptly in the tamed greenness of a well-tended landscape. Two rows of trees lined a white vinyl fence line on either side of the suddenly paved road.

The road curved gently up to an opening in the high stone wall that surrounded Angel Hills Assisted Living. In case passersby were in any doubt of where they were, there was an elegant, if large, brass sign on the metal gates that were open to welcome them.

They drove through the impressive entry into a prosaic parking lot laid out before a large, graceful building that looked very much like a high-end private hospital or school. A very tall stone wall spread out from either side of the building and swept behind it, encasing something very securely. Anna gave a thoughtful look at the open gates.

"All but shouts 'expensive place to store unwanted relatives,' doesn't it?" observed Tag.

"What do you do with grandma when she doesn't remember who you are and starts trying to spend all of her money on QVC buying synthetic pearl brooches?" agreed Anna.

"That was oddly specific," said Tag, sounding intrigued.

"My father represented just such a grandma after her intrepid teenaged grandchildren broke her out of a facility her son had locked her up in for her own good," Anna said, her tone a bit grimmer than she had planned.

She'd been doing homework when the two boys and their grandmother, still wearing stained hospital clothing and the remnants of plastic restraints, had knocked on her dad's door.

"From your face I gather that the son regretted his actions," Charles murmured.

"In his own way," Anna said, "my dad is kind of a wolf, too."

Anna had been heading toward a place near the main building when Charles made a soft noise. She glanced up at him, but he was watching the building.

"You think we should be wary?" she asked.

He nodded, so she drove back toward the gates. "Should I park outside?"

He gave the wall a look and shook his head. "We can get over the wall if we need to."

She took a parking place just inside the gates. They got out, and Charles took a slow, sweeping look around. Anna wondered what he saw. She knew that he didn't usually see ghosts, but she got the feeling he saw something here.

"Tag," he said slowly. "I think you should stay with the car."

"Watching our escape route," said Tag, sounding a bit more Celtic than normal. "Oh, aye."

"Magic?" Anna asked.

Charles jerked his head toward a light post. "We're being watched—and maybe listened to." Which wasn't a no, she noted.

She narrowed her eyes and finally saw what he had. An extra little bump on the bottom side of the post that arched over to hold the light—camera.

"Reasonable enough," she observed, "at a place that might have Alzheimer's patients, and—" Her breath caught. She had been so worried about her memory lapses and the grimoires that she hadn't actually thought about what it meant that Daniel was a relative of Carrie's the same way Dr. Sissy Connors was the daughter of Dr. Connors Senior. Witches tended to occur along family lines. "And maybe especially a patient related to Carrie Green," she said slowly.

If they were being watched, she couldn't ask Charles if he thought they were being stupid for going into a place designed to keep people in, maybe even to detain witches against their will. They didn't know if Daniel could tell them anything. *Charles has thought of all of this,* she told herself, and forced her shoulders to relax. All she had to do was not let him know that she hadn't figured it out until just now.

She wished she hadn't given the facility her real name. If this place was run by witches, that surname would alert people. Cornick was a good Welsh name, and there were doubtless hundreds of Cornick families in the US that were no relation to the Wolf Who Rules. But still . . .

In lieu of words, she reached out to Charles and stopped him when he would have walked toward the doors. He gave her a reassuring smile and covered her hand with his briefly. He didn't think that they were in any danger he couldn't handle. She slid her hand into the crook of his arm.

As they walked to the building, she saw that most of the windows were the kind with a metal mesh embedded in the glass, more discreet than bars but no less effective unless you were keeping in werewolves. She wondered how many of their patients were incarcerated here rather than held for treatment. Probably the same percentage of patients in any assisted living home, she thought. But the isolation of the place made it feel more like a prison than a place of healing.

Well, that and the surveillance equipment and escape-proof windows.

As if to make up for the imposing exterior, the glass-and-bronze entry would have done credit to a high-end hotel, an effect not lessened by the imposing reception desk. Anna gave their names to the young man behind the counter and told him they were there to see Daniel Green. He checked a list and gave them a bright smile.

"Dr. Underwood left a note that he wanted to escort you. Normally you would not be allowed in to see him at all. Daniel's one of our special guests—that means that he can be obstreperous if he is in a mood."

There was a hesitation before "obstreperous." Anna would have bet that the word he'd been going to say was "dangerous."

"It's not Daniel's fault." The young man looked suddenly serious. "Dementia is a terrible thing—scary for those who suffer from it."

The last few days had given Anna a visceral understanding of how frightening having undependable memories was. "Of course," she said.

"If you'll wait a moment, I'll go get him."

Dr. Underwood did not keep them waiting long. He was short, slender, and bearded, with warm blue eyes and a Mickey Mouse tie. He saw Anna's glance and laughed.

"My daughter gives me ties," he said. "She is eight. Yesterday's tie was from *Frozen*. One of our clients sang 'Do You Want to Build a Snowman?' to me every time I checked in on her." It didn't sound as though it particularly bothered him.

"Daniel enjoys the gardens in the morning," he said. "He's more lucid outside; we find that is true of many of our clients. Indoors can feel a little alien, with strange noises and smells, but a garden is always filled with familiar things."

He led them down a too-shiny-floored hall full of oversized solid-looking doors, most of which had dead bolts that locked the patients inside. The air smelled of cleaners that burned Anna's sensitive nose, so it could give her no further hint of what lay beyond those doors.

"Daniel was as cheerful as he gets this morning," Dr. Underwood said. "He had a good breakfast. I have every expectation you'll have a good visit. But if you don't mind, I will hover in view but out of ear-shot to make sure. Afterward, we should talk about Daniel's future."

"Of course," Anna murmured, wondering how they were going to manage that part. Maybe she'd just give him the check and Leslie's phone number and tell him to take it to the FBI.

The gardens were lower than the building, so when they stepped outside, Anna got a fair look at the whole thing. Five or six acres, she judged, completely enclosed by what looked to be a ten-foot wall. Hedges and the natural rise and fall of the land had been utilized to create small pockets of privacy. In the center of the garden was a good-sized water feature with a waterfall on one end and a natural-looking (other than it being aboveground) pond on the other end.

Charles gave her a thoughtful look as she started down the stairs ahead of him, following Dr. Underwood. She wasn't sure what that look was about, but she thought she was missing something. She tried to figure out what that could be.

Outside, her nose should have been of use to figure out what Charles had noticed, but she didn't find anything that shouldn't be there: plants, birds, insects, and presumably Dr. Underwood's after-shave or shampoo or something. He must have used a brand she didn't know that smelled spicy and . . .

She frowned, closing the distance between them so she could get a better sniff. It didn't smell like anything she had smelled before—and by now she was familiar with a lot of different scents. It was a blend of scents, she could tell that much—but none of the blend was anything she could pinpoint.

She couldn't imagine that look on Charles's face was because Dr. Underwood's cologne/aftershave/whatever was complex. She decided she should stay alert. Which was, she noticed, harder to do than it should have been. The aura in the garden was very soothing. Perhaps too soothing.

She eyed Underwood as she considered that. Assuming Daniel Green was witchborn—it definitely ran in families—it followed that any assisted living home that could keep him safe would not be a normal facility. It might, for instance, have an unusually peaceful garden.

Anna couldn't detect witchcraft anywhere around her, but she wasn't good at it on her own—she needed her inner wolf for that. But she was sure as damn it that something was trying to pacify her with unnatural persistence. That was her job, and she could tell when someone else had put their hand in to have a try at it.

She coaxed her wolfish nature out—which was a bit harder than normal. As soon as she did so, the effects of the garden's magic fell away. Her wolf told her that they were surrounded by magic so thick it felt as though she were breathing it. That was what she'd been smelling, but some spellcrafting had misdirected her into believing it was Underwood's cologne or the flowers or anything else with a scent she wouldn't pay too much attention to.

No wonder Charles had been wary.

Not all witches were evil. But she could not tell what branch of witchcraft had created the magic here, and there was something flattening out the smell. Even without her wolf close to the surface, she should have detected black magic under most circumstances. And if it was white magic they were using, there would have been no reason to hide what its origins were. It could have been gray magic.

But she didn't think gray witches would go to so much effort to hide what kind of magic was at work here—that was a fair amount of power to waste if all you were hiding was gray magic.

As they wound around hedges and down steep flagstone steps, she wondered if that soothing spell had been meant specifically for them—and decided that was unlikely. There were all sorts of reasons that someone would want to calm the powerful residents of an assisted living home, and not a likely magic they would throw at a pair of werewolves.

She reached for her bond with Charles and felt his high-alert status and also a touch of "Not now." Like the garden, Anna broadcast a soothing atmosphere almost unintentionally. Normally it was a useful—the *most* useful—aspect of her Omega condition. But calming Brother Wolf when he might have to fight was not ideal.

But his response gave her an answer of sorts. Charles felt that they were in danger. She probably should have been more worried about that. Maybe it was just the residual effects of the garden spell, but she thought it was probably her mate's solid presence at her back.

Underwood led them down to a seating area that overlooked the pond side of the water feature. Stone benches edged the concrete platform where a single figure sat in a wheelchair that was angled to give him a view of the handful of black swans drifting amidst lily pads and a scattering of low fountains that burbled around the edge of the pond.

The king in exile, Anna thought, taking in the proud cant to his head and the straightness of his shoulders. Power had once rested upon him, and his body remembered.

A nurse sat on a stone bench that angled toward Daniel Green, her back mostly to the pond. Anna could catch the cheerful chatter of her voice as she knitted something pink with yarn emerging from a woven basket at her feet. She was a tall woman, big-boned and gaunt, with a mouth that smiled easily. She looked up and saw them coming, and her smile disappeared.

"Daniel," she said, "you have visitors. I'm going to leave you with them for a while so you can have some privacy. But Dr. Underwood is here. If you feel any distress, you can call for him and he'll come."

She looked at Anna and Charles. "It is important for our clients to feel safe," she said. There wasn't active dislike in her voice, but she wasn't friendly, either.

Daniel growled something, but he didn't look around—or at the nurse, either. If Anna, with her werewolf ears, couldn't hear exactly what he'd said, she figured no one could.

"Of course," Anna told the nurse warmly, because her dad had been big on "You catch more flies with honey than vinegar."

"Well," said the nurse, whose name tag read Mary Frank, LPN, apparently taken aback by Anna's open friendliness. "I'll be back in fifteen minutes to take Mr. Green back to his room."

She frowned at Dr. Underwood and he bowed. Deferentially. A doctor to a nurse. Among the witches, it was usually the women who had the most power. Between Dr. Underwood and Ms. Frank, clearly Ms. Frank was in charge. Something in Underwood's posture, respectful as it was, told Anna he resented that.

Interesting, she thought, and wondered what unconscious social behaviors might betray the fact that a person was a werewolf.

Mr. Green made another noise, a grunt this time. Anna couldn't tell what kind of a grunt it was. He was facing away from her, and even with Charles she usually had to see his face to interpret his grunts.

"I'll be back to get you," the nurse said. "You behave yourself, Daniel, and we'll go have some ice cream afterward. Won't that be nice, dear?"

Dr. Underwood bent his knees a little so that he could look into Daniel's eyes. "I'll leave you with Anna and her husband, but if you need me, you can just call out." He stood up and said to Anna, "I'll just be on the other side of the fountain. I can see you—and hear you if you shout." It sounded like he knew that from experience.

She nodded—and waited until the doctor was well on his way before moving around the chair to where Daniel could see her. And she could see him.

Daniel Green's face was deeply lined, making his already prominent features seem larger—he reminded her of the ents in *The Lord of the Rings* movies. He'd been built nearly on the scale of Tag at one time, but age had winnowed away his bulk and left only the crags behind. His jaw was solid and his deep-set black eyes burned fever-bright. He had the eyes of a roadside evangelist, she thought—intense and slightly mad.

"I don't know you," he said, his voice surprisingly soft. He looked like a man who should have had a battlefield voice. "They said you are Carrie's sister-in-law. Carrie was an only child and she never married."

"I lied to them," Anna agreed. He was talking about Carrie as if she were dead, she noticed. If he was witchborn, maybe he could tell.

Based only on the way the young man at the reception desk had talked about him, she would place the odds of him being witchborn at about 95 percent. The way he carried himself made her think that he had been one of the rare men who were powerful witches. That made her very glad Charles was with her.

She sat on the bench that the nurse had abandoned, because it put her on eye level with him. "I'm Anna Cornick and this is my husband, Charles."

At her gesture, Charles, who had been casting restless eyes around the garden, came around so Daniel could see him without moving his chair.

"Cornick," the old man said, narrowing his eyes at Charles, who had moved to stand behind Anna. "I wondered if it was your family when they told me that name. But I did not really expect it. What do you think I've done this time?" He grinned suddenly at Charles, a wicked expression giving Anna a glimpse at the charisma this man must have once commanded.

He knew Charles and Charles knew him. She was sure that if Charles had known that coming here, he would have told her. She supposed that Daniel Green was a common name, or maybe Charles had known him under a different name.

"Plenty, I imagine," answered Charles, his voice equally soft.

"Don't worry," Daniel Green said, and waved his fingers. There was a popping noise, and something small and dark that might have been a miniaturized camera bounced through the air and rolled on the ground.

"That'll ensure our privacy. There will be a fuss behind the scenes. Look down there—he's getting the call." He gestured toward Underwood, who was putting his phone to his ear. "I have no intention of giving you away. They don't need to know that the son of the werewolf king is here in their power. Not yet, anyway. Have you come to kill me?"

He sounded, Anna noticed, almost hopeful.

"Not this time," Charles told him, and even Anna couldn't tell if he was just humoring the old witch or if he really regretted that Daniel's death wasn't Charles's aim today.

"We are here trying to find out what happened to Carrie Green and the rest of the people in the camp she lived in," Anna said, deciding that it was time to bring the conversation around to what they needed.

"Wild Sign," said Daniel. "She's dead. They are all dead." He didn't sound particularly broken up about it. "I suppose you've found the bodies."

Anna shook her head. "No. But the whole town is empty. We hiked in a few days ago to see it for ourselves. Do you know what happened? Are you sure everyone is dead?"

"She was a fool," he bit out, though he was still keeping his voice soft. "That's what happened. She was a fool living with a whole bunch of do-gooder, pansy-assed twits trafficking with powers they had no business dealing with. If my Jennifer had survived, she'd never have let Carrie grow up such a mealymouthed puling idiot. Now, that was a witch worthy of the Green name."

He rocked a little, lost in thought. Then he sighed. "But our only child was a son. He had no power at all, despite my own capabilities. He married a woman of good birth—it wasn't until later we found out she was a throwback, with no power, either. Jude knew, though, and kept it to himself. My Jennifer died when Carrie was six years old, and Jude and the damned fool woman he married turned their daughter into a 'moral' woman.

"Moral," he said again, his voice shaking with rage. "She had so much promise. She could have been a Power—but she was a Wiccan and would not break Wiccan precepts. 'An it harm none' and all that rot."

He made "Wiccan" sound like a swear word.

He took a long breath and seemed to regain some control.

"So she died," he said. "My only granddaughter. My only living kin. She died because she was a white witch, the last of our family—a mewling, moralistic weakling. Arrogant. I told her that they were all fools, but she wouldn't listen to me." He leaned over and spat on the ground. "I could forgive the rest, but not the stupid."

"Something happened in Wild Sign," Anna said. "What power did they traffic with?"

He narrowed his eyes at her. "Wild Sign was that place she lived in the mountains." He sounded a little worried—as if he needed her reassurance that he'd remembered it correctly.

Anna nodded. "That's right."

He rubbed the back of his wrist with the top of the other, as if there was something bothering him. A vague look crossed his face, but when he spoke, he sounded lucid enough. "They met a being there . . . a primordial spirit of some sort. Carrie called it the Singer in the Woods—which is a stupid name."

He watched her with suspicion, apparently waiting for her opinion.

"It sounds more like a description than a name," she said.

He grunted and gave a sharp nod. "A pretty name," he said. "And it made them think it was a friendly creature."

"It wasn't," Anna said.

"They bargained with it," he sneered. "Bargain with demons, bargain with the fae. That's usually fatal, too, but at least you know the rules. They treated this Singer creature as if it followed the rules of the fae."

"What was the bargain?" Anna asked the old man.

"Power," he said. "And safety. You know what life is like for a white witch. Carrie might as well have painted a target on her back and held up a sign saying 'All-you-can-eat buffet.'" He scowled, fisting his hand. "It promised them a safe place to live, free from being hunted." Green's face contorted. "A second bargain was that if they fed it, it would give them power."

He looked off at the pond—or maybe at Underwood—or possibly at nothing.

"Fed it with music?" asked Anna, remembering what Leah had said, also remembering what it had felt like to play music in the amphitheater.

"What?" he asked, turning his head to frown at her. "What are you on about? Who are you? Where is my nurse?" With each question, he became more querulous.

CHARLES KNEW THAT Carrie Green's dependent—be he father, brother, uncle, or lover—was a witch. It had only been a possibility until he put his feet on the asphalt of the parking lot, but at that moment he knew. This was a place of witchcraft.

The witches who ruled here must have done something to disguise it. He could tell that neither Anna nor Tag felt anything. But to him the very ground vibrated.

It was a prison, he thought, looking up at the carefully beautiful facade of the "assisted living" facility. Witches were practical people; they would not waste the power of family members just because those people could no longer be left loose to roam freely.

This place was, to the witches, what his da's pack was for the werewolves. The difference was that his da didn't feed on their old wolves. He'd heard rumors of places like this, but the witches knew how to keep secrets. He'd never managed to run one down.

When Underwood came to greet them, Charles let Anna take point, leaving him to guard her back. He was happier when they moved on to the garden. He was pretty sure that if they wanted to leave, the walls of the garden, spelled to keep witches in, would not be effective against a pair of werewolves.

He also let the spell be that Underwood had laid upon Anna, designed, Charles was certain, to bind her—and thus him—to talk to Underwood after they spoke to Daniel Green. If he had dispelled Underwood's will, it would only have warned him that he was not facing someone helpless against witchcraft. The Cornick name should have told the good doctor that much, and if it had not . . . well, Charles was happy to let his enemies make mistakes.

If he'd been thinking clearly when Anna had called, he would have had Anna use "Smith" or something else. But at that time, he hadn't yet found the grimoires that proved Carrie Green was a witch. Just because there were witches in Wild Sign didn't mean everyone living there had been a witch. Even knowing that Carrie had been a witch, until Charles had put his feet on the ground in the parking lot, he hadn't been certain that Daniel Green was a witch, too.

He still should have cautioned Anna to use a pseudonym.

Should have, would have. Matters are as they are, snorted Brother Wolf, impatient with Charles for trying to see how they could have worked harder to avoid conflict.

Brother Wolf enjoyed conflict, and his happy anticipation lingered in the back of Charles's mind up until the moment Charles got a good scent off the old man in the wheelchair.

Charles couldn't tell if the instant white-hot rage was all his or if some of it belonged to his wolf brother. He had long ago thought that his vow to hunt down and kill this witch was going to go unfulfilled.

Most witchborn men were far less powerful than their female counterparts. The man Charles had known as Daniel Erasmus was one of the exceptions.

Back in the 1980s, the Wasatch Pack had been subject to a series of attacks that had started out so subtly it had taken weeks for their Alpha, a cunning old lobo named Aaron Simpleman, to figure out they *were* attacks. Only when Simpleman's second, a wolf named Fin Donnelly, was found dead in his house with no sign of what killed him did the old wolf call the Marrok for help. There were, he'd told the Marrok, witches trying to take over his territory.

Charles had been sent down to find out what was going on. At that point the assumption was that the witches wanted a base for a drug operation, as Salt Lake had been experiencing an explosion of drug-related arrests. What he and Aaron had uncovered was a web of witches engaged in the trafficking of minors—such a clean term for what they'd found.

The witches had brought in children from all over the world—some of them in "adoptions," some of them kidnapped, and others sold by their families, who mostly expected them to go on to better lives. The witches used magic to condition the children, who were as young as six or seven, to obedience, and shipped them off all over the US.

He and Aaron had been able to save a few of them, with the help of Charles's brother, Samuel. But the damage the magic used on the children had done was irreversible after a few days. Most of those children had been unrecoverable.

Aaron had passed on his leadership of the pack and gone out witch hunting for the next decade or so. He'd significantly reduced the number of practicing black witches in Utah before one of them had killed him in Royal, a ghost town in Price Canyon.

Daniel and Jennifer Erasmus—and now that he thought on it, she had been born into the Green family—had been the masterminds behind the trafficking and the magic that broke those children's minds. Charles had killed Jennifer himself. He had hunted Daniel off and on for years, but even whispers and rumors of the witch's activities had died. He'd assumed someone else had managed to kill Daniel, but apparently not. Daniel had taken on his wife's name, possibly because the Green family had been a prominent one. Daniel was the only witch Charles knew of who carried the Erasmus name. Maybe Daniel had changed it to throw off the werewolves who were looking for him. If so, Charles was embarrassed it had worked.

Charles glanced up at the huge building looming behind them. Just walking through those halls had left Charles wishing for a shower to wash the ichor of foulness from his skin. They were torturing the old and infirm for magical power. He did not think that Erasmus, that Daniel Green, was an exception.

Charles remembered the first group of children he and Aaron had found in a mobile home out in the mountains. They had been looking for cocaine, and they'd found that—nearly half a million dollars' worth—stored behind the skirting around the building. They hadn't been expecting the children. They hadn't been able to save any of that group, though all of the children were still upright and breathing when they'd found them. Whatever the witches had done to them had destroyed their minds. Charles had laid them all to rest himself because Aaron hadn't been able to bear it that first time. The next time, the Wasatch Alpha had helped.

Charles could not imagine a better place for Erasmus to end up than this house of horrors. He hoped the old witch lived forever.

He was glad that Anna knew neither what Erasmus was nor what they were doing to him in this place. They needed the information that he had, and Anna's usual charisma was getting Erasmus to talk.

If she knew what the witch had done, she wouldn't be able to give him the smile that was keeping the weasel talking.

Charles kept quiet, kept his senses open, and stayed just out of the old man's sight.

"What was the bargain?" Anna asked the old man, her voice soft and coaxing, as if she were dealing with a human being instead of Daniel Erasmus. Doubtless she was more effective that way.

"Power," the old man said. "And safety. You know what life is like for a white witch. Carrie might as well have painted a target on her back and held up a sign saying 'All-you-can-eat buffet.'" He scowled, fisting his hand.

Charles wondered how Carrie had protected herself from the old man if she had chosen the least powerful path open to a witch. He had no doubt that Erasmus would have taken every scrap of power she had, granddaughter or not, once she had defied his wishes.

"It promised them a safe place to live, free from being hunted." Erasmus's voice was tight. "A second bargain was that if they fed it, it would give them power."

Something drew the old man's attention. Charles felt it, too, glancing to the source: Underwood. Erasmus had broken the technology that was listening in—but Charles had no doubt that Underwood had some other means of eavesdropping. Because he used his magic to tug on one of the spells wrapped around the old man.

"Fed it with music?" hazarded Anna, oblivious to the currents of magic in the air.

She'd made a good guess, Charles thought. Whatever lived in those mountains had pounced on Anna while she played "The Minstrel Boy."

"What?" Erasmus asked, turning his head to frown at Anna. "What are you on about? Who are you? Where is my nurse?" With each question, he became more querulous.

"What did they feed the Singer in the Woods?" Anna asked.

The old man snarled at her. "What the fuck do I care?"

Charles stepped in front of Erasmus, breaking Underwood's line of sight. Anna scooted over on her seat, but Charles went down on one knee in front of the old man.

"I am Charles Cornick," he said, his voice harsh as he used the old man's fear to brush away Underwood's cobwebs. "You know who I am. What did your granddaughter do for the thing in the mountains? What did it want in return for safety? For power?" There had been two bargains.

"Carrie?" His old voice was shaky, but the volume had increased to the point that Charles was sure Underwood could hear it from the path he was hurrying up. "She was a musician. A fiddler."

"She played music for it?" Anna asked, her voice gentle. Charles felt Anna's power encompass the vile old man, and he wanted to snarl.

It would be so easy to reach out and break his neck.

"They fed that thing music and it gave them power," said the old man, face twitching as he fought whatever Underwood's leash was doing to him. "It should have been *mine*."

We could tear out his throat, offered Brother Wolf.

His death would be too quick, Charles returned grimly.

We are not cats who toy with our prey, said Brother Wolf, but he didn't sound scolding. He was thinking about those children, too. *They hurt him here?*

Yes, said Charles. He had not seen absolute proof of that, but he knew black witches.

Good.

"What did the Singer in the Woods want from Carrie in return for keeping them safe?" Charles asked again. "What did it want that they didn't give it? How did they break their bargain with it?"

The old man blinked at him, his mouth opening and closing, a drop of saliva beading on the corner for a moment before he licked his lips.

Charles knelt, holding the old witch with his eyes, letting Brother Wolf brush aside Underwood's magic, which would have kept Daniel silent. "Daniel Erasmus. By your true name, I require you answer me."

The old man tried to break his gaze, his face twisting in pain at being caught between two magics. Charles didn't care about Daniel Erasmus's pain. At all.

Not until he heard Anna's unhappy intake of breath, anyway.

We will make this quicker, agreed Brother Wolf, drawing power from the pack to increase the pressure they were putting on the witch.

The old witch jerked his head forward and snarled at Charles, "It wanted walkers in the world. Walkers to find things out for it and bring back food."

"What is a walker in the world?" Anna asked.

Charles had a horrible thought—because he knew someone who was a walker.

"They come in the afternoon," Daniel Erasmus told Anna, then let out a sound of rage and horror. "Fuck you. Fuck you all. They come in the afternoon and they feed upon me until there is nothing left."

He laughed, a sly sound that made Anna sad for the lost titan. Charles could see it on her face.

"But I know something they don't." Erasmus gestured for her to lean closer.

Charles held her back with a hand on her shoulder; he wasn't letting his mate get any nearer than she already was.

"They thought that it bargained like the fae," Charles said. "That the words mattered. But this creature bargains with intent."

"Words don't matter to a god," said Erasmus. "Stupid bitch. She was a ripe plum ready for me to pluck. So much power for a white witch. I could have eaten her and taken that power. Then when they came for me, there would have been such a reckoning." He shook with frustrated rage as he spat out, "And then she got her stupid self killed. Fuck her." His voice dropped to a raspy growl. "And *fuck* you, Charles-fucking-Cornick, for not hunting me down and killing me like you should have done."

In the midst of his words, he flung out a hand, and a wave of oily black power poured out of him like a mist of darkness—as if Charles would let the old man harm Anna. Charles blew and the wind followed his request, dissipating the blackness into the air, where the hungry magic spells of the garden sucked in the power with more efficiency than a Hoover vacuum.

It would not, Charles thought, be a good idea to use magic in this place.

"Daniel," said Dr. Underwood in a soothing voice that was somewhat contradicted by the heaving of his breathing as he trotted up the last step. "We need to remember that these are our guests."

He is out of shape, observed Brother Wolf. *And there is something wrong with his lungs. Can you smell the illness in him?*

Brother Wolf was in full hunting mode.

Erasmus scowled and half rose out of the chair. The blankets that swathed him were dislodged, revealing the cuffs on his ankles and the binding around his waist. His arms would look unbound to eyes unable to perceive the world as it was. To Charles, the faint marks of a tattoo only a little darker than Daniel Erasmus's parchment skin stood out like a brand. The inked spell held him with greater sureness than the steel chain attached to his ankles.

"Rest now," soothed Underwood, touching the riled patient on the forehead. Someone else would not have seen the brutal magic that subdued the old man.

Yes, thought Charles, remembering the children, this was a very good place for the old witch. But the old man had been powerful and Underwood was not.

"She stole it from me," Erasmus roared, spittle spraying the doctor as the old witch rocked forward in the chair. "She was mine to feed upon. That power was mine. Mine. Mine, and she gave it to a fucking god that sings in the woods. Stupid little—"

"Danny, be a good boy," said the returning nurse, power in her voice.

Charles wasn't worried about Erasmus or Dr. Underwood, but the nurse was a different matter entirely. As Erasmus collapsed back in his chair and Underwood straightened, smoothing out his jacket, Charles put himself between Anna and the nurse. He pushed Anna (gently) to the edge of the concrete platform they stood on.

Mary Frank invaded the space in a cloud of Chanel No. 5. He still could not smell the black magic stink, but his skin and spirit knew what had created this place, what kind of witch she was.

And still, in his prime, Erasmus could have destroyed this witch with a few words. Now he subsided in the chair, listing to the left, dull-eyed and drooling a little out of the corner of his mouth.

"Were we being bad?" the nurse chided, straightening the blankets. She looked at Underwood and raised an imperious eyebrow. "We'll just head along to our room," she said. "It's time for Mr. Green's constitutional."

There was a bite to that last word, and Daniel Green, who had once been Daniel Erasmus, began to sob and mumble. As his eyes fell on Anna he said, "Help me, please. Such a nice lady. Help?"

Anna stirred, and Charles put a hand on her shoulder and made a soothing noise as the nurse rolled her victim up the garden path. Anna glanced up at him and he could almost read the words in her face.

Are they doing what I think they are? Why don't you stop it? Why don't you want me to stop it? The man I love would not let a helpless old man be tortured.

What she actually said was, "Charles?"

He touched her face lightly. "I knew him before," he told her.

She took that in and gave him a shallow nod. *Trust*, he thought, *but verify.* Her face told him that he owed her a good explanation when they were out of here.

9

"Ms. and Mr. Cornick, I believe you agreed to speak with me," Underwood said after Daniel and his nurse were well on their way. "Let me take you to my office, where we can talk uninterrupted."

He turned and headed out on a trajectory that wouldn't lead him to the path they had originally taken from the main building, making the assumption that they would follow. Which was a safe enough move, if not for the reasons Underwood expected. Brother Wolf all but purred with anticipation.

Anna followed him without demur, and Charles could see the frail net of Underwood's magic clinging to her, though it thinned more as the spellcraft worked in the garden fed upon it. Even at full power, Underwood's spell was indirect, relying upon cooperation from the person it was laid upon to have full effect. It was something Anna herself could have broken if Underwood had been asking her to do something she was actually opposed to doing.

Underwood's assumption of their compliance told Charles that the doctor hadn't realized Charles had largely neutralized the magic Underwood had been trying on Erasmus. If he had, he would have realized that Charles might be more than he could take on by himself. The desire to keep Underwood in the dark had been the reason Charles had kept his own working subtle. After watching Underwood trying to calm the old man, Charles could see how the doctor might think it had been the old witch himself who had pushed back Underwood's magic.

The predator in him took note that Underwood was so unskilled that he didn't understand his spell had not been able to dig into Charles at all. That hadn't been anything Charles had consciously done, but such a weak construct stood no chance against Charles's natural shields.

Charles didn't like leaving Underwood's influence attached to Anna, but he didn't want a confrontation just yet. Underwood was no threat. But the garden . . . that was another matter. He knew that most people who could work or sense magic thought of it as a lifeless power, but he'd been taught by a man who understood that the world was full of spirits, of life. Charles was sure that the garden, whatever the witches thought they had, was a living being.

If he and Underwood had a fight out on the stone walks of the garden, he wasn't sure either of them would survive intact. Even Brother Wolf acceded to Charles's judgment in leaving Anna bespelled, because fighting on uncertain ground was better avoided.

And it was necessary to find out what Underwood had in mind, what he wanted from them. Charles didn't like to think there was any kind of connection between the witches running this place and whatever had happened at Wild Sign. Black witches were not a fate he would wish on anyone.

Except Daniel Erasmus, Brother Wolf reminded him.

But the hungry expression on Erasmus's face as he ranted about the power his granddaughter had robbed him of highlighted the fact that the witches in this place might have a reason to be curious about Carrie Green. If the werewolves were going to find themselves going up against witches as well as the Singer, it would be a good thing to know.

Charles paced behind Anna, occasionally blowing the garden's tendrils of power away from her when they attempted to brush up against her skin. They were welcome to Underwood's spellcrafting, but he would not allow them to try to feed upon Anna. Anna was not witchborn, so probably the spells in this garden would have done her no harm, but Charles saw no reason to risk it.

The garden made no attempt to touch him.

FROM THE VANTAGE point of the window of Underwood's second-floor office, the hungry garden looked like nothing more than a well-tended green space. Outside of admiration for its outstanding design, the view elicited nothing more worrisome than the realization of how much money this place spent on labor to keep such an extensive space better groomed than a golf course.

Unless someone was like Charles, who could feel its soothing power reaching through the walls of the building. Funny how Anna, doing basically the same thing, made Brother Wolf content and peaceful, while the garden kept him in a state of near violence. Well, that and having to leave Anna under the influence of Underwood's magic.

Underwood's room was obviously designed to facilitate meetings with wealthy people who needed their problem responsibilities dealt with. Everything from the rich leather chairs to the subtle scent of tobacco was designed to inspire confidence.

"Please have a seat," Underwood said.

Anna perched on one of the leather armchairs, but Charles ignored Underwood's suggestion and stood behind her. He reached out and rested a hand on her shoulder, his thumb brushing the skin of her neck.

With that touch, Charles swept away the last of Underwood's spell-weaving. It was not a great feat to give Anna a little protection at the same time, and it soothed Charles. If someone else wanted to bespell her, they would have to make a real effort now.

Which we will not allow, stated Brother Wolf.

No, they would not.

He waited for Underwood to react to Charles freeing Anna. But he'd overestimated the witch. Underwood continued pulling out his chair and settling in it without pause. He straightened his desk in a manner that seemed to be calculated to prove to himself that he was in control of the situation.

When he looked up, his friendly, fatherly persona was intact. Then he saw Charles standing behind Anna and frowned a little, as if surprised that Charles hadn't followed his directive.

It might be, Charles thought, that with this place steeped in so much witchcraft, Underwood just wasn't sensitive enough to tell what was going on with his own spells.

Such an unobservant man, noted Brother Wolf, *working in a place like this is doomed. If we kill him now, we would just be doing him a favor.*

Brother Wolf was a lot more talkative than usual. Charles couldn't figure out if it was the emotional upheaval of the Singer's attack on Anna or Underwood bespelling her—or if it was a side effect of all the magic in this place.

This is a very interesting place, Brother Wolf enlightened him. *I have hope that we will kill some witches here before we go. This one would do.*

"Anna and Charles Cornick," Underwood said. "Your names are familiar to me. Very familiar." He gave Anna a sad-eyed look, and a soft billow of magic puffed out to land upon both Anna and Charles. "Carrie Green was an only child and she was not married. You are not her sister-in-law. But the Cornick name is well-known among people who are witchborn."

"Is it?" said Anna, who was, hit by Underwood's magic, supposed to feel guilty. But for now, her politeness looked close enough to guilt for Underwood, because he looked faintly satisfied.

"Charles Cornick, the scourge of werewolves, the Marrok's assassin—and the woman who rules him," Underwood said.

Was that what the witches were saying about his Anna? True enough as far as that went. He wondered who else was saying that. Maybe that was why the FBI agents had concluded that Anna was the Marrok. If Anna had wanted to rule them all . . . Well, Charles couldn't see his da giving over the care of his wolves to anyone while he lived, but Da listened to Anna. They all did.

She *could* have ruled them all, Charles thought, but only because she would never think to rule any of them. Being the ruler of all she surveyed was just not anything his Anna desired—which was one of the reasons they could let their guard down around her.

She was more than up to taking point against a second-rate witch like this. And she was better suited to get information out of him than Charles was. People liked to talk to Anna. People liked to run away from Charles. Both of those things pleased him.

"Yes?" Anna said in response to Underwood's I-know-who-you-really-are reveal. Her mild tone made Underwood's lips thin.

The best part, as far as Charles was concerned, was that the question in her tone meant that she wasn't lying to the witch. It wouldn't be her fault if Underwood misunderstood.

Witches couldn't smell a lie, but they had their own ways of detecting untruths, not that Underwood was using any of them. If Charles were to hazard a guess, it would be that Underwood did not have the magic to spare. He wondered how much of Underwood's magic went to just keeping him safe from the black witches who employed him.

As I told you, he would be better off if we killed him now, agreed Brother Wolf in a lazy tone that fooled Charles not a bit.

Underwood settled back in his chair and rocked it a little. "Did you think you could come *here*, into the heart of our power, and leave without a payment, Anna?"

Charles could feel Anna's intention to produce Carrie Green's check—though she knew full well that wasn't the kind of payment that Underwood was talking about. He tightened his hand on her shoulder to stop her.

It could be dangerous to give something to a magical being, especially something like a check, which was, in essence, a payment for things owed. Magic tended to be symbolic. It was the reason that Anna's gift of song in that amphitheater had allowed the Singer to attack her. She had offered a gift—and the Singer had taken her up on her offer.

He didn't think Underwood was powerful enough for that to be a real threat. But Charles was here to guard Anna against any possibility of harm—and Underwood wasn't the only witch in play here.

As if in answer to that thought, Charles heard someone cat-footing it down the hallway. Like everything else in this place, they did not stink of black magic, but the power that one carried . . . the last time he'd faced someone that strong, he'd nearly died. And witches only gained that weighty *realness*, the kind he could sense in his skin, from stealing death and pain from their victims.

Anna, apparently unaware of the more dangerous opponent approaching, asked, "What do you want from us, Dr. Underwood?"

The footsteps stopped. Whoever was out there—and he'd lay odds it was a woman, both because of the power she held and because of the faint smell of some flowery perfume—was listening on the other side of the door.

I am ready, Brother Wolf told him. And there was none of the unreliable violence in his voice that sometimes accompanied their encounters with witches.

Charles prepared himself for a quick shift. He could deal with magic at the level of a witch of Underwood's power. But he'd found the werewolf to be more effective against anyone of greater ability. It was hard for a witch to shape magic with fangs in their throat.

Anna knows the threat is outside this room, Brother Wolf told him. *She is prepared to deal with Underwood. Which she can. Some would underestimate her physical speed and power, but we do not make that mistake.*

The last was said with such pride in their mate's prowess that Charles had to work not to smile. Anna could handle Underwood.

"I want to know where Wild Sign is," Underwood said. "Carrie was nothing when she brought Daniel Green to us. She had barely enough magic to light a candle. Without that artifact she carried, he would have eaten her alive."

Ah, thought Charles, that's why no one had eaten Carrie Green. He had heard of artifacts, tuned to the witch who wore one, that could prevent power grabs by other witches. He'd never seen one himself and knew they had attained a mythical status among most white witches. But Charles had seen other mythical magic artifacts, and he was willing to believe Carrie had such a thing.

Anna did not speak into the silence Underwood gave her.

He gave Anna a real smile. "Without that artifact, we might have eaten her alive, too. If you find it, you should bring it to me—a silver necklace with a moonstone flanked by diamonds."

This influence spell was stronger. Precast, Charles assumed. A spell Underwood used often enough to make up for the trouble of setting runes under the oriental carpet or perhaps on the client chairs. But it wasn't strong enough to penetrate the protections Charles had set upon Anna.

The corner of Anna's mouth quirked up, which wasn't really the agreement Underwood obviously took it to be. Charles assumed that Brother Wolf was keeping her apprised of the magical attacks aimed at her.

Underwood tapped his desk with his hands. "Where was I? Ah, yes. When Carrie Green brought her grandfather to us two years ago, she was a powerless white witch with a necklace to keep her safe." He sounded like he was a little surprised the necklace had accomplished its task. "The last time Carrie Green attended to her grandfather, she was still a white witch with the amulet—yet she bore such a wake of magic that we all felt it when she walked onto the grounds of the garden." He licked his lips, and his hunger smelled almost sexual.

"Interesting," said Anna.

She was not wrong. It was verification that what Erasmus had told them had been true. Something had given Carrie Green more power. That it had been the result of an entity exchanging power for music was indeed interesting.

There was a link between music and magic. His grandfather had used music as part of his healing and his spiritual life. In the hands of such a man as his grandfather, the patterns of music rendered in chords, rhythm, and tone called and shaped magic.

"Ms. Cornick," Underwood said. "You will tell me the location of Wild Sign, or you and your husband . . . mate? Mate, yes. You and your mate will not leave this building."

Silence grew in the office while Underwood made the journey from smugness to anger as he realized Anna had no intention of giving him what he wanted. He increased the power of the magic he was using, breaking into a sweat with the effort.

Charles watched, but the magic continued to slide off the protections he'd laid on Anna. If that changed, it would be time to kill the witch.

"We are werewolves," Anna told Underwood when sufficient time had passed to make her point—he couldn't make her do anything. "Your magic does not affect us."

Both true statements, thought Charles happily. Maybe, depending upon who was listening, the witches here might start wondering if all werewolves had some undefined immunity to witchcraft. Then more witches would be told that. He could feel the intensity of the witch lurking in the hall, hanging on Anna's words.

"If you want to leave here," Underwood whispered, "you will tell me what I want to know."

"I don't think so," said Anna. "Besides, *I* don't deal with underlings."

Charles did not grin as she stole the tone directly from the most arrogant wolf he'd ever met—but it was a struggle. He would make her use it on Asil and see if that old wolf recognized his own medicine.

Behind them, called by Anna's words, the door opened, revealing a slender woman of much less than average height. She wore glasses, red lipstick, and a suit that seemed like it was supposed to make her appear businesslike—but actually made her look like a teenager playing dress-up.

Warned by Charles's abrupt grasp on the back of her chair, Anna picked up her feet. Charles dragged her chair around so that both of them had their backs to a wall and a good view of the witches. Anna put her feet down delicately as he released the chair.

"Well, hello," Anna said to the newcomer in dulcet tones. "Are you in charge around here?"

For a moment Charles could see the newcomer consider a "Who, me?" response, and then her personality lit her face. She gave him a wicked smile. Him, not Anna. Her mistake—and an interesting one for a witch to make. Exactly the opposite mistake Underwood had made.

Wolves were pack animals. It made them stronger. Both of them were dangerous.

"Not me, precisely," the witch said. "But close enough."

She looked at Underwood. "You are lucky that Mary Frank thought to tell me Daniel Green was to have visitors and who they were."

Underwood had gone white and he sat very still. If Charles hadn't been able to feel the woman's power, Underwood's reaction would have warned him.

"Carrie Green was something of a puzzle," she said, returning her attention to Charles. "It was inevitable that she would draw attention among the"—she glanced at Anna—"*underlings*. He is right about this: we certainly took notice of her sudden elevation in power without accompanying corruption. We all make choices. We give up some things for power. It is"—she smiled again—"a little bit enraging when someone seems to gain the prize without the sacrifice."

Is she trying to charm us? asked Brother Wolf. *Does she think we are stupid?*

Anna waited, giving Charles a chance to take over, since the newcomer was addressing him. He chose not to. When he didn't say anything, Anna spoke. "What do you want from us?"

"That is a proper question," the witch said, still speaking to Charles. "First, I will deal with my problem." She looked at the man behind the desk and sighed.

She walked past Charles and Anna. And as she walked, Charles noticed the way she balanced her body and the way the excellently tailored clothes were a tad bit loose around her waist. She was pregnant.

Well, that put a fly in the ointment. Charles had no qualms at all about killing a black witch—but a baby . . . a baby changed things.

The witch rounded the desk and put her hand on Dr. Underwood's. From the way his eyes widened until they showed the whites like a nervous horse, Underwood did not want her to touch him. But he did not pull away—and she was not using magic to make him stay where he was.

After a few seconds, the doctor's body relaxed. His expression softened to bemusement.

"Hey, Dr. Underwood," the witch said in a cheery voice. "I heard your daughter is missing you. I think you should call home and check up on her. Use the staff lounge for privacy because I requested the use of your office. Mom co-opted mine again. When you get off the phone, it will be time for your rounds. You won't think much about Daniel Green's visitors. They came and talked for a little, but it turns out he wasn't the person they were looking for. Daniel Green is a common name."

"Okay," he said. He gave Charles and Anna a mildly embarrassed look. "I hope you don't mind, but I have to go call my daughter." He smiled pleasantly and then hurried out the door.

When the door shut behind him, Charles spoke, having changed his mind about how to deal with this witch. It wasn't that he didn't trust Anna to handle the witch—Anna was much less likely to turn this into an unnecessary fight. But he did not know this witch, except that she was powerful. He decided to keep her attention on him and not on Anna. Against black magic, it was his job to be Anna's shield.

"You paid for your power with corruption," he told the witch. "Carrie paid for hers with her life—and she got very little use out of the power she gained. My father sent us to find out what happened. Daniel Green—who I know as Daniel Erasmus—"

The witch made a comical wince—yes, they had changed his name when he came here.

"—has given us the final keys to the mystery of what happened at

Wild Sign. My father will see this flawed avenue of power destroyed. It need not concern you further."

He had a reputation that he had carefully cultivated. It said that he did not lend himself to long, involved explanations to the enemy.

The witch gave him an amused look. She started to say something, but Anna spoke first.

"Is it Dr. or Ms. Hardesty?"

That made the witch pay attention to his mate. It also made Charles pay attention. Hardesty was a name they had come up against recently. How had Anna known this was one of the Hardesty witches?

"Ms.," the witch said. She smiled prettily. "My mother is the MD and PhD. You can call me Cathy if you'd like."

"Cathy, this is not the cross you want to hang your family on," Anna said, coming to her feet. "Your family has lost power this year already. Twice."

Once with them, once with Charles's foster sister, Mercy.

"Neither event involved a direct confrontation with Bran himself. You want to leave it that way." Anna gave Ms. Hardesty a sweet smile—a match to the one the witch had been throwing around. "Trust me."

Anna walked toward the door. The witch blocked her.

"Your people might be able to stop us leaving," said Anna in a low voice. "But not before my mate tears your throat out."

Charles took that as a hint and let the change from man to wolf rip through him. With the excess magic in the atmosphere, the change took even less time than usual. He smelled the witch's sudden fear at the speed of his shift—and perhaps at the sight of the big wolf. He snarled softly and enjoyed the stink of her fear spiking.

Anna stared at the witch. "Be smart," she said. Then she shrugged and said in a bored voice, "Or be dead."

When she started walking again, the witch moved out of the way. Charles followed her, but he walked so he could keep his eyes on Ms. Hardesty, who seemed to be amenable to allowing them to leave, though she didn't say as much. He wondered if her actions, like his, were hampered by her pregnancy.

When he got to the doorway, he gave the witch a careful, eyes-up-and-watchful bow. Then he resumed his human form, closed the door between them and the witch, and followed ten feet behind his mate all the way out the front door.

TAG WAS SITTING on the hood of the SUV playing games on his phone. He stayed there until Anna opened the driver's side door, and then he hopped down. There was a bit of a depression in the metal of the hood.

"Hope what you found was worth it," Tag murmured, passing Charles on the way to his door. "This place is a witch-hive, and they started swarming about ten minutes ago. They are giving me the creepy-crawlies for sure."

The parking lot was certainly fuller than it had been when they'd arrived, Charles noted, though Tag was the only person visible.

As soon as everyone was belted in, Anna—in a very un-Anna-like fashion—gunned the SUV out through the open gates, which swung shut behind them. There was nothing mechanical involved in their movement.

Charles wasn't sure of the exact message the witches intended for them to take from that. *Don't come back? We could have trapped you anytime we wished? Leave us alone?*

No one said anything until they were on the highway back to Happy Camp.

"Are you going to tell me what you found?" Tag asked. "Not that I'm curious about what the two of you got up to in Witch Central or anything."

Anna filled him in on everything. When she was finished, she said, "Tell me why we left that old man to be tortured."

"Daniel Erasmus—" Charles began.

"Erasmus?" roared Tag, jerking forward in a motion that threatened to rip his seat belt out of the Suburban. "You found Erasmus?" Then, calming somewhat, he growled, "Tell me that you left him in little pieces that somehow clung to life . . . or—" He paused, smiled in understanding, and relaxed like a big cat in the sun. "Or maybe you left him in the care of black witches who torture him every day and will eventually kill him and feed on his death to extract every bit of his power."

Charles had forgotten that Tag had been one of the wolves his da had brought to help clean up the mess in Utah.

"What did he do?" Anna said, but less like she was worried that she'd left an innocent man to suffer needlessly.

"Made me kill children," growled Tag.

"Trafficked in minors," said Charles.

"Sex trade," said Tag, in case Anna had misunderstood Charles's terms. "Erasmus and his wife got their hands on children and then used magic to eat their minds. Left behind puppets." He shivered. "Evil."

Anna gave a sharp nod. "So it couldn't have happened to a nicer guy," she said. By now she'd slowed back down to her usual grandma-going-to-church pace so she could safely take a hand off the wheel to rest it on Charles's leg. "Okay."

"How did you know the witch was a Hardesty?" Charles asked.

"Wild guess," Anna said. "But there were nameplates in that hallway of offices where Underwood's office was. One had 'Ms. Hardesty' and the other 'Dr. Hardesty.'" She paused, then said in a low voice, "And she had Sage's mouth."

"She was pregnant," Charles said.

His phone rang and he checked it. "It's Da," he told them, and hit the green button.

"Update?"

There was something heavy in that single word. Doubtless whatever lay under it would be made clear in Bran's own time.

"Charles found Erasmus," Tag said, his voice steeped in satisfaction. "And we left him helpless in the hands of a nursing home staffed by black witches who will make sure that he survives to suffer a very long time."

"*Daniel* Erasmus?" said Bran softly.

"Carrie Green's grandfather—the reason she was trying to mail a check to Angel Hills Assisted Living," Tag told him.

"He won't hurt anyone ever again," said Charles.

"Good."

That's what I said, agreed Brother Wolf, still caught in his oddly talkative mood.

Rather than going through their two days moment by moment, Charles gave him a more ordered version of the story they'd put together about Wild Sign.

"There are white witches who use the wilderness to hide from their predators," he said. "Some unspecified time ago—more than two years but fewer than five—one of them ran into the Singer in the Woods, Leah's nemesis. The Singer offered the witches two bargains. Power for music. Safety for—and I quote—'walkers in the world.'" The pause hung, then Charles continued, "Carrie Green's grandfather called the Singer a god. Whatever one's opinion of his character, his magical education was sterling. I am inclined to lean toward his assessment—this thing is at least a powerful manitou."

"It broke the bargain," observed Bran. "It did not keep the people of Wild Sign safe."

"Erasmus was under the impression that the white witches broke the bargain first," Charles said. "He implied it was a breach in the spirit but not the words of their bargain. What does the term 'walker in the world' mean to you?"

"It wanted some of the witches to go out and act and spy for it," said Tag.

"Walker," said Charles, with a little more emphasis.

"Like Mercy?" Anna said.

"I think so," said Charles.

His foster sister's father was Coyote, one of the primordial powers. Such descendants, though most of them were not first-generation, were called walkers. Charles now wondered if the original name had not been "walker in the world," which gave a different slant to the original purpose of such couplings. Certainly, Coyote had been making use of Mercy.

"Safety in return for progeny who would go out into the world and do its bidding, be its eyes," said Da. "It wanted the witches to carry its children." In his voice was the horror that Charles felt—and not for the missing occupants of Wild Sign, who were, after all was said and done, strangers.

They did not know for sure what had happened to Leah up in these mountains. But one of the babies his da had helped Sherwood bury had been Leah's.

Charles thought of the haunted feel of the amphitheater. If every person who'd lived in Wild Sign last April had been killed there, it would not have produced the layered feeling of tragedy that overlay the broken land. But the deaths of Leah's people might, especially if they were only the last people who had died there, not the first.

"She never said anything about her child," Charles ventured. It wasn't quite a question.

"No," Da agreed heavily. "And I never asked."

He should have, thought Charles.

Soul-wounded by Blue Jay Woman's death himself, Bran had not been a fit savior for Leah. Sherwood should have known better. It was a wonder Leah had not killed them all in their beds, Charles thought.

From the backseat came a thoughtful voice that cut through the heavy atmosphere. "I don't know about calling it a god. As a good Christian—" Tag paused, waiting for someone to make a derisive snort, but he was in the wrong car for that. "Anyway, as a good Christian, I'm happy to proclaim him *not* a god. That way we can go kill him. But the bastard is pretentious. 'Singer in the Woods' and 'walker in the world.' I wonder what he calls his shoes—'Slippers of Justice' or 'Protectors of Soles'?"

Charles appreciated Tag's intervention. Wallowing in guilt was never productive, but Charles decided to change the subject again before his da could decide how to respond to Tag's flippancy.

"That's all we found out about Wild Sign itself," he began.

"Not quite," Anna disagreed. "Daniel Green—Erasmus—said that the witches broke the bargain that guaranteed their safety. Correct me if I'm wrong, but given that witches have power over biological things, is it possible for a witch to keep herself from getting pregnant?"

"Yes," Bran said. "Even the most powerless of them could keep herself from getting pregnant—and a small group of them could ensure that no one in Wild Sign got pregnant."

"They kept the word of the bargain," Anna said, "but not the spirit. That would have worked had they been dealing with the fae."

"Not usually," said Tag, sounding like the voice of experience. "If you break the spirit of a bargain with the fae, they can figure out some way to make sure you lose even without breaking the word of the bargain."

"You had other news," Bran said.

"Yes," said Charles. "We found the storage locker that Carrie Green was paying for and bought the contents from the locker owner. And we found two witch families' worth of grimoires—the Greens and whatever family Erasmus actually descended from, I think. I thought it better to wait until we get them home before I examine them. For now, I have them warded in a hotel room in Happy Camp. I had to let the spells the witch had laid upon them dissipate before I could go through the rest of her property for smaller items. We'll try later today, but it might have to wait for tomorrow."

Da didn't say anything—which was odd. Whatever he was holding back was bigger than taking charge of a locker full of grimoires.

"There are some other things you should know," Charles said. "At least two of the witches involved in running the facility we found Erasmus in are Hardestys."

"Interesting," said Da.

"They found a way to disguise the scent of black magic," Charles said. "I could feel it—but not smell it."

"Yes," agreed Tag. "It's an odd sensation."

"I couldn't feel it or smell it," Anna said. "Not without bringing my wolf up to the surface."

"And Anna and I walked down a hall with what felt like proper torture chambers on either side of us, and I still couldn't smell it."

"That knowledge has been in the world a long time." Da's voice was restrained. "But apparently someone decided to sell it to the rest of the witches. Mercy ran into that effect when she encountered the Hardestys."

"Carrie Green had something that protected her from the black witches," Anna said. "Something that predated Wild Sign. It's the reason that Daniel Green—Daniel Erasmus—didn't take her down for her power."

"That is a different kind of thing," Charles told her. "Though I've never heard of anything that could protect a white witch against the likes of the Hardestys or Daniel Erasmus."

"There is nothing like that in the Green family," agreed Da.

"Carrie's father was Daniel's son, a man named Jude," Charles said. "Her mother came from a witch family as well, but she had no power. Maybe whatever it was came to Carrie from her mother's family. I'll research it."

"Is that all?" Da asked.

"Yes," said Charles.

"*Bright Things*'s Zander is selling snow cones in Happy Camp," Anna said.

"Really?" said his da, sounding dumbfounded. Apparently he knew who the photographer was as well. "What's he doing there?"

"I know, right? I mean, he has to be somewhere, that makes sense."

"But Happy Camp?" Bran agreed. He sounded almost as giddy as Anna did.

There was no reason to feel the slightest bit of jealousy over the pretty boy, Charles thought, looking at the excitement on his wife's face. He had been able to tell that Zander had been flirting outrageously with Anna when he and Tag had interrupted them—but she had not been interested in the photographer that way. Charles wasn't even sure that she'd noticed she was being flirted with.

It wasn't jealousy, really, he decided, or not the suspicious kind of jealousy. Charles only wished that he could be like that boy for his wife—someone softer, gentler. Younger.

She is ours, Brother Wolf reminded him smugly. *That one can find his own person. She already belongs to us.*

"I didn't ask," Anna was saying to Bran. "Maybe he's taking photos around the Klamath River, do you think? Anyway, he told me that he's probably headed to Colorado as soon as the season passes."

"Da," said Charles. "What's wrong?"

Silence filled the Suburban as they waited.

"Leah is gone," Da said, finally. "She was gone this morning. I thought she had gone out running in the mountains. This business has been hard on her, and she's taken to long runs. It wasn't until she didn't come in for lunch that I thought to look for her."

"She's coming here," Charles said.

"Going to Wild Sign, I think," Bran agreed. "That song she sang . . . it had the feel of a summons. I thought that— It doesn't matter what I thought. Our bonds, pack and mating, are still intact, but I can't open them further. Which is unusual. I am in the habit of keeping our bonds closed down, but I don't usually have trouble opening them if I choose. I don't have any sense of where she is."

"The Singer messed with my ability to open our mating bond," said Charles.

"Yes," Da said. "You told me that."

"I'll head up to Wild Sign as soon as I drop Anna and Tag off at the hotel in Happy Camp," Charles said. "I don't want Anna up there again."

"Leah won't make it today," Bran said. "I know she's still in wolf form—it changes the shape of our bond." He growled, and there was a crack as something wooden broke. In a velvet-soft voice he said, "I did not notice because it is my habit to leave our bonds closed. Has always been my habit."

"You can fix that," Charles said, "after we deal with the Singer. We'll deal with the locker today—I don't want to leave it any longer than we have to, because if there are any other artifacts there, they will start to attract attention now that I've taken down Carrie's protections. Tomorrow morning, I'll head up to Wild Sign. If Leah is running the whole way, she won't get there before I will." Even a werewolf had limits.

"I cannot leave here," his da said raggedly. "Asil is in Billings, dealing with a lone wolf."

There was no one else who could handle their pack.

"I will find her," Charles promised. "She won't get past us."

"She is a ghost in the forest," his da said. "If she doesn't want you to know that she is there—"

"Pack bonds," Charles reminded his da. "If I pay attention to the pack bonds, I'll feel her as soon as she is within five miles of me." Usually only an Alpha would be able to read pack bonds that well, but Charles could do it. His da was pretty upset to forget that.

"Yes," his da said. And disconnected.

"First, we check on the grimoires at the hotel," said Anna firmly. "Then we'll go to the storage locker and get that taken care of. You'll get a good sleep and go save Leah in the morning."

She caught his sudden attention and shook her head. "I don't think I should go up there, either. I opened myself up to that thing. I don't know if it can get a hold on me again."

Charles smiled, put a hand on her leg. "That's not what surprised me," he told her. His Anna was full of common sense. "It was your boundless confidence that I can save Leah."

It had come out in her voice like truth.

Tag snorted in the back, but he was quiet enough about it that Charles could ignore him.

Anna grinned. "My hero," she crooned—and that came out like truth, too. He wasn't sure she knew that, but he and Tag did.

Charles felt his cheeks heat—which was ridiculous.

CHAPTER

10

There was no more activity at the old gas station when they passed it for the second time that day than there had been the first. All three of them watched it go by. No one said anything about it, but Anna met Tag's grin in her rearview mirror.

They had passed the Sasquatch gift shop sign before something that had been tapping at the edge of Anna's instincts coalesced into certainty.

"Cathy Hardesty was pregnant," she said. "It didn't strike me as important at the time, but I think I was wrong about that."

Charles nodded, and from his face she knew that he understood what she had. Maybe he'd seen it from the start.

"She let us go too easily," Anna said. "And maybe that was because she was pregnant—and because you honestly scared her, Charles. But knowing black witches . . . If she, like Underwood, thought we were a path to greater power, she would never have let us get away without a fight." She paused. "They would never have let us go."

"Agreed," said Charles.

"Just like they wouldn't have let Carrie Green go, once they'd noticed the new power she carried," Anna continued. "I don't care what kind of artifact she had. And the Singer in the Woods—" She felt a flash of indignation. "I feel *very* unhappy that every time I say 'singer' I will have that thing in my head. 'Singer' is a thing you are, Charles, a thing we do that is ours. And I love the woods. I don't want to give that word to some creepy primordial god."

Charles gave her a half smile. "Creepy primordial god?"

"Whatever," she said with a wave of her hand. She got back to her original point. "That thing wants walkers. And we think that means children."

"It would have been easy enough for a witch or two to follow Carrie back to Wild Sign," Tag said, proving that he'd been thinking along the same lines that Anna had. "They can hide themselves pretty well from most things that aren't werewolves."

"Would the magic on the trail to Wild Sign have kept them out?" Anna asked.

Charles shook his head. "It's meant to keep mundane people from wandering in. Maybe if the Singer actively wanted to keep them out, it could. But the warding on the trail was easy enough to push through. A witch could do it without much trouble. Maybe even use the wardings to find what they were hiding, the way I did."

"How far along is she?" Anna asked. "It is late September, and whatever hit Wild Sign did it in April. That is five, five and a half months. She could be that far if the baby is small."

"I wonder," said Charles softly, "how many of the witches who run that rest home are pregnant. How long that garden has been alive. How long they've had the power to waste on covering up the stench of black magic. As a rule, not even black witches waste magic on permanent spells."

Chills swept up Anna's spine. That was further than she'd thought through, but it made sense. She didn't want to go up against witches again—not when they were also going up against the Singer. Maybe it was time to call in the troops.

"So maybe the witches followed Carrie back to Wild Sign," Tag said heavily. "When they got there, they informed the Singer that the witches of Wild Sign would never supply it with mothers for its children. A witch could tell what other witches had done to themselves—we are of the opinion that was how they broke their bargain, yes? The white witches of Wild Sign—" He frowned. "And doesn't that sound like a line from Gilbert and Sullivan? Anyway, those white witches had kept the women of Wild Sign from becoming pregnant—and the black witches told the Singer what they had done. What if black witches brought Wild Sign down—and offered the Singer a new bargain? Power for children who would be witches and walkers both?" He paused and said in a mild tone, "It is speculation, but that scenario would account for everything we saw up there, expect maybe for the pet graveyard."

"Cemetery," Anna said, the echoes of a long-ago monologue by her father ringing in her ears. He was something of a pedant. "Graveyards have to be next to churches."

"I know that," said Tag, with feigned indignation. "If that amphitheater wasn't Wild Sign's church, I don't know where they worshipped."

"I thought that you didn't consider the Singer to be a god," Anna observed.

Tag licked a finger and made an imaginary score in the air. "Point to you." He paused. "But since I think that they considered it a god, I stand by my nomenclature. No point." He put up the same hand and made an erasing motion.

"Proving you can believe two contradictory things at the same time," Charles observed.

"It's a talent," agreed Tag.

Anna went back to the original discussion. "We haven't found anything that sounds very good for the people who lived in Wild Sign. Are we counting them dead?"

"I think that's a safe assumption at this point," Charles said gently. "But we knew, given the length of time between when they disappeared and when we were called in, that this was unlikely to be a rescue. Our job was to get information."

"Which we did," Tag agreed. "So we tidy up our loose ends, and then what?"

"Intercept Leah," said Charles. "After we have her safe, then we'll lay it all out for Da. I don't expect that we are going to leave this alone. I expect we'll be back with more firepower to clean the Singer out of these mountains for good."

Anna thought that if it weren't for Leah's involvement, Bran was quite capable of letting the Singer prey upon anyone it wanted to as long as it left the werewolves alone. She had very few illusions about her father-in-law. Charles, however, would not agree to let it be. Someday he and Bran were going to find themselves on opposite sides of something like this, but she didn't think it would be this time.

She put her hand on Charles's leg, reassuring herself that he was safe. For now.

And aren't your current problems enough for you, Anna Banana? Her father's imaginary voice echoed in her ears.

Charles watched her with curious eyes, but before he could ask her anything, Tag spoke.

"There's another thing," the wolf in the backseat said. "No one else has mentioned it, so I have to think maybe you didn't notice. Dr. Connors is pregnant, too. I thought it odd at the time, but private business between her and her wife. They can do that nowadays. Have children without a man directly involved."

"You are an advertisement for modern sensibilities." Anna's response was automatic despite her growing horror at what Tag seemed to be saying.

"She is two months along, I think." He tapped his nose to show how he'd figured it out.

"When did she go up to Wild Sign?" Anna asked Charles urgently, her mouth dry. "This summer, right?"

"Yes," Charles said. "July."

"Does she strike you as the type of person who would give herself willingly to the thing that probably killed her father?" Anna asked.

"No." Tag grunted, and then swore as if the grunt hadn't been enough to express his feelings. "I can't even *get* pregnant and that is revolting. Shades of *Rosemary's Baby.*" Something about the lack of response made him pull himself forward to get a good look at their faces. "You two don't know *Rosemary's Baby*? Mia Farrow? Roman Polanski?"

With a huff of disgust, he dropped back into his seat with enough force that Anna could feel the SUV lurch. "You people. I get that it predates Anna's arrival on this planet, but it is a classic horror movie. Gave me nightmares for weeks after I saw it—and I'm a werewolf."

"What does it have to do with the present situation?" asked Anna to please him—though the title was a fair hint.

"Good Catholic girl is sold by her jobless actor husband to the Satanist neighbors, who need a vessel to carry Satan's baby," he said promptly. "Husband gets a part in a play. She gets drugged, raped, and then gaslighted," Tag said. "Do we need to tell Dr. Connors?"

Anna was never going to watch that movie. She'd had enough of being helpless and told that black was white for a lifetime. Maybe Dr. Connors and her wife had been trying for a child. Anna herself had been looking into reproductive alternatives.

It didn't feel like that.

"So the Singer is impregnating every woman who comes near it?" Tag said. "Do we need to start looking for its walkers?"

"That's why they kept everyone away," Anna said suddenly. "All those wards. It wasn't about keeping the black witches out—the Singer did that for them, didn't it? I had the impression that Dr. Connors the Younger thought it was out of the ordinary that she'd never gone up to visit her father while he was at Wild Sign. They were trying to keep possible victims away."

"The Singer isn't a new thing, though," objected Tag. "Maybe we are hip-deep in the Singer's walkers right now and just don't know it?"

"Maybe not," said Charles. "I don't think that it would be making bargains unless it needed to."

"She didn't act like someone who had been assaulted," said Anna.

"Rosemary didn't remember it, either," said Tag. "Not at first."

"You think it affected her memory," said Anna, keeping her eyes on the road so that Charles wouldn't read her face. She hadn't lost anything all day today. At least nothing that had left her with one of those odd teleport-feeling jumps. Nothing that she remembered, anyway.

Charles put his hand on her thigh, just above her knee. He'd felt her fear. She needed to tell him about that memory lapse yesterday. But before she could say anything, Charles spoke.

"We need to talk to Dr. Connors," he said.

He was right.

"Let me do it?" Anna suggested, though there were very few things that she wanted to do less. "If the situation is what we think, we shouldn't overwhelm her with men, right?"

She was aware of Charles's keen glance, but he didn't argue with her.

"I think I'll put a call in to Mercy," Charles said unexpectedly. "If I had my pick of who to consult about our current situation, it would be Coyote. Maybe she can tell me how we could make that happen."

ANNA HAD DEBATED about calling ahead, which would have been the polite thing to do. But she didn't think she could manage the proper tone. She dropped Tag and Charles off at the storage facility and headed back to the RV campground where Dr. Connors was staying.

She pulled into the spot she'd used before. The Volvo wagon, hatchback open, was backed up to the little cottage Dr. Connors and her wife were staying in. There was luggage piled inside the car. She was pretty sure that they had not intended to leave today.

She heard them before she got to the porch. They kept their voices quiet; someone with mere human senses would not have heard them at all. Even she could not hear the words, just the tone: hurt and anger with a fair bit of fear on both of their parts.

She thought, *Two months, maybe three, is about the time you'd have to quit denying what your body was telling you, isn't it?* She pictured Sissy's hollowed-out face and wondered if some of the grim control she'd shown was because she was fighting nausea.

Anna knocked briskly at the door. All of the talking stopped. Quick footsteps came to the door and it opened just a crack.

Dr. Tanya Bonsu bore very little resemblance to the cheerful woman Anna had met the day before. Her face was tight and her magnificent black eyes were reddened. "Ms. . . . . Anna," she said, evidently having forgotten Anna's last name. "I am afraid that this is a very bad time. If you could come back in an hour, I'll be out of the way and Sissy would, no doubt, be happy to speak with you."

"Have you," Anna said, her hold on the door keeping Tanya from pulling it shut, "ever seen the movie *Rosemary's Baby*?" She didn't know why she went with Tag's movie, but it did seem to cover all the bases and save Anna a long explanation with a hostile audience—assuming the movie was as well-known as Tag seemed to think.

Tanya quit struggling with the door. "That is not funny," she said coldly.

"It isn't a funny situation," Anna said. "Carrie Green, one of the witches in Wild Sign, had a grandfather. We spent this morning visiting him at a rest home. We know something more about what might have happened in Wild Sign."

"I don't care what the fuck happened in Wild Sign," said Tanya in a low, vicious voice. "Let go of the door and come back later. When I am gone."

"You care," Anna said, and she pushed out with the soothing Omega power. It seemed to her that things might go better with a little less anger. She wasn't as effective on humans as she was with the werewolves, but it could help.

She softened her voice. "Unless you and Dr. Connors have been making use of modern science, I think the creature who kept the white witches of Wild Sign safe got your wife pregnant. It wants children, and it can screw with people's memories."

Shock loosened Tanya's hold on the door, and Anna shoved it open with her shoulder, tempering her strength so she only moved the other woman back a few steps.

The cottage living room held a couch, a TV, and a two-person dining table. The kitchen was separated from the rest of the house by a door, which was open. Next to the kitchen was a narrow, enclosed stairway.

"Dr. Connors," Anna said, keeping an eye on Tanya, who had backed all the way across the living room. Evidently the shove had been hard enough to make Tanya reevaluate what she knew about werewolves, because she smelled frightened now.

Though Tanya had smelled of fear before, there was a difference between fear of losing the person you love and fear of a monster. The word was the same in the English language, but it didn't smell the same at all. A lot of emotions were like that. After years of Charles's teaching, Anna's nose was well calibrated enough to tell the difference. Anna just didn't know if the change in Tanya's fears was useful.

"Ms. Cornick." Dr. Connors's voice originated from upstairs. "This is a very bad time. Please go away."

"Do you remember getting pregnant when you hiked up to Wild Sign?" Anna called. "Or did it steal your memories from you first?"

Anna knew the answer to that, of course.

Sissy Connors rushed down the stairway. She was wearing Minnie Mouse pajama bottoms and a USMC oversized T-shirt that was the right size to have belonged to Tanya. She was barefoot and braless, and her face was a lovely shade between I-just-threw-up and watch-out-I'm-going-to-throw-up-again. Anyone who'd ever been to a college party would recognize it.

"What the hell did you just say?" she asked.

"Sit down," Anna said, and she glanced at Tanya. "You, too."

Tanya looked at Anna a moment and said, "*Rosemary's Baby*?"

Anna nodded.

Sissy must have watched old movies, too, because comprehension lit her face. She clutched her stomach and the scent of her revulsion might have made Anna's nose wrinkle if she hadn't been prepared for it.

It wasn't Anna's story that Tanya believed; it was the expression of shock and comprehension on her wife's face.

Tanya walked over to Sissy and wrapped her in her arms. They rocked a moment, cheek to cheek. Then Tanya whispered, "I'm sorry."

"How sure are you?" Sissy asked.

"That the creature that destroyed Wild Sign got you pregnant?" Anna shook her head. "Occam's razor sure. More certain after seeing your reaction than I was driving over here. I can tell you for certain that whatever that thing your father and the other white witches at Wild Sign made a bargain with, it can take your memories away."

Sissy looked up at Anna and raised her eyebrows. *You?*

Anna gave her a sharp, single nod.

"I should have believed you," Tanya said.

"It wasn't believable," Sissy said soggily.

"I should have believed you anyway," Tanya told her. "And I read that letter, too. I could have made some connections."

"It's still weird witch shit," Sissy told her. "I promised to keep it to a minimum. I broke my promise."

"That was just a joke," Tanya told her. She looked up at Anna. "She's been having nightmares. Ever since she hiked to Wild Sign. That's why I came down to stay with her." She shook her head. "*Rosemary's Baby*, huh?"

"You aren't leaving me?" said Sissy—and Anna was pretty sure the reserved woman was going to writhe later when she remembered that Anna had been in the room for that. Or maybe not.

"If you don't cheat on me, don't lie to me, you aren't ever getting rid of me," Tanya vowed. It had the sound of a well-used phrase.

Sissy stepped back and let out a sound that might have been a laugh if there had been any happy in it. "So a complete stranger comes over and tells you that Satan raped me—and suddenly you believe her?" Her voice was a little caustic.

"Not Satan," Anna said, though she didn't think either of them was listening to her. "This is going to take a while. You really should sit down."

She went to the table and got a chair. By the time she brought it back, the other two women had taken a seat on the narrow couch.

Tanya frowned at Anna. "I wish you'd dropped in to tell me this last night before I did my best to blow my marriage out of the water."

"Sorry," said Anna. "We only just worked it out ourselves this morning. And if Tag hadn't figured out that Sissy was pregnant, I wouldn't be here now."

"Tag?" Dr. Connors asked, frowning.

"Henchman," Anna reminded her. "The huge guy with the orange hair. He has a better nose than most of us do when we are running around looking human. He didn't think anything of it—we're used to getting all sorts of irrelevant but private information from our noses. It's rude to use it against people who aren't actively hostile."

Sissy gave a jerky nod—then her eyes widened and she bolted back up the stairs. Anna could hear her throwing up.

"Is she safe?" Tanya asked urgently, while her wife couldn't hear the question or its answer.

"Yes," Anna told her. Leah had had a child and survived, after all. And they were pretty sure that Mercy's conception was similar to what the Singer was trying to do with Sissy and the witches. Mercy's mother was still alive. But all they really had were educated guesses, and Anna didn't know what the Singer planned on doing with the mothers of its children. And "safe" meant more than survival.

She tempered her initial answer. "I think so, anyway. We'll try to find out—we are still learning about this creature, too. But I think anything else I have to say should wait until Sissy is able to listen."

"While we are waiting for her to revisit her breakfast and lunch—and possibly anything she has eaten this year—there's something you should have." Tanya got up and went to the little kitchen, coming back with a couple of sheets of lined paper filled with graceful, rounded letters.

"Sissy's brother had the code key," Tanya said. "She translated it last night. I'm not sure I'd have believed you about"—she nodded upward to indicate Sissy, her eyes worried—"if I hadn't read this letter first."

THE FEEL OF Carrie Green's spell casting and the weight of the grimoires had dissipated from the storage unit when Charles and Tag opened it again.

Charles nodded at Tag's raised eyebrows.

The whole unit was ten by thirty, a little larger than a single-car garage. Originally it had been packed in a dense but tidy fashion.

"What a mess," said Tag, looking at the room that had been a miracle of organization before the two of them had happened to it yesterday.

They had not worried about being either tidy or organized when they had moved boxes, furniture, and bins until they'd gotten to the grimoires yesterday. Then, wanting to get the books somewhere safe, they'd shoved everything back in with more haste than order. There was a pile of loose stuff, towels and clothing mostly, near the door where they had emptied boxes and bags to carry the grimoires in.

"How do you want to do this?" Tag asked.

"Can you find magic that a witch has tried to hide?" Charles asked. He had hunted with Tag before—Tag was very nearly the best tracker in the pack. But Charles hadn't had the opportunity to look for magic with him. Da didn't let Tag off pack land very often. And very few witches made it onto pack land.

Tag smiled. "My specialty." He tapped his nose. "What are we looking for?"

"I can make guesses about spellcrafted things, but I'm not a trained witch," Charles said. "I don't want to leave anything that could hurt someone."

"I can't tell anything other than it's been witched," Tag agreed. "So we need to take anything with a hint of magic and sort it out later." He looked into the depths of the unit and said, "At least she was a white witch—we aren't likely to run into anything too awful."

Charles couldn't help giving him an ironic look.

Tag shrugged. "Had enough horrible for seven lifetimes," he said. "I don't like adding anything to it unless I have to."

They worked in silence. Tag wasn't naturally quiet, but he was a little afraid of him, Charles knew. That was all right. His reputation, even among his own pack, was another weapon that Charles could use. And Tag was not wrong to be afraid.

Charles had paid for the entire contents of the storage locker, but he had told the manager that once they had gone through everything for what they wanted, he was welcome to sell the remainder. Charles had thought at first that they had been lucky, given that the check was six months old, that the manager hadn't already garage-saled or auctioned off the contents.

Then he'd shown them the locker. The manager hadn't even been able to get his hand near the lock. Charles had managed it, using the manager's key. Charles sent the unhappy manager, who had hoped to get a look at the contents of the unit, back to his offices before dealing with Carrie's spells so they could open the door safely. Working with her magic, and seeing how she'd dealt with Daniel Erasmus, had made Charles move from respect for her to outright liking.

Going through the unit now—without the driving need to pin down the grimoires—only reinforced his opinion. He didn't know if he'd have liked her if he'd met her in person—he liked very few people.

But her magic reminded him of the computer code written back in the early days, when memory space was at a premium. Programmers back then created elegant script without a wasted symbol to complete the necessary task. Carrie hadn't had a lot of power, but she'd made good use of what she did have.

Not that he knew how witchcraft worked—he wasn't a witch by

anything except raw ability. His father had offered to teach him once, but that offer had been full of such . . . horrific hidden emotions that even as a child he had known to refuse. He couldn't have reproduced Carrie Green's work, but he could feel its delicacy.

"Here," called Tag.

Charles found him crouched over a plastic bin filled with smaller boxes. He held one of the boxes in his hand and offered it to Charles.

The box was lined with silk and filled with dozens of charms. Handmade bracelets and necklaces crafted from inexpensive wooden beads. Each one marked with a paper tag that read *Health* and *$15*.

Together he and Tag sorted through the boxes of charms. *Health*, *Joy*, and *Luck* accounted for all but two of the boxes. One of those boxes held a single necklace, a jade bead strung on a silver chain. *Protection from Evil* had a price tag of two thousand dollars. And unlike the smaller charms, this one held real power. Made, he thought, after Carrie had been given more power by the Singer. He couldn't be sure that it was labeled correctly, but her magic had an honest feel about it. He supposed that this necklace was imbued with the same magic as whatever she'd had that kept her grandfather from torturing her for her power. It wasn't that one—Underwood had said it had been made with moonstone, and this necklace felt unused.

The final box held a bone shard strung on leather. Its label read *Death*. There was no price. He thought at first it was a murder weapon. But there was no feeling of darkness to the magic.

"Don't touch that," said Tag. "It's a cyanide pill."

"She didn't wear it," murmured Charles. "Unless she made a second one."

"It's not the kind of thing you'd make two of," Tag said. "One is

useful, but you can't commit suicide twice. She left it here in the end.
I hope she didn't regret that."

"I thought you said you could detect witchcraft, but you didn't
know anything about it?" Charles asked.

Tag shrugged. "Maybe I picked up a thing or two along the way.
But it's not anything like vast knowledge."

Outside of those two boxes, none of the charms would have been
enough to get anyone into trouble. Even taken together, there was no
harm in them. The purpose of each was very carefully set, and they
would have been impossible to use additively. One charm for good
health was as effective as wearing sixteen at the same time. It wasn't
Carrie's doing—it was just the nature of this kind of charm.

They could have left the bin, minus the two small boxes, to the
storage manager's care without worry. But after exchanging a brief
look with Charles, Tag moved it into the pile of things to take with
them. Charles wasn't sure what tipped the balance for Tag, but
Charles didn't want Carrie's careful work to go to people who would
not appreciate it.

Anna showed up, parking the SUV in front of the next unit over
because they had filled the available space in front of Carrie's unit
with approximately half the contents of her locker. Anna looked tired,
and the expression on her face when she got out of the rig made him
open his arms.

She walked into them and buried her face in his shoulder and
relaxed against him.

"She didn't know," she told him, her voice muffled. "They figured
out she was pregnant after we left them yesterday—apparently she'd
gone to see a doctor about her unusual tiredness and upset digestive

tract. On the good side, her wife now believes that Sissy didn't cheat on her and then lie about it. That is, believe me, the only good side."

"Abortion?" Charles suggested.

Anna shook her head. "Apparently Dr. Connors has protested and fought for reproductive rights for others, but finds the idea personally unacceptable. Tanya disagrees. I found them fighting about one thing and left them fighting about another. If they aren't careful, this will destroy them."

She stepped back and gave him a smile that was a little thin around the edges. "And there's nothing more I can do to affect that one way or the other." She rubbed her upper arms and said briskly, "Have you found anything interesting?"

She looked over at the smallish pile of things he and Tag had set aside and let out a pleased sound. She knelt by the antique spool cabinet. It was about two feet square and a little older than Charles was, clearly a family heirloom. It had six drawers, and Anna opened each one and took in the spools of thread set on individual dowels— organized by color, black in the top drawer working down to white.

"Is it the thread or the cabinet that is magical?" Anna asked, brow furrowed. "Even calling on my wolf, I can't tell for sure."

"Both, we think," said Charles. "But neither Tag nor I have a clue what they would be used for."

Her fingers traced the bird's-eye maple appreciatively, but she said, "What happens if Carrie wants her stuff back? Or one of her relatives?"

"I don't think Da will agree to give back the grimoires," Charles said in what he was fairly sure was a massive understatement. Anna's quick grin told him she agreed with him.

"As to the rest . . ." He looked at the spool cabinet, then shrugged.

"If she is not dead, we'll give it back. If she is dead and there is a will—we are not thieves. Anything that isn't dangerous we'll hand over."

She listened to his tone as much as his words—that was one of her gifts. "You don't think that there's anyone."

He shook his head. "It feels like she was alone." He tried to explain why he felt that way, but failed.

"Other than Daniel Green," said Anna.

"We wouldn't give him anything," Charles said. "But I don't think that will be an issue."

"I wonder," said Anna thoughtfully, "do you think that Carrie knew what she was doing when she entrusted him into the loving arms of the witches who run Angel Hills?"

"Yes," said Charles. Someone as organized and thorough as the woman whose life he'd been invading was not the kind of person who would make a mistake on that scale. He wondered what Daniel Green had done to his granddaughter.

"He said she was Wiccan," Anna said. "How does leaving him there jibe with 'An it harm none'?"

"Even the most peaceable people have their limits," Charles suggested. "And putting him there certainly reduced the harm that *he* could cause."

"You like her," Anna said.

He considered that. "I like what I know about her."

"You gonna sit around, or are you gonna work?" asked Tag, hauling a wingback chair out to the bigger pile.

Anna snorted a laugh at Tag, so Brother Wolf didn't remind Tag who gave the orders.

"Sissy translated the letter her father wrote. She said there were a few differences between the letters, but most of it was word for word." She pulled a couple of pieces of paper out of her back pocket and handed them to Charles. Tag took up a position where he could read them, too.

Dear Dr. Connors the Younger,

My daughter. So much has gone wrong I don't know how to tell you. I don't even know if you'll get this letter, but I live in hope.

First, I love you. I take joy in every day because I had you, your brother, and your mother in my life. I do not think that I will survive this coming night.

It discovered that we had broken our bargain, before I knew there was a bargain to be broken. Remember, if something is too good to be true—it is a lie. Do not come here.

I have not spoken to you about the Singer, have I? I suppose that must mean that I understood there was something wrong before I admitted it to myself.

We tried to kill ourselves, we tried to kill each other, and it would not let us. Nor will it let us leave.

I woke up this morning and I looked for your mother because I thought that it was the morning after we got married. I looked for her for an hour before the Sign Maker found me. He is deaf and it seems to make him immune to most of what the Singer has been doing to us. The Opera Singer has been crying for two days because she thinks that her daughter died today instead of twenty years ago.

It feeds upon music, but I think it also feeds upon emotions. I don't think it eats memories, because we wouldn't get our memories back if it could feed upon them. And mostly we get our memories back.

We all know there are black witches here now—but we don't remember them.

Sometimes some of us remember that it plans on killing us when it's done playing. We can't prevent that, but we need to prepare. We, Sign Maker and I, killed all of the animals last night because once we are dead, they will suffer. The coven lay wards around the bodies and we mourned. I don't think there was anyone there who did not wish to trade places with those animals.

I don't think we will meet again in this life, my daughter. I wish you joy and happiness. I am so proud to call you my daughter. So proud of the man my son is, too. Please let him know in case I don't get a chance to write to him tomorrow.

With love,
Dr. Connors the Elder, aka Dad

"It would have been nice if he'd spelled everything out," Charles murmured.

"At least we know what happened to the pets," Tag replied.

"Has Mercy called you back?" Anna asked.

"She says she'll try, but Coyote doesn't carry a cell phone and is usually disinclined to be useful."

"So no help there," translated Tag.

"Not yet," Charles said as he read the letter a second time, looking for anything that might be of use. "Mercy will figure out how to get in touch with him. After that, it's up to Coyote."

He folded the pieces of paper, and, as Anna had, he put them in his back pocket. "We should get back to work here."

"Is there anything I can do?" Anna asked.

Charles shook his head. "Carrie is pretty good at hiding her magic. I don't think you'd be able to find anything unless you changed to wolf."

"I can't open boxes or move them easily in wolf form," Anna said regretfully. "There's a pizza place down the block. How about I get some food for us?"

Tag staggered over—a huge old cauldron over his shoulder—and dropped to his knees in front of Anna. "Food?" he said in a quavery voice. "Food for us, mistress?"

He never played the fool around Charles unless Anna was present. Charles couldn't decide if it was because Tag only played like this in front of Anna or if it was because he figured Charles was less dangerous if Anna was in the vicinity.

She laughed at him. "Two large pizzas, loaded," she said. She rose on her tiptoes to kiss Charles and climbed back into the Suburban.

Tag waited until she was backing up before popping to his feet without effort. The cauldron was doubtless heavy—anything cast iron and that big had to be—but Tag was a werewolf.

"Magic?" asked Charles.

Tag gave the cauldron a surprised look, as if he'd forgotten he had it on his shoulder. "No—though it's old," he said, and carried it over to the proper pile. He set it down and contemplated it.

"Everyone should have a proper cauldron," he said, picking it up and putting it in their keep pile.

"You want to cook beans over a campfire?" Charles asked.

"Was that a joke?" asked Tag, sounding truly dumbfounded.

"Would I tease you?" Charles said, picking up a box of things that were not magic and hauling them to the pile of boxes they were just going to have to carry back.

The freshness of the breeze caught Brother Wolf's attention, and Charles looked up into the sky with a frown at the gathering clouds. "I hope the rain holds off until we get this done."

Tag glanced up, too. "Not supposed to rain, according to my weather app."

Charles said, "It's going to rain. Help me get the dining table out."

It wasn't heavy, but it was awkward. It marked the edge of how far they'd gotten in their hunt for what turned out to be the grimoires. When they'd refilled the unit, he and Tag had put the table over the top of where the grimoires had been. They'd found the books in the center of the unit, surrounded by a pair of room dividers and a chalk circle.

It had been a good circle, competently drawn—as far as Charles could judge. It wasn't a pattern that he'd seen before, but the intent had been obvious. Such a circle should have cut off the effect of so much magic—but he'd felt the grimoires when he'd stepped foot on the ground at the storage center. He didn't think it was a problem with the magic Carrie had used, only the length of time since she'd renewed her protections.

They had taken out one of the dividers and set it aside but left the second one up. Now Charles took down the second one—and found himself confronting a small open area that someone had clearly set up as an office.

Had there been a path from the door to here before they had destroyed Carrie's organization? He couldn't say one way or the other. He inhaled and caught a hint of vanilla and also a woman's scent. Carrie Green had definitely used this.

It was an area about five feet square, with a six-foot-tall bookshelf filled with books shoved in every which way, in direct contrast to the order Carrie had imposed upon her storage unit. But the battered old Steelcase desk—a relic of the Cold War era, complete with government serial plate along the edge of the desktop—was tidy enough.

On the upper left corner of the desk was a black coffee cup with *Witch* scrawled across it in red letters. It held two pens, a pencil, and a highlighter. On the lower left corner was a lined notebook. When he opened it, it proved to be blank, though roughly half of the sheets had been torn out.

On the upper right corner of the desk were three books that had never been commercially produced. He held a hand over them before he picked up the first one. It looked to be a handwritten diary, but he couldn't find the date because it was in Russian—or some other Cyrillic tongue. There were five bookmarks that each marked a passage that Carrie had highlighted.

"Do you read Russian?" Charles asked Tag, who had paused in his own work to look at Carrie's workspace.

"No," he said. "But the next one down is in English."

And so was the third one. Charles handed one to Tag and took the other. Charles's looked to be a detailed study of the deaths of various fae. It didn't appear to be a fae-hunter's diary but a scholarly study based mostly upon folklore. The methods of killing (or manner of dying) were all highlighted.

"How to kill a fae," Charles told Tag. "Though I didn't see anything that someone who wasn't armed with a supernatural weapon could manage."

"Her bookmarks in mine are all about how to kill vampires," said Tag. "Some of the methods I know are effective. Some of them I've never heard of. But there are enough here that I personally know do *not* work that it might as well be a study on how to get yourself killed."

He pulled out a folded sheet of lined paper that had been tucked in the back and showed it to Charles.

Back-slanted script, messy but easily readable, covered the page.

Interesting that wooden stake kills vampire when steel or silver does not. What is the difference in the materials? Silver is purifying—which is why it works on werewolves. So why doesn't it work on vampires? Wood doesn't work on werewolves. Why doesn't it work on werewolves?

Why does nothing not magical work on all fae? Not even cold iron.

Then in overlarge letters, as if in frustration:

How do we kill it? Will it stay dead? Emma thinks the Singer is like some of the Native American entities. In the stories, Coyote comes back if he is killed. How do we kill the Singer so he doesn't come back?

There was a lot of space, and then on the bottom were the words:

I figured it out. But do I have the courage? I don't know.

Anna drove up with pizza and water bottles—and when Charles kissed her mouth in thanks, she tasted like bubble gum. He pulled back and frowned at her.

"Bubble gum?"

She laughed. "While the pizza was cooking, I bought a snow cone." She gave Charles a smile. "But the reason I went there was to tell Zander I knew why his song sounded familiar."

They sat down at the dining table—it was handy—and ate.

"What song?" asked Tag.

"When I talked to Zander yesterday, he was playing guitar," she explained around a bite of hot pizza. "He was noodling around on a piece that sounded familiar to me—and he didn't know what it was, either, just something he was working on. You know how it is when you can't quite remember a song..."

Tag shook his head.

"And you know what it is now?" asked Charles. He was glad that the shadow of telling Dr. Connors what she was pregnant with had left Anna, even if he'd rather it hadn't been the pretty boy selling snow cones who'd accomplished that.

She laughed. "It is such a relief. It was the chord progression: D major, A major, B minor, F sharp minor . . ." She raised her eyebrows.

He closed his eyes and "heard" the progression in his head. "*Pachelbel's Canon*, among other songs," he said.

"And a dozen other songs at least," she agreed. To Tag she said, "It's one of those chord progressions that just sounds good—so it was stolen by a whole bunch of pop musicians. I have no idea what song Zander's mother sang to him—but I know Pachelbel." She mimicked playing the cello.

"Why didn't you pick it up sooner?" asked Tag. "It's mainly a cello piece, right?"

"For sure," she said. She shook her head. "I have no idea why I couldn't figure it out." She looked at the unit and asked, "Are you going to be able to get all the way through that before the rain hits?"

Charles said "Yes" and Tag said "No" at the same time.

"What he means," said Tag, "is that we aren't going to keep going through it. We're putting it all back. There's too much to put in the SUV. We found a cache of historical diaries written by the Green family of witches. They aren't magic per se, but we aren't leaving them for anyone. We'll get a crew in here to clear out the whole unit—take 'em home and sort them out there."

Charles nodded. "I'll pay to keep the locker and we'll take what we've already sorted out with us now. Once we do that, there isn't anything with enough magic left here to draw predators."

Tag tilted his head and then looked at Anna. "Do you know that he doesn't talk unless you're present?"

She laughed, and the sound made Charles and Brother Wolf happy. He wasn't sure he'd known what happy had felt like before they'd found her.

Anna and Charles went to the office to find the manager while Tag continued repacking the storage unit. The manager was not pleased to learn they had decided to keep the contents—but he was too intimidated by Charles to argue. Charles further softened the blow by paying him six months of rent, sixty dollars (refundable) for the key Charles had been using, and a hundred dollars for the manager's trouble.

"Bribery is bad," chided Anna as they walked back to Tag.

"Bribery will keep him happy and out of the storage unit," said Charles.

Anna shook her head. "I am saddened by your innocent belief that a hundred dollars would keep him out if he was the type of man who would steal things from one of the storage lockers."

Charles smiled, not unhappy to be caught out. "Then let's just say that I was sorry I got his hopes up."

They rounded the corner of the row of units where Carrie's was, and Anna stumbled to a halt.

"Anna?"

She didn't look at him but stared down the gravel road at Tag, who was loading his cauldron into the SUV. She reached out and grabbed Charles's arm.

Honestly alarmed now, Charles said, "Anna? What's wrong?"

She shivered, took a deep breath, and said, "Maybe a bit of a panic attack." She took her hand off him and put it into her pocket, where a stray piece of paper rustled unhappily. "I'm glad I'm not going back to Wild Sign."

"Anna?"

She shook her head and gave him a wobbly smile. "I think I'm just on edge."

They finished packing the storage unit, and Anna seemed to recover from whatever had bothered her. She teased Tag about his cauldron as she helped them get the last of Carrie's things back into the unit. By the time they were headed for the hotel, Charles was convinced that Anna was fine.

Tag and Anna carried in the items they'd collected from the storage unit and Charles added them to the collection of grimoires. He sent the other two out for a walk while he reinstated his safeguards. It was more difficult than it had been the last time, which he found worrying.

They are bored, said Brother Wolf in answer to Charles's silent grumbles.

"Who?" asked Charles.

The grimoires, said Brother Wolf. *They want to come out and play.*

Charles made very sure his wards were effective.

* * *

THE BED SQUEAKED again and Anna giggled. She hadn't noticed that the bed squeaked last night, but once she noticed, she couldn't quit hearing it. After a moment—during which she failed to control herself—Charles rolled away. She worried for a minute that she'd offended him. A giggling partner is hardly flattering when you are in the middle of lovemaking. But then he reached out and pulled her all the way on top of him, while she still snickered helplessly. He held out until the bed squeaked again, and then he was laughing, too.

Eventually she caught her breath. Charles's laughter was rarer than blue diamonds and more precious. She wouldn't have felt prouder of herself if she'd won Olympic gold.

She crawled up his body while he was still laughing and said, "I guess I can deal with three in the bed. Me." She gave him an open-mouthed kiss and felt the laughter flee his body in favor of something more urgent.

"You." She undulated. At the increased pressure, every muscle in his body tightened, and she felt the joy of being desired by him.

She almost forgot where she was going with this, but managed to hold on to her self-control. She leaned down and dropped her hips abruptly. He gasped—and the bed let out a shrill complaint. "And the bed."

She sank limply to his chest and started giggling again.

"Fair enough," he growled, rolling over, but there was a quiet joy in his eyes that made her want to bask in his gaze.

"But," he said, "I draw the line at three of us." As if to prove his words a lie, his eyes brightened with Brother Wolf's laughing spirit.

And then Charles made sure that Anna didn't have the breath to tease—or, after a minute or two, the desire to do anything but soften for him. He was a man who knew what to do with hands and mouth and skin—and he was not satisfied until she had much better things to pay attention to than a squeaking bed.

The end result left her limp, facedown on the bed, her hand in his, and the bed squeaking softly with the force of their breathing.

"You," she said, hearing the roughness of the past few minutes in her voice, "are dangerous."

"How so?" he asked—which was a ridiculous response from the Marrok's hit man, possibly the most feared and dangerous werewolf in North America.

She couldn't help but laugh again as she rolled over—and the bed squeaking didn't help with that. She had to let go of his hand to complete the maneuver, and felt ridiculously bereft until she rolled up against his damp side.

"To my heart," she said seriously. "To my soul."

He pulled her tight against him. "I will defend your heart and your soul with everything in me."

She felt her eyelids close even as her mouth turned up. "I know," she said. "Me, too."

"Even if you insist on inviting squeaky beds to our lovemaking," he murmured as she drifted off.

THE WIND WHISTLED outside, a forerunner to what felt like a fearsome storm. The energy overhead was wild and untamed. There would be lightning and thunder with this storm, she thought.

It was time.

She slipped out of bed, half aware of the big hand sliding off her hip. She felt hollow, as if there were nothing inside her except the music.

"Not *Pachelbel's Canon*," she said out loud. It felt like it was supposed to be defiant. But no one answered.

She dressed, not worrying about noise. No one would hear her. She wasn't sure how she knew that, but it didn't matter. Nothing mattered except that it was time for her to leave.

She pulled on clothing appropriate for a long hike in the mountains: jeans, hiking boots, shirt—and over that a red flannel shirt that was way too big for her and smelled like home. She fished the keys out of her purse but left the purse itself on the desk. She closed the hotel room door behind her with a feeling of accomplishment.

She got into the SUV and it purred to life. She smiled happily and petted the dashboard. How lovely to have the means at her disposal to complete her task. The smile stayed on her lips as she drove into Happy Camp.

She pulled over at the snow cone stand, which was dark and locked. But that was okay, too. She just had to wait a bit.

He knocked at her window and she opened the door.

"Hello, darling," said Zander, leaning over to kiss her mouth, one hand at the back of her neck.

That made her stomach tighten—and not in a good way. She stiffened under his hold.

"Shh," he urged, and kissed her again.

It still felt wrong.

"We'll give it a little time, shall we?" he suggested, and she could have wept in gratitude. She wanted to make him happy. She just . . . she just needed time.

He released her and gave her an odd smile. "Anna," he said. "How old are you?"

That was a stupid question, she thought. Who greets someone with a how-old-are-you?

"Jailbait," she said primly, to punish him.

He laughed. He had a beautiful laugh. She liked to make . . . well, it had to be him, right? She liked to make . . . people laugh.

"How old is that?" he asked.

"Seventeen," she said.

His eyes were soft and deep. Gentle. He was everything she'd ever dreamed of, she thought. Why was there some part of her that wanted to run? He wouldn't hurt her. He wasn't the kind of man to be afraid of. Not like . . . She couldn't quite complete that thought, and it made her worry.

"Of course," he said, reaching out to smooth her forehead with a thumb. It seemed as though her worries fled before his touch like birds flushing before a wolf. "Jailbait indeed."

"How old are you?" she asked, because turnabout was fair play.

"Older than you," he said with a wry smile. "Here, move over. I'm doing the driving tonight."

She climbed over the center console obediently and put the seat belt on. She pressed her face into the leather and inhaled. It smelled of mint and musk and . . . something familiar. Something safe.

"What are you doing?" he asked her, a smile in his voice.

"It smells good," she said, feeling as though she was being held, warmth against a storm. She pulled up the flannel shirt and found herself huddling down deep. Some part of her was lying low, and that part thought that the shirt was a way to hide.

"Are you cold?" asked Zander. He turned up the heat and then started forward without waiting for her answer. "I thought you might bring something waterproof. It's going to rain tonight."

"I don't mind the rain," she said truthfully, pressing her cheek against the window and staring out into the darkness. Her right leg began bouncing with her growing agitation. It was probably the storm that had her tense. There was such energy in the air.

The dash lights hollowed out his cheeks and hid his eyes. For a moment he looked like a stranger. She averted her eyes and saw the big Sasquatch statue.

"Do you think," she said, because it felt like the right question, "that Sasquatches are as big as that statue?"

"I've never seen one," he said shortly. He lied.

"I have." Which was a lie, too, right? But it didn't feel like a lie. She had never been in the mountains of the Pacific Northwest before.

What was she doing here? In this car with this beautiful stranger? She made a sound like a whine. There was something wrong. She wanted . . . not her dad. She wanted . . . She reached for the door handle, though they were going faster than the thirty-five-miles-per-hour speed limit.

He started singing. There were words to his song, but they weren't in English. Or any other language she'd ever heard.

"Not Pachelbel," she said as her hand dropped away from the door.

He didn't quit singing, but she could hear the smile in his voice.

No. This song that he had been working on did not have Pachelbel's chord progression at all. She wasn't sure why she'd been so certain that it had. Her hands moved, as if she were trying to play on her cello, though she wasn't certain if she wanted to play a harmony to his song—or Pachelbel.

Bereft of cello, she hummed its part in *Pachelbel's Canon*—which was boring. She had done it so often that she felt as though the notes were engraved on her bones. People liked to listen to songs they knew, her orchestra teacher used to say. We'll give our audience a few favorites among the unfamiliar pieces.

Everyone knew Pachelbel.

Zander stopped singing. "Anna, that's rude," he chided her. "Don't sing something else while someone is singing."

The tone of his voice set her back up. She had to remind herself that he was right. She pressed her hand on the glass as they drove past a hotel/campground on the river, and felt a sharp longing. She wished that she were sitting on a rock watching the river rush by instead of encased in this car heading into the darkness. It felt suffocatingly like the blackness was going to reach out and consume her.

She wasn't afraid of the dark anymore, she reminded herself. *I've met plenty of scary things in the light.* She heard that last part ringing in her ears in her own voice. As if she'd said it more than once.

But she had been afraid of the dark when she was seventeen. She was seventeen now, right? She couldn't remember when she'd learned to love the night.

Zander was singing again, and this time she politely hummed along with him. She preferred Pachelbel to the new tune, which was weird. There was nothing wrong with Zander's song, and, like many cellists, she was really very tired of Pachelbel.

But the music was soothing, and humming it made her feel better. When Zander quit singing, he asked, "So, what is your favorite subject in school?"

As she answered, she forgot that she couldn't remember how she happened to be traveling in the dark with a stranger who didn't feel like a stranger. Or maybe with someone familiar who felt like a stranger.

She was seventeen and headed to Northwestern in the fall, the daughter of a lawyer. Other than her mother's death, nothing bad had ever happened to her.

That was an odd thought, too. Why did she think something bad was going to happen to her quite soon?

"Tell me about your favorite family vacation," Zander asked. Before she could answer, he muttered, "You are obstinate, aren't you? I've never had this much trouble, especially not with someone my father has already caught. It's like everything just wants to flow off the top."

"Like an iceberg," agreed Anna. "There's a lot more under the surface that you can't see."

"Like what?" he asked.

But she couldn't answer him. It was a gut feeling. As if his music *should* slide off her. She had a big hollowness inside her head that felt denser than hollowness should feel. Something important was hidden there, something with fur and sharp teeth. She felt herself reaching toward that—

"You were going to tell me about your favorite family vacation," Zander prompted, putting a hand on her thigh. Warmth seeped into her flesh from that hand.

"Yes," she said hesitantly. "Um, I was about six and my brother was eight—"

And as the SUV turned off the paved road and onto a dirt track, she was lost in the feeling of lake water on bare feet and how her brother had tried and failed to teach her to skip rocks on the last vacation they'd taken as a family of four.

"That's it," Zander murmured. "Remember."

Something pulled Anna's attention away from the memory. A tug in her chest. She brought a hand up to rub at the spot, but the pressure didn't go away.

The SUV bounced and jostled over the ground, sides and underside scraping in such a way that she was glad it was this SUV and not . . . not some other beloved vehicle. Some thoughts just slid away from her in a way that was distracting.

She caught the reflection of a wild animal's eyes just past Zander's shoulder. She lost track of her family's vacation entirely and focused her attention on the darkness of the forest.

"Wolf," she said.

Zander glanced quickly in the direction she was looking in, but he had to return his attention to the road. They had already passed the place where the wolf had been standing anyway.

"I don't think so, not here," he said with assurance. "There is a pack a fair bit south of here, and there are some in southern Oregon. But not here. You probably saw a coyote. Size can be deceptive in the dark."

The wolf was gone from view, but Anna could feel her presence. She pressed a hand to her chest where that certainty lived. There was a wolf out there—and she was following them. It should have frightened her, but like the flannel shirt she wore, it gave her an obscure sense of comfort.

Pack.

The whispered word echoed out of that inaccessible hollowness. But she didn't know its import. Pack what? Her carry gun was in its usual holster. Was that what that inner voice had meant?

She didn't know how to shoot a gun.

"Anna," Zander's voice called her attention away from thoughts that made her worry.

"Are we there yet?" she asked cheerfully, in an effort to thank him for making her feel better.

LEAH WAS TIRED. It had dawned on her, not two hours after she'd started out for Wild Sign, that she should have taken the car. No one would have thought it unusual if she'd gone for a drive—and she'd have gotten here a lot easier.

But the need to move, the sheer strength of the summoning, had been so overwhelming. One moment she had been out running down the trail of a rabbit, and the next she'd changed direction and loped toward Wild Sign. That wasn't the name she'd known that place by, of course. And it wasn't exactly in the same location, either—though the amphitheater had been familiar. But she couldn't remember what it had been, so she held on to the designations she was given.

She was hungry, too. She'd eaten such things as had come her way on her run, mostly squirrels and rabbits, though she'd driven a coyote off of a deer and feasted for a half hour, letting her body recoup its strength. Most of the time, aided by the supernatural nature of werewolf endurance and speed, and her ability to draw upon the pack energies, she'd spent running flat out.

She knew that she could not, should not, arrive this tired. She needed to find a safe place to rest for a few hours, some food to eat, before she got any closer. She paused next to a fallen tree with a hollow under it.

She had started to burrow into the space when she became aware of the sound of an engine. Abruptly reversing direction, she shook off the dirt and looked toward the noise.

She watched the headlights bounce off trees and rocks, lighting a rough track she hadn't noticed. The engine sounded familiar, one of the pack vehicles. Charles had taken that Suburban.

She started off toward where her trail and the track the SUV was taking would intersect. As she approached her chosen vantage point, she was still debating whether or not to approach Charles. She closed her eyes as the SUV came over a rise, shining bright lights that would ruin her night vision. But the track dropped right afterward.

As soon as the lights dimmed, she opened her eyes in time to get a good look inside the cab.

She'd expected to see Charles driving, because Tag would already have wrecked on that track, and Anna would be creeping along at a quarter of the speed the SUV was making. But the face that the dash lights illuminated behind the wheel belonged to none of them.

She froze in her tracks, her eyes briefly meeting Anna's before the SUV's direction made it impossible to see anything inside the vehicle.

She heard herself whine, though it wasn't an intentional sound.

She had seen the face of the driver—and she knew that the man it belonged to was nearly two hundred years dead. There was something scratching in the memories she no longer had.

She took a deep breath and cut across country to the location that she could not have pinpointed on a map but her wolf had no trouble pointing her nose toward. That would be where he was taking her.

Where her father had taken her.

Where she had been summoned to return to. Where *he* waited. This chapter in her life would finally have a proper ending. She wasn't sure if the thought terrified her or left her exulted.

* * *

TAG WOKE FOR what felt like the hundredth time that night. He had slept fine out in the woods, but it had been a long, long while since he'd tried to sleep in a hotel next to a highway. Or anywhere the sound of a car was more than an occasional irritant, for that matter.

He rearranged his pillow in preparation to go back to sleep, but unease raised the hairs on the back of his neck and he reconsidered.

There was an odd feeling to this waking. As if he'd been very deeply asleep when the rumble of the semi's engine had broken into his slumber. He didn't sleep that deeply unless he was in his own home, and seldom even there. He would never have surrendered his defenses in a strange hotel room next to a weird-ass hoard of grimoires.

He inhaled and caught a trace of magic that seemed to him to be oozing through the wall—the connecting wall between his room and the room where the grimoires ruled. That was a little weird.

They all knew, the pack, that Charles could use magic when it suited him. Though not a one of them had the cheek to ask him about it. His didn't smell like witchcraft—and this didn't, either.

Tag was positive that it wasn't coming from the grimoires. That left Charles. Maybe he'd worked some magic to allow Anna to sleep without nightmares. Strange that it had seeped through the grimoires' hotel room and into Tag's, though. Charles usually had better control than that.

The magic made him restless. He was not inclined to try to sleep when someone was trying to make him sleep—even if the magic had not been aimed at him. He got up and dressed, feeling like a cat with its hair brushed backward. It was probably the result of resisting the spell, but it left him unhappy.

He was going to give Charles a bad time for not having better control of his magic. He snorted, aware that the chances of that actually happening were slight. He was more at ease with the Marrok's son than he'd ever been. With Anna around, the bastard was darn near human. But Tag wasn't stupid enough to tug that tail anyway.

Not unless he got in a mood.

Getting in a mood was how he'd ended up in Bran Cornick's pack for the Disorderly and Dangerous in the first place. His last pack had annoyed him . . . he didn't remember exactly what they'd done, something that had set off his inner berserker. But unusually (it was thankfully the only occasion his berserker had acted this way), it hadn't ever ratcheted up to killing-spree level, not quite. Instead, the mood had hung around for days. Maybe weeks. Time did funny things when his berserker was out.

He remembered challenging the first wolf who annoyed him— and killing him. And another. And another. Until he was going to have to make up his mind if he wanted to be Alpha pretty damn soon—if there were any more wolves left to rule. He'd killed seven wolves. He had disliked all but one of them, and he still felt guilty about that one.

And then Charles had come and told him to stand down. Tag had tried to eat his face instead—and found himself in the battle of his life. And Charles did not let him land a blow with his (mighty) claws or close his jaws on anything but air. He just put him down and pinned him over and over. Eventually Tag had sweated out whatever had been keeping him at a fever pitch, and when that happened, he'd been so tired he hadn't gotten up again when Charles released him.

When Tag had woken up, Bran had been there with an offer of sanctuary. Bran had even engineered the move of Tag's family, a few of the descendants of his sister's children's children. The caveat was that he would have to stay in pack territory unless he had permission to be elsewhere. He'd found that acceptable. A relief even, because what if after he'd finished the nasty pack of dishonorable werewolves, he moved on to killing innocents?

That could not happen in the Marrok's pack. Because Charles was in the pack, and Charles had been the demon who had taken on his berserker wolf and pinned him as if he were a child. No one else had ever defeated Tag when his berserker had the upper hand. He'd seen Charles fight now and again over the years—and he knew something that most people did not. In most fights, that old wolf didn't even break a sweat.

This trip had eased something in their relationship, but Tag wasn't sure it was a good thing. Tag had not gone full berserker since he'd joined Bran's pack. He didn't want to be friends with Charles. He wanted Charles to be the demon wolf who would keep Tag from doing anything terrible.

His mind kept trying to put pictures of the terrible things he'd done as a berserker in his head, so Tag started out of his hotel room. He'd run down to the river and then see if he needed to continue to run.

He was so intent on his aim, he almost missed it. He'd gotten halfway to the river before turning back to see what was nagging at him. And that was when he realized the Suburban was gone.

CHARLES WOKE UP with the splash of cold water on his face.

He blinked at Tag, who stood in the doorway of the hotel room, an empty glass in his hand.

"I couldn't wake you up any other way," he said, taking a step back. He grimaced. "Smells like magic in here."

Charles sat up and swung his feet to the floor. Tag wasn't wrong. The room reeked of magic, a cloying and smothering thing that kept trying to run over his thoughts and send him back to sleep.

Charles, using the time-honored tradition of "hot and cold," located the source in the pocket of the slacks Anna had worn yesterday. He extracted a small, crumpled piece of paper with a series of runes drawn on it, and shielded himself the best that he could from the immediate need to lie down and sleep again.

Charles closed his eyes and pulled on his grandfather's teachings. Breathing deeply, he made a fist around the paper for a beat of five. At the end of the count, he opened his eyes and his fist—which now held a handful of dust. Clarity of thought returned to him, along with an icy realization.

Anna was gone.

He dressed rapidly, assessing the room as he did so. She'd taken the flannel shirt he'd worn yesterday when he and Tag had cleaned out the storage unit. She'd taken her hiking boots and her carry gun. That didn't make him feel better at all. He walked to the bed and put his hand on the side of the mattress she had been occupying, but it was cold to the touch.

"What woke you up?" Charles asked.

"The sounds of the night are different here," Tag said. "A semi drove down the highway and I couldn't get back to sleep. I decided to go for a walk by the river, but when I got outside—the Suburban was gone. I knocked on your door and you didn't answer, though I knew damned well that you were in here. And that Anna was not." He growled. "I should have noticed when the Suburban started up. I think that whatever kept you sleeping seeped through the walls and got me, too."

Charles nodded and got out his laptop. "The SUV is LoJacked. I'll get someone working on locating it—I'm not up to such delicate work right now." Brother Wolf was frantic, and keeping him under control was an effort. "Could you see about finding us an alternate vehicle? Leave a card and we'll make it right." He thought about the hiking shoes. "Make it a vehicle that can go wherever the SUV could go. I think she's headed into the mountains. Back to Wild Sign."

Seeing the gleeful joy that lit Tag's face, Charles felt a moment of remorse for whoever had the best off-road-capable vehicle on the property. He grabbed his laptop and opened it up, then picked up his phone.

"Ben," he said. "I have a vehicle I need you to locate. It's LoJacked. ASAP."

BY THE TIME Tag drove around the corner with an early-seventies British Land Rover in pristine condition, Charles had the SUV's location—and the path it had taken to get wherever it was. The beacon transmitted to his phone along with his current location, so they could tell when they were getting close.

He climbed in the passenger seat and buckled in. "I need you to drive," he told Tag. "If you wreck this vehicle, it could mean Anna's life."

Tag nodded and put his foot down on the accelerator, heading toward the place where they'd camped that first night, though from the information Charles was getting from Ben, they would be turning off the road well before they made it to the campgrounds. Charles took the opportunity to call his da.

The cell phone went to voice mail. He left a very brief message and then called the house.

"Bran's phone," Asil drawled. "If this is anyone except Charles calling at this hour, I recommend hanging up now before I figure out who it is. If this is Charles, your father left for your location about two hours ago by air. About five minutes after I arrived from Billings."

"Thank you," said Charles. "If Da can't get in touch with us, we are on our way into the mountains, probably heading toward Wild Sign. Tag and I were spelled asleep and Anna took off in the Suburban. Presumably the Singer's doing. If he can't contact me, because cell reception is likely to be spotty in the wilderness"—which was one of the reasons why Tag was driving; when they inevitably lost contact, Charles wanted to be watching the location data so he'd have the most up-to-date information—"have him contact Ben Shaw, who has a LoJack trace on the Suburban that Anna took."

"Got it," said Asil briskly. "Will he know how to contact Ben Shaw?"

"Ben's in Adam Hauptman's pack," Charles said.

"Ah," said Asil. "That Ben." Then, with a fine tension in his voice, he said, "If it has harmed our Anna, kill it."

"I would be grateful for any advice you might have toward that end," said Charles. "Sherwood Post failed to kill it. And the witches of Wild Sign think it's immortal."

"Is that all?" Asil said. "A wise man once told me that the only way to kill something immortal is to remind it what death is."

"Suggestions?"

Asil sighed heavily. "Alas, that wise man died before he told me more. Killed himself. Your da is bringing the sword he killed himself with."

"Jonesy's sword?"

"Yes," Asil confirmed.

Charles felt the first hint of optimism. That sword had already killed one immortal being; it might be well suited to killing another. Bless his da for farsightedness.

"ETA?" Charles asked.

"He wasn't sure. He's flying into Bend, where the Alpha has a helicopter."

"Fortune favors the foolish," murmured Tag from the driver's side. Then "Blast" as both he and Charles realized that they'd over-shot the turnoff.

Charles disconnected and helped Tag spot where Anna had left the highway as they crawled past the area a second time.

"Here," he said, pointing to where two tracks broke the sod off the highway. It wasn't any kind of official road. It looked more like a trail that off-roaders had built.

"Yeehaw," Tag said as they left the pavement. He showed his teeth in a hunter's smile. "This should be fun."

Charles helped guide while he thought about how to kill the Singer if his da didn't make it in time. As far as he was concerned, this second attack—*third?*—on Anna had signed its death warrant.

HE GOT THE Suburban stuck—high-centered on a rock. Anna was pretty sure she'd heard the oil pan go. Certainly she smelled motor oil as she got out.

Run, something inside her urged.

She knew she could outrun Zander in the dark, even on the side of a mountain that he appeared to be quite familiar with. She didn't know where that confidence came from. She'd quit track in elementary school in favor of private violin lessons. She wasn't . . . shouldn't be in shape for a race in the forest.

She looked down and had no trouble seeing the hard muscle on her arms that looked as though she'd been in training for the Olympics or something.

She deserved an Olympic medal.

She waited for the strange thought to go somewhere. When it didn't, she continued to take stock of her oddly alien body. She'd never been the kind of girl who obsessed about being in shape. But this wasn't just her arms. She could feel the strength in her legs. When she reached up to touch her biceps, she encountered hard flesh.

For an instant she smelled pine and felt the snow give under her as she ran in joyous abandon.

While she was still processing that, Zander's hand wrapped around her upper arm just above her own. Relief washed over her. She was safe with him.

Run.

12

It started to rain. A light pattering rain at first, blown a little by a breeze. But it wasn't long before the rain was pelting down and the wind was blowing so hard that Anna had trouble keeping her hair out of her face so she could see.

"Are you cold?" Zander asked, concerned. "You should have brought a jacket."

She pulled the now-wet flannel shirt around her protectively. "I'm fine," she said. And it was true. Though the rain was cold, it didn't seem to be chilling her as she would have expected.

"In Montana," she told Zander, "a storm this late in the fall would probably be a snowstorm, not a rainstorm. A little rain won't stop me."

And then she wondered why in the world she'd been talking about Montana. She'd never been to—

She had a sudden vision of looking at a magnificent snow-covered landscape, unfolding below her in shades of blue. Of the cold biting her nose and the snow squeaking under her snowshoes, sounding a little like bedsprings.

She stumbled to a halt. *Bedsprings.*

"Stop lollygagging," Zander said, smiling as he tugged on her arm. "We've got a few miles to go and we're only going to get wetter."

Zander seemed to have trouble seeing their path through the night-dark woods, stumbling over rocks and roots that Anna had no trouble with. She scrambled up a steep place in the trail, and waited at the top while he found his own path up.

"The last person I took up here was part mountain goat, too," he complained cheerfully. "I've spent my life climbing mountainsides, and you show me up."

She shrugged because she didn't have an answer for him. She hadn't done anything more athletic than marching band, but this hike didn't feel as difficult as it looked. The few times she'd slipped as they climbed up wet rocks, she'd had no trouble catching herself. It felt like she'd suddenly turned into Spider-Man. But that made no sense.

If she'd been totally comfortable with him—and she felt bad that she wasn't—she would have teased him about being slow. She didn't know the elevation. Maybe it was lower than home and that was giving her an oxygen boost.

They emerged at last into an area that was a natural amphitheater, complete with seating that looked as though it had had some human help.

She stopped when she realized there were musical instruments scattered around the amphitheater.

Like sacrifices.

It went against every instinct she had to leave instruments to the mercy of the weather. Instruments were precious things. She broke away from Zander's chosen path to see if she could rescue any of them.

Zander grabbed her arm again in a way that she was beginning to resent and tried to jerk her away. She stiffened, and when he pulled, she stayed where she was, skidding a little with the force he used when she did not yield.

He stopped, took a breath. "Come on," he said, and she felt the effort he used to gentle his tone. "I've a dry place we can rest up in."

That false gentle tone made her plant her feet like a Missouri mule.

"Stop trying to drag me," she said. And then, with gritted teeth: "Get your hand off my arm before you lose it."

He met her eyes and took a step back, frowning. "I thought your eyes were brown."

They were. But she didn't care what color he thought her eyes were.

"Look," she said. "This has been a fun hike and all, but I think I am done. You go on." She needed to go back to that hotel by the river, the one they'd driven by, so she could sit on the rock and watch the river, waiting for . . .

She pulled the flannel shirt up to her face, not wanting to bury her nose in it with Zander looking on. But the smell of musk and mint and home was still there, rising from the damp cloth.

"Sorry," he said, and this time he meant it. "I am soaking wet, and even if you're not cold, I am."

There was a flash of lightning, and reflexively she started counting seconds—one thousand one, one thousand two . . . Thunder rumbled exactly at five. "That's a mile off," she said.

"Too close to stay out here," he told her. He held out his hand—and she heard music, though he wasn't singing. It came from the ground beneath her feet and shivered through her reluctant body, bringing with it the understanding of what she was doing here. That this was where she needed to be, with Zander.

She looked at his hand and couldn't remember why she'd left him standing like that. It was rude. She took his hand—his was cold.

"You *are* warm," he said, sounding startled.

"I told you," she said.

"You did indeed," he agreed. "Come this way, Anna mine."

That was wrong, she knew. But she didn't want to be offensive and tell him that he was mistaken. She didn't belong to him. She belonged. Belonged to . . .

She was sitting on a rock overlooking the river and felt his approach.

She would go to that rock when she and Zander were finished hiking, she decided. And her shoulders relaxed with that decision.

They walked another half of a mile, but they traveled now on an actual trail.

TAG HIT THE Suburban with the Land Rover. The Suburban gave way with a crunch and shriek of bending metal.

"Sorry," he grunted.

Charles didn't care about the damage done. They had lost signal ten miles before and he had begun to doubt that they were even on the right path. The sight of the Suburban through the trees had been welcome. He understood why Tag had punched the accelerator so they were going too fast to stop in the loose and muddy ground.

Even if the Rover had been destroyed—and he suspected it wasn't even dented, given the resiliency of old steel—it had already taken them as far as it could.

He jumped out of the Rover and into the cold rain. The Suburban's hood was warmer than the ambient temperature, but not by much.

"We're an hour behind them," he told Tag. "Maybe a little more."

"Scent isn't going to help us," Tag offered. "Not after an hour of this much rain." He loosened his shoulders. "Good thing that the two of us know how to track using mundane methods."

Charles didn't like it. Normally he could track darn near as quickly as he could run, but in the dark and in the rain, it was going to slow them down. Normally he could find Anna wherever she was by their mating bond, but right now all that he could tell was that she was alive.

"Here," said Tag, pointing up the slope. "They went this way."

"Wait," Charles said. He opened the Suburban, taking in the scents.

A man, but not one that Charles had met. Or at least not one whose scent he had taken in. He drew in another breath and got a faint hint of sweetness. Like a snow cone.

"Zander," he growled, though he wasn't really certain of that.

Another growl came from his left, and he looked to see that Tag's eyes were gold—and a little blind.

"Tag," he said sharply, putting a little push through the pack bonds when he did so.

If Brother Wolf wasn't allowed to go rogue tonight, Tag for damn sure wasn't allowed to go berserker. Not until they needed it.

Tag shook himself a bit. "Pip-squeak *human* boy photographer," he said in a voice that was very nearly a whine. "Our Anna wouldn't have left us for something like that. Is he a witch? He doesn't smell like a witch. How did he get her?"

Anna wouldn't have left him because of the blandishments of a boy, even a pretty boy like Zander. Not of her own volition. Dr. Connors had said that Zander had been in Wild Sign. Anna had stopped in to visit him while waiting for the pizzas, and when she'd come back, Charles had heard the paper rustling in her pants pocket. Ergo, Zander wasn't a normal human.

Not witchcraft on that paper, observed Brother Wolf. *Some other kind of magic.*

"Maybe he's one of the Singer's children. A walker. You were the one who thought there might be some of them around," Charles said. "Or he's another victim of the Singer who has been enslaved."

If the stories Anna and Dr. Bonsu had told of Zander the photographer were true, he had certainly been walking the world. According to Anna, Zander had told her that he'd met several of the people of Wild Sign before they'd come here. Charles wondered if they had come here because Zander had told them to come.

Tag had been running his own calculations. "Right." He looked back to where feet had disturbed the duff covering the forest floor. "Okay," he said. "She was kidnapped by this thing that wants to be a god."

It seemed to satisfy him, because he started off at a trot.

ZANDER PRESENTED ANNA with the mouth of a cave, a round hole about three feet in diameter. They were going to have to crawl or duckwalk to get into it.

"You can't mean to go spelunking now," Anna said, oddly reluctant to follow him. The cave was emitting a strange smell that raised her hackles. "What if there's a bear inside?"

Zander laughed and reached into the cave, coming out with an electric lantern. "There isn't a bear," he told her. "I promise."

"Well, if you promise," she returned, her lips quirking up. He had an infectious smile.

"I do. There's more light inside and it's dry and warm. Come on, just follow me."

After maybe a dozen yards the cave opened up so they could stand upright. The smell wrapped around them. It wasn't unpleasant by itself, but something about it bothered Anna. Zander hit a switch and illuminated a string of light bulbs that stretched out until the passage bent out of sight.

She frowned disapprovingly. "That's bad for the bats."

He laughed. "It's not used often enough to disturb the bats."

She wasn't so sure of that. She could hear the little creatures moving around restlessly. They didn't like the light—and who could blame them? But she shouldn't argue with Zander.

"How did you manage electricity in the middle of nowhere?" she asked instead.

"Solar panels," he said. "They put them in last year. I have to admit that it makes getting down to the main cave a lot easier."

There were a couple more narrow places—in one of them, she had to wait for him to squeeze through feetfirst, one arm up and one arm down. He held the lantern in his upward arm, lighting her way down because there was no room for the light bulbs that otherwise had marked out their path.

Tag would never make it, she thought, worried. And then worried more because she couldn't remember who Tag was.

As if he'd heard her thoughts, Zander said, "There's another way in, but I figured that if I could make it through here, so could you. The other way would have taken us another ten minutes, and there are worse obstacles in that direction."

She had an easier time than he did, scooting through and thinking about waterslide tubes instead of the mountain sitting on top of her. It helped that the floor was damp.

At the end of the rocky tunnel was a . . . well, a room. Complete with bed and battery-operated lights. At the far side of the room the cave had lighted passages to the left and right.

She would have expected a cave to smell of earth and moisture and bats. And it did smell of all of that, though they had left the actual bats up closer to the cave mouth. But it smelled musty, too—like old death and something weird . . .

Magic.

If they'd still been out in the forest, she would have scoffed at the idea of magic. But in the secret depths of the earth, it felt different. And the existence of the king-sized bed in a room she had gotten to via a tunnel that Zander had barely made it through was an argument for magic.

But it wasn't the magic that bothered her. She had been aware all night that her nose was a lot more sensitive than usual. Now she wished that she couldn't smell at all. That weird, dry smell that her brain kept labeling *death*, though it wasn't a putrid scent like roadkill or anything, was overpowering, as if the longer she was in this cavern, the stronger the smell got.

"What is that smell?" she finally asked.

Zander raised an eyebrow. "What smell? It smells like a damp cave. We left the bats behind."

She didn't want to tell him that there was something dead in his cave, and she didn't know why she thought she should keep it to herself. "Maybe that's it," she said. "I haven't been in many caves."

"The sound you're hearing is an underground river," he said. "There are some places in the cave system where it surfaces—I'll show you one of those in a bit."

She'd known that was what the sound was, she thought. Who doesn't know the sound of rushing water? But there was something about that last bit—the hint of anticipation in his eyes or excitement in his voice—that made her worry. And she could smell his arousal.

She breathed death and caught—something else, too, something that smelled like the depths of the ocean and the heart of a mountain. She had no idea what either of those would smell like—and she smelled them anyway.

She looked for something to distract both of them with. "How did you get a mattress down that tunnel?" she asked—and then thought that maybe a discussion about that bed wasn't where she wanted to take his attention, either.

The bed was covered with a pair of sleeping bags, unzipped so that they functioned more like giant blankets, one that you were supposed to lie on, one to cover you up. There were two pillows and two more electric lanterns that Zander had switched on while she had still been coming down the tunnel.

He grinned.

"There's not a mattress," he said. And lifted the corner of the sleeping bags to reveal a two-inch foam pad laid over a raised stone platform, as if nature had created a king-sized mattress here.

Or something else had, she thought, and didn't know why the thought was so compelling.

Anna hid her rising unease with a smile.

Because when she had wanted to get out of the moving car, and when she had told him, "This has been a fun hike and all, but I think I am done," he'd twisted her thinking so she suddenly decided it was a good idea to go along with him after all. And she didn't want him to do it again.

"You need to wait in here for me," Zander said. He leaned forward and kissed her, lightly at first and then openmouthed.

She didn't fight him—and that was an effort. But she wanted him to go away. Letting him kiss her seemed like the fastest way to that end.

She was also starting to feel panicky about the things that her nose was telling her. She had a bad feeling about what was going to happen in this cave that smelled of some primordial ocean. And *death*.

But she couldn't make herself kiss him back.

He pulled away and gave her a quizzical look. "Tough nut," he said, touching her bottom lip with his thumb. He'd figured out that she was starting to think for herself. Before she could decide what to do about that, he pulled her against him, as if they were slow dancing, and began to sing.

She could feel him aroused against her—and that focused her attention. She didn't want this—whatever this was. She needed to get out of here.

She was very much afraid that meant she needed to figure out what was beyond this room. What it was that smelled like death, and what smelled of magic and old power.

Wait.

If she had listened to that inner voice in the first place, if she'd run when they got out of the Suburban, she might be back in that hotel by the river. She thought of the miles they had driven and amended herself. She would at least be on the way to the river by now—though an odd part of her remained convinced she could have made it to the river.

He stepped back and shook his head, then walked over to a dark corner of the room and pulled out an instrument case. If he hadn't been standing between her and the tunnel, she'd have taken her chances. But without a head start, she wasn't going to be able to get far enough into the tunnel fast enough that he couldn't simply grab her ankles and drag her out.

She wondered why he'd brought her here. The kisses—and that bed—were making her very uncomfortable.

Wait.

He pulled out a mandolin that was a lot older than the case it was stored in. As he began tuning, he said, "You are not going to be hurt, Anna."

She'd had a dentist who used to say that right before he stuck the needle in. It was a lie then—and it was a lie now. Even if he thought he was telling the truth.

And then he began to play. She loved music—it spoke to her, and always had. It gave her joy when she was sad and comforted her when she was afraid. And she had been so afraid.

After a while he put the mandolin back in its case.

"Hello, Anna," he said.

"Hey, Zander." She gave him a shy smile.

"How old are you?"

She laughed. "Jailbait for you. Seventeen."

"Good," he said. "Would you go sit on the bed and wait for me? I won't be a long time. Maybe a half hour."

She didn't mind waiting. She liked to use downtime to work through the solo that she was going to play for auditions for Northwestern. There were a couple of spots that weren't as smooth as they could be. And she still wasn't sure that slowing down that movement in the middle a little more wouldn't make the music better, even if it might mean that the adjudicators thought she was doing it to make the piece easier.

He gave her a soft kiss she didn't pay much attention to and then gently propelled her to the bed. She couldn't help wrinkling her nose. The sleeping bags had been here long enough to absorb the smell of death and whatever that other weird scent was. It wasn't a pleasant smell. Her instincts told her not to react. There was something wrong here, and she needed him to go away.

"All right?" he asked.

She wished he'd shut up; she wanted to work on her music. If she'd been a mathematician, she would have solved equations or counted in prime numbers or something. Music would clear her head.

She gave him a perfunctory smile. "Yes, fine."

He watched her for a second, then he nodded and walked out.

As soon as he was out of sight, something rose out of the hollow place inside her, something vibrating with life and strength and rage. Her hands curled and every muscle in her body tensed. She needed to get out of here. Her head was foggy as all hell, but she knew that much.

She was on her way out, halfway up the squeeze-chute tunnel, when she heard a soft click and all the lights in front of her went out. She paused. Could she find her way out in the dark? The darkness of the cave was not the darkness of night. There was no light. She'd be able to make it out of the narrow passage, where there was only one direction to go, but after that? When her memory of how they had made the trip in was foggy?

She slid back out into the bedroom cavern. Improbably, given that it was presumably attached to all of the other lights, the single bulb was still lit, but the lanterns on either side of the bed were out. She picked one of them up and pressed the red button to turn it on. Nothing happened.

It had just been lit. It was a simple, battery-operated device. She tried the other one with the same result.

She was trapped.

And that was when she became aware of the sounds. Muffled scuffling noises with an odd wet edge to them. Groaning. A shushing sound almost like a croon that ended in a sound like grain spun in a basket. Then a wet squishy smacking sound, like someone had thrown a giant sponge out of an airplane so it could land on pavement.

She stood frozen, curiosity pushing her forward, curiosity and the desire to see what the hell was making that noise. But caution and that small voice in her head held her still.

And then the sound changed, becoming a rhythmical squicking, as if some film director decided to make a parody of sex. It was too loud and too . . . harsh, as if something huge and wet scraped over and over against a rough surface. Someone—Zander?—cried out in a mix of passion and pain.

It sounded, she thought, with a sort of revolted horror (and a weird desire to laugh), like the tentacle sex in the old anime movie that had been passed around the high school girls' locker room. Yes, she had watched it.

She and her best friend had consumed two buckets of popcorn and laughed themselves sick. Her dad had caught them. Being her dad, he'd grabbed a handful of popcorn and stayed to observe a tentacle enter a place a tentacle had no business being. He'd winced theatrically and then rolled his eyes before wandering out.

She wished her dad were here now.

A very distinctive odor hit her nose. The sounds did not lie. Sex was taking place.

She also caught a whiff of something else, musk and mint like the flannel shirt she wore as armor, but lighter somehow and vaguely familiar. There was a gentle scuffing sound just outside the cavern—and a naked, very dirty woman padded in on soft feet.

For a moment, she reminded Anna of Zander.

Then she came closer, dispelling the illusion—a thing of shadows and the shape of her eyes.

"Anna?" the woman said in a whisper so quiet Anna was surprised that she could hear. "Are you okay?"

The woman, even naked and dirty, carried with her an air of command that had Anna responding to her as if she were here to help. Anna looked at the bed, then pointed in the general direction of the sloppy wet noises—and shook her head definitively.

The woman nodded and then gestured for Anna to follow her

back the way she'd come—the direction that Zander had not taken. This section of the tunnel was still lit, and Anna couldn't help but look the way Zander had gone, but it dropped down and turned. All she could see was that the light from that direction had a distinct orange tinge and looked too bright to have been provided solely by ordinary bulbs.

The woman stopped and Anna stopped with her. There was something odd about Anna's own reaction to this woman—who was a stranger, a naked stranger, even. And she felt like a trusted comrade, if not a friend. But unlike the happy, safe feeling that Zander's music inspired, this felt *true*.

She turned to Anna as if to say something.

Anna spoke first. "Who are you?" she asked. "Have we met?"

The other woman's eyes flashed to icy blue, as if she wore some kind of contacts designed to make her look like a superhero or an alien.

Wolf eyes. And that thought felt true as well.

The woman didn't answer Anna's question, her voice still quiet—though she would have had to be singing full-throated opera to have pierced the noises coming from behind them. "You need music to clear your head. The wrong kind of music will make you vulnerable to him—anything soft or emotional. Music in general is dangerous. The Singer's powers are music and memory. But they can also be used to defend against him. You need something defiant. A war song. Maybe something like—" She hummed a little and Anna recognized the tune.

"Queen," Anna said. "I can channel Freddie Mercury."

"Wait until we get somewhere safer—or if the enemy appears.

Think defiance while you sing, or it will backfire. I hope it won't be necessary, because we are going to try to make it out before they are finished back there. I warn you, though, this next cavern is bad. Stay beside me."

"What if he cuts the lights?" Anna asked.

"I have a flashlight," the woman said. "I picked it up at the cave entrance." For the first time, Anna noticed that she was carrying a small black flashlight in one hand. In the dim light, it blended with the dirt on the woman's hands.

"Something killed the electric lanterns back there."

"Well, then, Anna," said the woman in a biting tone—so familiar. *Who was this woman?* "I guess we'll have to fight in the dark, or"—she nodded her head toward the disturbing sounds behind them—"you can go back and wait until he gets done in there."

Anna followed her into the next cavern without another word.

This cavern was huge. Though it was lit by dim bulbs on a string down the middle of it, Anna had to judge the size of the cave by sound as much as sight, because the edges were hidden by stalagmites rising from the ground like giant malformed trees. Some of them had broken over the years—or perhaps those were stalactites—and lay like broken marble columns in an ancient Grecian temple.

The fallen cave giants weren't the only things strewn broken over the floor. Anna found the source of the musty smell of death.

The mummified bodies of maybe a dozen people lay scattered around. It took her horrified eyes a moment to register that they were all dressed in modern clothing. They lay in small groups—two men face-to-face, holding hands. Four women who looked as though they'd been sitting cross-legged and also holding hands when whatever had done this to them had hit. It looked as though they had all sat down and awaited their doom without a fight.

Just when she thought she'd reached her limit of horror for the night, she realized that some of the bodies were children.

She turned in a slow circle, though she still followed the other woman, who was picking her way across the cavern, walking backward as her eyes found new bodies in the shadows. There weren't just a dozen; there were at least twice that many.

There was a soft airy noise—and it took Anna a second to realize that the noise was coming from the bodies. They were breathing . . . or at least they had all exhaled, pushing the musty scent of death into the cavern.

"This is how he punished the rebels," the woman said grimly. "We need to get out of here."

"Are they alive?" Anna asked numbly, forgetting to be quiet.

She didn't realize she'd stopped moving altogether until her comrade grabbed her wrist and pulled. "I don't know," the woman answered. "Worry about them later."

"Anna?"

Zander's voice came from the direction of the bedroom cavern.

"Sing, now," said the woman. "Run."

One of Anna's voice teachers, a woman who had been in *Cats* for five years on Broadway before retiring, liked to make her students sing while they were running. She said it taught them abdominal control.

Singing "We Will Rock You" at the top of her lungs certainly challenged Anna's diaphragm control. But she still did better than the other woman, whose volume changed with her footfalls.

"Think defiance," the woman said at a break in the song—and as she spoke, the lights went out.

Anna heard the flashlight hit the ground, so apparently that hadn't worked any more than the electric lanterns back in the bedroom cave. But a hand wrapped around hers in the darkness and tugged. They had to quit running, but the other woman led the way with apparent confidence. Anna assumed that she knew this cave system, had bat radar, or was guiding them by something other than sight.

There was a soft noise and the other woman staggered. "Low ceiling," she growled in a rough voice.

She was a head taller than Anna, but Anna put her free hand up so that if something were hanging down, she'd have some warning. She couldn't tell if anyone (Zander) was following them, because she was singing.

She sang the second verse of the song as they stumbled in inky darkness, thinking that it would be a hell of a beacon for anyone or anything trying to figure out where they were.

As she sang a generation's hymn to defiance, the go-to score of almost every high school pep band since 1977, the huge hollowness that Anna had been contending with all night dissolved, the fog on her memory cleared, and the challenge in her voice quit being any kind of acting.

Anna staggered, stumbling to her knees on the damp stone as she tried to reconcile the memories of a lifetime with the past few hours. Her song broke off, but her memories remained.

"What the freaking hell, Leah?" she growled angrily, though none of this was Leah's fault. She wasn't angry with Leah.

"Sing now, talk later," Leah told her, yanking her to her feet. "And be careful. This is a weapon that can bite back. Music is meant to be a gift to listeners—but it can't be that here. It has to fall on him like an axe. Make your music a declaration of war."

Leah started with the first verse again, moving at a quick walk. Keeping Anna behind her so that if someone were going to stumble or run into something, it would be her. Leah protected her people.

Back in her own skin, her wolf so close to the surface Anna was a little surprised she wasn't already starting to change, she could catch the faint whiffs of fresh air—which had to be what Leah was following.

They ran out of verses for "We Will Rock You," and Anna went for another classic with Pink Floyd's ode to juvenile delinquency, "Another Brick in the Wall."

Without electric guitars, though, that one took only about a minute. Anna tried Twisted Sister's "We're Not Gonna Take It," but it was quickly obvious that Leah didn't know it. So Anna sang only the first two lines. In desperation she went back to Queen. They could just sing the damned verses over and over again, she thought; that's what they had done when she was in high school.

The lights came back on, ironically blinding her so she tripped and fell down hard. She popped up, throwing her weight back so she could come to her feet balanced and ready. Leah was stock-still in front of her. And twenty feet beyond that, Zander stood with a black handgun aimed at them.

He'd gotten in front of them, presumably traveling by a different path. Maybe that way had had lights so he'd been able to run.

Hiding her movement with Leah's body, Anna pulled her own

gun, releasing the safety as she did so. The Sig was matte black and small; Anna kept it against her leg and kept that leg behind Leah.

Ten shots, she told herself as she belted out Brian May's lyrics. *Keep count and use them wisely.*

The lights were brighter than she remembered. Either the stint in the darkness had made her more sensitive or there was magic at work, but she could see Zander as if he had a spotlight on him.

He was barefoot and shirtless. His only clothing was his jeans, and they were unbuttoned and unzipped. His skin was damp and a little shiny, as if someone had covered him in oil. On his collarbone and navel, the shiny substance thickened to clear blobs that clung to him as if it were something sticky.

There was a roundish red mark on his hip, visible because his jeans were riding low. Another of those marks was halfway up his throat. He was breathing hard and he smelled like sex.

His face had been flushed with triumph, but even as Anna watched, his expression went blank. He stared at Leah like a rabbit in the face of a hungry wolf.

"Mother?" he said, voice raw.

Leah didn't say anything. Anna couldn't read anything from her body language. Leah had a pretty good game face; she probably wasn't showing what she thought there, either.

Anna, on the other hand, promptly forgot where she was in the song, so she started the chorus up again. On the whole, it had been a good thing she hadn't found a song with words she'd have to think about.

Mother.

She remembered that when she'd seen Leah enter the bedroom cave, for an instant she had thought the woman looked like Zander.

"I thought you were dead," Zander said. Anna noticed his pistol was a Glock, though she wasn't familiar with the model. It was something a lot bigger than her own. She was pretty sure he wouldn't have bothered with silver bullets—he hadn't known Anna was a werewolf—but a head shot would probably still be fatal.

"I knew you were not," Leah said, speaking for the first time. "Though I had hoped so. He needed you too much."

"You betrayed him." Zander's voice cracked out and he gestured with the gun, as if with so much emotion he could not contain his body. "You helped the Beast come into our home and kill all of Father's children. All of them except for me."

"I intended for it to be you, too," she said. To someone who did not know her, her voice would have sounded flat.

But Anna had heard Leah's flat voice before, and this time she heard the roughness in Leah's consonants. Leah was feeling something powerful—the echoes of it washed up through the pack bonds and made Anna's wolf spirit tense in readiness. But Anna suspected that not even Leah would be able to put a single name to those roiling emotions.

"What did you get out of it, Mother?" Zander snarled. "My father told me that you let the Beast transform you, that you became like one of them. Did he bribe you with immortality? I have that, and I don't turn into a monster with the full moon."

"No," said Anna grimly. "You just go out and rape women. Someone is a monster here, and it isn't Leah."

She went back to singing before the fog could take her again.

"Bitch," he said to Anna. "You would have been the mother of—" Here he said a name that Anna, classically trained to sing in languages she didn't speak, could not have begun to put together.

"Mother of the Singer's children, his walkers who go about his business in the world. There is no greater honor."

"I'm a werewolf," Anna told him. "I can't bear a child."

"He could fix that," Zander told her. "Your children would have been pleasing to him. They would—"

"Grow up to be rapists?" Anna said dryly.

He sneered at her, but he wasn't really interested in Anna. He returned his attention to Leah. "You don't understand what you did. He was on the verge of Becoming when you betrayed him. Our lord and master nearly died under the teeth of the Great Beast—and I was left alone to wander."

The Great Beast must have been Sherwood, Anna thought.

"I was a *child*, Mother," Zander said. "And you abandoned me. If I am not what you wanted me to be, the fault is not mine or my father's."

Leah flinched a little before she caught herself.

"As to the charges of rape—" He held Leah's eyes and said emphatically, "I have never taken an unwilling woman. Such would be an abomination to the Singer."

He made a finger gesture that Anna didn't quite catch. "My father was trapped in the waters beneath the ground for nearly two centuries healing the damage the Beast had done. And through it all he kept me alive at great cost to himself. If he had not loved me, I would be dead and he would have healed himself much faster.

"As it is, he cannot sing, Mother, because the Beast took his tongue. He cannot leave this place until his Becoming, and he had only me to find worshippers for him. We offered them a fair bargain and they accepted. It was not rape." He raised his chin.

"What about Dr. Connors?" said Anna.

"She was not unwilling," he said. And he lied.

"I see." Anna kept her voice soft with an effort. "He has the witches—the ones who told him what Wild Sign had done—they are bearing his children. Why did you need Dr. Connors? And me?"

"Do you think that those children will be his as I am his?" Zander's voice was bitter with something that sounded very much to Anna's ear like jealousy. "Those creatures are selfish. They will keep their bargain—because they know the Singer does not trust them. But they are black witches. Evil. Their children are taught vileness with their mothers' milk."

He paused. "He trusted the people of Wild Sign. They gave him form and they worshipped him with music. My father loved them and they betrayed him. I told him not to trust them, that he could only trust me. That I am the only one who loves him. *Now* he believes me."

His gun had been gradually lowering as he spoke, but he jerked it up, aiming it at Leah's head. "I told him that he would need children better than those the black witches will carry. Children who will love him. My children. He told me to find women to bear them. So I have."

Anna wondered if there were other unsuspecting women carrying the Singer's children.

"Nonconsensual sex is rape," Leah said. "Twisting someone's memories around makes them incapable of consent. You are a rapist. We are done here."

He said, "Yes, we are." He pulled the trigger a hair slower than Anna did, even though she had to step around Leah first.

Anna's initial bullet hit his hand, making his shot go wild. She'd considered the dangers of that before she'd fired and chanced it anyway. Better being hit by a chunk of rock than a bullet; the rock would do less damage. Her second and third shots went through his left eye. She hit him in the heart, too, as he was falling.

Six left, she thought. She shoved Leah, who had not moved.

"Out, out," she sang instead of "rock you." She had no intention of letting her memories get stolen again.

They had to step over Zander to escape.

Leah had quit even trying to sing. But she was running with Anna in the right direction, so Anna figured that Leah was in charge of her own mind.

Rain was still pelting down sideways as they scrambled out of the cave—a different opening than Anna and Zander had used to enter earlier. Lightning flashed and thunder boomed too close together. Anna quit singing.

Leah said, "If we head directly to the highway, we can make it faster than if we take your SUV."

Anna shook her head. "The SUV is dead anyway. Pretty sure he took out the oil pan on a rock. But we don't have to make it to the highway before we get help." She pointed. "Charles is over there. Maybe a quarter of a mile away."

Leah half lidded her eyes—Zander's eyes. Once Anna had noticed the resemblance, she didn't know how she could have missed it. Then Leah nodded. "Okay, I feel them, too."

Anna gave her the damp flannel shirt with about the same amount of reluctance with which Leah accepted it. They jogged along the side of the mountain, skirting heavy undergrowth where they found it.

"I don't really remember him," Leah said suddenly, her voice tight. "I remember I had a child named Alexander. I remember we weren't able to get him out, and that he wasn't there when the rest of the children were killed. I don't remember any more."

And that was only partly a lie. Anna wasn't going to call her on it. "What made you come here?" she asked, hoping it was an easier thing for Leah to talk about.

Leah said, "I dreamed. The night before I left Bran to come here. Buffalo Singer, Charles's uncle, told me that the time had come to finish my battle. I didn't know what he meant, not until . . . I heard the Singer's call again. And I decided that I would go to the Singer after all. I expected a battle, I think. I did not expect Alexander."

She sounded . . . broken. Voice hoarse, she continued as if the words were being forced out of her mouth. "I didn't tell Zander that I don't remember why we left him, did I? I told him, told my son, what I thought would make him angry enough to raise that gun so that I could make myself kill him before the Singer came after us in his stead." She paused. "I wonder why he did not come?"

Anna did not regret Zander's death. But she was very glad it had been her who had killed him and not Leah. The other woman would have done it, but Anna thought that Leah was going to leave this place with enough battle scars. She didn't need to add killing her son to the list.

Anna groped for something she could say.

Don't feel bad; he was a rapist asshole who stood by while the Singer did whatever he had done to the people of Wild Sign that turned them into what we found in that cavern didn't strike quite the right tone somehow.

He took great photographs and fought for the environment didn't seem . . . on point, either.

Leah was not someone Anna could give a hug to, even had it been appropriate to the situation. Sage was the only one who might have been able to do such a thing—and Sage had been a lie. And a hug was only useful if there was time to cry—and the person who gave you a hug was someone you didn't mind crying in front of.

"I am not sorry" was all that Anna managed.

Leah didn't reply to that.

Anna felt Charles's nearness and increased her pace without considering that the much more fatigued Leah—who had apparently *run* here from Montana—could not keep up. The trees thinned out a little and she caught sight of Charles and Tag.

Charles saw her, too, and broke from the jog he'd been moving at to a full-on run. She could have flown down the hill. She didn't slow as she neared, just threw herself at him, wrapping around him, arms and legs and heart—knowing he would catch her. He would *always* catch her.

And for a moment, with his hard arms around her with bruising force, she wasn't a badass who had just killed the minion of a would-be god. She was a shivering fearful woman who had narrowly missed being Rosemary. A woman who had seen a cavern of living mummies—and that was a memory she might not fight too hard to keep if someone wanted to steal it from her.

Hugs were dangerous in that way. He held her tight—and she could feel in the too-rapid beat of his heart and the slight shiver of his arms that he had been frightened, too.

"We need to go," said Leah. She sounded pretty tough, but she had it worse than Anna, and she didn't have anyone to hug her.

Anna dropped back to the ground.

"Leah," said Charles. "Da is worried about you. I'm glad to see you safe."

An odd expression crossed Leah's face. "Is he? And 'safe' is a matter of degree, isn't it?" She looked over her shoulder. "We should go."

They set off down the mountain toward safety. Anna and Charles took the lead and Tag the rear, surrounding the usually indomitable Leah with what protection they could.

"Tell me," said Charles.

And because the pace didn't preclude talking, Anna did. When she had finished, Charles glanced over his shoulder at Leah so that it would be clear that he was speaking to her.

"My da called Asil back from Billings and left for here in the middle of the night, as soon as Asil returned to care for the pack. His intention was to fly to Bend and then requisition a helicopter and fly to Wild Sign. If he was able to do that, he should be here sometime in the next hour or so."

Because Anna knew her mate, she felt that there was a lot more he wanted to say. He saw her gaze and shook his head. "Some things my da is going to have to put back together or not," he told her.

"Should we wait for him in Wild Sign?" Anna asked.

"No," Leah said, though Anna had been talking to Charles. "We need to get out of here."

"No need," Charles answered Anna. "Pack sense will tell him where we are. We should just keep going. We'll come back and hunt when we have a better idea of what we are dealing with. We can bring some allies along—and a better way to protect ourselves than singing Queen at the tops of our lungs."

Leah stumbled as they came to the amphitheater. She recovered quickly and took up the pace again, but her running had lost the easy rhythm she'd had before the stumble.

"Leah," asked Tag, "would you let me carry you?"

"No," she said. "Twisted my ankle. It will heal in a minute. Keep—"

There was a rumble, louder and longer than any of the thunder they'd been hearing, though it was the same kind of sound.

"Earthquake," said Tag.

"It's him," Leah said, despair and fatigue in her voice. "We were too slow."

"Look," Charles said.

The ground that formed the amphitheater lost solidity, dropping down like ground zero of an underground nuclear detonation. Dirt flowed downward like a waterfall, punctuated with the boulders and stumps that had been the pews in the Singer's open-air house of worship.

Nothing emerged from the pit. After a moment, they all—well, they didn't relax, that was for damned sure. But they regrouped.

"Should we leave?" Tag asked. "Come back with more fire-power?"

"It has the witches," Anna said. "And all the power they can muster from hell's own assisted living facility. Are we sure we want to give them time to get here?"

Charles didn't say anything, just tested the ground with his feet as if making sure it wasn't likely to open up into a pit anytime soon. Anna didn't find that reassuring.

Instead of waiting for an answer from Charles, Tag nodded, as if Anna's comment had been enough. He started stripping out of his clothing in preparation for shifting to wolf.

"We have no choice," said Leah hollowly. "He won't let us leave. He can't afford to."

"Do you have any insights about what we'll be facing?" Charles asked Leah.

She looked like she hadn't heard him. Anna gave her a few seconds and then told Charles what she knew.

"It messes with your memories." Everyone already knew that, but Anna had very recent personal experience. "The first time it attacked me, it took me back to one of the most traumatic times in my life and removed all of my memories from that time until this. I felt like it replaced who I am now with that earlier version of me. It was very disconcerting. I don't know how you can guard yourself against that."

"He tried to do that to me as we left the cave," Leah said unexpectedly. "But he had trouble with the wolf in me. I think that might mean that the hunting song may shield us—at least a little."

The hunting song was an effect of the pack bonds, connecting all of the wolves who had a common goal into a tighter team, allowing them to share knowledge, power, and strategy in real time until the object of the hunt was achieved.

Anna glanced at Charles. "It can mess with your short-term memory, too. I lost about fifteen minutes the first time we drove to our hotel."

"You didn't tell me," he said softly, and she knew she'd hurt him.

"I'm sorry," she said. "It felt like just a glitch. Over and done." She looked at Tag and Leah, because they didn't have time to waste with her guilt. "It might cause you to falter. Maybe if you know it's coming, you can push through it."

"Did you see the Singer? What does it look like?" Charles asked. "Best-case scenario, we bring this down to a physical fight, because that is where our weapons lie."

Anna looked at Leah, who was resolutely not looking at Anna or Charles.

"Uh," Anna said. "I never saw it. But from what I overheard . . . and I know this sounds really stupid out here—but I think that it is some kind of cave squid. Or cave octopus."

Tag froze. "Cthulhu? We're fighting Cthulhu? Up in these mountains?"

His incredulity forced Leah to speak. "I saw him," she told them in a low voice. "Before I found Anna in the caves. I couldn't be sure of his size because it was dark and some of his body was underwater—and at the time I needed him not to be aware of me. She's right about the tentacles. I also think he's huge."

"Cthulhu," said Tag happily, discarding the last of his clothes. Apparently his incredulity had not signified reluctance. His eyes were wolf eyes and slightly unfocused in a way that, under other circumstances, would have made Anna nervous.

Charles turned to look at the pit. His head tilted and Brother Wolf said intently, "Listen."

Leah frowned and then drew in a breath. "The pit is filling with water. Smells like salt water. Ocean water."

No one asked aloud where the salt water was coming from, but Anna figured that they were all thinking about it—and what that said about the thing they were facing.

"Cthulhu," chortled Tag as a popping sound signaled the start of his change. "I get to fight Cthulhu. Asil is going to be so jealous." His smile, like his eyes, looked a little wild.

"Cthulhu," Anna murmured, because that was an interesting observation.

"It's not Cthulhu," Charles said dryly. "That's a character from a book."

Well, yes. Anna thought that actually might be the point.

"Leah?" Anna asked. "Did it have tentacles when you were here? Before?"

"I don't remember," Leah said. Then she held up a hand, asking them to wait. She turned her face into the rain for a moment, closing her eyes. When she opened her eyes, she said, "No. The Singer looked like one of us—human, I mean. He was"—she shook her head—"he looked like someone you could trust. I don't know where the tentacles came from."

"I think I do," said Anna grimly. "Do you remember when Zander said the people who settled Wild Sign gave it form?"

"Yes," Leah said.

Charles's eyes became suddenly intent. "That bookshelf," he said.

"The big yurt in Wild Sign has a bookshelf of Lovecraft-themed books," Anna told the others. "Not just cheap paperbacks or that all-in-one leather-bound collection you can buy for twenty bucks around Christmas. Original editions of Lovecraft and Chambers. Nineteen-thirties editions of *Weird Tales*. I think one of the first Wild Sign people was a Lovecraft fan. And that's why we have a cave squid. Or possibly a cave octopus."

"Not Cthulhu," said Charles slowly, "but inspired by those tales."

There was a short, appalled silence punctuated by the sounds of Tag's ongoing change.

"It could be worse," Anna said. "At least it's not the Stay Puft Marshmallow Man."

Charles grinned suddenly. "A pop culture reference I know." He looked at Leah, his smile lingering around the edges of his mouth and eyes. "Anything you can add?"

"If he could sing, we would be in a lot more trouble," she said. "But Sherwood ripped out his tongue." There was satisfaction in her voice, but Anna felt a sudden stab of concern. Leah looked tired and cold—and about fifteen pounds underweight. Running from Montana had burned calories.

"Zander implied that the Singer had not healed from that," Leah continued. "I don't know if that means he can't still attack us with music, but he can't sing."

She scuffed her bare foot in the dirt and gave them a grim smile. "And that's all well and good. But what I don't know is how to kill him so that he stays dead. I don't know that he is something that *can* be killed."

"Asil told me that the only way to kill something immortal is to remind it what death is," Charles said. "Da is bringing the sword that killed Jonesy—an immortal fae. The Dark Smith's weapons carry the memories of the deaths that they have brought."

Leah rubbed her bloodshot eyes. "Good. All we have to do is stay alive until he gets here. I wonder what's taking the Singer so long." She frowned thoughtfully—as if, Anna thought, she might have a clue about what that was. But instead of telling them, she looked toward the pit, where the sound of rushing water had quieted now that the water was deeper. "Don't let him pull you into the water."

Werewolves couldn't swim.

Tag stood up on four legs—huge, even for a werewolf, his thick, shaggy coat a shade more orange than his hair. Leah stretched her neck and began her change, and only then did Anna realize she'd been waiting for Tag.

Charles saw her look. "When there are so few of us, and there is opportunity, we try not to have all of the wolves shift at the same time. That way no one can attack us when all of us are hampered with the change."

They waited, Anna tucked against Charles's side, as rain poured over their heads and lightning cracked in a brilliant show that would have rivaled a Fourth of July display. When Anna counted the distance between lightning and thunder, she could only count to two. She hoped nothing caught fire—because one thing she could think of that would make this fight even harder would be if they were trying to do it in the middle of a freaking forest fire.

Eventually Leah, like Tag, stood on all four feet. The rain had already drenched her gold-and-silver coat, darkening it to gray. The combination of weight loss and wet fur made Leah look small, an effect not helped by the hunch of her shoulders.

Anna let go of Charles and untied her boots, because Leah's shift was finished. The pit was now a dark pool filled to the brim, its surface rippling with the driving rain.

CHARLES KEPT AN eye on the newly formed lake as he waited for Anna to change. The water was inky black, even when the lightning struck, briefly illuminating the whole forest as if it were daytime. It might have been an effect of the night sky or the turbidity caused by the rapid fill of water. Or something else.

There was so much magic in the ground under his feet that he felt blinded. A thousand forest spirits could be tugging at his hands and he would not know it because his senses were already overwhelmed.

It was a testament to the power of the creature they faced. Charles did not find it reassuring.

Sherwood had not been able to kill the Singer, and Charles did not think that the four of them were as formidable an opponent as Sherwood had been all by himself, not against something like the Singer. Perhaps in a purely physical fight, it would have been different. But if the Singer was—to steal Anna's term—a creepy primordial god, he did not think that a physical fight was how it would die.

He hoped Da got here soon, but found himself doubtful he would be in time to help. Time was running out—Brother Wolf could sense the nearness of battle. Without his da, without the sword, Charles did not think they were going to win this fight. Pessimism was not going to be useful, however, so Charles gave his worries to Brother Wolf, who was adept at keeping their secrets away from the pack, even in the throes of the hunting song.

As if in response to Brother Wolf's assessment of the nearing conflict, Charles felt the pack bonds shift. Between one breath and the next his senses expanded, and he, Anna, Leah, and Tag were caught up in the mad exhilaration of the opening moments of the hunt. Anna was not quite finished with her change when the song took them, so their combined magic pushed into her, rushing the last moments painfully fast. Charles changed. And when his change was complete, he was in charge of the hunt.

He had not been sure it would be him. Leah had more experience—and more involvement with the Singer. As his father's mate, she outranked him in the pack. His da thought that leadership went to the wolf the majority of the participants wanted in charge. Charles wasn't sure that was true. He often felt that pack magic—and, by extension, the hunting song—had its own intelligence.

His body still, he processed the information flooding into him, knowing that once the fight started, instinct would guide them more than thought. But for now, he assessed his pack.

Tag's eagerness for battle overlaid the song. They all felt the addict-level strength of his need to give in to his berserker. Charles lent Tag some of Anna's Omega-born quiet and felt him settle.

Charles considered the method of the Singer's attacks and how Anna explained it had affected her. Tag, he thought, would be least affected among them. The berserker was difficult to distract.

Tag's amused agreement sang through the hunting bonds, because the flow of information went both ways.

Leah . . . Charles had probably been in a thousand hunts with Leah, though none so dire and none with so few wolves. He was in the habit of keeping as far from her as he could, both physically and in the bonds themselves. Given his success in avoiding her, he suspected Leah did the same. He'd never been in a hunt with her in which he took the lead position.

And still he had expectations based on his previous experience. Through the pack bonds, Leah had always felt like a lethal, whip-quick weapon—cold, controlled, and deadly. He had expected that this time, too—but if he had not known better, he would have thought she was a different person entirely.

Leah's surface displayed only ripples of her wide, deep, and violent emotions, but the hunting song gave Charles deeper insight; he knew the power of her rage. She would do anything to see the Singer dead. It was a craving so deep it felt like obsession.

But Charles also knew that she had used most of her reserves getting from Montana to here. Any other werewolf of his acquaintance would have been down for the count already. She needed a day's rest and a lot of food before she would be back up to reasonable fighting trim. Food and rest she wouldn't get.

He had no doubt that Leah would keep going until she dropped—but he was afraid she was close to her limit. Exhaustion would slow her. What he knew, the hunting song knew. The pack understood Leah's current limitations, understood they made her vulnerable.

He would keep her at the edges of the battle when he could, if he could. It was impossible to really determine tactics before the Singer emerged. They knew something of its magic—though the power still rising from the ground worried Charles. And they had only a vague idea of the Singer's physical being—as he thought that, Leah's glimpse of it filtered through their bonds.

Anna's bright presence lit the hunting song with purpose and calm. It wasn't like her usual Omega effect—Anna was still embarrassed about the time that a hunt had ended not in a kill but in all of the wolves lying in a meadow, basking in the sun. She had a lot more control now, but that didn't mean she had the predatory need to kill that the rest of them did. Not normally. But, like Leah, Anna's presence felt different. She felt . . .

Deadly, said Brother Wolf.

Charles could feel the surprised agreement of the others. Like Charles, they weren't used to seeing Anna in a killing mood.

She felt like Da. Implacable will directed toward the death of the Singer. In her own way, Anna's drive was as deep as Leah's.

She is very unhappy about the people of Wild Sign, Brother Wolf whispered to him, so the others could not hear.

Brother Wolf was the only one who knew that Charles didn't think they would live through this. Charles did his best to keep it that way. He would not hurt his pack's morale going into this arena. Instead, he let Leah's and Anna's determination and Tag's fierce joy in the fight ring through the bonds and set the stage for their battle.

And still they waited.

Leah, Charles understood, thought she knew why they waited. But when he asked, she did not tell him. He had to trust her. They both were surprised to find that he did.

They were patient, his pack, as hunters need to be. They waited unmoving, a dozen feet from the edge of the saltwater lake, coats settling against skin under the pouring rain. The lightning storm came and went, but the unrelenting precipitation never decreased. Charles utilized all four sets of eyes as they watched the surface of the water for something more than the disturbance of the weather.

Tag saw the edge of a solid body breaking the surface, a quiet announcement that the star of their battle was here. Charles never did figure out how the Singer knew where they were—he never caught a glimpse of an eye or any other organ of perception.

But there was no question that it saw them somehow.

The tentacle that broke the surface was as big around as a Volkswagen bug, and it stretched a distance of nearly twenty-five feet to slam down on the ground where Leah had been standing. Unsuccessful, it did not pause. Moving with vicious speed, it disappeared back beneath the roiling waters as quickly as it had come, leaving long strands of mucus to mark where it had been.

The whole attack had been incredibly quick. Charles assimilated the observations of the pack.

The skin on the tentacle had been a light-pink-tinged gray, mottled and darker on the upper surface than on the lower. The underside of the tentacle, which only Tag had seen, had round ridges similar to—if not exactly like—a squid's, suction cups that would allow the Singer to attach itself to the underwater edges of the pit, giving it stability in the water.

A second tentacle struck at Tag, landing with a hollow boom that echoed like a rumble of thunder. Charles leapt on top of it. He had to dig his claws through the thick slime to give himself traction. Bearing in mind the speed the last tentacle had shown, he wasted no time biting down, burying his fangs into the tough flesh—and releasing the flesh instantly. He jumped off the moving tentacle and landed on the ground not two feet from the steep edge of the lake.

He ran, coughing up slime that seemed to grow inside his mouth. When he was a reasonable distance away, he rubbed his face in the wet grass. The slime tasted vaguely familiar—and unpleasantly fishy.

Hagfish, supplied Brother Wolf, who never forgot anything they had tasted. To the others, Brother Wolf suggested, *Use your claws.*

He was right, though that effectively lost them half of their attack capability. But that loss didn't bother Charles now. His earlier grim assessments forgotten, fierce excitement lit his veins as his focus, and his pack's focus, narrowed to the here and now. Charles was always most alive when he and Brother Wolf fought a worthy enemy.

Brother Wolf threw them into the fight with a joyous abandon, wishing that this battle, this song, might last forever, an eternal dancing with the pack against an enemy that demanded every skill they had. Tag's berserker spirit lay over them all, but spread out so that it only gave muscles more strength, speed, and endurance instead of the suicidal madness it could become.

A different sort of limb snuck out of the water and wrapped itself around Anna. It was darker colored and round, like the snakes children made with Play-Doh, maybe six inches in diameter—but at least as long as, if not longer than, the tentacles. It tried to haul Anna into the water, pulling her off her feet with a jerk.

Charles was on the far side of two of the big tentacles and couldn't even see what had happened, but what the others knew, he knew.

It was Tag who got to her and bit down savagely on the rubbery flesh, which was devoid of slime. Had Tag known that, the hunting song understood, he would not have done a bite-and-release. But the bite did the trick, and the arm went momentarily limp, allowing Anna to scramble out of it. She freed herself and rolled to her feet as the Singer's limb gave a sudden twitch, then withdrew to the safety of the dark waters.

They watched for those sneaky dark limbs after that.

Unable to use their mouths on the tentacles that were the Singer's main physical means of attack because of the slime, and unable to stay for a concerted attack because of the danger of being flung or dragged into the water, the wolves were reduced to delivering minor wounds in the hope that they would eventually weaken the creature.

They were further hampered by the mental attacks. They all understood when Leah missed a strike because she thought she was still waiting for the first attack. The hunting song offered her what it knew of the past few minutes, and she made her second strike count. Anna took the next mental attack, but Charles would not have known it bothered her without their bonds because she never slowed down, his graceful, deadly warrior. Hit and run suited her style of fighting because she was fast.

Charles had been right about Tag's resistance to the Singer's magic. Though the hunting song told him that the Singer attacked Tag's memories as frequently as it did Anna's or Leah's, the only effect on the old wolf was the deepening hold the berserker spirit took on him.

Charles had to work to make sure that it didn't spill onto the rest of the pack. Tag knew how to use the berserker in his soul; if it attached to one of the other three, it could be a disaster.

But the larger part of the Singer's attempt to steal memories settled onto Charles, as if the Singer was well aware that Charles spearheaded the wolves. If it had not been for Brother Wolf, Charles suspected he would have fallen.

Trust me, Brother Wolf told the twelve-year-old Charles, who found himself in wolf form trying to keep upright on slick ground in the middle of dodging an unlikely giant tentacle when just a moment before he had been on two feet and talking to his grandfather.

The only possible answer when Brother Wolf asked for trust, no matter what the circumstances, was for Charles to give it. He allowed Brother Wolf ascendance, and the wolf got them away from the danger. It was Brother Wolf who coordinated the others in Charles's place while Charles battled in a different arena.

For the next ten minutes, by Brother Wolf's reckoning, Charles was tossed from one reality to another with only brief sojourns in the current time. Then something changed.

A very distinctive drumbeat pulsed through the ties of the hunting song as Anna brought her steel-trap memory for music to bear. There were no lyrics—only Brother Wolf could speak through the hunting song's bonds, a quirk Charles had been unaware of until this battle. But "We Will Rock You" didn't need words.

The Singer's attacks on their memories lessened in effect—and then, as if it had become aware of their new inefficacy, ceased altogether. The fight continued as the rising dawn, muffled by the storm clouds and the rain, brought only faint shards of light onto the battleground.

As Charles had feared, Leah fell first. She saw it coming, but exhaustion slowed her more than she'd expected. Her right front foot slipped in a patch of mucus—the ground anywhere near the lake was becoming dangerously slick. She mistimed her dodge. One of the smaller dark arms whipped out and wrapped around her back leg, jerking her off her feet.

Charles got his jaws on the tentacle a second later and severed it in a spray of clearish fluid that seemed to be the Singer's version of blood. But the damage was done. Leah's leg was all but ripped off.

Charles did not see a mouth in the frothing water of the lake, but something must have surfaced, because the Singer shrieked, an ulu-lating, ear-piercing noise that rose to the point of pain on sensitive ears. The searing agony of the sound dropped on the pack, and for a moment they were still.

Then Brother Wolf took advantage of the temporary motionless-ness of the three tentacles currently onshore and opened a four-foot-long wound that was as deep as he could manage given the length of his claws and the toughness of the Singer's rubbery skin. In apparent response, the Singer jerked all of its parts beneath the water.

Directed by the needs of the hunt, Anna grabbed Leah by the scruff of the neck with her teeth and pulled the wounded wolf well out of reach. Leah did not object to either the pain of Anna's teeth breaking through hide and into flesh or the bump of her damaged leg on the ground. The hunting song knew that to heal such a wound would weaken the pack too much to continue the battle. So the song withdrew from Leah, leaving only three wolves in the fight.

ALONE AND SHIVERING from pain and exhaustion, Leah tried to start her change. The shift should heal most of the damage to her leg on its own. The sooner she got this done, the sooner she could get back into the fray. Nothing happened. She simply didn't have the resources to change again without rest or food.

She cast an anxious glance at the ongoing battle. They weren't going to win. The Singer was simply amusing himself with them. Leah couldn't bear being the only survivor a second time.

Desperately, she reached out to her distant pack for a boost of energy to help her change. They should have been too far away for her to reach. And they were.

But Bran wasn't.

Rich energy pulsed through her mate bond, making the change almost easy, certainly quicker than she was used to. As her body burned and stretched, she felt Bran begin to open their bond.

Buried with pain and the confusion of the shift, she reacted with utter and instinctive honesty. She shut it tight, cutting off the feed of energy, which she might not have done if she'd been more cognizant. It didn't matter; she had enough to finish the change on her own.

When she lay faceup in the mud, the falling rain keeping her eyes closed, she heard the faint sound of an approaching helicopter. Proof that Bran was near—had she needed further confirmation.

He brought hope with him. She knew of no other being who might accomplish what Sherwood had failed to do. Charles said he was bringing Jonesy's sword, and that was certainly a weapon that might kill a god—it had killed Jonesy, who was a son of Lugh, after all. If Bran joined them, they stood a chance.

With the wracking physical pain that was only just beginning to die down replaced by the accumulated mental wounds that could not be healed by magic, Bran Cornick was the last person in the world that Leah wanted to see. The pain of his presence might be the straw that broke her.

There was a sudden brilliant flash and a crack as lightning struck a tree on the far edge of the pit. And a second crack as one of the Singer's small limbs, the ones that hid in the shadows, smacked out and hit Tag, knocking him on his side—and one of the huge tentacles followed, staving in the berserker's side.

THE FIRST BLOW had not done much; Tag was a tough old wolf. But the second strike was another matter entirely.

The hunting song meant that Charles felt the sharp edge slicing Tag from nose to flank, laying him open to the bone. But it was the crushing blow of the rest of the tentacle that did the real damage, splintering bone and flattening organs.

What Charles did next wasn't an impulse. He and Brother Wolf had been engaged in a back-channel discussion from the beginning.

Remind it what death is, Asil had said. Jonesy had told him so, and Jonesy had been the son of a Celtic god, so he should have known. Charles had been hoping for his da to arrive with Jonesy's sword, but there was only a faint chance that he would get here before they lost this fight—a chance that had become significantly smaller now that Tag lay dying.

If he could pull magic from Leah through the pack bonds—and he wasn't sure that wouldn't kill her—Charles thought that they could probably save Tag. As long as they did it soon, before he or Anna sustained further damage. Between the time it would take and the drain of energy, such a decision would mean conceding the battle to the Singer.

Which meant they would lose what might be their only opportunity to kill something approaching godlike powers that would bear a grudge against his family and owe allegiance to the Hardesty witches—who also bore a grudge against his family.

It would be loosing evil on the world, Brother Wolf said.

But if they chose not to save Tag, they had a different opportunity.

Charles released that knowledge to the hunting song, which was already reeling under Tag's wounds. It was a pragmatic choice. If the pack rebelled, if Tag refused, Charles would listen.

Yes.

Tag's wolf spirit gave eager consent. Taking one's enemy down with one's own death was more than acceptable to the berserker spirit, but the single word had a bit of Tag's laughing amusement in it, too.

Anna waited. When a tentacle struck from the depths of the pit, she began a swift and brutal attack in the faint hope of keeping the Singer's attention on her. She didn't have to do it for long. This would not take much time.

With the Singer occupied with Anna, Charles ran to where Tag lay in the slime-covered mud. It was still Tag, not his corpse yet, though they could all feel the separation beginning.

Charles put his human hand on the horrendous wound, coating it in blood. He could not have said when he had changed back to human, only that he needed a hand for this, so that is what he had. Then he ran to the tentacle that was trying to kill his mate. This one had a long wound and Charles plunged his bloody hand into it, pressing Tag's lifeblood into the Singer. And then he tied them together—like the first step in bringing a new member into the pack.

He felt what he had done in the pack bonds, but Tag lay between the Singer and the pack, keeping them safe. Tag had always been a protective wolf. Dying, he was no less a guardian, dragging the Singer through that final veil with him.

THE HUNTING SONG waited for Tag's death.

Leah wasn't a part of that anymore, but she was a pack mate, and she knew how to read the signs. It had been a ruthless decision—and something inside her told her it wasn't going to work anyway. The Singer was too alien.

Not in body; it did not matter what body it wore. But pack magic was specific, and there had to be some affinity for Charles to find if he was going to bind the Singer to Tag.

She forced herself to her feet. Her hip hadn't healed completely in the change, but she was satisfied that it was only outraged tissue she had to deal with. She ignored the pain.

Even through the lesser window the pack bonds gave her, she could feel Tag's joy in achieving a glorious death. The idiot. It made her want to bite him.

THE TENTACLE WRITHED and Anna ran for safety, knowing Charles was doing the same thing on the other side. It didn't matter; they both knew their last chance had failed. Tag was still dying, but the bond Charles had fought to forge had not taken.

Only then did she realize that the noise she was hearing was a helicopter, flying in close. The hunting song had failed to notice it sooner because Tag was dying and Anna and Charles were both numbed with exhausted failure. Three wolves were not usually enough to keep a song going, and the magic was fading.

Bran's helicopter didn't land in the meadow in the center of Wild Sign, the only place with a big enough clearing to put the machine on the ground. Instead, it flew over—and Anna could almost hear the sigh of relief as the hunting song renewed itself and reached out for its king.

Bran dropped out of the hovering helicopter into the forest, because it was necessary to keep the helicopter out of reach. Tied to Bran with intimate closeness, Anna felt—they all felt—the momentary pain of his impact on the ground. But Bran healed himself as soon as the damage took place—filled with the power of not only the hunting song but also his pack, his wildlings, and a huge distant well of strength that was all of the wolves who owed him allegiance.

CHARLES LET THE reins of the hunting song go with relief and a renewal of hope. Da was here; all would be well.

He is not a god, said Brother Wolf dryly, but Charles knew his wolf shared Charles's faith.

Bran had assessed the situation before his feet hit the forest floor, and Charles knew what he needed to do as soon as his da did.

Anna waited for Bran beside Tag. Da wanted her human because he might need her hands to help save Tag, so she began her change. Charles felt the power that poured to her from the bonds of the hunt, felt her surprise at the speed of her transformation.

For his part, Charles ran toward the lake. About halfway there, he jumped into the air and raised his hand. Jonesy's sword, tossed by his da, landed in his clasp as if it wanted to be there.

* * *

DRIVEN BY THE wishes of the Marrok, the hunting song tried to engulf Leah again. Her initial rejection was instinctive. She could not bear being that close to Bran right now, raw as she was with the pain of the memories that the Singer had returned to her—only to snatch them away again, leaving her with just the remnants of the emotional upheaval. She did not have the strength to deal with the careful distance Bran maintained between them.

From her vantage point maybe fifty feet from where Tag lay, Leah watched her mate prepare to save them all. He threw the sword he'd brought into the hands of his son, then dropped to his knees beside Tag. Because, she understood, either he or Charles could have wielded the sword—but only one of them had a chance to save Tag.

Leah was not necessary.

She gave up the fight and let exhaustion, emotional and physical, overtake her, watching Charles with a gray numbness that approached disinterest. The silvery sword, which was not a long sword, looked more like a knife in his hand from this distance. It had been forged by the Dark Smith of Drontheim, and it had killed a son of the god Lugh.

The exhaustion-born numbness was swept away by the sudden certainty that she still had a role to play.

In her dream, Buffalo Singer had told her that this was her battle. Watching the great fae sword in Charles's hands, she finally understood what those words meant. Bitterness engulfed her and gave her the power to get to her feet.

If Buffalo Singer ever came to her in a dream again, she would make sure he regretted it.

*   *   *

AS IF IT understood the weapon Charles bore, the Singer had with-drawn under the water. Left without a target, Charles came to a wary stop three or four body lengths from the lake.

He could feel his da pouring power into the dying wolf behind him, using the hunting song and the pack bonds to keep Tag with them. Other than his da's cursing of stubborn werewolves, the dawn held a waiting quiet.

There was a bright silvery edge to the sky, but where they stood the rain still poured. Charles was glad the pilot had gotten the heli-copter down safely, because the storm was once again filling with the electric quality that told him the lightning was preparing for another round.

Charles felt a great calm sink into him. It wasn't the kind of calm that Anna gave him. It was the calm of battle, when all was at the ready and he would either live or die. It was Brother Wolf's favorite place to be.

Without warning, the tentacle whipped out of the water directly in front of him, snaking forward to slap down on him.

Charles moved aside. He was very tired, and he moved more quickly on four feet than on two. But he was fast enough. He buried the sword, driving it through the tough skin until it was haft deep.

The Singer screamed once more, the tentacle knocked into Charles, and he lost his grip on the sword.

He landed in a crouch. With no forethought at all, he raised up a hand and shouted . . . something. It didn't feel like he needed a word—just the cry, the sound of his voice.

And a bolt of lightning struck the sword in the center of the old blue stone at the top of the pommel. And the balls of lightning that spun off improbably in all directions knocked Charles off his feet again.

The tentacle, the entire visible upper skin crisped black and smelling like burnt fish, lay limp on the slime-covered mud.

After a while, Charles staggered to his feet. He looked at the tentacle and the twice-blackened sword. Leaving it, he headed back to where his da and Anna still fought to save Tag.

"Change," growled Da, both of his hands buried in Tag's bloody fur.

Charles put one hand on his da's shoulder, releasing all the power at his disposal to Bran's use. Anna wrapped a hand around Charles's wrist and did the same. He couldn't remember if she'd known how to do that, or if the hunting song showed her how.

Tag fought to live now, and that had taken a good deal of effort. Da had a grip on Tag that would, Charles was worried, bind Tag's soul to his bones if his body gave out before he was able to change and heal.

But Tag wasn't changing. Da gathered himself for another effort, and Anna put her free hand on Tag's forehead.

She bent down and whispered in his ear, "We have had enough death this night, you stubborn bastard. Change."

Charles felt her draw on the power of the hunt, on Charles, and on the Marrok. She did something tricky with her own Omega power, too. *"Change."*

Tag changed. It took a very long time. Long enough for the storm-drenched skies to lighten to full morning. Long enough that the rain gentled and the thunderstorm moved off.

"I can see why the FBI thought that Anna ruled us all," said Da, sitting in the mud. The hunting song had died down to a more subtle thing, but Charles could still feel his da's amusement trickling through it.

"Is there a reason," Da asked delicately, "that Anna is using the hunting song to project Queen?"

"Yes." Anna was staring at the limp tentacle. "It's not dead. Is it?"

Da sighed. "No."

THERE WAS ONE more flashlight inside the cave entrance. Leah turned it on and concentrated on her footing as she retraced the way she and Anna had taken earlier.

Memories of Zander flooded back. A gift, she thought bitterly, from the Singer.

Zander had been four when Sherwood came. He'd been a bright-eyed, affectionate child. Her new baby had been colicky. When she lay him belly down across her legs and patted his back to make him more comfortable, Zander would pat his tiny shoulder.

She had loved her children as she had never loved anything else in her life. Of course, back then, she had not remembered how they had been conceived. She remembered now.

She still loved her children.

The flashlight fell on a trail of blood, following it to the man propped up against the side of the cave. The light fell on his face and she looked her fill.

The adult Zander could have been her own father's double. Line breeding did that. The Singer could supply the spark of life—but required two human vessels to complete the act.

None of that was Zander's fault.

His eyelids wiggled and then his eyes opened. His mouth moved and she read his lips. *Mama.*

This was what the Singer had been occupied with while they

waited for him to attack them. Memories and music were his powers, not life and death, so keeping Zander alive had taken the Singer time and power.

"I almost told her that the bullets wouldn't kill you," Leah said, kicking the Glock out of his hand. He didn't have the strength yet to use it—but she didn't know what would happen when the Singer became aware of her here. Maybe he'd be preoccupied with Charles and the sword. "The Singer couldn't afford to lose you yet. Those new children are not even born—and he cannot leave these caves. Not until he Becomes."

Becomes something more, she thought. A god. A more powerful being. She thought of the damage that the Singer might cause once free of the caves, and found the determination she needed.

"I thought I could give you a chance." She knelt beside him and put her hand on his face. Leaning forward, she kissed his forehead at the same time that she unsnapped the sheath he wore on his belt and took out the knife.

ANNA WAS WAITING for her when she came out of the cave. Like Leah, Anna wore her human shape, though she was clothed. The perceptive Omega wolf did not say anything, just walked at Leah's shoulder. Leah raised her face to the blessed rain so that it could bathe away the evidence of the price she'd paid to kill the Singer.

Bran and Charles both stood up and left Tag to trail after her. Jonesy's sword rose out of the blackened flesh like a cross on the top of a hill. Crosses made her think of her father, and Leah had the odd thought that she might at last make peace with that memory.

Her father had been weak. He'd believed his god had forsaken him in the wilderness—no matter that all of the choices that had led them there had been his own. It was no wonder that when faced with another god, one that required nothing more difficult than obedience, her father had not even struggled with the decision.

She jumped on top of the tentacle. The weakness in her damaged leg and her inability to use either hand made her wobble. Bran caught her elbow and steadied her. Then he let her go.

It took her a moment to realize that she was going to have to set down the knife before she could pull the sword out. It was truly stuck. Why had Charles felt it necessary to bury the damn thing? But she managed—Bran steadied her again.

Then she shoved her right hand deep into the cut the sword had made. She took a breath and then crushed her son's heart until it quit trying to beat. She stood up and fumbled because both of her hands were slick with blood, but she managed to get the point of the sword into the cut and shoved it back in.

She jumped down—but would have fallen to her knees if Charles hadn't held her up. He released her and she took a step, stumbling because sometime in the last few minutes her leg had gone from being painful to not working right. When Bran put his hand on her arm, she jerked it free.

"Okay," he said, glancing up at the sky. "But we need to get back."

"Here," Anna said. And Leah was able to let her daughter-in-law help her, because Anna didn't make her feel any uncomfortable or hurtful things.

They stopped when Bran quit walking. Then they all turned to look back at the lake and the cross on top of the hill.

Bran looked at Charles.

"I didn't do it on purpose," Charles said. "There's no reason for it to work again."

But when Bran didn't say anything, Charles grunted. Then he raised a hand to the sky and said, in a quiet voice but one that carried power that reminded Leah of the scent of the Singer's magic, "Now."

Lightning struck the blade of the sword. And after that, it seemed to Leah as if nothing happened quite as it should have.

The strike should have blown the metal to pieces, she thought. Then she remembered who had built that sword.

Lightning should be instantaneous. A crack and then gone. But the blinding light lingered, emitting a buzzing sound that made the bones of her skull vibrate. She had to look away from the brilliance. Only then the thunder rolled and the ground grew so electric that it bit at Leah's bare feet.

When the sound was gone, the forest was darker, and it felt so very quiet after the endless thunder that even the wind whistling through the trees seemed like a whisper. Leah looked toward the lake and saw the sword slowly falling over in the ashes that were all that was left of the Singer. And her son.

Leah managed to control her fall so that she simply sat where she'd been standing. But that didn't work the way she'd expected, either. Because she kept falling until her wet cheek was pressed into the slime-covered mud, and her eyes closed.

She might have fought to stay conscious, but she thought it might be nice, just for a little bit, to quit hurting.

SHERWOOD POST SAT up in his bed and remembered his name.

14

Da slipped off the light waterproof jacket he'd been wearing and covered Leah's limp body with it. He scooped her out of the mud and stood up, hesitating for a moment as if contemplating what to do next. He looked as though he hadn't slept for a week—though nowhere near as worn down as Leah was.

"You take Tag and her back home," Charles suggested as Brother Wolf shut down the hunting song, because it didn't appear that his da was going to do that, and it wasn't doing it on its own. Tag was out of danger; the pack bonds were sufficient to keep him on this side of death now. Da gave Charles a sharp look, but didn't interrupt when Charles kept talking. "Anna and I can clean up the leftover mess here. It might take us a couple of days. More if you want Anna and me to deal with the storage unit."

Da shook his head. "I can't spare you. I'll get the pack in Bend to send down a team to clear it out. Do you want everything sent home?"

Charles nodded. "Yes."

"I will make it so," Da said. He looked at the sword.

Anna strode over and picked it up gingerly. It had been buried in ash and slime. She did the best she could to clean it off in a clump of wet grass, but the results were mixed. It had been scorched and blackened when they'd found it in Jonesy's body. It had been hit by lightning twice today—and it still looked scorched and blackened, now with an added coat of slime and ash. Anna used the bottom of her shirt to clean off the cool blue cabochon stone in the pommel. It looked odd in the framework of the filthy sword, but it seemed to satisfy her.

When she reached them, they all started hiking toward Wild Sign, where the helicopter waited. Charles picked Tag up along the way. Like Leah, Tag was skin and bones—healing that much damage took energy. They walked the whole way in silence; Charles figured that his da had a lot to think about. Anna was just exhausted.

There were blankets at the helicopter as well as water and some emergency high-protein bars. They roused both Leah and Tag enough to eat and drink. Charles helped the pilot get Tag wrapped in a blanket and strapped in. Da did the same for Leah, who batted at his hands like a very tired toddler.

He gathered her bloodstained hands in his and said, "Stop."

She let him buckle her in then, but she didn't look at him.

A week ago, Charles would never have imagined himself feeling protective of his stepmother.

She saved us all, at great personal cost, Brother Wolf said.

"Do you mind if we keep the sword and bring it back when we're finished?" Anna asked. "I want Charles to look at the . . . the people of Wild Sign."

"You found them alive?" Da's eyes widened in surprise.

"I don't know," Anna said; she sounded every bit as tired as she looked. Charles had managed to get a couple of protein bars down her, too. "They smelled dead, looked like mummies—and they were breathing."

Da's eyebrows shot up.

"I just . . ." Her voice trailed off.

"I'll go with you to check things out," Charles said. The caves would need to be cleaned out in any case. He didn't want to be explaining bodies found on Leah's land to some law officer fifty years in the future. That would be a task for later. And if it had been up to him, he would get a good night's sleep and return. It might come to that, depending upon what they found. But it wouldn't hurt to look at things now. To his da he said, "If Leah . . . if you need a rundown on today's events, we can talk later."

"Can I take the sword?" Anna asked again.

Bran nodded. Charles had the distinct impression that Anna could have said, "I want to throw it in the ocean," or "I want to give it to the owner of the local gas station," and she would have gotten the same response. Da wasn't thinking about the sword just now.

"You should go," Charles said.

Bran nodded. "I will see you when you get back." He lifted a hand in good-bye and started to walk around the helicopter to take the copilot's seat.

"You should talk to her," Charles said, and saw his da's steps falter. He did not say, *You should have talked to her a long time ago. She was hurt and you did not see it. You should have seen it.* But he had no doubt that his father heard those words, too.

"Yes," Da said, without looking around. "We will need to talk."

Anna tucked herself under Charles's arm and leaned her cheek against his chest. "Do you think they'll be okay?" she asked. He knew she assumed that the sounds of the helicopter powering up would hide her voice.

He was pretty sure that wasn't the case, but he told her the truth anyway, because his da should hear it. "I don't know."

THEY WERE VERY nearly stymied at the mouth of the cave because he'd forgotten that they would need light to travel inside.

"There was one left," Anna said.

"There are flashlights in the Suburban," Charles said. "Or we could come back tomorrow."

"No," Anna said stubbornly, but there was a wobble to her voice.

It surprised him—and he took another good hard look at his mate. They were all exhausted, in need of food and sleep. She didn't look as bad as Leah, or Da after he'd kept Tag from dying. But that was just a matter of degree.

We need to get her home, Brother Wolf said, and he didn't mean the hotel. Her jaw was set and she had her lower lip caught between her teeth to keep it from trembling. Charles could tell she knew she was being irrational.

But she was tired, worn to the bone mentally and physically, and he wasn't going to argue with her when she was in that state. Briefly he worried that they were going to have to go into the cave system in the dark.

Happily, before that happened, Anna spotted a flashlight that had rolled into some shrubs. She wiped the blood off it and headed into the cave.

They came to a place where three tunnels met, and Anna stopped. She pointed to a pile of ash. "I think that's Zander," she said.

"Good" was probably the wrong thing to say, Charles thought. She'd liked Zander, loved his photography—though perhaps she didn't like him as much since he'd kidnapped her so she could carry Cthulhu's child.

"Good," he said anyway.

She put her forehead against his biceps and gave a laugh that was nearly a sob. "Good," she agreed huskily.

Her flashlight fell upon a Glock pistol. Charles picked it up, took out the clip, and checked the chamber, which was clear. He put the clip in one pocket and tucked the gun in the back of his jeans. He couldn't leave a loaded gun lying around for anyone to find.

The cavern of the dead was not far away.

Anna's flashlight found the face of the first body just as the gem in the pommel of Jonesy's sword flared with light. He didn't blame it. Magic was so thick in here that he could barely breathe.

The Singer had been feeding on these people, had set up some sort of construct that pulled . . . something from them. Charles wasn't sure what it was, only that he could barely perceive it. But with the Singer dead, the cave was filled with power.

Anna had been right. It had been important for them to come here now.

Anna's description of the people of Wild Sign was right on target. As they stood in the entryway, every body he could see in the cool light of the gemstone sucked in a breath and let it out again. And she was right about what it smelled like, too.

"Are they dead?" Anna asked in a small voice.

He wished he could tell her yes. He knelt beside the closest one and put his hand on her forehead, then on the skin over her heart.

"No," he said. "But there is no going back for them, either."

She lifted the sword in question, shifting her grip as she did, so that she held it properly.

He held out his hand for the sword, and Brother Wolf spoke aloud. "Please."

Because Brother Wolf was as tired as Charles, he reverted to speaking through their bond. *Let us do this terrible, necessary thing.*

"I can do it," she said, raising her chin.

"I know," Charles said. "But it will cost me less to give these poor souls the coup de grâce"—he saw her draw in an indignant breath and completed his sentence—"than it will cost me to watch you do it."

She closed her mouth and gave him a disgruntled look. "That is so sexist it leaves me speechless."

But she had heard the truth in his statement.

"I know," he said apologetically, which made her sputter.

"And manipulative," she said.

He bowed shallowly in acknowledgment. "I am my father's son."

She looked around the room and then held the sword out to him. Her eyes glistened wetly in the blue light.

He took the sword, then kissed her. "Thank you."

It took some time. Charles wasn't sure that Jonesy's sword had been necessary to break the spell that held the bodies to a semblance of life, but there was no question that it accomplished the task.

When they found no more bodies, Anna said a quiet prayer.

Then she said, "Do you think they are at peace?"

He didn't know how to answer that. Their bodies were dead, but he had no idea what the Singer had been doing to them.

Anna had her back to him—and a motion caught his eye. He looked over to see a narrow-faced, sharp-nosed coyote. Coyote.

Bless Mercy, he thought. She'd managed it.

"Yes," he told Anna. "They are safe now."

COYOTE WATCHED THEM go. He had not paid much attention to the Marrok's son, his daughter's foster brother. He was more interesting than Coyote had thought.

But they were not why he was here.

He trotted into a damp cavern that held a clear, cold pool in its center. He nosed around until he found what he'd been looking for. A small squid-like creature, no bigger than his toenail.

Immortal things were truly difficult to kill.

It tasted like eel.

WHEN ANNA AND Charles emerged from the cave, the rain had stopped, though the chill that lingered in the air had an edge of winter in it. The next rainstorm in these mountains was going to carry snow, Charles thought.

He smelled the witches before they came upon them.

"Is something wrong?" Anna asked.

"Witches," he told her quietly. "Black. Over by the amphitheater. The lake."

Neither of them slowed—or sped up, either.

He pulled the Glock out of his waistband and loaded the clip. Their best weapon against the witches was likely to be the sword. He wanted Anna to have it, but he hadn't taught her swordplay yet. If his da was going to continue to break out swords from his store of weapons, Anna needed to learn. But for now, it meant that he kept the sword.

"You still have your gun?" he asked, keeping his voice soft.

She nodded. "Six bullets."

Brother Wolf thought there were fewer than six witches waiting for them. Charles handed the Glock to Anna, too.

"This is a Glock 21. It's a .45 caliber. Thirteen shots—there is not one in the chamber right now. You've shot this gun before." She hadn't liked it. It hadn't fit her hand as well as her Sig did.

We could just kill them, observed Brother Wolf. *There are three of them.*

Anna checked the Glock herself, then tucked it next to her carry gun in the small of her back. "We don't want to start a war," she told Brother Wolf. "They don't have anything to gain by our deaths—and a lot to lose." She looked up at Charles. "They'll know the Singer is dead, right?"

"Probably," Charles said. "If it was feeding them power, that would have stopped the moment it died."

They quit talking. Charles wanted to get this encounter finished as quickly as possible. He was tired and so was Anna.

He was, under the circumstances, unsurprised to find three witches standing next to the lake. He hadn't expected that they would be standing in the ashes left by the Singer's tentacle, and didn't quite know why he found that disconcerting. He suspected they did not realize what they were standing in, and he had no intention of telling them. Who knew what mischief they could brew up with the ashes of the Singer?

One of the witches was the pregnant Ms. Hardesty, which he thought had been a mistake on their part. Her pregnancy gave them something they wanted to protect.

Brother Wolf snarled in his mind; he did not like witches. Especially when he and Charles were so tired. It made Brother Wolf worry that they could not protect Anna.

"This is private property," Anna said. "You are trespassing." It was better if Anna talked, because Brother Wolf might say something they would regret later.

Ms. Hardesty, her lips white, strode up to them while the others hung back. Either she was in charge, or she was rash. Since she was here, he was betting on the latter.

"You killed him," she said, her voice low with rage. "You will regret that."

"We told you our intentions," Anna said. "Why are you surprised? The Singer was unfinished business that belonged to my family. Ours to deal with. You have no claim."

"He was mine," the witch snarled, one hand wrapped around her belly.

For some reason, Brother Wolf thought it was important to make Anna's case. To show that they had justice on their side. So Charles said, "No."

Charles couldn't see justice making any inroads on the intentions of the pair of older witches who were chanting—softly, as if they thought that he, a werewolf, wouldn't notice them gathering power. Perhaps they didn't care what Charles knew.

"He was mine," Cathy Hardesty's voice was raw. "He was the father of the child I carry."

"That did not make the Singer yours," Charles said, despite the knowledge that Anna would be a better intermediary. Brother Wolf was adamant. "You belong—belonged—to it, not the other way around. It was on our lands. Its walker carried my Alpha's mate's blood and was accountable for his crimes to my family. This land has been in my family's name for two centuries. His death was spoken for long ago by my family."

The magic the witches were conjuring increased in strength, and Charles had just about decided he needed to do something about that when it died as if it had been a candle flame smothered by a snuffer. One of the witches stifled a cry of pain.

A man strode out of the trees—and Charles was sure that there had not been a man anywhere near this place. This man smelled quite human and he moved that way, though obviously he was at home in the woods.

This is why you needed me to speak, Charles said. *Why didn't you tell me the Sasquatch was here?*

Brother Wolf was smug.

"Felt a disturbance," said Ford. "And under the circumstances, I thought I should come check." He looked at the ground the pair of older witches were standing on, and then away. He knew what the wet ashes were.

Sasquatches were the guardians of the forest. Tag had been worried about their physical strength, Charles knew. But when they were acting for justice in their territory, they had other power that was much more impressive. They could, for instance, make it impossible for these witches to work their magic.

Normally, Sasquatches would not concern themselves in a fight between witches and werewolves—unless possibly they considered one or the other as part of their territory. He didn't know why Ford was doing so now.

We killed the Singer, Brother Wolf said. *He owes us a debt.*

Indeed, Charles and Anna had just rid the forest of a disruptive force—he paused and thought about the events surrounding the death of the Singer and had an interesting idea.

"I believe," Charles told the witches softly, "you were told that you were trespassing. If I were you, I would leave—and not come back."

"Who are you to say so?" asked Cathy Hardesty, though she'd felt the magic die as well, Charles thought. He could hear it in the wariness of her voice.

One of the witches approached Ms. Hardesty and took her arm. That one kept a sharp eye on Ford, though she took time to give Charles a foul look.

"Come, daughter," she murmured. "This is unproductive."

Ms. Hardesty jerked her arm free. "Where is Zander?" she demanded harshly. "What have you done with him?"

Charles did not reply—and was glad that Anna did not, either.

"Go now," said Ford. His voice was not ungentle, but there was force behind it.

"Come," said the older witch. "We cannot win this battle on this ground."

Ford gave her an affable smile. "Common sense is a rare commodity."

They stalked off in the direction of Wild Sign, and after a moment Charles heard the sounds of dirt bikes revving up.

Ford shook his head. "They came through the wilderness area on those. We'll see that doesn't happen again."

"Thank you," said Anna. "We would not have been happy to have another fight today."

Ford slanted an amused look at Charles. At Brother Wolf, maybe, because he said, "I'm not sure that is entirely true." He glanced in the direction the witches had taken and said, "You have made yourself enemies there."

"We have always been enemies," said Charles mildly. "Water is wet. Black witches are our enemies."

Ford nodded. "Fair enough." He took a deep breath, then said, "We owe you thanks. This one has long been a foulness in our home."

"Team effort," Charles said.

Ford smiled. "This is your land, Charles and Anna Cornick. This forest welcomes you here. But I think, today, you have accomplished all you set out to do."

"Yes," agreed Anna.

"We found a couple of vehicles a few miles away." He jerked his chin in the general direction of where the two cars had been left. "One of my nieces said that she knew the owner of one of them, who might be surprised to find it where it was. She has taken it back where it belongs. She is something of a tinkerer." This was said with a look of pride. "She fixed what was wrong with the other rig—the one that brought you to the Trading Post. Good as new, she said."

Charles, surprised, said, "Thank you. I believe a card was left with a phone number, and if the owner of the Land Rover would use it, we'll see that they are compensated for the use of their vehicle."

Ford smiled and nodded. "Good. Good." He tilted his head at Charles. "You and your lady, when you come back here, you should stop in for more pie."

"We'll do that," Charles said.

* * *

WHEN THEY FINALLY made it back to the hotel, they showered and went to bed. Charles slept for a couple of hours but woke with the sun in his eyes. He was still tired, but he'd have to wait for nightfall to get more rest.

Anna was deeply asleep. She'd curled away from him at some point, though she had a foot pressed against his calf to make sure she knew where he was. He took a moment, while she couldn't see him, to watch her, to convince himself that she was safe.

She was going to wake up if he got out of bed. He stayed for a few minutes more before acknowledging that he wasn't going to be able to lie still—and so would wake her up anyway.

He slid out of bed and dressed. Anna rolled over and half opened her eyes.

"Shh," he said. "Go back to sleep."

She looked at him with wolf-blue eyes for a full second. Then she rolled over to his side of the bed, grabbed his pillow, and went back to sleep.

He made sure the door was locked behind him. He stopped by the room next to them and pressed a hand against the window. He felt nothing. His wards around the grimoires were still holding.

Driven by restless thoughts, he took the path down to the river and was somehow unsurprised to see Anna's rock occupied by a compact man who had his back to Charles. The man was, however, wearing buckskins and had his black hair braided and hanging down to brush the rock he sat upon—so Charles had a fair idea of who he was.

"Coyote," he said. "Better late than never."

"Do you think so?" said Coyote, turning to look up into Charles's face. He had been chewing on a stick, and he tossed it into the river without looking. "I think I came in exactly when I wanted."

"Too late to help?" Charles said. He hadn't quite kept the growl out of his voice.

Coyote laughed heartily and slapped his leg. "You sure are a happy camper, aren't you?" He took in Charles's expression and laughed some more. "You get it, right? We're in Happy Camp, but you aren't a happy camper. I have been waiting all day to say that."

"Why," Charles asked, "are you here now?"

Coyote held up a finger. "Wait a moment." He looked expectantly up the trail.

And Anna came hurrying down the path, sleep-tossed and bleary-eyed. "Where were you—" Her eyes fell on Coyote and she quit talking. She stopped a little to the side of Charles, giving him room if he needed to defend them.

She is smart, said Brother Wolf.

"She is," agreed Coyote.

Charles wasn't sure how he felt knowing Coyote could hear Brother Wolf.

"Well," said Coyote impatiently, "are you going to introduce us?"

Then, without waiting, he said, "I'm Coyote. You're Anna."

"You are he," she agreed. "And I certainly am."

"I could come," Coyote said, "because you put right what was wrong here. And because I didn't want to have to deal with the Singer. That is two 'becauses.' I will answer two questions. One for you." He looked at Anna. "And one for you. You were here first. Ask your question."

To his surprise, Charles did have something he wanted to know.

"Mercy is a walker," Charles said.

"Ah, excellent question," said Coyote, even though it hadn't been a question at all. "Yes. We have children so they can go out and do our will. They walk in the world, messengers and . . . What's that word? Ah, yes, henchmen. And henchwomen, of course. My walkers tend to be disobedient and more effective than other walkers." He preened, then raised his eyebrows at Charles, inviting him to speak again.

Charles decided they might get further if he waited for Coyote to tell them what Coyote wanted to tell them.

"You talk like words cost money," Coyote observed sourly when Charles didn't speak. "Wolf is like that, too."

"What happens to your children if one of you die?" asked Anna suddenly.

Coyote gave her a surprisingly sweet smile. "That's the right question, even if it's the one Charles is supposed to ask. My death would not kill my children." He looked coy. "I've tried that. But the Singer had not yet Become. He wasn't quite like me. He required Zander—or some other living man—to even get women pregnant. When he died, the life force in those children he fathered on mortal women died, too."

"All of them?" Charles asked.

Coyote gave him a narrow look. "You are pushing the extent of your one question with all of your questions."

Anna started to speak and Coyote waved a finger. "Uh-uh. Not yet. You have a different question you want to ask." He looked at Charles and sighed. For the first time, Coyote looked truly serious. "I want you to know this, so it can still be part of your question. None of the children the witches bear will survive. Your Dr. Connors miscarried about an hour ago."

Charles nodded slowly. He could not be sorry. He *should* not be sorry.

"Walkers reflect some of the aspects of their parentage," Coyote said. "Wolf's children are fierce—and not too bright, for instance." He gave Charles a smile that showed his teeth. When Charles did not react, Coyote heaved a sigh. "You really are not any fun at all, are you? Fine. Zander reflected the Singer's aspects—I cannot find it in me to feel bad that there will be no more of his walkers in our world."

Anna nodded.

"You have a question?" Coyote asked.

"I've seen too many horror films," she said. "Is the Singer dead?"

"Absolutely," Coyote said. "And now that I have answered your question, I have a task for you."

He leaned over until he could reach his back pocket and pulled out a silver necklace with a single moonstone in a very plain setting. "She said—and I quote—'Tell them that I didn't have the power to make the other one very strong, but you are welcome to try it. This one my great-grandmother made. I have no daughter to pass it on to. I would very much like Sissy Connors to have it. Her father worried about her so.'"

Charles took it gingerly. "From Carrie Green."

"Yes," Coyote said.

"I'll see that she gets it," Charles promised. He knew that Anna would want to check on Dr. Connors before they left for home anyway. This would be a good excuse.

"Why didn't it protect Carrie?" Anna asked. "It's protection from evil, right?"

Coyote gave her an exasperated huff. "Two questions. Two. We might as well sit down and have an entire conversation. Ah well, I don't like rules very much anyway. The necklace is protection from black witches who want to steal your magic. That's all."

Anna nodded at him. "You spoke to her? To Carrie Green?" There was a wobble in her voice.

Charles put his hand on her shoulder.

Coyote nodded and gave Anna that sweet smile again. "They are all safe now." He tipped his head up toward the sun, closing his eyes. "We're done now. You go away. I think I will sit on this rock and digest my breakfast. Maybe dream a bit, who knows?"

Charles knew stories of Coyote. "Isn't that dangerous?" he said.

Coyote smiled at Charles this time, his eyes laughing. "You do have a sense of humor. I knew it." He turned his back on them both, wrapping his arms around his knees as he stared out over the river.

As they headed back to the hotel, Charles heard Coyote singing "We Will Rock You." He decided he wasn't going to think too hard about what that might mean.

THAT NIGHT, THE coyote easily hopped over the stone wall that encased the garden. He trotted over to the raised pool, looked at his reflection backlit by the moon for a moment, and drank. When he had drunk his fill, he hopped on the ledge—no longer a coyote, but Coyote in his human guise.

He hadn't lied to Charles and Anna, but he had concealed this thing from them. All of the Singer's children had not died. This one last child had survived.

"Heya," he told the listening garden. "I am Coyote. I think we should talk."

* * *

LEAH LEFT TAG sleeping in the guest bedroom. He would recover, though it would be a week or more before he was up and moving with anything like his old strength. She was distantly glad of it. The pack was safer with Tag in it.

For lack of other tasks, she wandered into her bedroom and caught sight of herself in the full-length mirror. She walked over and stared.

She'd showered and put on makeup. Like Tag, she had weight she needed to regain—though nowhere near the same amount. Outside of the gauntness and a hollowness in her eyes that might only be her imagination, she didn't look any different than she ever had.

But now she remembered. The moment the Singer died, she had remembered everything. And yet that woman in the mirror was more of a stranger than she had ever been. She reached up and put her fingertips against her jawbone, just to make sure that it was really her.

Bran didn't make any sound approaching her room, though like the good werewolf she was, she knew he was there. Of course she knew. She closed her eyes briefly, trying to find a center of normalcy. But she had killed her own son and used his heart to kill a god. She wasn't sure where normal was in that.

"We need to talk," her mate said.

And that quickly, she couldn't breathe. She did not want to have this talk with him. With anyone. Her chest ached as she forced herself to calm.

She might be a stranger to herself, but she knew Bran. Her mate. He had violated his own rules when he had forced her to live through her Change and convinced her to be his mate. For two centuries both of them had ignored that. These last few days had shoved his sins down his throat. Now he would need to fix it. And that terrified her.

"I don't want to talk now," she told him truthfully. She looked down at her fingers and regretted painting her nails red. Like blood. It had seemed fitting at the time—but she regretted it now.

"Nevertheless," he said.

She bowed her head and closed her eyes, but forced herself not to hug her chest, too. He would already know how unhappy and defensive she was, but she didn't need to shove it in his face.

She inhaled to give herself strength and could have cursed because her breath hitched. Damn it.

She turned around.

He hadn't come all the way into the room, but leaned a shoulder against the doorframe. He watched her with hooded eyes. Started to say something and clearly reconsidered.

"You have been greatly wronged," he said finally. "Not just by me, but I did my part. And I don't want to lose you."

That first part she had expected, but not the second. She would have to be very stupid not to have understood that he did not particularly like her. He needed her—or someone in her place. Someone to balance his fierce and too-powerful wolf—and also someone to bear some of the burden of his various offices: Marrok, Alpha, guardian of the wildlings. She was useful.

She'd thought that he would take this opportunity to set her aside "for her own sake." He had wronged her, forced her because she had not been in any condition to give consent, either to being Changed or to mating with him. She deserved better. She should go out in the real world and find better. And then he could find someone he'd be happier with.

Maybe she could convince him that she wanted things to stay as they were because she was ambitious. Any role she held after being the Marrok's mate would be lowering her position. Both of those things were true.

She did not want to tell him the real reason she wanted things to stay as they were. She had loved, really loved, three people in her adult life. One of them had died before he had a chance to live. One of them had grown up into a monster that Leah had killed. The third was standing in her bedroom, and she was fairly sure he'd spent nearly two centuries hating her because she was not Blue Jay Woman.

"Leah," he said when she'd been silent too long. "I don't want to lose you."

She gave him a sardonic smile. "Why the hell not?"

He tilted his head and she saw the shadow of his wolf pass through his eyes. Then he opened the mating bond—which had always been tightly shut, always—and showed her.

EPILOGUE

Outside, the first snowstorm of the season was whistling through the trees, turning the world white. Inside, Charles had a guitar out and was singing Gordon Lightfoot songs. Anna was knitting an afghan that she intended as a Christmas present for her dad. Flames danced in the fireplace.

Someone knocked fiercely on the door, startling both of them.

Charles put his guitar aside. He didn't make it to the door before it opened—letting in a blast of arctic cold and a fair amount of snow before his brother, Samuel, shut it. Seeing him home and safe relieved a worry that always lurked in Charles's heart when those he loved were away.

"Samuel," Charles said. "Welcome."

Samuel looked rough. He hadn't shaved for quite some time, and there was a white scar that ran from his temple down the side of his face and disappeared into his scruffy beard. It took a lot to scar a wolf; Charles was pretty sure that anything connected to Doctors Without Borders wouldn't manage it. He had no doubt that his brother had worked with the organization, but Charles decided the feeling that they weren't getting the whole story of where Samuel had been and what he'd been doing was verified in his brother's face. Samuel's eyes were tired.

"Would you do something for me?" Samuel asked.

"Yes," said Anna immediately. "Samuel, what's wrong?"

"Anything," Charles agreed. "You know that."

"Keep her safe," he said. He unzipped his coat, dropping it to the floor so he could take off the sling he wore across his chest. He handed the baby, still the size of a newborn, to Charles.

She blinked up at Charles with vague baby eyes. Like most babies' eyes, they were blue. She was warm and dense, as babies were. Her skin was a little flushed from being tucked against Samuel's body.

Charles lifted his eyes to Samuel's.

"I told you I might have a solution for you. For your need for a baby," said Samuel. He tried to smile. Charles saw that it wasn't just the weather making the whites of his eyes red. "I need you to take care of her. To raise her as your own. No one can know she's Ariana's daughter."

"We'll protect her with our lives," Anna said firmly. "You know that. You and Ariana could stay here with her. Our pack will do anything to make you safe. Bran would do anything."

"She's a maker," Samuel said. "The fae have not had a maker since Ariana bound her power into the last artifact she made. One of the fae found out—Ariana will take care of him. But if he knows, if he told anyone . . ." His voice trailed off. "If the fae have the ability to make great artifacts again, that would be a game changer for them.

She is safer with you. My daughter, Ariana's daughter, has to die. Our child would never be safe."

"Are you hungry?" said Anna. "Can you stay for the night?"

Samuel shook his head. "It's not safe for her. No one can know I was here."

"Da?"

Samuel lifted his head, staring in the direction of their da's house. "Da already knows. He's on his way, but I can't stay. Give him my love." He hesitated and his eyes found his daughter's face. "I'll come when I can. Uncle Samuel can visit."

"Okay," said Anna. "We will keep her safe for you, Samuel. What's her name?"

"Call her what you like." Samuel picked up his coat and put it on. "Her mother gave her a name, but the fae don't use their true names for a reason." He gave Charles that heartbreaking almost-smile again. "I don't have to tell you to love her."

"No," Charles agreed.

She is ours, said Brother Wolf. Samuel hugged Anna, resting his head on top of hers for a moment, as if drawing strength. Then he hugged Charles, too. Samuel kissed the top of his baby's head. He rested his face against hers, inhaling audibly. Then he backed away several steps before he turned on his heel and went back out into the storm.

ACKNOWLEDGMENTS

My gratitude to the following people, who helped put this book together:

My crew at home: Collin Briggs, Linda Campbell, Dave Carson, Katharine Carson, Ann Peters the Trusty Assistant, and Kaye Roberson.

And to the professionals: Anne Sowards (editor), Miranda Hill (assistant editor), Alexis Nixon (publicist), Jessica Plummer (marketer), Judith Murello Lagerman (art director), Michelle Kasper (production editor), Christine Legon (managing editor), Joi Walker (production manager), Tiffany Estreicher (design supervisor / text designer), Kristin del Rosario (interior designer), Dan dos Santos (cover artist), and Christine Masters (copy editor).

As always, any mistakes that remain are mine.

ABOUT THE AUTHOR

Patricia Briggs graduated from Montana State University with degrees in history and German. She worked for a while as a substitute teacher but now writes full time. Patricia Briggs lives in the Pacific Northwest.

Find out more about Patricia Briggs and other Orbit authors by registering for the free monthly newsletter at orbitbooks.net.